Susan Arnout Smith is a third generation Alaskan now living in California. Winner of the Stanley Drama Award, she has written television movies that have aired in the United States and other countries. She has been a playwright at the National Playwrights Conference, Eugene O'Neill Theater Center, and an essayist for National Public Radio.

THE TIMER GAME

A reluctant CSI detective with the San Diego squad, Grace Descanso is summoned to attend a seemingly routine crime scene. Hours later, two detectives have been brutally murdered and Grace herself is under investigation for shooting the killer. Her daughter Katie is five years old. She's all Grace has got. But when Katie is snatched, Grace is thrown into a nightmare world of timed riddles that she must solve in order to find her daughter before it's too late. She has twenty-four hours before Katie dies. Welcome to the Timer Game . . .

SUSAN ARNOUT SMITH

THE TIMER
GAME

Complete and Unabridged

CHARNWOOD
Leicester

First published in Great Britain in 2008 by
Harper Perennial
an imprint of HarperCollins*Publishers*
London

First Charnwood Edition
published 2009
by arrangement with
HarperCollins*Publishers*
London

British Library CIP Data

Smith, Susan Arnout
    The timer game.—Large print ed.—
Charnwood library series
    1. Women detectives—California—San Diego
—Fiction 2. Criminal investigation—Fiction
    3. Kidnapping—Fiction 4. Suspense fiction
    5. Large type books
    I. Title
    813.6 [F]

    ISBN 978–1–84782–505–6

Published by
F. A. Thorpe (Publishing)
Anstey, Leicestershire

Set by Words & Graphics Ltd.
Anstey, Leicestershire
Printed and bound in Great Britain by
T. J. International Ltd., Padstow, Cornwall

This book is printed on acid-free paper

For my husband, Alfred Toulon Smith,
with love and gratitude —
every day with you is a blessing.

Beware the fury of a patient man.
— JOHN DRYDEN, *Absalom and Achitophel*

1

Sunday

'If somebody's following us, would you know?'

Grace Descanso glanced at her daughter as they squeezed past an inflatable ghost at the entrance to Party Savers. Katie's dark eyes studied her gravely. She was almost five, small for her age, her honey-colored curls bouncing in two high ponytails under a Padres baseball cap.

'You mean right now this second?'

Grace kept her voice neutral but her gaze shifted to the salesclerk ringing up a line of customers and a group of teens clustered by a rack of spiders. The store was busy. Nothing jumped out.

'Why, honey? Do you think somebody is?' Grace picked up a shopping basket.

Katie shrugged. 'I don't know. I finally decided. I want to be a doctor.'

'When you grow up?' Katie shifted gears at dizzying speed, and Grace trailed after her, trying to keep up.

Katie slowed at a rack of pumpkin lights and kept moving. 'No, silly. For Halloween. That way I can wear that thing of yours.'

'Stethoscope,' Grace said. She blinked. 'I'm not sure I can find it, Katie. I haven't seen it for a long time. You could be a princess. They get to wear sparkly pink.'

The cell phone in her pocket rang and Grace's

1

first instinct was to ignore it. She'd put it on *High* and *Vibrate* and now it whirred in her pocket like an angry bee. It was Sunday, her first real day off in almost a month from the San Diego Police crime lab, and she wanted to spend it with Katie.

Katie cut a look at the phone and walked ahead down the aisle. They shared the same dark Portuguese eyes and angular grace, but Katie was tawny as a golden cat. Next to Grace's ivory skin and dark hair, Katie always looked sun-kissed and radiantly healthy. Sleeping helped, too, Grace figured. She hadn't been doing much of that lately.

They were both in shorts; for October in San Diego it was humid, and the store smelled of dust and suntan oil. The phone stopped ringing as Katie paused at a rack of fuzzy bat pencils, picking up one and examining it closely.

Katie's birthday was coming up Saturday, the day before Halloween, and Grace didn't have a lot of money to spend on treat bags. It embarrassed her that she was so tight for cash, but she was a single mother with no margin for mistakes, living in the house she'd grown up in, paying off her brother for his half, shoring up the leaky roof and splintery steps, repairing the gargling refrigerator and wheezing car, trying hard not to completely lose her mind.

'Those are fun,' Grace offered. And affordable, she added silently.

Katie nodded and put the pencil back in the rack.

The phone rang again and Katie looked at her.

2

'You're not going to get that?'

There was something tight in her young voice, and Grace knew that even at her age, Katie knew how much their fragile security depended on this job, on things going well.

Grace flipped open her cell and recognized Dispatch. She smiled reassuringly at Katie.

'Grace Descanso.'

A man's voice crackled over the line, his voice unrecognizable.

'I can't hear you.'

In Grace's ear, the voice was irritable, distracted. 'Sergeant Treble, headquarters. We got one. Let's roll.'

'I'm not on rotation this week.'

She transferred the phone to her other ear, watching her daughter. Katie was counting out seven pink erasers in the shape of porpoises and putting them into the shopping basket, along with a set of fake teeth.

'Hell you are; you're secondary after Larry and he's not answering his beeper.'

'You're working the wrong sheet.'

'I don't give a rat's ass, sort it out Monday. You answered the phone, you're It.'

'I'm not on duty,' she insisted.

'Yeah, but I say you are.'

She swallowed her rage. The lab was set up so someone was on call a week at a time. Her week wasn't there yet; it started Tuesday morning at seven-thirty. She'd been pulling overtime in the lab lately, processing two homicides and a particularly messy frat party that had left one participant with his little toe shot off by a naked,

3

unknown assailant wearing a Bart Simpson head mask. She had been looking forward to this free day with Katie.

On the phone Treble was saying, 'Patrol responded to a complaint, usual deal. High traffic, bad smell. The duty judge is sending through the warrant.'

'We don't process meth busts, you know that. Call the DEA.' The Drug Enforcement Agency handled cleanup in San Diego.

'Already ahead of you, Grace. These scrotbags left a bucket of blood in the living room. No body.'

'And you want to know if it's enough blood for somebody to have died.'

'Doesn't look like a nosebleed.'

He paused, and Grace could hear the scorn dripping from his voice. 'Or I could just run it by Sid. Your level of cooperation.'

Grace grew very still. It had taken her six months to get back on CSI rotation after an inquiry into slopped samples and falsified data, an inquiry that had cleared Grace but left her feeling vulnerable and defensive, and after five years on the job, needing to prove herself all over again. She didn't want to find herself stuck again in the lab. CSI meant overtime and that meant money, but she needed to plan things like a general, not be ambushed in the party-favor aisle.

'You're really an asshole, you know that?' Grace said it low into the phone, so Katie wouldn't hear.

'Save it, Grace, I'm already married.'

4

'Who's the DL?' She fished in her purse for a pad and pencil.

'Lewin. Not a duty lieutenant, a sergeant. Western substation. He's at the site.'

Katie looked at her, comprehension and resignation flooding her eyes, and Grace realized in that instant how much the day had meant to Katie, too.

'What's the Thomas page?' Grace said into the phone.

Katie blinked and looked away.

★　★　★

It was a shady street in Ocean Beach, with shaggy palms and houses flecked in DayGlo colors, just close enough to the ocean to smell of salt water and kelp. The house stood halfway down the block, cordoned with yellow police tape. A ripped sofa sat in the front yard and trash clotted the tall weeds. Bedsheets obscured the front windows and a faded sticker clung to the front door: NEIGHBORHOOD WATCH! CRIMINAL BEWARE!

A carved pumpkin adorned the junky yard and Grace felt a pang of guilt. Katie had been after her for weeks to buy one. She kept putting it off, and here even unkempt lowlifes living in squalor still made quality time for their kids.

A crowd was starting to gather as uniforms hustled three gaunt men out the door, hands cuffed, and pushed them into waiting patrol cars, followed by a wailing toddler on the hip of a Child Protective Services officer.

Grace pulled into a space vacated by a patrol car and locked up, the list already going in her brain on why this was a better career path than her last choice. *You see dead bodies but you don't* make *them dead, that's a big one.*

She reached into her trunk, rooted past Katie's T-ball bag, a dirty soccer sock, and a spilled carton of Legos, and lifted out her evidence collection kit and pearly white Tyvek protective gear. *You're offered shapelier work clothes in attractive designer colors.*

The front door opened and Detective Sergeant Vince Lewin emerged, flipping his mask off his face so it dangled on the front of his Tyvek suit. Plodding down the steps, he looked like a scowling Pillsbury Dough Boy. He gripped a cage covered in tight mesh wiring and held it as far away from his body as possible. A large snake banged against the wire, fangs bared. *You sometimes get to interact with nature.*

'Show's over. That's it. It's done.' Lewin handed the cage to a uniform who stowed it in the back of a patrol car.

Lewin was in his midforties, with graying hair and a permanent crease between his eyes, made more pronounced by his scowl. Grace had worked with him maybe a dozen times, and the combative edge he carried into every conversation made her instantly tense.

'Dr. D. Takes forty minutes to get here.'

Grace took a slow, irritable breath. 'Thirty-nine. I clocked it.'

'I expected Larry.'

'Yeah, well, I had better things to do, too,

6

Vince, but they rescheduled my kidney dialysis so I could come.'

'You're kidding, right?'

She pulled on her Tyvek suit and looked past him toward the house. 'What'd you find?'

'A shitload of nasty. Two pit bulls, assault rifles, six snakes — big ones.' He gestured toward the cage. 'That guy was booby-trapped to the kitchen cabinet. Missed him the first time around.'

'That inspires confidence.'

'I'm not paid to hold your hand, Grace.' He was still grumpy about the dialysis joke. Too late, she remembered his mother-in-law had died of renal failure.

A balding man in his midtwenties detached from an assistant DA in the crowd and trotted over. He was wearing wire-rimmed glasses and a Tyvek suit in a muddy tan color that signaled he worked for the DEA. Agents apparently hadn't gotten the memo about looking spiffy. The suit looked a size too small.

'You guys met? The new DEA chemist Chip Page; Chip, Dr. D.'

'Grace Descanso,' she corrected pleasantly. She pulled on a bootee.

'Yeah, fine. Grace Descanso. She's been a police forensic biologist for — I don't know, what?'

'Five.'

'Five years. Sol retired early and moved to Florida so we got Chip,' Lewin answered her unasked question and tapped his clipboard, as if the small effort at pleasantry exhausted him. 'Set to live here the next few days?'

'Sure,' Grace lied.

'Then welcome to amateur hour. These guys didn't go to the Cordon Bleu.'

A taco van turned onto the street and the driver grinned at Grace and gave a jaunty thumbs-up as if he knew her. She took a good look at him as she pulled on the other bootee.

He had a narrow face and glassy eyes and a thatch of black hair and seemed to be about her age, thirty-two. The taco van veered — he'd been staring at her rather than the road ahead — and the uniform on crowd control bellowed at him to move it along. Things could be worse. She could be driving a rancid food truck, trying to stay one step ahead of the Department of Environmental Health.

'Heard some bozo blew up a trailer park in Reno drying down acetone in an oven.' Lewin pulled on a second set of gloves and passed the box to Chip. 'They found body parts in trees. Chip, any questions, ask. Don't want to send you home in a box. Several.'

Chip blanched and Lewin looked away, satisfied. Grace smiled at Chip in what she hoped was a reassuring way.

'You were really a doctor?' Chip asked. It was a blurt. 'What happened?'

'Double glove, Chip.' Grace passed him the box again, her good humor gone.

The crowd drifted off and stationed themselves in nearby yards, talking quietly. Vince Lewin turned back to Grace and Chip, all business.

'Chip, you got residue but nothing exciting, no pounds of product. Grace, work your magic. There are enough spatters in there to keep a busload of Rorschach head shrinks happy for a year. The house is sealed and it's going to stay that way. We're clear on phosgene. We're gonna dust, collect. Be smart and stay alive. Ready?'

Grace cinched the hood of her suit and attached her bug mask — an air-purifying respirator — and followed him up the stairs, Chip lagging behind her. Grace let him go past her through the door. An armed patrol officer stood at the door, feet spread, another one at the perimeter, and Grace remembered hearing how they'd once busted somebody who'd wandered into a meth house after the task force had secured it. He'd come to do a buy, realizing too late that Joe and Jim and Rudy were already downtown rolling their fingers across ink pads and that the nice man inside with the wide smile wasn't selling anything except a felony conviction.

The interior was dark, windows covered in duct tape and sheets, and it took a moment for her eyes to adjust. A dark stain saturated a sliver of ratty carpet and spattered a nearby wall.

'Chip, don't come near this, okay?'

She squatted down carefully out of reach of the stain and roved her flashlight beam over the wall. The drops curled like exclamation marks in a hurry, which meant that whoever was bleeding had been moving. Or blood had scattered from a weapon that was moving. Or maybe it had been an earthquake and the wall

9

had been moving. Something had moved, and whatever it was, it meant work on her end, and a lot of it.

'Lovely.' She'd never see Katie again.

Grace stood up. Already her arms inside the Tyvek were damp as boiled hot dogs. The suit sealed her like a deli chicken. Too bad she hadn't wrapped herself first in secret herbs and cellophane; she could lose six inches in an hour. She wondered if women losing inches in a spa wrap suddenly exploded like a hot sausage the instant they drank a glass of water. She had to stop thinking about food.

'Any ideas?' Lewin stood at her elbow.

'Yeah, Vince, somebody bleeding was in here once.'

'Ha-ha, very funny.'

She turned her attention to the rest of the living room. The floor was littered with asthma inhalers, so thick it looked like an army of oversized, hard-shelled insects. Bedding lay tangled across a stained mattress. A child's dump truck climbed a hill of fertilizer. A meth pipe tilted out the toy cab of the truck. Matchbook strips, ripped down to the red phosphorus, were scattered across a table, along with boxes of diet pills and stiffened coffee filters. Red, as if they'd been dipped in blood.

'What do you think?' Lewin looked at Chip. His voice was tinny in the mask.

'Nazi method,' Chip said, thinking it was the same cooking the efficient Germans had used during the war, to keep the troops awake and ready.

10

Lewin made a buzzer sound. 'Wrong.' He looked at Grace.

'Red phosphorus reduction method,' Grace said. She turned to Chip, shrugging it off. 'Nazi method's lithium and ammonia gas; it's white powder.'

Lewin looked disappointed that she'd gotten it right. He turned toward the kitchen, motioning them to follow. Under his mask, Chip's face was a pasty gray and dots of sweat sprouted on his upper lip.

'You okay?' She stopped walking. 'Chip?'

'Claustrophobic. Always have been. Even when I was a kid.' Chip's voice was muffled in the mask. He shrugged, embarrassed. 'Don't tell Sergeant Lewin.'

She nodded. She could tell by the way his hand kept going to it that Chip carried a gun. Most criminalists opted against it; it was bulky and unnecessary. Police controlled the scene and afforded protection, but occasionally Grace ran across a wannabe cop. They always carried.

Her bootees made a snicking sound on the filthy floor. Pyrex pans littered the stove, and a jug of what looked like denatured alcohol lay on the grimy table. The cabinets were empty except for lighter fluid, Drano, duct tape, and a half-opened box of Froot Loops.

Chip was swallowing, his face shiny with sweat. 'Okay to take off my mask?'

Lewin's head shot up from inspecting residue in a pan. 'You mean safe? Yeah, but — '

The rest of the sentence died as Chip tore off his mask and screamed. His eyes bulged and he

11

shoved Lewin out of the way and raced for the paint-blistered kitchen door, yanking it open and pelting down the steps into the backyard. They could hear him taking great shuddering gasps.

'Stupid kid,' Vince said.

Grace shrugged, looking around. 'He'll learn. They don't call it *cat* for nothing.'

Methamphetamine cooking smelled like cat urine, if the cat were as big as a town car and the box hadn't been changed in months.

Outside, Chip uttered a sharp strangled cry that cut off abruptly into silence.

'I'll check out the other rooms. Leave the sheets up. I'm going to document the blood spatter.'

'Have at it.' Lewin put down the search warrant, along with the hazardous-waste forms. 'I gotta go babysit.'

'Hey, Vince — he's a chickie. Go easy on him.'

Lewin grimaced through his mask and stepped out the kitchen door. Grace looked around. It was going to cost the state a bundle getting it cleaned up.

Something large slapped against the house and slid to the ground. It was a sound like a piece of rotten fruit hitting clumsily and hard. She straightened, listening. Silence. A thin, reedy whistling grew in the silence, followed by a muffled moan.

She swallowed. 'Vince?'

The whistling escalated, the sound wickering through the air like a broken electrical circuit, and the hair on the back of her neck pricked. She moved silently to the kitchen door and down the

12

stairs, yanking off the breathing mask, her head light without the weight.

It was a small yard with rusted cars up on blocks, obscuring the alley. She stared blankly. There was supposed to be a uniform out back protecting them, just like there was out front, but if he was there, she couldn't see him.

From deep in the yard came a bubbling sound. She'd only heard that rattle in ER and it didn't sound any better now. She eased around the hulk of a car. Chip Page lay clutching his throat, his fingers slick with surging blood. He stared up at her mutely, his eyes wide and terrified, his glasses askew.

She could see into the alley now. A uniformed officer lay facedown in a pool of blood, his legs at odd angles. Blocking the alley was the taco van, its motor running.

Her throat closed and she dropped to her knees. Chip's windpipe had been sliced. His mouth opened soundlessly. *Establish an airway. Make sure the victim is breathing.* His eyes flicked to a spot behind her and she looked over her shoulder.

Pain exploded across her jaw as she was broadsided by a fist and yanked to her feet. It was so unexpected all she felt was a dazed terror and blinding pain behind her eyes and a shooting fire down her arm.

'You lose.'

He was taller than he'd looked in the taco van, pulsing as if he'd been hot-wired. His breath smelled minty fresh. In his other hand, he held a butcher knife.

13

He jerked her higher, dragging her backward toward the house, his arm gripping her throat, closing off her airway. Her lungs roared and pricks of light exploded in her eyes. He stumbled, cursing, and she stepped down hard on something mushy.

It was the partially severed head of Detective Sergeant Vince Lewin. The mask had cracked off and lay to the side. His lips were gray, eyes wide, startled. The butcher knife had cut through his Adam's apple and it lay, like a small oyster, in a bed of blood.

On the ground, Chip feebly pointed his finger like a gun. His eyes had started to film. A gun. Dying rookie Chip Page was trying to remind her that he carried a gun. She banged her elbow hard up into her attacker's throat and slammed her boot back into his shin, and for an instant, he loosened his grip and she wrenched free and stumbled over to Chip, ripping open his Tyvek suit and scrabbling his gun free. It was a Glock 30, slippery with Chip's sweat and blood, unbelievably heavy. She lunged to her feet, bringing the gun up as she chambered a round and pointed it in a blur of motion fueled by terror and a primitive rage.

'Freeze, asshole. If you think I won't squeeze it, you're wrong.'

He blinked once, refocused on her face. 'He's coming for you,' he whispered.

'Shut up.' Sweat leaked into her gloves and she tightened her grip.

'He's the Spikeman. He transmits orders from outer space through the wires in my brain.'

'I said *shut up.*'

'I came to save you, warn you. He's after you, the Spikeman. You need to run, Grace, now, before it's too late.'

A chill shot through her. He knew her name. How did he know her name?

'Don't you want to know what he's going to do to you?'

She hesitated a split second and saw the knife winking through the air and she pulled the trigger, kept pulling it, emptied it over and over, until he toppled, the back of his head blown off, and still she kept clicking the trigger, firing some phantom bullet, sobbing.

2

Grace couldn't stop shivering. Dark was settling over Ocean Beach, the sun a fiery ball sliding into the Pacific. Four blocks away the sand on the beach would be cold now, latched in kelp, the good-natured mothers and toddlers gone, the tourists with white legs sucking Diet Pepsi and eyeing the tattooed volleyball players gone, everyone to their own warm rooms and hot baths and Olive Garden dinners. The beach belonged to the skittering creatures of the night pushing Safeway carts and muttering, runaways with studded ears and vacant eyes, the predators. The world she worked so hard to keep away from her daughter.

And now look what happened. Look how good she was. She couldn't even give the kid a dad, and now she'd almost made the kid an orphan.

Her stomach hurt, acid roiling up. She gripped her knees and bit her lip to keep from wailing. She should be home now, that was the deal, that was the whole thing. Katie had that pen pal assignment she'd been postponing, had to get it done tonight.

'Did you hear me?'

Grace pulled herself back, looking through the window of the squad car, refocusing. The crime scene glowed yellow in a surreal splash of police car lights, television crews, crime scene technicians. The neighbors were back in force, smoking

16

cigarettes, drinking beer, and joking. The two cops on traffic detail pressed the cars forward, gesturing savagely, sweat and weariness on their faces.

Grace chafed her hands together under the thin wool blanket and shifted on the backseat of the patrol car. 'I've already gone through it. I gave my preliminary statement. I'm coming in tomorrow to sign it.'

'Grace.' Sid Felcher, her crime lab boss, sighed heavily and swiveled in the front seat, his face oily. It wasn't his squad car, it belonged to the detective who'd taken her statement, but Sid had climbed into the front seat when the detective had gone inside the meth house, and now he rested his arm along the top of the seat as if he were polishing the leather with his forearm.

'Another study just released, found it on the Internet, two biggest stressors for supervisors. Causes ulcers, heart attacks, groin injuries.' He raised his eyebrows and they inched together like furry mating caterpillars. 'Well?'

'Sid, I need to call Katie. I need to go home.'

'We already took care of that, remember? She's fine, your daughter's fine. Okay, so the answer is, *ta dah!*' Sid waved his hands expansively. His nails were bitten. 'Two main stressors for guys like me, poor working-class schmos just trying to make a living, is having to discipline, take action, against a subordinate. That means you. Huge stressor, stroke city. Other one is having to deal with the public, explain what the subordinate did that was so wrong we're going to have to apologize for about

17

a million years and maybe even pay big bucks to get things straightened out.'

This couldn't be happening. Even with Sid at his most dysfunctional.

'Sid, in case you forgot, he had a butcher knife.'

'But he wasn't swinging it, right? I mean, not *at* you. Just that little side-to-side thing, you said, but not actually *at* you.'

She sat back in the seat. 'Is there something I don't know?'

'Grace, be more specific. What you don't know could — '

'About what just happened,' she interrupted. 'Is there something I don't know?'

'Like what?'

'Like have they ID'd him?'

He hesitated a beat too long. 'Whoever it was, it was a human life.'

She felt rage surge under the exhaustion. 'Are you suggesting I did something wrong shooting a man with a butcher knife who had just killed a drug agent, a sergeant detective, and a uniformed cop?'

'Whoa. I'm not suggesting anything, Grace, I'm just passing the time, sharing a survey I downloaded from Yahoo.' He grinned. His gums were receding.

'I need to go home.' She pressed her fingers into her temples, fighting the impulse to bite him.

'See, this is what they call a critical incident.'

'I know what a critical incident is,' Grace snapped.

A man darted out of the house and under the police tape, Paul Collins from Trace. Bags sagged under his eyes, heightening his resemblance to an aging basset hound on speed. He lumbered toward his car, face grim and an evidence kit clenched in his hands.

'Thing is, another study.' Sid unwrapped a toothpick and massaged his gums. 'Some shooters, they get permanent emotional trauma, they go a little cuckoo, they visit la-la land and never come back.'

He sucked noisily on the toothpick and twirled it. His lips were wet.

'Supervisors — we're responsible, I'm responsible — as your boss, like it or not. I mean, I don't take you in, get your head examined, you could sue me for mondo moola, retire to Florida, you and your kid, how old is Katie now? Two?'

'Five this Saturday. She's already in kindergarten.'

'Even better. Closer to college.' Sid fished car keys out of his Hawaiian shirt pocket and jangled them. 'See, the thing is, you don't have a choice. Nobody wants to see a shrink, ever, fillet out their personal life, spill their guts to some stranger with a clipboard. I wouldn't. Who would? You'd have to be crazy.'

He grinned at his little joke.

'So the way it comes down, the department policy is, you have to go whether you want to or not.'

'You haven't answered my question.' She shifted in the seat.

'Which was?'

19

'Who'd I shoot, Sid?'

Sid looked out the window and stared at the sky. Grace saw it seconds before she heard it, the heavy *whup whup* of rotor blades. A helicopter.

In Guatemala, they'd brought the girl in on a stretcher, off a helicopter. Same sound.

The wind was picking up and it hurled loose trash across the yard. A palm tree tilted crazily back and forth like a metronome.

'Yeah, actually. They have an ID. Eddie Loud. Mean anything?'

She shook her head.

The helicopter circled and landed delicately in the flattened grass. Grace stared at the man in the passenger seat.

It was a California U.S. senator. Albert Loud looked older than his pictures, haggard, the lines around his mouth deep grooves, his nose hooked and ridged. He stared at her without comprehension.

'I'm getting you out of here. Sit tight.' Sid raised his voice over the roar of the blades. Senator Loud was crouching and running away from the slowing rotor blades, toward the meth house, a phalanx of officers crowding around him, keeping the press at bay.

'Why is he here?' Her head felt light. 'What's going on?'

In front of her on the lawn, the reporters turned, eyeing her. It only took a split second. They wheeled, lunged at her.

'Holy shit.' Sid pulled her out the other door, gripping her arm in the blinding flash of lights and clamoring reporters. 'Head down!' he screamed. 'Head down.'

She ducked and he pushed her through the tangle of cords and microphones.

'He's here, Grace,' Sid barked, as they burst onto the street and ran for her car, 'Senator Albert Loud is here because it was his son back there. You killed his son.'

3

She pulled into the driveway and her headlights revealed her house in pitiless relief, like in a police lineup. Hers was the ratty one in the middle, squeezed into a row of minimansions.

The house on the right belonged to a retired osteopath and his wife. Blocky pink stucco, gated and electronically locked, with a metal fence spiking into iron bulbs every few feet. Nobody came in or out of that house. Even the mailman used a cement slot built into the fence.

The house on the left cascaded in white cubes amid designer palms. A stoop-shouldered attorney Grace's age lived there, with a blond wife and two kids in private school uniforms. She'd hear them in the back sometimes through the natural barrier of high succulents that separated their properties. At night, the motor in their swimming pool gargled like an old man.

On her house, the dormer window flaked, the front door bulged with moisture, the second step leading to the door splintered and sagged. Even the trees looked bad. Leathery and overgrown, they shed gray leaves like molting birds onto the green tar paper roof of the garage clamped onto the left side of the house.

She watched as a squirrel darted across the front yard and sprinted along the splintery picket fence, diving into a shrub under the bay window. The bay window hung over a yard she was too tired to tend, the window made of cramped squares of glass leaded and soldered, looking as if it had been assembled by some parsimonious contractor cousin of Dickens — *please, sir, may I have one more pane of glass, sir, a little larger, if you please, oh, you're too generous* — flanked by two narrow windows that actually opened, providing some relief in the summer when she sat in the living room and contemplated her life.

Not much relief, considering what she had to work with. Cramped, untidy, spilling with dog hair and scraps of paper, vagrant Cheerios and missing shin guards wedged under sofa cushions. Home.

Not that she could complain. From the street it looked like a broken-down fire hazard, but inside, her home held an amazing secret. She had no illusions about ever being able to afford a new roof or granite countertops in her lifetime. It was enough, plenty, more than enough that the house sat on an actual beach in a section of San Diego in Point Loma called La Playa, and that the back of the lot faced out over the harbor and gently tilting sailboats, while across the water the glass and chrome towers of downtown San Diego twinkled on the horizon like small crystal boxes.

Only thirteen homes shared the beach that had once been a staging area for seamen melting tallow. They were whalers, Portuguese immigrants transplanted from the Azores, sturdy soldiers of fortune who rode the seas and started a tuna empire. They'd all lived together; their kids had gone to Cabrillo Elementary and they'd shopped at family-run stores and eaten at small restaurants clustered along Rosecrans, the main thoroughfare. Now the fishermen had moved a few blocks inland, and real estate along La Playa beach had skyrocketed.

She'd never sell, despite increasingly clamorous offers from Realtors and sometimes people just out for Sunday drives. The view always calmed her, but it wasn't only the view that made Grace fight so hard to stay there. The house was all she had left of her dad.

Thoughts crashed. She turned off the ignition and sat in the dark. Once, her dad had taken her alone to Lake Morena to catch fish. He made his living doing that, in deep waters, but this was vacation, and he was spending part of it with her. She'd crawled eagerly into the boat. Six years old, still small enough so the wooden sides seemed high. He'd heaved the boat into the water and jumped in after her, her hands clamped around a tin can of worms. That was her job, he'd said, keeping the can safe while he climbed into the boat. He plunged his hand into the black soil and pulled out a worm. It glistened plump gray and magenta, pulsing in his hand. It was the most magnificent thing she'd ever seen. Her dad's other hand flashed into his tackle box and in the same fluid motion pierced the creature with a hook. Blood spurted and it thrashed, trying to get away. Her throat closed in fright. It was alive just like she was. It had blood and it hurt. She burst into tears and begged him to take her home. She didn't mean for it to die, she whispered.

24

And now she'd put a bullet through a man's skull. Several bullets. There had been a fence next to Eddie Loud, and the force of the gunfire had splashed it with bits of brain and flesh and blood. The raw stink of fresh meat had hung hotly in the night air.

Now she couldn't seem to get that smell out of her nostrils. Heavily, Grace stepped from the car and locked the door. She could hear them inside as she went down the service alley on the right side of the house. Helix banged against the porch screen door, whining.

She unlocked it and Helix bounded toward her clattering on his fake leg, tail wagging in a frenzy of doggie devotion. He was a mix, a mongrel stray, part shepherd and collie, hit by a car as a puppy and left to die. Grace had rushed him to the vet, who'd informed her that fixing him up would cost the equivalent of a small developing country's entire gross national product. Grace had made the mistake of going into the death chamber to say a weepy good-bye. Five minutes later she was scheduling the operation that had saved his life.

'Some alarm system.' Grace scratched him behind his ears, and he rolled over and yipped. She rinsed off her Tyvek suit and filled the sink with water and bleach, spying a discarded pizza carton tucked behind the wastebasket. Helix followed her through the kitchen, his doggy nails clicking across the linoleum like a flamenco dancer.

The calamity of being a parent was that there was no off switch, no time-out for personal disaster. Schoolwork still called, lunches had to be packed, reprimands administered. Her head pounded.

In the family room, Katie was belting out a country western song, standing on the piano bench wearing a pink flowered nightie, Mickey Mouse ears, and cowboy boots, almost dwarfed by the Gibson she was strumming. Her fingers were so tiny she only played the bottom string of the chords. Lottie stood crouched over the piano, banging the rhythm, her silvery blond head moving in time. She was wearing orange vinyl hot pants and white go-go boots with tassels and a vest with beads that shimmied as she moved.

'No, honey,' Lottie interrupted, 'that's a C chord you're playing; it's a G.' She broke into song, demonstrating, '*We don't share the same time zone . . .* '

Katie focused, nodding, tried it again, her voice clear and treble. '*We don't share the same time zone . . . you're not my phone-a-friend . . . and all the special features I like best you never do intend . . .* '

Lottie nodded, banging out the chords with force. 'That's right, kid, milk it, honey.'

Helix bounded across the carpet and skidded into Lottie. He still had trouble stopping properly.

'For Pete's sake. How'd he get out . . . '

Grace smacked the empty pizza carton against her thigh and Lottie snapped her mouth shut.

'Busted,' Katie said.

Lottie guiltily banged the lid down on the

26

piano. Katie turned toward her mother to plead her case. She froze on the bench, staring.

'Mommy, are you okay?' Katie's voice was small, and too late, Grace remembered her face.

At least Katie hadn't seen her on TV. Lottie's idea of television news was watching psychic pets find missing jewelry.

'I'm fine.'

'Your jaw is all purple.'

'I just had a little accident, but I'm fine. That's not what I want to talk about. What I want to know is . . . ' She lifted the pizza carton as if she were signaling the ships in the bay beyond the sliding glass door. 'What is this? Lottie?'

Grace waggled the carton at her and Lottie sneezed.

'You know I'm allergic to that dog.'

'Answer the question.'

Other people had mothers who wore suits and went to the Wednesday Club, where they drank tea and listened to lectures on Quail Botanical Gardens. Grace's mother was still in her midfifties, with a smooth, unlined face, stuffed into a pair of hot pants so tight that her rear looked like two cantaloupes squeezed into a plastic bag.

'You weren't supposed to see that pizza carton,' Lottie said.

'You know she had pizza for lunch. Lottie, you promised you'd fix her a real dinner. Something with vegetables in it.'

'It's rude to call your mother Lottie,' Lottie said. 'It's not respectful. Is that what you want your daughter to call you when she grows up?'

'Latte?' Katie squealed. 'You want me to call Mommy *Latte?*'

'Sure, like one of those coffee drinks,' Grace said.

'It's not like you're a Roller Derby queen.' Lottie's eyes traveled over Grace's face. 'A mud wrestler. Look at you. What did you do? Walk into a wall? You know, you can't spend your life running through jobs like they were a pair of hose.'

'We're not talking about my face or career choices. We're talking about dinner.'

'Jeez, Grace, lighten up,' Lottie said.

It was like having two kids, only one of them could drive and order take-out. 'Where's your homework, Katie?'

'A four year-old child — '

'Five,' Katie said. 'I'll be five on Saturday.'

'A five-year-old child in kindergarten shouldn't be expected to do homework,' Lottie said. 'You should change schools. I bet you'd like more recess, wouldn't you, honey?'

'So where is it?' Grace repeated.

Katie said brightly, 'Grandma's taking me to Disneyland for my birthday.'

'You're having a party on your birthday,' Grace said. 'You're not going to Disneyland.'

'Not right *then*,' Lottie said. 'Of course, not then. I have to miss her party, I told you. Terrell and I are going out of town.' She leaned down toward Katie and cooed, 'And that's why I'm taking my sweet little sweetums to Disneyland upon my return. I personally know one of the dancing dwarfs, who's prepared to give us a

28

behind-the-scenes tour of the Magic Kingdom.'

'Goodie,' Katie cried.

'You did make her do her homework, right?' Grace pressed a finger against her temple. A vein throbbed.

Lottie pulled on her lip.

'The one thing I asked you to do.'

Lottie shot her a wounded look and fiddled with her hair. Her bracelet clanked. It was fake turquoise that looked like gobs of used chewing gum. 'We were getting around to it.' She opened her mouth, threw back her head and sneezed. 'That dog. I mean it.'

'When, Lottie? It is now after eight on a school night and all you've done so far is pump up my child on caffeinated soda and yellow grease.'

'Grace, you're just not fun anymore. You need to work on your people skills.'

'I want you to sit, Katie.' Grace's voice was icy calm. 'I want you to sit at this desk and not move until you finish your homework. Is that clear?'

Katie stomped to the desk.

Grace yanked open a drawer and got out Katie's stationery. It was pink and orange and had psychedelic ponies gamboling. She positioned a purple crayon in her daughter's limp hand.

'This is fun,' Grace said. 'We're having fun learning about the mail. You send this to somebody, you get something back. You're going to like it.' It sounded like a threat.

Katie started to whimper. 'You can't make me.'

'Oh, for Pete's sake,' Lottie protested.

'I don't have anybody to write to!' Katie burst into tears and put her head down, dampening the stationery.

'Write to Clint, honey,' Lottie said, 'he'd be happy to have you — '

'She is not writing to Clint,' Grace said, and Katie wiped her eyes and raised her head, interested at this turn of events.

'Who's Clint?'

'She's not writing to some hick singer who shellacs his hair until it's the size of a turkey rump.'

Grace couldn't believe she was having this conversation after the day she'd had, except that it was with Lottie, so it made sense. In the kitchen, the phone rang.

'Hick!' Lottie said in a hushed, stricken voice. Her unnaturally violet eyes brimmed with tears. 'I want you to know Clint's hosted the first hour of the *Grand Ole Opry* seventeen times, and I mean the first hour that's broadcast, too, not the one that warms everybody up. Not even George has done that.'

'She's not doing it,' Grace said.

'How do you spell Clint?' Katie asked.

'Katie, enough. And Lottie, would you *please* get that phone?'

Grace waited while Lottie stalked out of the room, muttering about personal maid service.

'Remember that girl Mommy told you was her friend when she was in high school?'

Katie shook her head.

Grace reached around Katie to rifle through the desk.

30

'We haven't gotten a pumpkin and you promised. We never do anything.'

Novels made it look easy. Heroines, they had a kid, they had problems, the kid got farmed out for long stretches, just dropped conveniently out of the story, while the heroine — always taller and skinnier than in real life, too, it wasn't right — got herself out of trouble in some plucky way and came back to the kid and the kid was relaxed and happy and clueless about how close her mom had come to being turned into roadkill.

'Nothing fun. I'm just a little kid. I'm supposed to have fun.'

'You're having a party Saturday.'

From the kitchen, Lottie sneezed and trilled into the phone, 'Hello? Helllooo?'

'And no goodie bags ready yet either. None. Not one.'

'Oh, good, here.' Grace pulled out her address book and started thumbing through it. It was slow going. Somehow, she'd mixed up the *R*'s with the *S*'s. 'Well, Mommy had a friend named Annie and she grew up and got married, and they had a kid and he lives on a farm in Iowa and that's who you can send your drawing to. And you can tell me what to say, if you want, and I'll write it down.'

'And a costume. You said you'd make one this year. You promised.'

Grace had. Months ago it sounded like a fine idea, she just couldn't remember why. In the kitchen, Lottie banged down the phone, cursing.

'You promised and you forgot. Just like you

31

forgot to take me to see the panda baby at the zoo.'

'The panda baby was sleeping, Katie.'

'You promised and we didn't.'

Katie had the instincts of a pit bull. She just lunged and clamped hold, dragging Grace back over every thing she'd promised and failed to deliver. Grace would be on her deathbed and Katie would kneel and clasp her wizened hand and stroke the purply veins, lean in close and murmur, 'You promised popcorn and we were out.' Then Katie would pull out a *list* of wrongs, and it would be on one of those long computer paper rolls, and she'd settle in for a nice, long chat.

Death would be a relief. Grace kept looking through her address book, ignoring the expletives coming from the kitchen. 'He's nine. A Cub Scout, I think.'

Her finger stopped. 'There. Here it is. His name is Dusty Rhodes. He'll enjoy getting a lovely drawing from you.'

'No, he won't. He's a boy.'

Nobody ever told her it would be this hard. This constant and this hard. 'They have animals and he has a paper route and he's nine,' she repeated. 'Or ten. Anyway. That's who you can send your letter to.' She block-printed out the address onto the envelope.

'I could write to Daddy.' It hung there. Grace looked at her. Katie stared at her hands. Katie tried lots of things to get out of what she didn't want to do, but never the trump card, her dad.

Grace had created this longing in this small, beautiful girl, this empty space that nothing filled. She'd promised herself she'd be better than Lottie, and she'd turned around and created the same ache in Katie that she'd had, growing up.

'We've been through this, honey,' Grace said gently. 'Remember? Daddy died before you were born. It has to be a real letter. Not one to heaven.'

'Tell me again.' Katie stood up and Grace settled into the chair and pulled her onto her lap.

Katie's eyes were a rich brown, a Portuguese color that spoke of sailing ships and rough seas and High Mass said in lonely places.

'We loved each other very much.'

'Uh-huh. Jack. You met him at a Padres game. They were playing New York.'

'Right. We got pregnant and were going to get married, which is not the right order to do things in, and I don't want you doing it that way either, but I'll still love you no matter what.'

'Only there was a car crash. That's what happened.'

'That's what happened. And he would have loved you, honey.'

'A lot.'

'Over the moon. That's what he would have been, having you as his daughter.'

Lottie appeared in the archway. 'Wrong number. He hung up.'

'You're sure it was a he?'

'I could tell just the way he breathed it was a he. I know how men breathe, Grace.'

'So this Dusty kid,' Katie said. 'That's a silly dilly stupid name.'

Grace glanced uneasily toward the phone, her thoughts elsewhere. 'What? Try and leave that part out, Katie.'

★ ★ ★

An hour later, Lottie mercifully gone, Grace finished the carton of yogurt she was eating standing up. She bent down and kissed her daughter on the forehead.

Katie's hair was a curly cloud on the pillow. Her favorite doll nestled in her arms, a Katie doll built to look like her, an extravagant birthday present Grace had given her for her fourth birthday. It had a recorder inside, so that Katie's voice came out in short staccato sentences that Katie periodically changed. The voice was so lifelike that Grace sometimes thought it was Katie herself and dropped whatever she was doing to answer, much to Katie's great amusement, which made Grace want to permanently injure the Katie doll's vocal cords in any one of a number of unfortunate accidents.

Katie's eyes were closed, along with the doll's. They were dressed in matching pink nighties, caramel-colored hair tangled in wild manes, dark long lashes against pink cheeks. On the vanity lay the drawing, smudged and crinkled with violent splotches of color. It appeared to be a giant smiling orange head floating over a pink and orange lake. Katie had dictated a short message to go along with it.

Dear Dusty: How are you? I am fine. This is Cinderella who is riding in a big pumpkin. She is inside. That is why nobody can see her. Mommy says you came to our house and broke your arm. You need to write me back right away so I can pass kindergarten. Sincerely, Katie Descanso.

Impulsively, Grace ripped a piece of paper out of a wide-lined notebook she found in Katie's bookshelf and added a quick note of her own:

Dear Annie: We missed hearing from you at Christmas. Hope you're okay. I know this is a lot, but could you prod Dusty to answer this right away? Katie's had this pen pal assignment looming over her for weeks. Of course. Love you, thanks. G.

'We get to play the Timer Game tomorrow, right?' Katie's voice was blurred with sleep.

She'd forgotten about the Timer Game. 'Right.'

'Good.' Katie shifted and licked her lip, eyes closed. 'You're wrong about one thing, Mommy.'

'Only one?' Grace sealed the letters in an envelope and dropped it on the dresser. She opened the drawers.

'He's not dead.'

'Who?' She pulled together shorts and a top and underwear. There was a long silence, and Grace thought Katie had dropped off to sleep.

'Daddy,' Katie muttered. Her lips went slack. She breathed in through her nose.

A prick of unease darted through her. She put down the clothes. 'Honey. Katie.' Grace touched her shoulder gently. 'What are you talking about, sweetie? With Daddy.'

'He visits me sometimes.' Katie shifted under the covers, punching the pillow down, trying to find a comfortable spot.

'Visits you?' Grace shifted her weight. She adjusted the quilt. They'd bought it on sale at Penney's, small pink squares of pink and white rosebuds.

'Uh-huh. I'll wake up. He'll be there, at the end of my bed. He talks to me, too.'

'What does he say?'

'Stuff. Just private stuff. He's coming back for me.' She yawned hugely. 'Night, Mommy.'

'Night, sweetie.'

'Wait till I sleep?' Katie's voice was faint.

'Sure.'

The room faced out over Scott Street. In the dark, the soccer and T-ball trophies on Katie's bookshelf were indistinct soldiers. The half-opened window was a small black square hanging over the eaves slanting down to the front porch. The dotted Swiss curtains moved gently, caught in an invisible breeze.

Grace stroked her daughter's hair. 'Katie? You do know he doesn't do that, right? Sweetie, you do know that?'

Katie's mouth opened into a slack O. One small foot hung out of the pink quilt. Grace cradled it in her hands. It was warm and delicate as a shell.

She kissed the arch, tucked it back in, and

gently eased the window shut.

Across the street, a shadow moved. Grace tensed. It was a dog, nosing in the trash. Screens. She had to spring for screens.

Helix was dreaming on the braided rug when she entered her bedroom at the end of the hallway, his fake leg spasming the air. From her bedroom sliding glass window, the harbor spread out before her, glittering with boats tethered in black water. She pulled the sheer curtains and locked her bedroom door. She could feel her heart banging dully in her chest as she went to her closet and found it.

It was a small hard box made of enamel and she kept it on the top shelf under her sweaters. She was breathing through her mouth now and Helix cracked an eye open to look at her blearily before settling back into sleep. She lay down on the bed and put the box on her chest and felt its small cold heaviness, and her finger slid into the crack of the box and she sighed deeply and opened it.

The phone rang.

Helix jerked out of sleep and growled once deep in his throat. 'It's okay, boy, it's okay.'

She stared at the machine, wondering if this was going to be another night where she was plagued with hang-ups. She heard Jeanne's voice leaving a message, and she put the box aside and rolled over and picked up. 'Hey.'

'My God, I can't believe what you've been through.'

'Did you call earlier?' Grace sat up. Helix stretched and got up, taking a few steps and flopping down next to her ankles, his ear cocked, watching her.

'What? No, why?'

'I keep getting hang-ups. Never mind.'

Her eyes strayed to a group of photos on the wall and found the one of a beaming nun holding the hand of a shy Guatemalan kid who looked to be about ten. She frowned and reached down to scratch Helix behind his ears. He made a small sound of pleasure and his tail thumped the wooden floor.

'Are you watching the news?'

'What channel?'

'All the channels, kiddo.' Jeanne's whiskey-ravaged voice dropped into a phlegmy rattle and Grace could hear her sucking on a lozenge. 'They're withholding your name for the time being, there's that at least. Some wild man in a Hawaiian shirt's pushing you out the squad car and screaming at you to duck.'

Grace felt drained. 'Sid. My boss. I've told you about him.'

'Oh, so that's Sid. I always pictured somebody taller.'

Grace tried to smile.

'Who was taking care of Katie?'

'You mean while it happened? Lottie.'

Jeanne groaned. 'God. Oil on the fire. You need to take a meeting? I could stay with Katie.'

'I'm okay, Jeanne.' An edge had crept into her voice.

Jeanne was silent, except for the sound of crunching. 'I could come anyway.'

Grace shifted the phone and sank back,

stretching out on the quilt. A pain jolted her midriff, and she massaged her side.

'Grace?'

Tears welled and leaked down her face, wetting the quilt and pooling near her ears.

'Honey?'

'I'm here.' Her voice was desolate, lost.

'Talk to me, honey.'

Grace curled into a ball and rocked. 'I can't. I don't.' Her voice was low, fighting it.

'Start anyplace. Start with what happened.'

Grace squeezed her eyes shut. 'Can't. Too soon.'

'Then start with how it feels.'

Her belly was on fire, her head throbbed, her shoulder felt wrenched from the socket, and everything safe in the world was gone. She was in Guatemala again, and the world was on fire. It happened fast, when it came, with a force that never failed to derail her. It was close now and she was running hard ahead of it, trying to break free.

'Oh, God. Pain. In my gut. Lost. Nobody here. Afraid. Like my body's been torn apart. I'm free-falling, Jeanne.'

'Honey, stay with me.'

Her lips were numb now and she felt a pounding behind her eyes; all the bad horses had been unleashed. A flicker of fire darted across her vision, the screen behind her eyes blinding, and she heard the crackling noise that always presaged a bad attack.

'Stay there. Right there. I'll be there in ten minutes.'

'Door's locked.' Her lips were turning numb.
'I've got a key, remember? I'll be right there.'
'Don't. Don't go. Don't leave me.'
'I'm right here. Take a breath. Come on.
Come on, sweetie. Come on back.'

Grace made herself open her eyes and she stared at the ceiling and forced her breathing to calm down. Her skin felt damp.

'Where are you now? What's happening?'

Grace shook her head and closed her eyes. Her feet were cold and she burrowed them under the pillows. 'If I drove. I could.'

Jeanne crunched down hard on the lozenge and the noise made Grace wince.

'Sure. There's Vons on Rosecrans but why mess around pretending you need milk? Just hit the first liquor store you can find and get it over with. There's one two blocks away.'

Grace exhaled. Her breath was shaky. 'Too hard, Jeanne. This.'

'Don't give me that crap. You know drinking's not the answer.'

Grace took another unsteady breath and the dark thing in her mind slid back to where it lived.

'You heard me, right?'

'Tell me again all the reasons.'

'Katie.'

'That's one.'

'That's five or six million, all bunched up together, Grace. That little girl is your only responsibility. That's all that matters. Doing right by her.'

'My only responsibility?' Grace licked her lip.

The ceiling had stopped moving, and she took a deeper breath. 'Easy for you to say. You have alimony and a house in Mission Hills with a pool, and AA when you want to go slumming.'

'An *empty* house, Grace, an ex-husband who would have gnawed off his own foot to get away, two kids who hate me, neighbors who talk about me behind my back, and yes, AA, but not when I want to go slumming.' Jeanne stopped. 'You okay now? You better?'

'Yeah, I'm fine.' She rolled on her side and took a deep shuddery breath, her eyes on the door, the door that led down the hall to Katie, that sweet bundle of laughter and darting energy, prickly feelings and blazing joy.

'That's it. I'm coming over.' A click. Dial tone.

'Thanks,' Grace whispered.

In her mind, she still heard the whispery voice, the silky question:

Don't you want to know what he's going to do to you?

Going to do to you?

Going to do to you?

41

4

Monday
The CNN reporter had been following the taillights of a battered pickup truck for almost an hour as it headed into the Tohono O'odham Nation, a hundred miles of desert stretching from Arizona into Mexico. It was two in the morning, and stars spangled the night sky.

Mac McGuire was traveling a road he'd taken half a dozen times, but a sudden rain the night before had cut gullies through it and left part of it a mire. He was relieved to have a guide.

On the seat next to him Pete Hildebrand snoozed, a burly arm around the camera. Mac felt a flash of irritation. One day, the car would hit a bump and that camera would fly out of his arms and smack the dashboard like an egg. In back, Aaron Spense stretched out, arms crossed, wearing his dad's Marine boots, iPod earbuds in his ears. Next to him lay a mixer in a tangle of cables and snarl of mikes. Aaron was twenty-two, Pete not much older. It made Mac feel tired. He was thirty-eight, his last birthday.

Usually, CNN would have sent at least one producer, but Mac had insisted on keeping the size down, instinctively understanding that the fewer people pushing into their world, the greater likelihood he had of getting what he'd come for.

He thought through how it was going to go,

what he was going to say, where the overhead boom mike needed to be positioned, and when exactly he wanted Pete to come in close for a tight shot. The mechanics kept his mind off the shoot itself, how important this one was.

Hekka Miasonkopna was a Yaqui Indian girl, three and a half years old, who was born with a damaged left ventricle. What had started as a piece about the nightmare of getting expensive cardiac care when poor had evolved into a series about the complexity of culture shaping worldview and the ferocity of a parent's love.

Hekka's parents knew she would die. They accepted it. So it became Mac's fight, for her. She was now in end-stage and would die without a transplant, something they'd resisted considering. There was another thing they could try. Something so new it was still in experimental trials. So new nobody in the media except Mac and his producers and video team even knew of its existence.

His job was laying out the options and stepping back to record what happened next. Part of him came here wanting to nudge her parents into action, a move that was right at the edge of stepping over the line, and he knew it.

He and his colleagues joked about the special hell reserved for reporters. Someplace where they'd be forced to sit for eternity with the hapless fools they'd talked into doing something — a giddy kid he'd once coached early in his career into getting a tattoo on camera came to mind; that one still gnawed at his conscience — and the problem was that even with the most

43

altruistic of pieces, like this one, there existed a small part inside himself that was looking at it coldly, evaluating it not just for its emotional wallop but for its ability to be a *Mac* piece, helping him — just like that old American Express ad — go everywhere he wanted to go.

Unlike local stations keyed to November sweeps, CNN tracked ratings all the time. TV viewing was higher in the fall, and Mac was working on two series simultaneously that would get big play: a graphic and disturbing one about child porn on the Internet that was close to being in the can, and this one with Hekka, culminating in her ground-breaking surgery and its aftermath.

Providing they went for it. Or not. Either way, it was a story. He hated himself for even thinking that. Mac sincerely wanted her to live. He'd grown attached to the little girl and her family. But part of him, almost equally as strongly, knew if they chose to let her die, it would tug at the audience just as much.

Horrible business, news. Someplace along the line, he'd sold part of himself and he couldn't figure out how to get it back.

Clouds of dust rose and seeped into his vehicle, making it look as if Arturo's truck was floating in a puff of magic. Mac's eyes burned. In the lights, the Coyote Mountains rose like an apparition of shaggy cliffs and granite bluffs.

The pickup veered off road and Mac shifted into low, bumping across a dry riverbed. The Swiss Army knife on his key chain clinked like wind chimes.

The mother was in his pocket; he knew that. She'd try anything to save her kid. The grandfather, Don Jose, was the challenge. Maybe he wasn't even there anymore and it would make things easy. Somehow Mac doubted it. This one hadn't been easy from the first.

The land crumpled into arroyos of creosote bush and cactus. Bony cattle, picking their way among the scrub, flared in the lights and disappeared. Tin houses flashed and were gone.

The truck slowed and disappeared over a rise and Mac followed. The hollow was pitch black, except for a lightbulb hanging over a wooden porch that outlined the sloping roof of a house. Moths banged into the light and an oak stood like a sleeping giant, one branch hanging low over the house.

The truck cab opened and Arturo got out, with his long braids and dusty jeans, a younger version of his elderly father. Kids spilled out of the flatbed. Maria stood in the doorway, a baby on her hip, dark hair streaked prematurely with gray. Worry had etched fine lines on her face.

'Showtime,' Mac McGuire said softly as he pulled to a stop. Pete and Aaron yawned and scratched and rolled out of the vehicle, shivering in the cold. Aaron's dyed hair tips looked like white dandelion tufts in the dark.

'Inside.' Maria pulled Mac over the doorsill and switched on a light.

Hekka's bed sat in the middle of the front room. The kids from the truck crept silently into the room and slid into the corners. The room smelled acrid and old. Hekka's breathing was labored, a bubbly sound that alarmed Mac. Her hair lay limply across the gray pillow. A vein in her neck pulsed. She'd always been smaller than normal, but now her fingers were clubbed and tipped in blue and her lips were ashy. He went to the bed and took her hand. It was icy.

'Hey,' he said softly. 'It's Mac. The reporter.' She moaned in her sleep and her eyelids fluttered. 'Yeah, I know, that's what everybody says when they hear it's me.' He gently slid his hand free and surveyed the room.

An old man close to eighty was sitting in a chair near the window. Mac nodded. Cords of sinew roped Don Jose's arms and most of his teeth were gone. His few remaining teeth were yellowed tusks. He patted a pouch strapped to his belt, extracting a piece of guasima wood and a small knife. It was a half-carved figure three inches tall, the legs of a man, the head of a deer. Nicks outlined where the legs and feet would go. He set to work, ignoring Mac and the tangled cables at his feet as Pete and Aaron moved through the room setting up equipment.

The important thing right then was how quickly Pete and Aaron could get things ready, and Mac took the offered cup of water from Maria and stepped back as his crew adjusted the lights and checked audio levels. After a few moments, Aaron nodded to Mac, signaling they were set. Once they were inside this dusty wooden room, things always moved quickly, and Mac had learned the hard way he could never redo a moment if it wasn't captured on video.

'She's dying,' Arturo said abruptly, daring

Mac to contradict him. Pete hoisted the camera and came in for a tight shot of the father's wounded face.

'I'm not a doctor,' Mac started.

'But still. You were one of those reporters in Afghanistan, you said. You saw death all the time. Even sewed some people up. Stopped that one guy from bleeding to death. You told me the story,' he insisted. 'You can hear it, same as me.'

'I can hear it,' Mac agreed.

In the corner, the blade snicked through the wood, popping shaved curls into the air.

'She needs to go to the Center, Arturo,' Mac said. 'She can't stay here anymore. That's what the doctors say. They have a bed for her. They've told you it's her best chance.'

'But not for that!' Arturo said. 'Not for that heart-that-is-not-a-heart! She will die! Don Jose is certain.'

Maria buried her face in her infant daughter's neck. Pete swung the camera onto her face and held. Maria shifted the baby in her arms.

'You've changed your mind about the heart-in-a-box?' The parents had enrolled Hekka in the experimental program four months before, only the second child out of a possible ten to be admitted, and time for her was running out.

'It is a lie,' Don Jose said from his chair. His voice was gravelly. The camera swung and steadied on his implacable face.

'It's brand-new,' Mac countered. 'But Dr. Bentley's done it once before and that child is now strong.'

Mac thought of the piece he'd just finished

47

editing that was part of the series. Eric Bettles was a five-year-old boy who'd been within days of dying a year ago when his lab-built heart had been implanted, a heart made from his own cells. He'd come back so dramatically that when they'd taped him last week, Eric was playing ball with his dad. During that year, his family had been sworn to secrecy until the series aired this week. It was a new procedure. Risky. How risky was the question. No one had an answer.

It was a crap shoot; a gamble. Eric Bettles looked strong, but no one could accurately predict what waited for him down the road. A developing heart in a fetus acquires tensile strength from the rhythmic beating of the mother's own heart. In a lab-created heart, electronic pulses were used to simulate that movement; scientists still weren't sure if Eric's heart wouldn't some day fray. If that happened, he'd die immediately. No turning back.

But Mac's job wasn't explaining the downside to Hekka's parents. Doctors had done that and he'd caught it on tape.

'It's a heart built just for her,' Mac reminded him. 'I'm wondering why you're rejecting the advice of doctors. They say it's time to bring her into the Center and have that new heart put in.'

And then the series would air. And life forever would change across the world for transplant patients. Two lab-created hearts made out of tiny patients' own cells and successfully implanted were enough for the center to risk a firestorm of publicity and the attendant clamor of those wanting to enroll their kids in the experimental and risky program.

Enough to bump Mac up to whatever he wanted next. Maybe an anchor job. He wasn't sure.

'Except it's a lie.' The video whirred, the shot tight now on Don Jose. 'I dreamed a black hole in Hekka's chest. A heart not hers, evil found and lost. I dreamed her with wings, singing with a *tuik kutanak*, a good throat, and a strong heart in heaven, finally hers.' He rolled the carving and knife between his yellowed palms and the outline of a foot emerged.

'If she doesn't come in, she will die. That's what they say. It's that simple.' Mac's voice was flat.

Don Jose carved in silence. Finally he said, 'I carve the deer dancer. I carve this not for life. But for the *usi mukila pahko*.'

Mac searched his memory for Yaqui religious symbols and found it. When he'd first met the family and discovered the elder Don Jose was a devout Yaqui, he'd bought books through the University of Arizona to better understand the culture. Hell, use it. Why lie? Especially to himself. *Usi mukila pahko*. The funeral of a child.

'You go now. We prepare for the *sea ania*.' Don Jose sniffed, already done with him.

'The flower world,' Mac pressed. 'But that's east, beneath the dawn.' East meant life.

Don Jose tipped the carving. The deer dancer stooped, caught mid-dance, elbows out, head angled, so his deer face and antlers looked

49

behind him over his shoulder.

'The dancer looks behind him. Toward the place of life. But his feet, still unformed, move in the opposite path. He dances west,' Don Jose rumbled. 'Toward death.'

'No!' Maria cried. Her voice was unexpected and shrill. The men froze. It was not seemly to behave this way, even over the dying of a child. 'No. She is my daughter, too. I will not. I will not. She will go in.'

Arturo took a step toward his wife but Don Jose held up a gnarled hand, stopping him.

'Hekka's on the UNOS list. Maybe there will be a regular donor heart for her,' Mac offered. 'Arizona and California are both AREA 5 on the UNOS transplant map so that means you can stay at the Center while you wait.'

Not reminding them that because of specific immunity problems, doctors had pegged Hekka's chances at finding a compatible heart at less than 15 percent. Only saying, 'If she stays here, they say she doesn't have a chance.'

They waited. The camera whirred.

'Very well. Hekka goes to the Center with me,' Don Jose said finally. 'I shall be her guardian. But this heart-in-a-box, it will not save her.'

Great video, Mac thought, and felt equal parts shame and euphoria.

Pete and Aaron dropped him off at La Cholla Airpark northwest of Tucson near the Tortolita Mountains. The pair kept driving toward Tucson International, where they'd catch the same commerical flight that would carry Hekka and her grandfather back to San Diego.

50

The office was a modular building, sided in stucco and framed by a cement walkway larded with stepping-stones. An acacia and two bristly mesquite trees offered slight shade. Even this early, the smell of heat rising from the cement mingled with the faint scent of sage.

The pilot, Jeb Shattuck, punched in a code at the French doors and pushed them open. He was wearing black Doc Martens and his hair under his trademark Sacramento Kings hat was turning gray.

'There's a computer in the pilots' lounge, if you need to go online before we leave. I'll be outside.'

Mac nodded and stepped inside. He drank coffee out of his thermos as Jeb went through the check-list on the Cirrus. The room had lavender-gray carpeting and two sofas littered with aviation magazines. A bulletin board to the left of a small office was crammed with ads for planes, spaces to lease, and tie-down information.

Mac went to the window and looked out past a row of corrugated metal hangars and shadeports. It was just after four in the morning and the sky held the faint pearl color that came an hour before dawn, suffusing the mountains in pink. A light rain fell. In the distance, tidy homes sat amid a vast desert landscape, and horses drowsed along a corral fence.

Jeb was squatting under the plane with what looked like a shot glass and metal straw, poking the straw up into the underside of the plane, taking a fuel sample. He was based out of

51

Sacramento but Mac always used him for trips when he could pry money out of his expense account. Jeb routinely flew media stars who wanted a low profile, and sometimes celebrity pilots whose insurance policies insisted on the presence of a second pilot on board. Mac had heard he flew with Angelina Jolie, but he'd never hear it from Jeb. And Mac liked that, how discreet and trustworthy Jeb was, and how unswayed by star power. Liked the man.

Jeb held the cup up to the light and checked for contaminants, discarding the thimble of fuel in a quick toss onto the tarmac that left a faint streak of shine. He half waved and mimed checking his watch. He held up five fingers. Mac nodded and turned away from the window.

He knew from experience Jeb still needed to check the control surfaces, making certain the safety wires were secure, tweak the wheel parts to see if they moved, eyeball the static port, a quarter-sized metal piece flush on each side of the sleek white body, to ensure that the pin-sized hole at the center wasn't blocked. More checks than that, but that was enough to know he had five minutes at least.

He walked to the computer desk and found the mouse amid a stack of papers. He drank the rest of his coffee and sat down, fingers clicking over the keys, looking for breaking news stories, an occupational curse.

He found a Web stream of a local news station out of Tucson, anchored by a stocky man with darkly handsome features and a much younger woman wearing a crisp suit. The female anchor, hair stiff with gel, was introducing a piece out of San Diego. Mac had seen a flash the night before. Something about a California senator's son being shot in a meth bust gone bad.

He turned up the sound. He knew that part of San Diego, Ocean Beach — a funky hippie holdout with bead shops and tattooed panhandlers usually accompanied by pit bulls. He saw her darting out of a squad car into a jostling thicket of reporters and felt his throat close.

Grace Descanso.

Grace. Her hair was shorter than he remembered. But her face still held a curious mix of intelligence and warmth and a kind of raw sexuality, the kind no woman could manufacture. It came from some molten liquid place deep inside.

It had been over five years since Guatemala, and yet he instantly felt the roiling emotions he'd experienced standing next to her in that makeshift shed assisting her as she doctored, felt the remembered cautious optimism, the laughing connection, and then the quiet certainty, born of hope and fostered in every act of kindness, every molecule of her hard, clean presence, that they belonged together then and always, that neither time nor space nor act of God could separate them.

That she was the woman he was willing to die for.

Die for, perhaps, but not give up the story for.

And so it is, and was, and always shall be, amen.

His career was not a cold thing. It was a sinuous presence, alive, a shape-shifter, luring him always with the next seductive thing just over the horizon, the eternal quest to get to the bottom of things, to get it right.

For a brief moment he'd been certain he could have it all.

She was the one who got away. She was his great What If.

They'd been in a dangerous spot and he'd left her there; he knew it was dangerous and he'd left her there, to meet whatever fate was hers while he went into the next country, and then the next, dogging a lead that melted into lies, that changed form, that became a breathless and sensational story that faded away into a yellow dawn, leaving him stunned and awake for the first time in months, with a bitter taste of fear and regret in his mouth. And afraid for her, for what he'd done. For what he had not.

He'd come back for her then and she was gone and there was nothing but scorched earth, and she'd stayed gone for the longest time and to be honest, *It wasn't all bad*, his work murmured, *She was a distraction, an inconvenience, a minor character in the play of your life*.

And now there she was like some apparition, standing there with her head tucked, rushing away from the cameras into a waiting car.

He watched the piece straight through and turned it off.

Jeb poked his head inside the door. 'Ready?'

Mac nodded.

Jeb zipped up his leather jacket. 'We might get whapped around a little up there. Expect some turbulence.'

Mac already knew that.

5

He's coming for you. I came to save you, warn you.

It played through her mind all night, darting through her dreams, leaving her troubled and drenched in sweat.

He's after you. The Spikeman.

A warning, specifically for her. How else would he have known her name?

You need to run, Grace.

And if it was a legitimate threat, it meant she'd killed the only person who could lead her to the truth. She was a sitting duck now, stalled in the crosshairs, easy pickings for whatever fresh lunatic came lurching out of the muck whispering her name.

She gave up trying to sleep as dawn washed the boats in the harbor a pale shade of gold. The water was a gunmetal gray and the sand looked cold. She took Helix outside and walked him quickly, sticking to side streets, eyes darting, looking for danger, wondering if when it came she'd even recognize it. Helix was no help; there wasn't a person that his joyous broken body didn't love. The street was quiet when she unlocked the door afterward and let him in, and she was relieved to be done, wondering if that's the way it was going to be now, always looking behind her, scared.

She took a shower and studied herself in the

closet mirror. Her skin looked unnaturally pale, and smudges accented her dark eyes. She lifted her black hair off her neck and studied the damage. The bruise on the right side of her neck was as big as a fist, and her jawline, still strong — although at thirty-two, time was waging its inexorable battle — was faintly discolored. The bruise was turning an interesting shade of purple. She smiled bleakly into the mirror. At least he'd missed her teeth.

He's the Spikeman. He transmits signals through the wires in my brain.

Yeah, right. Not anymore, sweetheart. She put on a turtleneck.

Jeanne was still sleeping on the foldout sofa in the family room as Grace carried Katie's clothes into the kitchen and made coffee. She could hear the scratchy sound of Jeanne's gerbils stirring in their cage. The gerbils were Jeanne's pets, lab animals from her old life as a medical researcher. They'd never worked at the same place, but when Grace had been ready to get a sponsor, Jeanne's connection to science had been one of the things that made Grace trust her. Science didn't lie. Both women appreciated that.

Grace got out a pencil and tablet, her mind blank. Months ago, she'd taken a game from her own childhood and tweaked it, using it to make Katie's transition into the school week easier. It had morphed into Katie's favorite, the game they always played on Mondays to get dressed.

The Timer Game involved everything Katie loved: clues, a race against time, and at the end, if she beat the timer, a small treat to kick-start the day. It was helping Katie identify words and begin to grasp the passage of time, but now, October, all the easy combinations of rhymes and hiding places had been exhausted. Grace kept the old clues in a kitchen drawer. She riffled through them. It reminded her of sorting recipes, wondering if it was too soon again to try the meatloaf.

She found some clues she could modify and worked silently, concentrating. Jeanne appeared in the doorway arch, hair springy, a pink kimono cinched around her waist. She was in her midfifties and looked older. Alcohol and too much time in the sun had thickened her skin into a deep web of lines. She had dyed her hair a defiant shade of red that both moved and amused Grace. This was a woman who would not go quietly. Soberly and with a bad knee, but not quietly.

'Coffee.' Jeanne eased into a chair. Helix woofed a greeting and Jeanne absently scratched his head as he settled himself at her feet.

'Bad night?' Grace poured a cup and gave it to her.

'When are you going to tell her?' Jeanne stared at the clues. 'Oh, God, Monday.'

'Yeah, I have to hide all this stuff before she wakes up.' Grace scooped up Katie's clothes and bent to pick up *Spot Goes to the Farm*, splayed open on the kitchen floor. She folded Katie's T-shirt into the book, putting them under the kitchen sink along with the correct clue.

'Mommy?' The voice was coming from the stairwell upstairs.

58

'I'm coming,' Grace called. 'I'll be right there.'

'You don't want her finding out at school.' Jeanne stared at Grace across the cup rim.

'I'll tell her, okay?' Grace said irritably. 'But not right now.' She ran into the living room and hid Katie's underpants along with a clue. From upstairs came the sound of a toilet flushing.

'I'm using your shower.' Jeanne was making her way to the stairs, leaning on her cane.

'Go for it.'

'Mommy?' Katie's voice was imperious, the queen summoning her court.

'Coming!' Grace shouted as she trotted into the kitchen and grabbed the timer. She stuffed Katie's shorts and a clue into the family room bookshelf behind a tub of clay, dropped Katie's Air Walkers next to the cage holding Jeanne's gerbils, and scanned the room, trying to find some small treat. She settled on a pack of balloons she'd bought for the party and slid one into the final note, putting it under a shoe and covering everything with the cage blanket.

'Mommy!' Katie bellowed from upstairs. Helix perked up, ears lopsided, and trotted off to join her. Grace took a slow breath and climbed the stairs.

Katie waited in bed, eyes closed, pouting, Helix next to her on the quilt. 'If you played this game, you'd lose.'

Grace stood the first clue on the top bookshelf next to the Peace Beanie Baby. 'Well, guess what? Keep your eyes closed, honey; Helix, *down*.' She pulled him off the bed and he grunted and flopped on the floor. 'I played this game with my dad and your Uncle Andy when I was a kid and I was really good at it.'

She slid the scalloped socks she was holding under the bed ruffle along with the last clue and stood at the side of the bed, her hand on the timer.

'Okay, at the count of three, I start the timer and you open your eyes. One . . . two . . . '

Katie's eyes popped open. She scanned the room and spotted the note. 'Three!' She scrambled out of bed and flew to the bookshelf.

'Three,' Grace finished, giving the timer a brisk turn. Sixty seconds. Katie snatched up the first clue and opened it.

'Today . . . is,' Katie sang out.

'You can read that?' Grace settled onto the floor.

'Mommy, that's how all the clues start, so now I know those words.' She stabbed her finger at the next word. 'Mah . . . mah . . . Mommy?'

'Today is *Mommy*? That's silly.'

Katie grinned and threw her arms around Grace. 'Today is *Mommy*, silly dilly Mommy.' She beamed, her goodness radiating, at making this small joke.

From down the hall came the sound of a shower starting.

'Who's here?'

'Jeanne. Remember? You have Show and Tell today with the gerbils.'

'I just want to be with you.' Katie crawled into her lap. 'I need you to read these today. You pretend I'm little and I can't read anything yet. Read the whole thing.' She smiled sunnily.

'Okay. Look at the words while I point.'

Katie repositioned herself and Grace smelled the ripe sleep smell of her young skin. Grace pointed and read aloud:

'*Today is Monday*
Here we go
Your socks are close by
Someplace low.'

'Someplace low, someplace low,' Katie muttered, rolling to her knees and scanning the carpet. Grace saw a wink of hot pink under the bed ruffle. Katie scrambled to it. 'Aha!'

The timer dinged. 'You beat it. You beat the timer. I didn't hide those very well, did I?'

'Nope,' Katie said cheerfully. She pulled on both socks and trotted back to Grace with the second clue. Grace reset the timer and read:

'*Far from here*
Is underwear
Near a window
Down the stair.'

'Down the stair!' Katie urged. 'Come on!'

'No running on the stairs!'

Katie shot ahead, running. Helix joined her, his leg banging on each step. The staircase opened into the living room and by the time Grace had made her way down, Katie was yanking on a pair of flowered underpants under her nightie, Helix prancing and yipping in tight circles around her.

'Come on, hurry!' Katie thrust a clue at Grace, and Grace reset the timer and read aloud:

'Your T-shirt's pink
And if you look
Under a sink
It's in a book.'

'This is too easy today,' Katie protested, heading for the kitchen.

'Maybe you're just too good.'

Katie bent and opened the door under the kitchen sink and pulled out the Spot book and the T-shirt. She squirmed out of her nightie and pulled the T-shirt over her head. 'Read,' she commanded, her voice muffled.

Grace reset the timer and read the next clue as Katie's face breathlessly emerged.

'So take the book
Put it away
Then take a look
Behind the clay.'

'I didn't leave this book out.'

'Helix likes to read at night when we go to bed.'

'You're funny.' Katie carried the book through the archway into the family room, glancing at the rumpled foldout bed and covered cage. She stood for a moment staring at the shelves jammed with games, books, abandoned dolls. She found the clay bin and moved it aside, snatching up the shorts and a clue.

'Put the book away!' Grace reminded, as Katie pulled on her blue shorts. A thumping sound like a heavier Helix signaled the approach of Jeanne, making her way slowly with her cane down the stairs into the kitchen. Katie shoved the book onto the shelf as Grace reset the timer and read:

'*You're almost done.*
To find your shoes
Look by a cage.
No time to snooze!'

'Well,' Katie sniffed confidently. She pulled the blanket off the cage and sat down next to the gerbils. Yin padded in a revolving wheel. At almost five, he was elderly, and his back was a slow-moving checkerboard blur of brown and white fur laid out in a neat grid of alternating squares. Helix nosed the cage and yipped.

'Stop already, Helix,' Grace said. 'It's not like you've never seen gerbils before.'

Through the archway in the small, sunny kitchen, Jeanne poured kibble into a porcelain bowl and the sound brought Helix clacking into the kitchen as Katie put on her first shoe and adjusted the Velcro straps. She found the note and the balloon under the second shoe and put it on before she handed the note to Grace to read out loud. Grace had written in block letters:

'*You have fun!*
At school, at play
And know I love you!
All the day!'

63

'That was fast today,' Katie said wistfully.

Grace was silent, thinking about how she still had to tell her daughter what had happened, how her instinct was to delay. 'Come on, sweetie, maybe you can practice at breakfast.'

⋆　⋆　⋆

'Okay, so the front page is the section you don't want to read,' Jeanne said. She turned to a new section. 'Oh, and also Metro. You can skip right over that part today.'

Grace shot her a look.

'Why?' Katie asked. She looked up from her bowl, where she had been picking out all the letter *M*'s and putting them in a soggy row on the table.

Grace reached for a hairbrush on the counter and moved behind her. 'Tip your head.'

'Why doesn't Mommy want to read the front page or Metro, either?' Katie said more loudly. Grace brushed through a golden tangle, snapping a tie around Katie's ponytail.

'You want to practice now? Pretend you're holding Yin up in front of the class?'

Jeanne glanced pointedly at the kitchen clock. She was wearing a blue muumuu that matched her vivid blue eyes. Her eyebrows rose in penciled wings that waggled, giving Grace the clear message that time was passing and she had a job to do. Katie was absorbed in the soggy cereal, oblivious.

'I'll tell everybody Jeanne did it. She's a scientist and she did it.'

'Was,' Jeanne corrected. She reached across the table and snapped a dead leaf off an iris. She'd brought a bouquet the night before. Jeanne's home overlooked a canyon and she cultivated flowers in her backyard.

Part of what Grace had learned from her sponsor during the three years they'd been paired in AA was the names of flowers. The other part was more subtle, and had to do with how to live life. Grace was working on not beating herself up so much. She'd never drunk when she was pregnant, no matter how bad the flashbacks; that was the big one. But she was still working on facing things head-on. She had no idea how she was going to tell Katie.

'And it didn't hurt them,' Katie said.

'No,' Jeanne said.

'Okay, pretend I'm holding Yin.' Katie stroked a finger down an imaginary back. 'See, we each carry these things inside — these fighter things . . . ' She looked to Jeanne for help.

'T cells.'

'Right. And they're like commandos, like Rambo or something, and they fight with everything they think's bad. So . . . ' She stopped, her knowledge exhausted.

'So what happened was,' Jeanne picked up the thread, 'scientists figured out a way to make it be okay.' She hesitated and cut a quick look at Grace. 'Your mom actually did this kind of thing when she was a doctor.'

Grace froze over the paper, waiting, always waiting for Katie to ask why: why she'd quit doctoring. Jeanne shot her a look of apology, a

65

shrug, a *what was I thinking?* look.

Katie beamed at her mother, oblivious, and crowed, 'But now she does CSI, like on TV.'

Jeanne's shoulders relaxed. 'That's right. So. This little guy started out brown. And Yang, the one in the cage — '

'He bites, that's why we left him there. He's the all-white one,' Katie said.

'Usually you can't take white fur and put it on a gerbil that's brown.'

'They'd fight,' Katie said. 'Not gerbils. Those fighter things. Those T things.'

Jeanne nodded. 'So we figured out a way to fool the brown fur into thinking the white fur was okay. It's called breaking the immunity barrier and it's a pretty big deal.'

Katie grinned and Jeanne reached across the table and gave her a high-five.

'Great, you did great,' Grace said. She hesitated and took a sip of coffee. 'Honey, you know how we had to leave Party Savers yesterday?'

Katie's eyes warily shot up. 'You want to put the treat in my shoe?'

Grace took the curled balloon off the table, lifted Katie's feet easily onto her lap, and pried apart a tiny pocket on the shoe. There were two secret pockets on each shoe, flat and sealed with Velcro, where Katie liked to stash emergency treats. Grace reached in and pulled out a dime.

'Something bad happened yesterday. At work.'

She felt a small tremor run through Katie's foot. She sealed the dime back up and opened the next pocket. Bubble gum. She closed the pocket and opened one on the other shoe. It was empty. She rolled the small pink balloon and stuffed it carefully into the pocket, sealing the Velcro, taking her time.

'That's why I got the bruise. I'm fine. That's the thing. I'm okay.'

Katie's eyes dilated to almost black. Grace knew it was Katie's oldest fear, losing the only parent she'd ever known.

'A man hurt some people — '

'No! I won't hear!' She clamped her hands against her ears.

' — and Mommy ended up having to hurt him.'

'NO!' Katie scrambled out of her seat and flung herself into Grace's lap, her small arms tight. Grace held her and could feel her heart beat.

'Don't talk. Don't.'

'I won't. But somebody might at school. That's why I brought it up.'

'What happened?'

Here it was. In a perfect world, no terrified kids ran screaming out of schools, no splintered car bombs mangled babies, no planes crashed into buildings crumpling into a blue sky.

'Some people died yesterday.'

'Oh.' It was a wail, low and heartrending.

'Mommy's fine.'

'Daddy died.'

'It wasn't like that, honey.'

'No, no,' Katie moaned. 'Daddy died. You can't die, you can't.'

Grace murmured over and over like a song, a prayer, 'It's okay, Katie, it's okay, everything's fine, Mommy's fine, nothing bad's going to happen.'

Another lie.

6

Grace stopped at the post office on Cañnon and mailed Katie's letter, feeling a sharp stab of anxiety. Katie should have nothing more important to worry about than holding Yin by his neck so he didn't nip her during Show and Tell, not thinking about whether something terrible would happen to her mother.

He's coming for you.

Not if Grace could find him first.

The vehicle-processing storage facility was across from Lindbergh Field on Aerodrive. Grace parked, identified herself to the guard to on duty, and told him what she needed.

'Can't miss it. It's outside around back.'

The taco van was wrapped in a tent of visqueen supported by a wooden frame. It was a mideighties modified Volkswagen, originally dark blue, layered with grime and paint. She caught the reek of stove grease and Super Glue.

'Grace.' Paul stepped around the van, gripping a bologna sandwich. 'You okay?'

'Little shaky. Nice.' She surveyed the tent. 'Christo should be worried.'

'He is,' Paul said mildly. 'Looks just like the Reichstag after he wrapped it in silver fabric, only smaller and cheesier.'

He took a bite of sandwich and his eyes went to the bruise on her jaw.

'It's taking what? Twenty pouches to print it?'

The police Super Glue came in foil pouches, simple to use, but costly on something this big.

'Nah, the bean counters wouldn't approve that, even on this one. I got creative. Used aluminum pie pans at each corner with a couple of vaporizers and squeezed out Super Glue I bought at Long's Drug. Everybody wins.'

'Yeah, right, except Eddie Loud.'

'Hey, he's the whacked-out bad guy, Grace. Not you.'

Looking at the tent made her realize what Paul wasn't saying. How much the department was putting into processing this one. And the reason why.

'Not many senators' sons drive taco vans and wind up dead.'

'You can play this one through any way you want, Grace, but it's still going to stink. We should have good prints by late afternoon.'

'What do you expect to find?'

'At this point? I'm not sure.' His jowls sagged and his eyes dropped, his usual look after a good night's sleep. 'I heard the first toxes from the ME said Loud was cranked.'

'Makes sense.' Grace had a flash of Eddie's jangly energy. 'Mind if I take a look?'

'Have at it. There is something you might find interesting.' Paul put down his sandwich and positioned his face against the cloudy plastic, looking through the window into the dim interior. Grace squinted next to him. She made out vague shapes, open chip bags, the stove. Soft white particles dusted the grill and cabinets.

'What am I looking at?'

Paul pointed at something through the filmy visqueen and Grace took another look.

'The kitchen timer? Is that it?' It was a small white timer with big black numbers, sitting on the counter next to an open bag of taco shells. Grace had used an almost identical one that morning playing the Timer Game.

Paul shook his head. 'No, that.'

She still didn't see it.

'Loud was wired.' Paul pulled a Dr Pepper out of his jacket and drank.

'Wired. What are you talking about?'

'Right out of the Spy Shop Catalog. A tiny video cam attached to his shirt button. We think from the setup, there was a mixer right there on the counter, and I don't mean the Martha Stewart kind.' He pointed. 'Whoever was in here left behind a connector cable.'

'You think somebody was in here? Recording this?'

Paul shrugged. 'Too soon to say. Eddie Loud's minicam button in his shirt could turn out to be a prop, not real, not with a signal transmitting what was recorded.'

He took another swig of his drink.

'Or it's out there, in cyberspace, the killings.'

She stared at Paul, her gaze troubled.

'You okay?' he asked again.

'He said my name, Paul, right before he tried to kill me. He warned me about somebody called the Spikeman who was coming to get me.'

'We don't know yet what we have here,' Paul reminded her. He finished the sandwich and drained the can, crushing it and tucking it into the pocket of his brown polyester jacket.

A short fat man rounded the building, moving like his hip joints were killing him. His shiny bald head caught the light and for a second, Grace saw the taco van reflected like a miniature hologram. Tan work pants ballooned over a huge belly, cinched with suspenders the colors of a Portuguese flag: green, red, yellow. He was scowling and waving his fists.

'Oh, shit. I told the guard not to let this guy in.'

The man was yelling in a torrent of Portuguese, fury mottling his face.

'Calm down, Mr. Esguio.' Paul moved forward cautiously, his palms raised and flat.

'Calm down!' Esguio cried in English. 'You have stolen my van! My work! How can I calm down when you have stolen my van and won't give it back!'

'Okay, Mr. Esguio, I know you're upset — '

Esguio lunged toward Paul and shoved him backward. They grappled. It was like watching a strongman contest where the leading contestant was charged with pushing a semi. Paul skidded a half step back, losing ground as Esguio moaned and smacked a hand to his heart and flopped forward. Paul managed to brace himself and catch Esguio before he toppled.

'Oh, my God,' Paul said. 'He's having a heart attack. Is he okay? Ask him.'

Grace asked him in rapid-fire Portuguese. Esguio cracked open an eye and answered, his voice pitiful. His eyes were the same dark brown as hers, making him look vaguely familiar. He

72

was as old as her aunts. They probably all went to school together. Dated. Divorced each other at least once.

'What's he saying?'

'He wants to know how long you're keeping the van.'

'About his health.'

'He's fine.'

'The van,' Esguio prodded. Paul tipped him to his feet.

'Try two or three years,' Paul said. 'He's okay, though, right? You okay?'

'Two or three years!' Esguio moaned in English.

'You should have thought of that before getting a killer to drive it,' Paul said. 'Did you even check Eddie's license? Did Eddie even have a license?'

'Now listen here,' Esguio bristled.

Grace laid a hand on his arm and smiled winningly at him. 'How about I take you out for breakfast. Would you like that, sir?'

Esguio stiffened with pride and yanked his arm free. He started moving through the cars and Grace fell into step next to him.

'Wait.' Paul trotted after them. 'Mr. Esguio. Sir. You can't go with her. You're not supposed to tell anybody anything.'

'Paul.' Grace stopped, her voice reasonable. 'Say for a second maybe there was a TV-remote setup in there. Was there audio and video equipment in your taco van, Mr. Esguio?'

'What?'

'TV stuff. To take pictures.'

73

'No TV. Just a grill and a refrigerator. What are you talking about?'

She turned back to Paul. 'Say there was a TV-remote setup. Say Eddie really *was* trying to warn me. That means somebody very bad might be after me. And if he is, Eddie's made it clear the bad guy doesn't have plans to invite me to his mother's house for dinner either, unless she lives in the Bates Motel. So if Mr. Esguio can help me find the bad guy first, before he finds me and kills me — and that could be the plan here, Paul, to kill me — that's good. Works for me.'

Mr. Esguio looked from Paul to Grace. His chins moved like a hula dancer.

'I could use a cup of coffee. Decaf.'

7

Esguio tapped three pills into his hand and swallowed them dry. 'Thyroid, heart. Cholesterol. Take my advice. Never get old.'

'I'll remember that.'

They sat in a vinyl booth at the back of Denny's on Rosecrans, a couple of blocks from where Esguio said he lived. Grace ordered French toast; Esguio stuck with coffee. He had wide lips and took small sips of air as he talked, as if breathing was hard work.

'Descanso. You one of Francisco Descanso's grandkids?'

'You knew my grandfather?'

'Sure. Everybody knew him. Terrible thing, what happened to his son.'

Grace blinked and looked away.

She could feel his face change. She should have expected it. Esguio was Portuguese. Of course he'd know about her father. Back then everybody Portuguese lived in a tight community in Point Loma, fished on boats passed down to their sons.

'Must have been, what? Thirty years ago?'

'Twenty-one. I was eleven when he washed overboard.'

Eleven when Lottie dragged her and her kid brother, Andy, out of the warmth and safety of Point Loma, into a life on the road. Grace had spent the last of her childhood shuttling from one beersoaked bar to another, living out of cardboard suitcases while Lottie warbled in bars, living out her fantasy of becoming a country-western singer.

If her father had lived, Grace wouldn't feel so damaged today. By any standard but her own, Grace had done well, but every step along the way had been punctuated with failure and despair and terrible doubts. Goodness was a fragile thing chipped daily out of the rocky soil of her spirit. Lottie, on the other hand, soared like a vast overwrought blimp, gliding over the wreckage of Grace's childhood, never coming down to earth long enough to be tethered to anything as pesky as consequences.

'Your father was a good man,' Esguio said. 'You know that.'

Grace shrugged. 'Thanks. Always good to hear.'

Esguio sipped his coffee. She could feel him watching her, probing the pain, and in a courtly way stepping back. He frowned and shifted gears.

'Wait. You're the one we sent to Guatemala, right? From the parish. We were in Portugal that year. We heard she died over there. Sister Mary Clare.'

'Yeah. Yeah, she did.' The bad things crowded into her mind, fresh from their naps and grinning, wanting to play.

'We heard there was a fire.'

A bad thing bared its blunt teeth and cocked its shaggy head, and Grace could feel the whiff of its breath on her face. Her heart was starting to hammer. She took a deep breath and let it out, trying to find her quiet place, quiet the demons.

'We heard you were going to be a heart doctor. Work with kids. Then you quit.'

Grace studied her hands and looked up. 'Mr. Esguio, I'm sorry about your van. They have to process it for prints and — '

'That doesn't take two years.'

The waitress put down the plates. Esguio gazed longingly at her French toast.

'No, but when something's been used in the commission of a felony, when somebody's been murdered and that was the vehicle used to transport the suspect . . . '

Esguio watched as she poured syrup, a slow dawning growing across his face. He looked pained. 'I'm never going to see that van again in my lifetime, am I?'

'Probably not.' Grace shoveled in a forkful of food and washed it down with orange juice. 'Mr. Esguio, somebody bad is after me. Somebody Eddie knew.'

'No kidding,' Esguio marveled. 'Do the police know?'

'I am the police.' Or close enough. 'That's why I'm asking these questions and why it's important you tell me what you know. How did you come to hire Eddie Loud?'

'This recruiter came to the Portuguese Hall. Trying to place these folks. I got a card here someplace.' Esguio fished it out of his wallet and passed it over the table.

NEW LIFE
giving those ready a second chance

77

'He told us how the Center sounds like a science place, but it's got a big hospital there, too. Where they do research, helping people. Eddie had problems, but he'd been in a halfway house three years, no incidents. It was all monitored. He'd never even had a parking ticket, Grace. Nothing. He even liked to cook.' A small lost laugh.

'Can I keep the card?'

'Sure. I'm not going to be needing it. Know how much money is tied up in that van? I can't believe it. Gone, poof, just like that. Damn. Two in one day.'

Some antenna tweaked. 'What happened to the other van?'

'Wasn't a van, just a food cart, thank the good Lord and all His Saints.' Esguio crossed himself. 'Still.'

'Tell me about the other guy you hired for the food cart. What happened to him?'

'Woman.' Esguio made a face and drained his water glass. 'Heartburn. Acid reflux.' He eyed her untouched water glass and Grace passed it over.

'Thanks.' He took a deep drink and crunched ice. 'Where was I?'

'The woman you hired to work your food cart,' Grace prompted. 'Something went wrong with it.'

'Jazz Studio, that was her name. Should have been my first tip-off, right? Somebody with a fake name isn't going to think twice about

78

trashing the cart. I blame Eddie, though.'

'How's that?'

'They had a big fight right beforehand. I think whatever he said got her stirred up.'

'How'd they know each other?'

'Hired them from the same place.'

Grace studied the card.

'So this Jazz Studio and Eddie Loud are both outpatients at the Center for BioChimera. What were they being treated for?'

'They never said what exactly. 'Patient confidentiality.' That's where they get you over the barrel. I should have stuck to distributing turkeys to St. Vincent's at Christmas.'

'Did Eddie Loud ever talk about video, or TV recording, or hidden cameras?'

'Never. Although when he was really tired, he'd start acting like he thought somebody was after him, out to get him.'

Grace mulled that over. 'Where'd you have Jazz working?'

'The Center. Nice easy job, no stress. Everybody loves the food cart, right? And I thought it would be familiar. They had Jazz working in Records for a while so she knew the building.'

'What happened?'

'Her first day on the cart's yesterday, Sunday? Gave her that on purpose, because it's a light day at the Center, only people there are those who have to be. So she takes the cart to Records, where she used to work? Hadn't been there ten minutes when she causes this ruckus and her old boss has to call security.' Esguio shook his head.

'Ever find out what set her off?'

'No. But something scared her. Bad.'

Grace pushed the plates out of the way. 'Any idea where she lives?'

Esguio shook his head. 'Or Eddie either. They keep that part quiet. Jazz could be living at the Center now in a nice padded room, for all I know.'

'Could I have your home number, if I have any more questions?'

He scribbled it on the back of a napkin and passed it over. 'Know where it is? That Center for BioChimera?'

She looked away. 'Oh, yeah.'

8

The Center for BioChimera was part of a strip of high-end biotech research centers, hospitals, and the University of California, San Diego, in an area of La Jolla known as Biotech Mesa. Grace took 5 North to Genesee and Torrey Pines Road and made the familiar climb.

The view sweeping to the Pacific didn't engage her; Grace was preoccupied with what she'd learned. Eddie Loud was mentally ill. How did a mentally ill outpatient at the Center for BioChimera driving a taco van get her name? What did Eddie Loud have to do with her?

The Center slanted in two wings facing the ocean, its back in a V toward the road. Three stories low to the ground, it resembled a Frank Lloyd Wright structure hewn out of the side of the ridge. Research labs and administrative offices fanned out in one wing; the other wing was a hospital specializing in transplants and immunological disorders.

The entrance to New Life was tucked behind Emergency in the hospital wing and faced out over a damp lawn, a tangle of trees, and the high Plexiglass fence closing off the steep drop leading to the waves smashing four hundred feet below. Grace wondered if they had jumpers.

She parked the car and entered the New Life waiting room, giving the receptionist her name. No, no appointment. Yes, she'd wait.

Pastel plaid chairs faced a coffee table covered with magazines. Grace read the bulletin board, a crammed assortment of admonishments to take meds, numbers to call if a client fell apart, a map of the hospital with an 'X: *You Are Here*,' and tips on 'How to Put Your Best Foot Forward' when going after that special minimum-wage job.

She sat. Five minutes later, a short man in his forties with glasses and a crew cut came through the door from the back rooms, face pink with exertion. 'Grace Descanso?'

She stood up and extended her hand. 'Yes, and you're . . . '

'Curtis Crumwald.' A hard grip for a soft man. 'Sorry for the wait. Had to drive my wife to a hair appointment. We're down to one car.'

Crumwald made a face and motioned her through the door to the back. He wore neatly pressed Dockers and a shirt under a Stanford sweater pushed up his freckled arms. They passed a room set for a group — chairs in a circle, a second room with a copier, ratty sofa, and a Mr. Coffee. Tossed newspapers and Styrofoam cartons littered the laminated coffee table.

'Harriet said you were interested in our program. Have job opportunities?'

'No. Just questions.'

Crumwald stopped walking. 'Are you a reporter?' His voice was flat.

'I was the forensic biologist Eddie Loud tried to kill.' It hung there. *So I killed him.*

Crumwald took off his glasses and wiped them

on his shirt. 'Come in. Close the door.'

Client photos covered a large bulletin board in his office: grinning McDonald's workers, a city employee stabbing trash at Shelter Island, a singing telegram dressed as a hot dog.

'Where's Eddie? I want to see his face.'

Crumwald pointed him out. Eddie Loud stood stiffly in front of the sparkling taco van, hair combed, pride and anxiety blazing across his face. He was wearing a pair of blue pants and a pressed shirt. He was gripping a bag of tacos, but gently, it appeared, so they wouldn't crush.

'Believe it or not, he was a kind man. Not violent. His poor parents.'

Grace shot him a measured look. 'He killed a DEA chemist, a detective sergeant, and a uniformed police officer yesterday. Good men. And he did this to me.' She raked down her turtleneck so he could see the purple mark left when Eddie had grabbed her.

Crumwald blinked. 'I'm sorry. Please. Have a seat.'

She took one across from the desk, and he sat heavily in his chair and placed his hands flat on the desk as if to compose himself.

'I was hired on faith, understand? To cobble together a program assisting those the world has no interest in helping. And now — '

'He was in a halfway house. And this program for work. Was he in rehab?'

'I can't answer that. That's confidential.'

'He'd dead, Mr. Crumwald. It's going to come out.'

'When you . . . saw him. Did it look like Eddie

83

was on some kind of drug?'

'He was amped like a light show. Cranked so high his brain was frying. I'd bet money.'

The air went out of him and Crumwald slumped in his chair. He had a squishball stress reliever next to a photo of a placidly smiling woman. He picked up the ball and squeezed. He looked defeated.

'That's so unbelievable. He knew if he tried that he'd be gone. He really wanted to stay.'

'Did Eddie ever bring up anybody called the Spikeman?'

Crumwald shook his head. 'But I'm not the one he talked to. When he did talk. He didn't do too much talking when he was medded properly.' Crumwald looked up, still back on what she'd said about drugs. 'He could have just stopped taking his meds.'

'I don't know what was wrong with him, Mr. Crumwald, but if not taking meds is enough to get him to hack up three men with a butcher knife and start on me, then sure, stick with that.'

'They feed off each other energywise. Yesterday he was agitated in group and later, another client fell apart. Not as spectacularly but . . . big mess we're still cleaning up.'

Jazz Studio.

'Did Eddie Loud say anything in group that would have alerted you?'

'You mean, so I could have stopped it?' Crumwald sounded defensive and aggrieved and he squished the ball harder. It made a squelching sound like a trapped mouse.

'No, just — '

'Just what, Ms. Descanso? I run this place on a shoestring and a prayer, and if I stopped every client from going out that door who thought sometimes he was God or the next Bill Gates — or Bill Gates himself — I'd never have confidence to send any of them out. They're trying. Beset by demons, but trying. They haven't given up. Where are you going with this?'

'Is there any reason Eddie should have known who I was?'

'None that I know of.'

'Because he did. Right before he tried to kill me, he said my name and warned me about somebody he called the Spikeman.' She couldn't keep the tremor out of her voice.

Crumwald looked genuinely shocked. 'He said your name? I don't understand.'

'That makes two of us. If you have anything, anything at all, I need to know it now.'

Crumwald stood heavily and looked out the window. 'Anything else needs to come from higher up the food chain, if you know what I mean. Warren Pendrell is the head of this place.'

He said the name as if that should scare her.

'Warren Pendrell,' he repeated.

9

Talking to Warren Pendrell was the last thing she wanted. It's what she'd been trying to avoid by going to Crumwald first, and already she could feel the familiar constriction in her throat.

She walked out of the outpatient facility and got in her car, driving across the parking lots that connected the research and hospital sides and reparking so she could make a speedy getaway afterward. The dignity of her exit would be lost if she had to tramp across the gravel and succulent beds back the way she'd come. Not that he'd be watching.

But maybe someone was, out of the blank-faced windows in the high granite building, and that was troubling. A faint wire mesh covered a set of windows on the second floor, and Grace snatched another glance, disquieted. The wire was new, she was certain, and she wondered if that's where she'd find Jazz. The building rose like a granite monolith under a vivid blue sky with a faint tracing of clouds. A perfect San Diego day, covering what?

He's coming for you . . . He's the Spikeman.

She locked up and entered the building under an imposing sign etched in granite: CENTER FOR BIOCHIMERA.

Next to the sliding glass doors was a smaller sign in black letters: WARNING! THIS IS A LATEX-FREE SITE. ALL LATEX PRODUCTS

STRICTLY FORBIDDEN!

Grace scanned the lobby. A young woman sat reading at the information kiosk in the middle of the room. A small coffee and pastry area lay to the left, most of the tables occupied by interns and nurses, none she recognized. On the walls hung pictures of the groundbreaking, Nobel laureates who did research at the Center, and an unseemly number of photos featuring Warren as the beaming centerpiece, his shock of white hair glowing along with his teeth.

The V of the building opened into floor-to-ceiling windows, revealing the view. Here the ocean was a churning presence, a gray and blue highway carrying Navy traffic and fishing trawlers out to sea. The skyline of La Jolla glinted in the bright sun, and far to the south, Mexico's Coronado Islands rose like the purple humps of a prehistoric sea monster.

On scattered sofas people waited. They waited in the halls, milling around. On chairs by the entrance. They waited in pairs and family groupings and alone. It seemed to Grace as if that waiting defined the essence of the Center. It was saturated with a pain born of that waiting, and a longing so intense it seemed distilled, the longer she was away from it.

She headed past the information kiosk to the elevators. A family marshaled a boy of about ten out into the hall, his wheelchair sticking as it bumped over the elevator groove. His younger sister hopped next to him in excitement. The mother had a trembly half-smile on her face, as if smiling even that much was too costly.

Grace rode the elevator alone to three. The joke was, the Center was built on a bluff and run on one, and Grace had heard it repeated more times than she could count by jealous colleagues of Warren's who didn't realize they knew each other personally. She never repeated it; it was petty, but it spoke clearly to the empire he had built and the enemies he'd made.

Damaged adults and children wounded by disorders and limping from attacks leveled against them by their own immune systems flocked to the Center for specialized treatment, hoping for the miracle cure that would stop their bodies from viciously destroying themselves. Warren Pendrell promised nothing, but something in his manner must have communicated hope. People lined up for clinical trials.

She'd spent part of her residency on loan from Johns Hopkins working in the Center's sophisticated pediatric heart transplant unit, and Warren had taken her immediately under his wing. Those were the giddy days when she was a rising star and everything was working, but that was a long time ago and when she'd left medicine, part of what she'd jettisoned was the safety of his mentorship, the easy way doors opened and the belief that anything professionally was still possible. Now she approached his offices with the caution and respect they deserved.

The elevator opened and she faced smoked-glass doors with Warren's name engraved in brass: DR. WARREN PENDRELL, DIRECTOR.

Another name was inscribed in smaller script underneath: LABS OF DR. LEE ANN BENTLEY.

88

Grace felt the beginning of a headache, seeing the name. Lee had been a coldly amoral researcher hungry for grants and recognition when Grace had known her five years before. Now she'd moved up to the major leagues, sharing lab space with Warren himself. Grace had managed to avoid seeing Lee in earlier visits. But today she didn't feel lucky.

Grace opened the heavy door leading to the reception area. This smaller lobby glowed in a soft shade of gold, the center of the room dominated by a carved marble statue of an angel and child. A drug salesman looked up incuriously from a trade magazine and went back to reading, his briefcase of samples bulging at his feet.

Grace went to the counter and waited as the receptionist finished a call. The receptionist was middle-aged, efficient, with a helmet of dyed black hair and a chest that jutted forward like the prow of an immense ship. She put down the telephone and turned to Grace.

'Yes?' Her face was neutral. She'd missed a spot with her eyebrow pencil, and one of her brows had a small, disconcerting patch of white in the middle of what otherwise was a perfect walnut brown arched wing.

'Cynthia. Could you please alert Warren I'm here.'

'And you are?'

Cynthia knew exactly who she was. This was a petty humiliation she put Grace through every time. 'Grace. Descanso.'

'Identification?'

Grace pulled out her crime lab ID instead of her driver's license and was heartened to see a quiver of surprise in Cynthia's eyes before she recovered. *Good. Let her think I'm here on official business. Serves her right.*

'Do you have an appointment?' She touched her pearls. The necklace was so long she could hang herself.

'No.' Grace stared her down and felt a sharp surge of victory when Cynthia turned away first. She really needed to play more board games.

'He's very busy.'

'He wants to see me.'

'I'll let him be the judge of that. Sit and wait.' It was an order.

Grace smiled thinly and went to the window, looking out. Far away, hang gliders floated over a blue expanse of sea, and clouds threaded the soft sky. Behind her, she heard Cynthia whispering into a phone. The steel door behind the counter slid open.

'Grace!'

Warren had a forceful way of dominating a room, his energy thrusting itself into the place moments before he spoke, which gave her the unsettled feeling of being constantly in the presence of a sonic boom. He was in his late sixties but tall and fit-looking. His silver-white hair was precision cut, and he wore dark linen trousers and a blue cashmere sweater that matched his eyes.

He bared his teeth in a smile. The door wickered shut behind him. He stepped into the lobby. 'Cynthia taking good care of you?'

Grace shot a smug smile at Cynthia but it was wasted. Cynthia shuffled papers, pretending to be busy.

Warren didn't wait for an answer. He gripped Grace's elbow gently and moved her out of harm's way as he stood for a moment under the retina scanner. The red light beamed into his eyes. He blinked and the door reopened.

'Quickly, quickly.'

He led her back into a hallway as the steel door closed behind them. They were in a corridor with laboratories. Grace could hear a synthesizer whirring softly in a lab down the hall, and the muted sound of voices coming from a conference room.

Warren turned and studied her, and the heartiness in his face fell away and was replaced with anger. 'He could have killed you, damn it. I've left three messages since yesterday. You couldn't pick up the phone and let me know you were all right?'

'I wanted to come in person.' She wondered if he could tell she was lying. 'I have questions about Eddie Loud.'

Warren glanced quickly at the conference room and Grace realized Warren didn't want whoever was in there overhearing them.

'Follow me. I've got a meeting going on so I don't have much time.'

In all the years she'd known him, he'd always had a meeting going on. Something big.

Warren had started the Center as a shoestring biotech company thirty years earlier, and hit the jackpot with a drug that became widely used in the treatment of rheumatoid arthritis, inhibiting the immune system from attacking the body's own cartilage. He'd taken that money and bought land, eventually building the Center for BioChimera. Now the company had grown to over three thousand employees worldwide, with manufacturing plants scattered across the globe.

But it was the hospital side that had attracted her. The chance to work with pediatric heart transplant patients and pursue new methods of controlling transplant rejection. When she'd been offered a residency, she'd jumped at it.

Warren had immediately singled her out, something that stunned her and made her uneasy at the same time. She had no interest in following Warren Pendrell into hospital administration, but she soon learned his interest was more complicated.

He'd lost a daughter about her age, he confided finally. Warren's pain at losing his daughter Sara, and Grace's need to have a dad, melded during her work at the Center. That and a mutual passion for research and healing. He'd personally recommended her for a position at Cedars-Sinai after her residency, and had helped set up the two months she'd spent in Guatemala working in a remote mountain clinic.

And then she'd come back from Guatemala and dropped out of medicine and taken a job at the crime lab.

She'd never told him why and Warren never let it drop, how her place was back at the Center leading the assault on transplant rejection and doing heart surgery on kids, instead of wasting her talent in some two-bit job with the police, barely scraping by.

She'd delivered Katie at the Center when the time came, and later Katie had ear surgery as a baby there, but the relationship between Warren and Grace had grown increasingly strained until it had erupted in a frightening outburst of pyrotechnics, Warren insisting she tell him why she'd given up medicine, Grace holding to silence. He'd apologized but she sensed lurking beneath the surface a fierce need to control, a need he was barely able to keep in check. Now their contact was relegated to stray lunches and occasional phone calls.

'Do you know how many people I've mentored here in all these years? Exactly two.'

'Warren.' It was the opening volley of a familiar war and she didn't have the taste for it.

'Fine, fine, I'll stop.'

She followed him into his private library and waited as he scooped up an open reference book from a leather sofa. The room was large, airy, painted Italian custard.

A plaster fireplace vaulted in sweeping simplicity, surrounded by chairs in a rich palette of gold and red, accenting his favorite painting, a Degas that hung near his Italian rosewood writing desk. Two walls held floor-to-ceiling bookshelves. It was here he kept his collection of science journals, books on philosophy and religion and first-edition nineteenth-century European novels.

'Sit anyplace.' He turned his back on her and went to the window. 'I'm relieved you're all right, by the way,' he said gruffly. 'More relieved than you'll know.'

She sank into the leather sofa. Soft sunlight floated through raw silk panels, spilling wide bands of light across the tiled floor.

He turned and she saw how tired he looked under the tan. 'I don't mean to be short. I'm under more pressure than usual this week, that's all, and then when I heard how close you'd come to dying — well, it seems to have unhinged me. What do you need?'

'Answers. You knew him personally, didn't you? Eddie Loud.'

He gave her a long, measured look. 'I think I'll have a drink. May I get you something? Perhaps fresh papaya juice?'

'Sounds wonderful.'

He went to the sideboard, glancing at the photograph of his daughter he kept in a small gilt frame. Taken years ago, it revealed a young woman with a strong jaw and merry eyes. She was lost in a corn maze, laughing, not sure which way led to the exit. It had been shot from above looking down, and the exit was within reach. She just couldn't find it.

Losing her way seemed to have been a chronic problem. Sara had been a sophomore at Brandeis when she'd fallen in love with a foreign exchange student who police discovered was traveling with false papers and had a criminal record. He was deported and six weeks later, she'd dropped out of school and followed him to Central America. Warren sent a former Green Beret to capture her and drag her home, but she'd run away again, and this time he'd left her alone.

Warren's gaze left the photo and settled on Grace. 'I'm sorry,' he said quietly. 'What do you need to know?'

She told him what Eddie Loud had said right before she killed him.

The color drained from his face. 'Good God. You're sure he said 'He's coming for you'? Those exact words?'

'Yes. I'll never forget it.'

Warren fixed their drinks, his face troubled. He handed Grace her glass and sat down, taking a long drink of scotch and rolling the heavy glass between his palms, studying the amber liquid. ''Run. He's coming for you. The Spikeman.' Any ideas?'

She shook her head. 'I was hoping it made sense to you.' She took a sip of juice. It was sweet and wonderfully pulpy.

He was silent, mulling something over. He looked up.

'He's dead. Under the circumstances, I guess I can tell you some things.'

Warren drank some more and the ice clinked. He studied the glass.

'Eddie Loud was schizophrenic. You know on the research side of the Center, we specialize in immunological disorders and treatment. We do the usual — arthritis, lupus, MS, transplant compatibility, but the last few years, since you left, we've added schizophrenia to the list. That's what we do behind those wire windows on two.'

'How can schizophrenia be an immunological disorder?'

'Might not be, jury's still out, but there's a possibility that a simple virus in the fourth month in utero could contribute to a wiring problem significant enough to create it. We used magnetic resonance imaging and found structural defects in the temporal lobes, some cell changes. Anyway, we're exploring whether we can reverse that damage on chromosome six — not just throwing drugs at the problem after the fact. It's delicate and difficult.'

'You were experimenting on Eddie Loud?' It sounded colder than she'd intended, and Warren flinched and drained his glass.

'Yes, he was enrolled in our experimental program and yes, the combination of gene therapy, drugs, and behavior modification seemed to be helping. I've known his dad four years or so. Eddie's bounced around other treatment centers and Bert — that's his dad, Senator Loud — heard about the work we were doing here and pleaded with me to take him. Big mistake. Clearly.'

Grace's glass was empty and she put it down and slid her hands under her legs to warm them. 'I don't understand why he fixated on me.'

'I don't either.' He shrugged. 'There's a chance he could have made it up. Eddie had a peculiar fascination for video. When he fell off his meds, he believed himself to be a hotshot reporter, going after the big story. In his room at the halfway house, they'd find equipment he'd ordered over the Internet and squirreled away, and once even props from a Hollywood set he'd managed to buy off eBay.'

She could see the headline: ALCOHOLIC CRIME LAB FORENSIC BIOLOGIST KILLS ALMOST DEFENSELESS MENTALLY ILL SON OF SENATOR.

'That still doesn't explain how he got my name and matched it to my face. And knew I was going to be at that particular meth house.'

Warren scrubbed his jaw with his knuckles. 'God, what a mess.'

He put his glass down and moved to a wall of books. Long thin windows had been built into the shelves, revealing sudden views, as surprising as if the views themselves were a work of art. Soft clouds filtered across the narrow stamp of blue sky.

The shelf held a wooden toy of Sara's that always reminded Grace of a parking garage, a series of small wooden ramps and painted wooden penguins. Warren absently touched the spring and the penguins clicked up a ramp, and the first one began its inexorable slide down the first chute into the turn. He wasn't watching it. He was looking at her.

'I have to tell you something in confidence, something that factors into all this. Want anything else to drink? Or a muffin or something?'

'Thanks. I'm set.'

He made himself a second drink. The last penguin was ratcheting up a ladder to the top. It dipped its head and dove down the chute. He took a chair across from her.

'Have you any idea how much this company's worth?'

She shook her head.

'The Center has developed, won regulatory approval for, and marketed over ten drugs dealing with specific immunology disorders: diabetes, Crohn's, MS, transplants, cancer, AIDS.'

He paused. 'It's worth close to eight billion dollars, Grace. I know that because I just went through an extensive process of determining assets and liabilities. I'm selling.'

'What?'

'Just what I said. I built a world, and now I'm tired.' He smiled dryly. 'And perhaps a little old. I've never publicly traded the Center so it frees me in some ways to do slightly unorthodox things. Of course I have a team of high-priced experts, many of whom are sitting around my conference table right now wondering where the hell I am, but we've passed due diligence and it's in escrow. We close at the end of the week. Everybody's signed confidentiality agreements and noncompete clauses, and we've played it close to the vest. I've already signed off at the secretary of state's office on a release of the name, so the new owners can continue using it.'

There was a quiet knock on the door and Warren's assistant, a striking black woman named Karen, stuck her head in the door.

'Sorry to interrupt, sir. The eastern sector pharmaceuticals rep has a plane to catch.'

Warren stood. 'I'd appreciate it if you could stay. This will only take a minute.'

Grace nodded. Karen smiled neutrally and held the door open for Warren, closing it after him. They both retreated down the hall. Grace heard Warren's voice in the conference room, muffled and hearty.

Eight billion dollars, Grace thought. To her it was Monopoly money, not real. She wondered what he was going to do with his share. His wife had died years before. All he had was this place. His telling her about it matter-of-factly, his trusting her with such a significant secret, troubled her. It had nothing to do with Eddie Loud and brought her no closer to finding Jazz Studio, and she feared it was his way of trying to hook her back in.

The door opened and Warren reappeared. He closed the door. 'Sorry about that. I wouldn't have told you if it wasn't necessary, and of course this information is confidential and not to be shared.'

'I understand.'

'It's a Swiss company called Belikond. They have their own marketing arm in place to smooth the way. They've pledged no personnel changes in the first twenty-four months, which makes it somewhat more palatable.'

'The Center's worth close to eight billion dollars?' She was still on that.

'Not just the Center. The manufacturing plants are in the mix, too, but the most significant assets are patents. The deal's gone hard.'

'Excuse me?'

'Belikond's had to put hard money down, and whether the deal closes or not — and it will close, I assure you — the seller gets to keep the deposit.' He paused. 'Ten percent of the total purchase price is typical.'

She did the math in her mind and wished she were still drinking. She could use something a lot stronger than papaya juice.

'And that seller getting to keep the hard money would be you.'

'And others. Underwriting the Center are drug development companies, a cluster of university research deals, and some investment bankers willing to take huge risks. I'm the director but six others sit on the board, and getting them to agree on anything is like trying to get a bag full of cats to stop fighting. We've jumped through hoops the past ninety days — proof of title, physical inspection of the lands, the buildings, improvements — worldwide, Grace, not just here — and due diligence inspection of the IP's. Intellectual properties. Checking that all the patents have been properly registered, and that there are no existing or potential claim infringements, and then dividing up each investor's share. Oh, and then the lending bank sends over its own team and we do the dance all over again.'

'And you're closing when?' She was certain he'd told her, she just couldn't remember. She was on the verge of taking out a second mortgage on her house, just to repair the roof.

'Delivery of assets, titles, full custody, and control gets turned over at the end of this week. I don't have to be present, but I have to be on top of it.'

Under the tan, there were dark circles under his eyes.

'My chunk — minus whatever part the government's going to chip out for taxes — I want wired to an account in the Caymans. And since nobody but me has that access code, they're going to electronically link me as the deal closes. I'll have thirty seconds on my end to enter the access code, releasing my funds into my private account. If I miss that window, my share gets sent to my bank stateside, but for tax reasons, that's something I'd like to avoid. My share is worth several hundred million dollars.'

The shock must have shown on her face. She looked around the immaculate space, studying his daughter's photo so she wouldn't have to meet his eyes. She wasn't afraid of money and people who had it, but power tripped her up sometimes, and she could feel herself starting to fall.

'So. You sell. You leave. Eddie Loud acted alone as a crazy person, God knows how he got my name. Nobody else is after me.'

'Not exactly. I told you it was complicated. Yesterday, I got this.'

He went to his desk and unlocked the drawer and came back with a postcard. 'Hand-delivered, left in a manila envelope for me downstairs at Information.'

The postcard was faintly blue in color, on handmade paper stock, with streaks of heavier blue weaving through it. There was no address or postmark. Warren Pendrell's name had been typed on the message side, with a single typed sentence underneath: *He's coming for you, the Spikeman.*

She turned the postcard over. Warren's picture had been cut and pasted onto the postcard. It was blurred, shot as he stepped through the front door of the Center, a hand shading his eyes.

Imbedded in his chest was a crudely drawn butcher knife, dripping with blood.

''He's coming for you, the Spikeman.' And the butcher knife. It's the same threat, Grace. The same. One thing science teaches, there are no coincidences.'

'You're saying somebody could be after both of us? Who? Why?'

He shook his head. 'I have no idea.'

'I could take this in. Get somebody to run tests.' She and Paul Collins were colleagues, but Marcie had worked next to Grace in the forensic biology lab for five years, and they were friends. The tall, emaciated, jumpy woman would figure out a way to have the postcard tested if Grace asked, even though fibers and documents were not handled in their lab, and the paper wasn't saturated with biological fluids.

Warren shook his head. 'The last thing I want is the police involved while I'm negotiating this deal. Businesses run on rumors and innuendo, Grace. The total valuation of the business has been in flux over the period of time we've negotiated, and I'm talking a flux that could cost us millions. I don't want to hand Belikond anything else its team could use.'

'Marcie's very discreet.'

'Grace, I'm serious. I want things quiet and on

102

schedule. I'm telling you this because I want you to protect yourself. Let me rephrase that. I want to protect you. And Katie.'

'We're okay.'

'God, you're impossible. If you change your mind . . . '

She nodded. He held out his hand for the postcard and she reluctantly gave it to him. He relocked it in his desk and rang the receptionist.

'Yes. Cynthia. Please alert Lee Bentley we're on our way.'

Grace felt a visceral surge of panic and anger. He was doing it again. Broadsiding her.

'Warren, you should have asked me first.'

'So you could say no?'

'I don't have time.'

'Make it.' He reached for her hand.

10

Warren walked down the brightly lit hallway toward a lab at the far end of the corridor, Grace seething behind him, the images of Lee tumbling one on top of the other.

When Grace had been tapped to work the pediatric side of heart transplants at the Center, she'd immediately come into conflict with a leggy young researcher, Lee Ann Bentley, doing postdoc work on kids.

There had been a whiff of scandal that Lee had falsified lab results before coming to the Center in an effort to prove the effectiveness of a new immune suppressor used on chimps in heart transplants. Two primates had died before anything conclusive could be determined, the bodies conveniently cremated. Lee had been exonerated of any wrongdoing, but it had left Grace feeling there was something creepy buried under all that perfection.

Lee was concentrating on xenografts and xenobiotics, genetically altering animal hearts so that one day, they'd be recognized as human by a transplant recipient. Grace was going another direction completely: chimerism. Mutual cell assimilation. Tricking the body into accepting a new, human heart as if it were its own.

She'd stumbled onto it by accident years before during her internship — that if she first transplanted bone marrow from the donor, the patient's immune system could be tricked into accepting the donor heart almost as if it were its own. That meant lower doses of immune-suppressant drugs. The patient would still have to be on a rigorous drug program for the rest of his life, but at lower doses. Since the immune-suppressant drugs were so toxic, the lesser the dosage the better.

Later, that groundbreaking research was validated when transplant surgeons in Lyon, France, infused an Australian patient with donor marrow cells before performing a successful hand transplant, and then again when a woman in Paris, infused first with marrow cells from a donor, had a partial face transplant.

But when Grace was trying it, she was among a small group of surgeons and the only one at the Center. She'd been working there only a couple of weeks when she butted heads with Lee over a patient, a six-year-old boy who needed a heart transplant.

Lee talked the parents into putting a genetically altered pig's heart into his small chest. Grace had passionately argued with her in private beforehand. It was too experimental. Risky. Safer options hadn't been exhausted yet. Lee had shrugged and smiled, and the smile had been a cold thing.

'It doesn't really matter, does it? If he dies?'

She'd said it so quickly, matter-of-factly, Grace wasn't certain she'd heard correctly. 'It does to his parents,' Grace said. 'It does to me.'

In the end, the parents prevailed, signing off on the surgery. The boy died three days later. A week afterward, a human heart became available that would have worked, and Grace had never forgiven Lee for killing him.

The research side of the Center had always been Warren's particular interest, and Grace had a growing suspicion that Warren was willing to sacrifice patients on the hospital side to be used as guinea pigs for research that was still experimental.

Or she could just be jealous that Lee was Warren's favorite now, and had been for some time. Part of her still missed him.

A sterile tray the size Grace used for making cookies glowed in purple light as Warren pushed open the door to the lab. 'Don't turn on the light. She's got cartilage cells that are light sensitive.'

A green light cast a glow over the counters. It was a narrow, windowless room and Grace felt slightly claustrophobic. Out of the gloom, Lee Bentley emerged, her hair gleaming.

'Well, well. We meet again.'

Her hair had grown long since Grace had last seen her, and she wore it in a thick braid that shone the color of wheat and made her cheekbones look high. She had the talent for smiling with her teeth and never having the smile ease up her face. Her eyes were pale green, humorless and cold. Somewhere in Lee's genetic code, marauders clambered in fur boots over a dung hill, swinging mastodon thigh bones and shattering the skulls of slumbering children. She was taller than Grace and just as slender and could have easily modeled. Whips

106

and chains, probably.

'Still killing chimps?'

'Please,' Warren said.

'She's a lab tech,' Lee said. 'She couldn't find the jugular if she Googled it.'

'Biologist,' Grace said. 'They call us forensic biologists.'

'Both of you.' Warren held up his hands in a classic gesture of peace. 'Lee, I'm sorry.'

He was siding with her. How could he side with her?

'I want Grace to see this.' His voice held a pleading note.

Lee narrowed her eyes, debating something with herself, and then whirled and went down an aisle. She walked past what appeared to be an ear floating in gelatin and stopped before a large metal container the size of a Crock-Pot, connected by a snarl of tubes to the wall. It was a bioreactor, for growing things. A monitor attached to the tubes beeped in a steady pulse, and Grace saw at the far end of the counter a printer spitting out a stream of data.

The human ear meant Lee was focusing now on an entirely different direction in her research, and it made Grace queasy. 'What am I looking at?' she said irritably.

Lee slid her hand over the outside of the bioreactor, caressing it. 'First, a few thoughts. There are almost three hundred kids — just in America — waiting at any given time for a heart. Often a heart that never comes.'

'And the neck bone's connected to the chin bone. I know the stats, I know how many die waiting. Can you leave the theatrics for your Nobel prize speech and cut to the chase?'

Lee lifted her chin and looked at Warren. 'She's impossible.'

Grace thought she saw him nod in agreement and she snapped, 'Good. I'm gone.'

Warren clamped a hand gently on her shoulder and she bit off her sarcasm when she saw the pain and tenderness in his face.

'Grace. Please. I need your help.' His voice was low and urgent. He was turned away from Lee so the researcher couldn't hear their conversation, and Grace felt again the connection with this aging man. 'I need you to see this.'

She nodded and he took a breath, relieved. Grace moved primly down the aisle and stood next to Lee, noting that her perfume held a mix of citrus and musk, and something fainter.

Perhaps gunpowder. 'What's in there?' Grace said.

Lee lifted the lid. Inside the vat floated a human heart.

It was the size of a tiny fist. It swayed gently in a thick, viscous liquid. It was an odd tan color and floated in a soupy nutrient sea the red color of Jell-O. Grace felt a wave of nausea. The last time she had seen a human heart was in Guatemala. She closed her eyes and steadied herself against the counter.

'Grace? Are you okay?' Warren said, alarmed.

'I need to leave. Go into the hall.'

She patted her way blindly past them toward the door and burst through it into the hall, taking gulps of air and leaning against the wall.

Her legs felt unsteady. She wiped her lip and swallowed hard, a faintly metallic acid taste in her throat. She heard the lab door close.

Warren joined her in the hall. 'What can I do?' he asked quietly.

She shook her head, took another gulp of air, opened her eyes. 'Sorry. Just took me by surprise.' The pale print on the hall wallpaper slowly stopped moving.

'You want to sit?'

She shook her head and took a steadying breath. 'I haven't heard anything about that. A human heart. Extraordinary.' Her legs had stopped trembling and she risked straightening up.

'You're one of only a handful of people who know of its existence. That's why we have the steel door and retina scanner. It is the most explosive research breakthrough in decades. Did you know that the biotech field is the fastest-growing business segment in the world? It's going to be worth billions, Grace. Let's go back in my office. I'll get you some water.'

After he got her settled he said simply, 'It's the motherlode. It's the thing, frankly, that Belikond wants. That they're paying big money to get.'

'I thought Lee was working with xenografts.' She was still feeling queasy and Warren refilled her glass with water.

'She stopped five years ago, right about the time you left. Scientists all over the world have been working on growing specific parts of hearts, valves especially, but Lee hit on something, utilizing a set of over a hundred different patents

109

we've been quietly acquiring, that made growing a heart in a bioreactor a reality. She's just started experimental trials. That heart is only the second one in existence.'

'If I hadn't seen it there with my own eyes . . . ' Her voice trailed.

'I know. It's extraordinary. And the reason I showed that to you — well, there are a couple of reasons, Grace.'

He hesitated. 'I needed you to know how this whole thing with Eddie Loud has complicated everything.' He held up his hands, cutting her off. 'And believe me, I don't blame you for killing him. If I'd lost you, I don't know what I would have done. But it's definitely not the kind of publicity I was hoping to get during the week I'm selling.'

She waited, wondering where he was going with it.

'I'm bringing this up because I need you to watch something on CNN tonight. A piece about the work Lee's doing.'

She tensed.

'There'll be some blood, Grace, but not too much.'

She worked with blood all the time. That wasn't what bothered her. Medical reporting on CNN was Mac's world.

'It airs tonight,' he repeated. 'You've been a medical doctor. You work with the police. Somebody is targeting me. And you. And maybe, in some way I don't know, trying to derail the sale. Someplace, there's a connection, Grace. That's what we have to focus on. Finding it.

Before we run out of time. Can you do it?'

'I need something, too. The owner of the taco van, Mr. Esguio. He told me he'd hired somebody besides Eddie Loud from the Center, a woman named Jazz Studio, who had problems with a food cart this past week. I need to find her.'

Warren's face colored scarlet. 'You've been asking questions about my patients?'

'She knew Eddie. Maybe she can tell me what the warning about the Spikeman meant. It's for both of us, Warren, remember that.'

'Eddie's dead, Grace. And I hate to point it out, but the best chance we had of finding out who's after you — and me — died when you shot him. Jazz is still a patient. I can't let you talk to her. I'm sorry, but I can't. She's emotionally fragile now. She needs her privacy.'

He got up and took her arm and escorted her out into the hall. At the steel door, he pressed a button to open it and hesitated, pulling out a business card and scribbling on it.

'Please, for both our sakes, watch that program tonight. Find whatever the missing link is between the two of us. Before it's too late.'

He thrust the card into her hand. 'Home number, private line into my office, cell — although I'm the only man in America who doesn't seem to remember to carry one. I'm serious, Grace. Take care of yourself. And if you need my help, I can have somebody on you in a heartbeat, but leave Jazz Studio alone.'

Hearts again. She nodded and stepped through the opening door.

111

11

The Spikeman was targeting her and Warren. Why?

Exhaustion clouded her thinking, born of the terror of the meth bust and its sleepless aftermath. A small kernel of anxiety had lodged in her chest and it was a cold thing, even though the day was warm.

Grace made a stop and returned to the Center half an hour later, the gray stone and blank windows a cipher. She went directly to the information desk in the hospital lobby. She was carrying a mediumsized pepperoni and cheese pizza, the receipt taped to the front with JAZZ STUDIO written in block letters. Jazz had just started working the food cart after being in Records; Grace was banking on that job change not being recorded yet at the information desk.

'Delivery for . . . ' Grace ripped off the receipt and frowned. 'Jazz Studio in Records.'

'Jazz Studio? You've got to be kidding.' The woman at the desk was in her early twenties, with thin pink lips spackled with glitter. Her name tag read TRINA TAYLOR. She pushed aside the book she was reading: *Television Production Handbook*. A USED sticker adorned the spine. A college kid moon-lighting.

'That's what it says. So where's Records?'

'There are lots of records departments here. I don't know if I can help you.' The odor of warm cheese bit the air. Trina wet her lips and stole a glance at the carton.

'Come on,' Grace pleaded. 'Comes out of my pocket, somebody stiffs me. You got a roster, right? I'll look it up myself.'

'I can't. Against Center regulations.'

'Look, I get by on tips. I'm just trying to stay in school.' It was an inspired lie and Trina immediately looked sympathetic.

'Where do you go?'

'Point Loma Nazarene.' If Grace was going to lie, may as well throw in God.

Trina chewed her lip and left a pink lipstick chip on her tooth. 'I got a friend in security. Maybe he can help.'

Grace shifted her gaze to the gift shop while Trina made the call, watching an old man shuffling to the cash register with a rose. He had a bad hip and the rose took a sharp dip every time he leaned on that foot, as if he were conducting an invisible symphony.

'Uh-huh. Yeah. Okay. Sure. I'd like that.' Trina put down the receiver and pointed toward the hallway on Grace's left. 'Jazz Studio works in Deep Six.'

'Deep Six?' Grace ripped off the receipt with Jazz's name on it and crumpled it up.

'South wing, basement, door at the very end. Use that elevator, it's easier. And good luck, okay?'

Grace looked at her, confused.

'With school.'

'Oh, yeah. You, too.'

Trina smiled wanly and reached for her book.

113

Grace pushed open the door to Deep Six and put the pizza she was carrying down on the counter. The room was cramped. Behind the counter hung shelves of color-coded books holding bound volumes. An archway led to a deep cavern of filing cabinets. Nobody was there.

Grace leaned over the counter. 'Hello?'

'Goddammit all to hell!'

Grace craned her neck and could just make out a glimpse of a woman kneeling amid an explosion of scattered charts.

'Hello?' Grace said more loudly.

The woman jerked up, slamming a hand to her heart. She had sallow skin and faded, wispy hair and pale, watery eyes. The cream-colored knit she was wearing made her look as if she'd been dipped in a vat of lemon juice.

'God. You stopped my heart.'

'Sorry.'

The woman clambered to her feet and slammed a file drawer shut with her hip. It was a large hip, and the cabinet rocked as if it had been caught in a ground swell. She came through the arch, her chunky beige heels beating a brisk tattoo. A brass tag identified her as Rosemary Melzer. Her chin was holding up, but her neck was starting to go. Grace in another ten years.

'If you need microfiche, Eileen can download in 212 if you have the chart number, but if you're looking for inactive hard copies, you're out of luck.' She gestured at the mess behind her and then scrutinized Grace more closely. 'You look familiar.'

Grace extended her hand. 'Grace Descanso.'

Rosemary's handshake was boneless and cool. Her puzzled glance went to the pizza.

'The guys at New Life thought you might need this, after yesterday.' Grace shoved the pizza across the counter.

Rosemary grimaced. 'Nice. Jazz goes psycho on me and Curtis thinks he can wipe the slate clean with a deep dish. Not that I won't devour it, although after yesterday, I could use something a whole lot stronger.' She cracked the lid open and the sharp smell of pepperoni wafted out. 'Want a piece?'

'I'm set.'

'You're Jazz's new caseworker? I wasn't expecting you for another hour.'

'Whenever there's an incident with an employee — '

'That's what you're calling it, an incident?' Rosemary opened the door in the counter and motioned her irritably through. 'Look at this mess. Just look at it.'

Grace followed her back into the filing room. Jazz had systematically emptied a steel filing cabinet. She'd dumped the first two drawers on the floor, scattering and ripping apart charts in a blizzard of medical information ankle-deep in front of the gaping filing cabinet. A row of gold stars, the kind Katie brought home on tests, had been pasted to the front of the empty cabinet.

'I'm going to talk to the board, I really am. I know their position on hiring, but I'm tired of being a guinea pig. These are charts, people's lives. What's to stop a crazy person from taking this information out into the street? She is, you

115

know. She's totally crazy.'

Grace was silent. 'Well, she does have . . . '
Waiting to see what Rosemary would fill in.

'Yes, exactly. And I just don't think it's a good
fit with my department, you know?'

'I can understand that,' Grace said neutrally.

'When I was hired, Dr. Pendrell himself
explained to me the importance of trying to
reintroduce clients back into the workforce, but
why can't they put somebody on the janitor
crew, or dishwashing in the cafeteria?' Rosemary
took a breath and rolled her shoulders. 'I'm
done. Okay.'

'What's this filing cabinet hold?'

'You mean the one she wrecked? Charts for
pediatrics we're about to transfer into deep
storage at a secure warehouse.'

Grace wanted to ask if Rosemary had ever
seen Jazz with a guy named Eddie, or if Jazz had
ever talked about him, but she didn't want
Rosemary remembering where she'd last seen
Grace, on television after killing Eddie Loud.

'Frankly, I was relieved when Jazz was
transferred out of Records, I really was. I'd
already taken her off the shredder — didn't want
her hurting herself — and assigned her
something less stressful, but when Curt told me
he was moving her on to some food cart, well, I
thought, it's about time.'

'She brought the food cart here first thing.'

Rosemary nodded as she walked back to the
counter and reached for the piece of pizza. Grace
spotted the Rolodex tucked on a shelf under the
counter.

'I was here early. We're instituting a new computer system, and we're backed up, which is why I came in on a Sunday. She was waiting for me. And then, get this, she wouldn't even let me buy a cup of coffee or a pastry. Said I had to wait until nine, like everybody else. She backs the cart right up next to the counter, too, so I can get a good look at what I can't have.'

Rosemary took an aggrieved bite of pizza. 'Did you bring any Coke?' she said hopefully.

'No. Sorry. So Jazz is there with the food cart first thing but won't let you buy anything.'

'You try waiting, smelling that coffee smell, and some little twit not letting you buy a cup because it isn't time. I went down the hall and got a cup from the machine, and when I came back, she'd smashed up the office and was dragging the cart out of there. I called security.'

'What number do you have for her?' Grace flicked a glance at the Rolodex.

'You don't have it?'

Grace froze.

Rosemary's eyes narrowed in suspicion.

'I just want to make sure you have the one that's the most up-to-date.' Grace smiled in what she hoped was a convincing manner. A split second passed while Grace thought, *This is it, she's not going for it*, and then Rosemary nodded and put down the pizza slice and reached for the Rolodex, flipping through it.

'Did she say anything while she was doing this?'

'Not to me. But while she was leaving she kept muttering, 'I'm the keeper. I have to keep them

117

safe. Hold them until the Coming.' '

' 'Keep them safe.' Any significance?'

'None. Oh, here we go.'

Rosemary detached the card and passed it over to Grace. A phone number and an address on Pacific Highway near the Old Town trolley station. Grace passed it back. 'Current. Anything you want me to tell her? I'm going over.'

'Yeah. Tell her she sets foot on this floor again, I'll have her arrested, and not just by a security guard either. I don't care what they say.'

12

Jazz Studio lived near Old Town in a faded house tucked between ramps for 8 East and 5 North, cement overpasses arching like apocalyptic cathedrals, blotting out the sky.

He's coming for you.

Eddie had been so *sure*. Yeah, paranoid schizophrenics usually were.

Cars whined overhead as Grace parked next to a late-model car with government plates. She got out and surveyed the yard. A bike stood chained to a willow shading the front of the house. A crate of desiccated geraniums lay tilted next to the door, like a UPS package waiting for pickup. She stepped around the geraniums and read the mail slots nailed to the siding. J. Studio was in 2C.

Grace tried the front door. It wasn't locked. The living room was small and surprisingly cheerful, with scattered comfortable-looking sofas and chairs, and a shelf of novels and board games. A television muttered, tuned to a soap.

'Hello?' No answer. She stepped into the living room and glanced into the kitchen. An eight-burner stove stood next to an empty table holding an abandoned chess game. Grace took the stairs leading to the second floor. Voices and muffled crying came from a room closest to the stairwell. Two doors down, 2C stood ajar.

Grace rapped softly. 'Jazz?'

She pushed open the door. A woman lay crumpled on a bed. She was in her midtwenties, skinny and East Indian, with glossy black hair and high cheekbones. She peered up at Grace, her stare vacant.

'Jazz? I'm Grace. You don't know me, but I'd like to talk to you. You've had a hard couple of days.'

Jazz shifted, eyes red, unfocused. 'Eddie. Eddie died. Shot right through the head. Splat. He was my boyfriend. Wanted to work on the railroad.'

'No kidding. I'm sorry.' Grace wet her lips. 'Did he like to play spy games? Maybe with little cameras?'

'We were getting married. I was going to wear a dress. Pretty one. White.' Jazz spoke mechanically, as if it were something she'd memorized.

Grace nodded, her gaze searching the room. 'When he drove around in the van, did he like to spy with a camera?'

The room was a jumble of pill bottles, makeup, tossed clothes. A large, scratchy-looking stuffed lion with shiny button eyes sat on the bed, its smile faintly menacing. Grace didn't see any medical charts but a photo lay in the debris on the dresser top.

It was a Polaroid of Jazz and Eddie, arms around each other. Jazz was gripping the lion. A faded wooden ramp jutted behind them. Grace recognized it immediately: the historic roller coaster at Belmont Park in Mission Beach. Katie wasn't tall enough yet to ride it, but she loved the noise and caramel corn and crowds and how close it was to the beach.

The Eddie in the picture looked skinny and vulnerable. Not the Eddie in Grace's mind. That one burned with insanity and juiced-up rage.

'Oh. The camera.'

Grace locked eyes with her. 'You know about the camera.'

Jazz nodded. 'He could see things with it. Just walking around. We were famous on the Internet. We were.'

'Who gave him the camera, Jazz?'

She shook her head 'A secret. Can't tell that one, no no no.' She took a deep, shuddery breath. 'He was my boyfriend and somebody bad got him.'

Yeah, me.

'I'm sorry.' Grace waited until Jazz's attention faltered and palmed the photo, apologizing silently for taking it. She slid it into her pocket and came over to Jazz's bed. 'Mind if I sit?'

Jazz didn't answer so Grace sat gingerly on the edge of the bed. Jazz smelled like vanilla.

'I heard you had a fight with Eddie the other day.'

Jazz raised her head cautiously, like a cornered animal. The whites of her eyes were almost a milky blue, making the irises look black. 'He told me it was my job. I told him no, but he wouldn't listen.'

'Really. What job?'

'The keeper. I have to keep them until the Coming. Eddie made me see. The Spikeman told him all about it.'

Grace smiled encouragingly but the hair on

121

the back of her neck rose. 'You know the Spikeman?'

Jazz clutched Grace's arm. Her fingers were bits of damp seaweed. 'I'm his messenger now, the only one left. Eddie was trying to warn her. Save her.'

'You mean at the meth house. He was trying to warn the tech.' Her.

'Bad spacemen were there, bad bad in space suits, and the Spikeman said kill kill kill, all the bad men in space suits, but not her, her you warn first, that one.'

Spacemen. Detective Sergeant Lewin and DEA chemist Chip Page were wearing Tyvek protective suits. Had someone told Eddie to kill the spacemen? Kill them and toss in the uniformed cop standing guard in the alley as some kind of bonus? Grace was in a Tyvek suit, too. Would Eddie have killed her next?

'You know the Spikeman?' she said again.

Jazz nodded slyly and a sheaf of black hair fell over her face.

'Jazz, this is important; does he have another name?'

'Does who have another name? What are you doing?' The voice came from a heavyset woman standing in the doorway.

She was middle-aged, with limp hair she wore skinned back into a navy blue bandanna. Coverall shorts stretched over her lumpy body, exposing creeping cellulite in her knees. She carried a mop like a rifle.

Jazz flinched and cowered on the bed. 'I didn't tell! I didn't.'

122

'Who are you?' The woman banged the mop butt hard and it rang like a gunshot. She looked vaguely familiar and Grace wasn't sure why.

Down the hall, a door burst open and Grace heard the sound of feet coming fast.

'I asked you a question.'

Grace eased off the bed. She'd seen that woman somewhere. She rapidly added a different hair color, subtracted weight, put her in a suit. Something was on the edge of awareness, if only she could retrieve it.

'What's your name?' Grace asked.

'I don't have to tell you squat. This is private property. Get the hell off.'

A man appeared in the doorway behind the woman. It was Senator Loud. He looked twenty years older than he had in the helicopter, hollowed and gray.

He locked eyes with Grace and emotions flashed across his face: Recognition, followed by pained disbelief and an anger so raw it made Grace take a step back.

'I know who she is, Opal. I'll handle it.'

'I don't want trouble.' Grace inched toward the door. There was no way out. The woman with the mop was acting as a sentinel and Senator Loud stood right behind her.

'Trouble?' His voice dropped to a fierce whisper. 'You killed my son. You come here the day Pat and I have to clear his things, how dare you.'

'I didn't know he lived here! I was coming to see Jazz!'

Lighter footsteps pattered down the hall and a

123

thin woman in her late fifties appeared, her head peering around the senator. Diamonds studded her ears. She wore a trim black pantsuit. Her hand stole to the senator's arm and tightened, her nails turning white with pressure. Her eyes were slits in a face swollen with grief, and Grace could see her son in the dark hair, now streaked with gray.

On the bed, Jazz stared wonderingly at Grace. 'She killed him? You killed my Eddie? And you come to my room? You ask me questions?'

'He was trying to kill me,' Grace said. It sounded small.

'Oh, God. Bert. This is the woman who killed him?' Shock coursed across Mrs. Loud's face. The skin under her eyes creped into hairline cracks, as if her entire face had been made of flawed porcelain that was starting to crumble.

Senator Loud made noises deep in his throat, saying her name over and over: 'Pat, Pat.'

Pat pressed a hand to her mouth. Her face convulsed and she ran into the hall.

'Honey?' Senator Loud followed his wife, and Grace saw her opening and ran. Senator Loud spun and shot his arm out, blocking her flight. 'Not so fast.' He pushed Grace into another bedroom.

Pat slumped at the window, weeping. Cars droned up the cement arches. A dead tree stood in the backyard, cracked and broken. A faded yellow motel anchored the corner, and a kid on a skateboard practiced banging up the curb.

'Take a look. This is who you killed.' Loud's voice was raw. 'He didn't have anything,

124

understand? Look how small his life was. The littlest things . . . ' He choked.

The bed was stripped. A Rubik's Cube sat on the dresser. A clean uniform and fresh hat for his taco job hung neatly on a row of empty hooks. A cardboard box lay at the foot of the bed, half filled with folded clothes, a faded pair of jeans on top. Grace had interrupted them packing.

'You see? Eddie had health once and it went; he had dreams and they got smaller until the only thing left for him was here in this room, and now it's gone.'

A Polaroid wedged into the rim of the mirror, taken the same time as the one in Jazz's room, his arms around Jazz and his face pressed against hers, a look of possession and joy on his narrow face. He was cradling the stuffed lion like a baby.

Grace looked from the senator to his wife and tried to steady her voice, but it was coming out as angry and cornered as she felt. 'I didn't kill three men. Your son did. You might not want to believe it, but he did. I have a life, too, and your son almost made me lose it. I'm sorry for what happened, but he was going to kill me.'

'He had a little sister. And a life and a girlfriend for the first time and a good job and people who loved him and you took it all away.' A line of white banded Pat's mouth. 'You didn't have to kill him. He wasn't very strong. He's not even much taller than you are.'

Grace thought of Katie, and how much her daughter needed her. 'Maybe he just looked taller slashing the air with a butcher knife.'

'That's enough. Get out of here and don't ever

125

come back.' Loud shoved her toward the door.

She was almost at the car when she realized the hooks hammered into Eddie Loud's wall to hold his clothes weren't really hooks.

They were spikes.

13

She had lunch in the Gaslamp district and parked in the employee lot at the police station, already feeling like a visitor. Katie's school got out in forty-five minutes, and Grace took the stairs rather than wait for the elevator.

The homicide cube farm on four was a honeycomb of stalls, empty except for Detective Theo Sullivan's partner, Stella, and a couple of detectives busy on the phones. Grace tried hard not to inhale. The room smelled like bad cheese and ripe gym socks.

Stella glanced up and went back to working the phones. Her hair was tied in a blond ponytail, roots gray. She was short, packed into a pinstripe suit. Trophies for bodybuilding competitions lined her desk.

'Theo around?' A crystal paperweight slivered with family photos sat on Theo's desk. His day-timer was open and the cursor on his computer blinked. Coffee stains ringed a legal pad where Theo had picked up and put down a cup of Starbucks, now empty.

Stella shot her a look. 'Oh, yeah. He's armed, Grace. Better sit.'

The mood in the room was heavy. Killed yesterday were a rookie drug agent, a police detective, and a uniformed cop, and here was the tech who lived through it. Grace sat and leaned on her knees, staring at Theo's navy and burgundy tie looped across the back of his empty chair.

'Grace.' Theo scowled over a partition.

Lines grooved his forehead and his jaw was clenched. He wore a soft blue shirt unbuttoned at the collar that set off his dark skin. An elegant man with silver threading his black hair, always in a suit, he held stapled papers and he smacked them against his palm as he came around the partition, yanked his chair back and sat. Last night, when she'd sat in the rear of his squad car and given a statement, his voice had been gentle. Now it rang with anger.

'What part of last night didn't you get?' He leaned across the desk.

'I was just trying to — '

'You were under clear orders that this one goes through channels. And here you show up while they're clearing out Eddie's things? What was that? Do you have any idea how you've upset the senator and his wife? Senator Loud went all the way to the chief, Grace.'

'With what?' She could feel her face grow hot.

'With how his son was killed by an alcoholic with a documented post-traumatic stress disorder.' He delivered it low, directly at her.

She blinked. 'That's private, that's not supposed to come out of my personnel file.'

'A little late, Grace. Reporters have chewed a hole in it, it's all over the place.' He rubbed a finger violently into his eye. 'If you had a PTSD going in, God knows what this is doing. That's what they're saying.' He scowled and added softly, 'That's not what I believe.'

128

She couldn't breathe. A beefy detective at a nearby desk banged down a phone and scooped up papers as he brushed past the American flag on his way out the door.

'That's what this is? I'm getting thrown to the sharks?'

Theo slapped the papers down and squared them. 'It's a senator's son, Grace. Lawyers are probably crawling all over this, smelling fame and movie deals and slots on Court TV.'

She felt faint. A tight band constricted her chest. She took a gulp of air. 'Eddie Loud had a knife, Theo. It was justified. You know it and I know it.'

'Oh, yeah, and there's the gun. Not certified to carry, and here you're firing a drug agent's weapon. Good aim. Right between the eyes. And the shoulder. And the chest. And the — '

'I get it, I get it,' she said irritably.

A vein in his forehead pulsed and Grace wondered if he had high blood pressure.

'On the off chance you missed it, Senator Loud's got a running battle with local California police departments, San Diego one of them — '

She opened her mouth to protest and he held up his hand. His palm was light and spidered with lines.

' — that they're exerting undue force in arresting and subduing minorities.'

'Eddie Loud was white, Theo.'

'He was a schizophrenic, Grace.' He looked at her sharply. Too late, she realized he was checking to see if she already knew that.

'I already knew that.'

'I saw.' He sighed, and when he spoke, his voice was dangerously quiet. 'You're not going to interact with the senator again, end of story. I don't want to see your face until your lab boss, Sid Felcher, tells you to come back. You're going to sit at home on your skinny Portuguese ass and watch your tax dollars at work as we climb our way out of this mess.' Theo slid the pages over to her. 'Now sign your statement and get out of here.'

'Half Portuguese.'

'What?'

'Just on my dad's side. That makes me half Portuguese.' She skimmed the statement, a page and a half, single spaced. 'What about the blood?'

'At the meth house? Slimeball number one knocked around his old lady and she split. She came back the next day with a fat lip.'

'So Eddie wasn't part of that group?'

'Doesn't look like it. He was selling tacos to old ladies down the street, using that knife to slice onions before he stopped in the alley.'

'Theo, he said my name.'

'Yeah, I know, it's all in the statement.'

'It was a warning, Theo. What if somebody really is after me?'

Theo grimaced and pulled a folded newspaper out of his drawer. Grace recognized it immediately. It was the piece written six months before, accusing a fibers tech in the crime lab of slopping samples, the worst thing imaginable. A slopped sample was enough to get a case thrown out of court. The accusation came after the tech had been caught on a crime scene video inadvertently dragging the tail of a victim's shirt through an unidentified footprint after being up processing the scene for almost twenty-four hours. That tech had been fired and all the cases she'd been involved in were still mired in review.

It had been a nightmare of a case, a double homicide, and Grace had been on site doing the tedious, meticulous part of evidence evaluation: examining clothing, stains, the room itself for the presence of biofluids, taking detailed photos and measurements, and cutting stains out for biotesting. Except it had gone on too long, and Grace's babysitter had gotten antsy. A frantic call to Marcie, and her friend stepped in to relieve Grace so she could go home that night to Katie. No samples of theirs were involved or proved to be contaminated, but it had been enough to get them taken off the CSI rotation, and even more galling, to have to have everything they did rechecked by another lab tech before Sid signed off on it. Grace had only just gotten off restriction and back onto CSI detail when she'd shot Eddie Loud.

'Not the article, this.' Detective Sullivan flipped the fold and pointed. It was a picture of Grace and some of the others, working in the crime lab. 'Your name, Grace. Right here, along with your face.'

'You're saying he got it from that.'

'Looks that way.'

'Theo, he drove by!' she protested.

'He drives by, sees your face, stops. Know where I got this paper?'

131

She folded her arms. 'Dying to find out.'

'It was in Eddie's room, Grace. Senator Loud himself dropped it off. This guy wasn't trying to warn you about anything. He was too busy being crazy.'

She thought about it. Maybe Eddie Loud had seen Warren's picture in the paper, too, and had sent him a postcard with a knife sticking out of his chest. It could have happened like that. It was possible. A cloud was starting to lift.

'Eddie had spikes in his room, Theo. Wanted to work on the railroad.'

'There you go. Spikes. Spikeman. Can we go now?'

The door opened. It was Sid, wearing a pink shirt with flamingos and a string tie. 'Grace. I'm so glad I caught you before my walkie.'

He actually talked like that. He pulled a chair close and sat, gripping her hand and clamping his other on top of it, as if he were making a Grace sandwich. She moved her knees so they wouldn't touch any part of his body.

'How are you?'

'Fine, Sid, couldn't be better.'

Sid clicked his tongue against his teeth, making little *tsking* sounds. 'Grace, you can't kill somebody with a famous father and expect your life ever to be the same.'

Grace removed her hand from Sid's grasp.

'Want to know what's going to happen to you?'

'No,' she lied, and picked at a nail. 'Not particularly.' She had Andy as a younger brother. She knew how this game worked. If she acted

132

interested, he'd never tell. She yawned.

'What happens is, you're on administrative leave from the crime lab. I might stick you someplace else, but maybe not. The DA will send around an investigator to sift through all the statements and evidence, and then the department puts together a shooting review board, and those guys, along with the DA, decide whether there's a case to make you criminally liable.'

'Is that all?'

'Well.' Sid frowned, a difficult quiz. 'You'll have to surrender your evidence kit.'

She glanced pointedly at the door. Sid got up.

'Another thing. Word's come back you haven't scheduled time yet with the police liaison.'

'The what? Oh, you mean a shrink.' She shrugged. The last place she'd dump her guts was in the lap of a shrink paid for by the department.

Sid walked to the door and cocked his head. He was a small man with a porcine belly that today strained the flamingo on his shirt so that it looked as if the long neck and beak were gulping and swallowing some large foreign object. His hair tufted in wings over his broad forehead, giving him the appearance of having fluffy horns.

'Grace, everybody suits up, they want a shot at the ball.'

'I ran cross-country.'

Sid pursed his lips, processing it as he went through the door and it snicked closed behind him. For an instant, she thought she saw an amused look flash across Detective Theo

Sullivan's face before it returned to its neutral penetrating gaze.

'I need to touch base with Marcie before I leave. You okay with that?' She stood. Her legs felt a little tingly.

Detective Theo Sullivan stood. 'Funny thing, I'm going that way.'

'And you'll be conveniently in the hall right about the time I'm leaving, right?'

'Most likely. Almost forgot. Got a visit this morning from some top gun at CNN, saw you during the coverage of Eddie's shooting. Claims he knows you. Mac McGuire.'

Grace felt her face grow hot.

Theo sucked his teeth. 'I thought so. Dammit, Grace, you're just one problem after another.' He fished a folded scrap of paper out of his pocket and handed it to her.

★ ★ ★

He'd found her. That added to the anxiety she was already feeling. Something wasn't ringing right about Eddie Loud, and she couldn't put her finger on it.

She studied the slip of paper. Mac's handwriting was still familiar after so many years. She felt Theo watching her and tucked the paper into her purse as they rode the elevator to the sixth floor.

The elevator opened and they went past a door marked CS UNIT and stopped at Forensic Biology. The lab was quiet except for the hum of a centrifuge machine. Long white counters, workstations with stacked court papers, coded vials, cabinets overhead. Everything tidy, silent. They were probably in a staff meeting. That always happened after a shooting.

'So,' Theo said, surveying the quiet.

'So,' Grace agreed. 'I'll just leave her a note.'

Theo nodded and let her walk down the long row of stations by herself. Her lab station was bare. The active-cases pile at her station, usually high with bulging files, was empty and she felt a flash of humiliation mingled with loss. Already her work had been divided up.

Grace and the others toiled in a swamp of grimy fibers, blood-soaked clothes drying in racks, semen swabs, gunshot residue, narcotics spittle, smeary prints. It was part of a hive humming with experts delicately dissecting the dark tracings left behind after violence erupted and sheared apart whatever flimsy safety net was rigged to keep the bad things at bay, a world of long hours, catnaps on cots, exhaustion, mistakes, rechecking results, tight time frames, and the terror of missing a court deadline and getting called in to explain themselves in front of a judge.

Then having most of it discounted because a jury couldn't understand its relevance anyway. But it was a job, a good job. Already she missed it.

She spotted a rape case of hers in Marcie's pile, and a double homicide she'd been working on in a stack of files belonging to Nolo, another biologist. That file was open at his station, as if he'd disappeared in a levitated puff of smoke

135

while reading. A small Asian with a mullet, she could see his exhausted face in her mind's eye. The CSI she'd taken should have gone to Nolo; it was his week on call. She wondered again how the sheets had gotten screwed up.

A small sound made her look up. It was Marcie coming around a corner with a rack of test tubes that had just come from the centrifuge. She was a tall, emaciated woman with close-cropped hair, wearing a billowing violet peasant skirt under her lab coat. Exhaustion made her look even more gaunt. She stopped in her tracks when she saw Grace.

'Oh, my God, you're here.' She put the rack carefully down and bent to embrace Grace. The hug was a little too hard and Grace stiffened.

'I'm sorry, I'm sorry,' she said in a rush. 'I didn't mean to hurt you.'

'Marcie, get a grip. I'm fine.' Grace half laughed as she pulled away. Leave it to Marcie to need calming down after Grace had almost gotten killed.

Marcie wet her lip. 'I feel really bad. So helpless.' She averted her eyes.

'You didn't do anything wrong.' Grace felt a flash of exasperation mingled with affection. Marcie didn't handle emotions well, especially those that involved other people.

'I mean, we were always afraid this could happen,' Marcie nattered. 'Some whacko coming at us, but I never — '

'I'm okay,' Grace repeated.

'I really never thought — whoever thought it would really happen, right?' Marcie went on as if

136

she hadn't heard. 'How many CSI's have we been out on?'

'Not many lately,' Grace said crisply.

That seemed to jerk Marcie back. She nodded too hard. 'Right, right, that's right.'

Grace changed the subject. 'You and Frank and the kids still coming to Katie's party, right?'

'Wouldn't miss it,' Marcie said heartily. She uncapped a tube, rechecked its label, reached for a slide and picked up a pipette, carefully squeezing up a pellet of cells and delicately expelling the cells onto the slide, as if by ignoring Grace long enough, she'd go away.

She didn't.

Finally Marcie said, 'You want help, writing out clues for the Timer Game?'

'I'm set.'

Marcie glanced longingly at the incubator where she'd be drying down slides. She wasn't the least bit interested in the Timer Game, Grace knew. She just wanted Grace gone before everybody got back.

'Tell me the truth,' Grace said.

'The truth,' Marcie said faintly.

'Tell me what they're saying about my killing Eddie Loud. I'll leave then, I swear.'

Marcie breathed through her nose. 'Okay, it does seem like maybe you jumped the couch on this one.'

'That's what they're saying?'

'He was shot five times, Grace. Doesn't that seem a tiny bit excessive?' Marcie readied a Christmas tree stain of nuclear-fast red dye and green picro indigo carmine.

'I wanted to make sure he was good and dead.' Grace looked away and her gaze settled on the high stack of work orders at Larry's station.

'If Larry had picked up, none of this would have happened.'

'What are you talking about?'

'Yesterday. That's why I got the call. They'd screwed up at headquarters and were using the new sheet. If they'd been working the right sheet, they would have called Nolo, but they thought it was Larry's turn in the box and he wasn't picking up. So they went to me.'

Marcie frowned, preoccupied, readying another slide. 'Larry was here the whole day. We both were. We were backed up on a court date.'

The temperature in the room dropped. A cold draft of air moved across her neck.

Grace had been contacted because Larry couldn't be found. That's the way it worked.

'Well, he wasn't picking up his pager,' Grace said more loudly. 'That's why I went out. He wasn't answering.'

Marcie raised her head and locked eyes with Grace. Her voice was low. 'He was here. I was working, so was he. His pager was on, I saw it.'

'But all the time?' Her voice rose a notch. 'Couldn't it have been turned off?'

Marcie shook her head more vehemently. Her shoulders looked bony under the lab coat and Grace wondered if she was eating regularly.

'It was on the counter, I saw it. We worked together all afternoon. He was standing right here when his pager went off and we got word that a drug agent and two officers were down.'

138

'Oh, God.'

The two women stared at each other. Marcie looked as sick as Grace felt. In the hallway, Detective Sullivan shifted his weight. Grace lowered her voice.

'The bottom line is, somebody wanted me out there. Somebody wanted me to work this meth bust, intersect with Eddie Loud. They wanted all this to happen to me.'

'But who, Grace? Who's after you?'

'And more to the point,' Grace said, 'why?'

14

Every local channel carried her face and the story of the carnage at the meth house, and she channel-clicked and kept it on mute until she found the right station, turning the sound to a low mutter. It was the commercial break right before he came on. She was curled up on her bed, the shades drawn. She could hear Katie sighing in her sleep down the hall. From his standard place on the rug, Helix yipped softly, his eyelids moving as he tracked invisible quarry.

Her eyes strayed to the closet and she got up and rummaged through her sweaters until her hands closed around the box. Her chest felt constricted but she was used to that, and she sat in her rocking chair and opened it. The inside of the lid was bright enamel yellow. She stared at the contents for a moment without touching anything. The lily had dried long ago, but when she lifted the box, closed her eyes and inhaled, she still caught a faint sweet scent that always reminded her of the Guatemalan highlands.

On television, the show's intro started and she blinked and refitted the lid, stowing the box back on the shelf. Her body felt cold, the way it always did afterward, and she crawled into bed and pulled the quilt up, adjusting the sound.

Mac was standing in front of the Center for BioChimera. Tall, big through the shoulders, nose broken and healed crooked, his gold hair still thick and unruly, he was several lifetimes removed from stringer bylines for AP. Now he had real time slots as a CNN science reporter and blurbs in the gossip columns about the starlets he was bedding. His voice was strong.

'There's a dirty little secret about heart transplants nobody wants to discuss. Donor hearts die. They wear out. The meds used to keep a heart from being rejected eventually kill it. The meds might buy a patient ten good years if he's lucky. That's great if you're a sixty-year-old man. But what if you're a four-year-old kid? What then? The transplant gives out before you even get through high school. Or learn to drive or fall in love. If you're lucky enough to get a heart.'

On screen there were shots of sick kids in hospital beds as Mac said, 'This is about one kid who got lucky. But in an unexpected way.'

The visual changed to a shot of a yellow-skinned, glassy-eyed kid about Katie's age, covered in chest bandages. 'A story about Eric Bettles, a kid with a bad heart living — and dying — in Poway, California.'

Lee Bentley, her shining blond braid dancing, leaned over a bioreactor. She was wearing a lab jacket over a soft cream-colored silk suit, cut short, exposing tanned legs as Mac said, 'And it's the story of a brilliant San Diego researcher willing to take chances, working on something so out there it sounds like science fiction. A heart-in-a-box. A heart created out of a patient's own cells. A heart that never needs toxic antirejection drugs to keep it alive. Science fiction, except to the kid who's had one in his chest for a complete year.'

A tight shot now of a healthy Eric Bettles in baggy shorts, a five-year-old with his dad playing catch in his backyard. 'To Eric Bettles and his parents, it doesn't sound strange, it sounds like a miracle.'

Mac was good. Grace had to give him that. Her mind wandered as Eric talked about his life, how he could play now. And then a two-shot of his parents, bubbling with gratitude.

Replaced by shots in a lab with researchers. 'Within the last year, scientists have grown human bladders in labs and successfully transplanted them into patients. Within the last decade, they've grown skin, teeth, ears, nose cartilage, thumb bones, heart valves.'

On screen, doctors leaned over a patient's opened chest and Grace closed her eyes to steady the nausea that flared now when she glimpsed hearts. Mac continued: 'Over fifty universities have tissue-engineering programs. The field is exploding into a multibillion-dollar enterprise. But the big one is, and has always been, building a human heart.'

On camera, Lee opened a stainless steel drawer and Grace glimpsed a stack of objects wrapped in transparent sterile cellophane. Lee took one out and closed the drawer. With a shock, Grace realized the object in Lee's hand was shaped like a small human heart. Lee said earnestly, 'The problem is — well, there were several, but the most difficult was figuring out how to grow the blood supply. Without arteries, capillaries, and veins, oxygen only goes down a few hundred micrometers into tissue. That's what was killing off the first hearts we tried to grow — they didn't have oxygen. Most cells can't live more than thirty minutes without it.'

'And that's a problem not easily solved,' Mac said. On screen, a wave smashed onto a beach. 'Dr. Bentley took long walks along the La Jolla shoreline, trying to clear her mind. Then it came to her; the answer had been right there, all along.'

'Seaweed,' Lee said. 'That stuff is tossed around under the water but still gets the nutrients it needs to grow. I needed to build a scaffold — that's what this is,' she hefted the object in her hand, 'just like that seaweed. Porous on the inside. And you don't even want to know how we came up with this.'

'But she did it. Working with a team around the globe, she created this small, airy, porous scaffold capable of growing cells. On the inside, it looks like this.' On screen, a 3-D model of a heart split open, revealing a spidery network as eerily transparent as a jellyfish. Grace wiped her mouth.

Lee had unwrapped the cellophane and now the spongy scaffold lay exposed in her hand. It was small as an apricot. She blinked twice, just enough times, Grace thought, to emphasize her long eyelashes. She raised her eyes. Her pupils were dilated.

'It's made of biodegradable collagen,' Mac said.

'Polymer,' Lee corrected. 'I took cells —

endothelial cells that live on the inside of blood vessels — and grew clusters in a petri dish. I'd etched an outline of blood vessels — like a road map — onto silicon wafers, and added the cells I'd grown. Before long, I had 3-D capillaries, so tiny they were one-tenth the size of a human hair.'

Lee flicked her braid over her shoulder and it caught the light.

'I grew heart muscle cells, too, in a dish, and then I seeded those cells onto this polymer scaffold. Squirting what amounts to a soup of living cells and nutrients onto this scaffold so they'd have a chance of growing.'

Lee turned and moved down the aisle as Mac trotted after her. Grace had made that identical trip earlier in the day, and she took a steadying breath as Lee said, 'Then I took the scaffold and put it into a vat fed by nutrients, and waited as cells multiplied and the polymer frame itself disintegrated, leaving behind' — Lee pulled off the lid — 'this,' she finished simply.

Inside the bioreactor, a small, tan-colored heart pulsed gently, the same heart Grace had seen, floating in a soupy mix that looked like red Kool-Aid. Grace dug her nails into her palms and took a slow, steadying breath.

'But not everybody's a true believer,' Mac continued, and the screen filled with a fat, aggrieved scientist from La Jolla, Dr. Newt Poundstone, director of a lab called In/Or/Gann Inc.

He looked greasy compared with Lee, and when he spoke, his voice was shrill.

144

'Did Dr. Bentley tell you what happened to the model she let us see? The lab heart pulverized, unable to withstand the violent pressure of real blood pounding through veins. What's going to happen long-term to these kids? She's never let anybody in behind that steel door. She could be doing anything in that lab.'

Back with Eric throwing the ball to his dad, Mac wrapping things up. Eric's folks defending Lee. Their proof was there, playing ball.

Then a reference to a second child, a poor Indian girl. Mac closed with a shot of that second patient's parents in a remote site under a star-swept sky, the house ramshackle and broken down, the girl a small gray body limp in a tangle of sheets.

The parents bracing themselves for surgery that would remove Hekka's diseased heart, replace it with a second heart-in-a-box, grown from her own cells, the heart Grace had seen in Lee's lab. The father was graying and exhausted; the mother had dark, fearful eyes. Both hoped a year from now Hekka Miasonkopna would have the same story to tell as Eric Bettles.

Mac talking about how eight other kids, waiting for the same miracle, would soon be added to the program. A tight shot now of Eric Bettles blowing out the candles on his one-year anniversary, his parents clapping.

Grace clicked it off and turned off the light. In the dark, she got up and pulled the sheers back from the windows, letting in the harbor lights. She stood silently staring out across the dark shadows of bobbing boats. She could still smell a trace of lilies. Across the bay, downtown San Diego stood in sparkling relief.

She thought about the CNN program, laying the pieces out in her mind, rearranging them. What did Mac's report about hearts-in-a-box have to do with Eddie Loud warning her about the Spikeman? Or about Warren getting the threatening postcard? Nothing that she could see.

When she finally slept, she dreamed of talons and teeth and a long braid swinging.

15

The blue-colored package sat on the redwood table in the backyard amid a small array of perfectly wrapped gifts.

Later, Grace tried to remember exactly when she'd first seen it, clumsily wrapped in clown paper and tied in loose string, but by then it was too late.

She'd worked hard since early that morning getting ready. The party version of the Timer Game involved advance heavy lifting, requiring Grace to invent two different sets of eight clues, hiding the clues, squirreling away sugar treats in unexpected surprise places as rewards, getting two timers that worked, as well as blowing up balloons, checking the oven to see if the cake was falling, putting out the treat bags, all the while Katie asking if it was time yet and could she please have a meal that involved actual preparation, not just one out of a can.

Now crepe paper and balloons flapped smartly in the breeze along the redwood fence, separating the yard from the runners jogging along the path by the boats. It was late Saturday morning, and the air was filled with children's squeals, the banter of weekend boaters, and the rich smells of barbecued meat.

Grace was so tired she felt as if she'd been clubbed by a mallet; ever since Katie was born,

147

she'd been tired; she couldn't remember ever being rested, alert, on top of things. That was another country, one she couldn't visit anymore; she'd misplaced that passport under a load of clothes to be washed and papers to be filed and more recently, locked doors that had to be rechecked late at night.

Not that she wanted to trade her life for one without Katie. Just one with a little sleep.

She rubbed her arms against the sudden chill; San Diego was famous for small, damp shifts in temperature. She'd never get Katie into a sweater over her costume, or the others, either, even though their parents had hurled sweatshirts into a pile in their rush to get away. Grace thought that's how you could tell a true friend: at kids' parties, they stayed behind to help.

'How many are there?' Jeanne sloshed a pitcher of lemonade onto the picnic table, next to the packages. She was wearing shorts that exposed flaccid thighs and a green gauze top that revealed part of a wrinkly heart tattoo, done decades ago, when only bikers and drunks sat for the needle. She'd come late, after a sleepless night from her bad knee, and gotten right to work in the kitchen, mixing juice and tidying up.

'Two teams of four. Seven girls, one boy. One team's inside, Katie's is here. They only look like more with Helix yipping between them.' Helix was dancing up and down with such force, his fake leg sounded like a tent stake being driven into the ground.

Jeanne reached for a paper cup, filling it with

lemonade. 'That mutt's going to break that thing one of these days.'

'Can you do the burgers next and be the clue reader for Katie's team?' Grace's timer had less than sixty seconds left before it went off again.

'If you find the briquettes. They're not under the sink. I'm done walking for the day.'

Leaning against the redwood table was the walking stick called Willa that Jeanne used for bad days. Made out of oak, it was topped with a knot that resembled an eye and ended in a froth of yellow woody fiber that looked like a bad hair day.

'And take that timer with you. That dinging is making me crazy.'

Grace grabbed the timer and dashed for the sliding door. Other mothers she knew didn't run back and forth like a demented party planner on speed. But other mothers she knew had husbands and nannies and calm children — medicated at times perhaps, it was true, but whatever it took — with straight teeth and shiny hair who appreciated the color choices their mommies laid out for them. Grace had Katie, mouth open like a shrilly demanding bird, *feed me, entertain me*, and a brown and white yappy dog pounding across the living room floor.

The other team of girls spilled into the family room. They were four girls Katie played soccer with — tall compared to Katie — skinny and blond. They'd marry well and stay in Point Loma and fifty years from now scientists would study them for articles about inbreeding.

And Grace really needed to stop passing along

her deep-seated animosity toward skinny tall blond girls who just happened to be perfect, and get a life.

She took a breath.

The blond team swarmed into the kitchen and out again, through the family room and into the living room, pale, giggling blurs in sequined Spandex costumes, as remote as sparkly fish. They were busy taking the cushions off the sofa, monitored by Marcie and Frank. Marcie was half a head taller than Frank and swung their team's timer like a javelin.

'Sixty more seconds, girls.' Marcie wore a plum-colored skirt and a loose midnight blue sweater that fell over one shoulder. Frank was in dark maroon slacks with a blue sweater, and as Marcie leaned into her husband, Grace realized their colors matched completely, their sweaters, hair, even their eyes. Everything matched. The world was going two by two into some great twinkly beyond, color coordinated and cheerful, and Grace alone would be left behind, scraping gum off the bottom of the picnic table.

She found the charcoal bag in the kitchen, shoved behind the overflowing trash bin, and she pawed through a drawer and discovered matches, running them outside with the timer and slapping them down on the table next to the package. Something had stained the clown's smile on the blue wrapping paper so that his teeth looked discolored. Grace hoped whatever was inside wasn't already broken. Returning broken presents wasn't high on her list of ways to relax.

Helix nosed her, licked her hand and wagged his fluffy tail, growling deep in his throat as if he were in grave sexual pain. Great. The only male in her life who understood her completely drooled and bounced on four legs. Three, if she didn't count the fake one. Which, now that she was staring at it, she could clearly see was beginning to splinter along some invisible doggie fault line.

Along the fence, Katie and her teammates turned over rocks and checked bushes. Katie was wearing her Velcro sneakers under her princess costume. The good thing about taking time off from the crime lab was that it gave Grace the chance to actually make a costume. They'd gone together to a fabric store and Katie had hand-picked silk ribbons and pink organza and hot pink satin, her faith in Grace's ability to sew never wavering, despite the fact that the sewing machine was four years old and still in its original plastic wrapper. They'd had a perfect afternoon, Katie stretched on the floor, her arms out like a snow angel, as Grace outlined her body onto the fabric with a pencil and cut around it.

It had turned out exactly as she'd feared, which had given her the time to find a pink princess costume at Costco and hand-stitch bunches of satin, puffs of organza, streamers of ribbons, onto every available surface. She was smart enough to have removed the tags, and if Katie had figured it out, she never said. Her eyes had glowed when she'd slipped it on.

'Am I pretty?' she'd asked.

'Way past,' Grace had answered. 'You're the most beautiful birthday princess anybody has ever seen.'

Katie had smiled back and Grace had thought that she'd sew a hundred costumes to see that smile again.

A small piece of folded paper winked from under an upturned rock. Katie pounced, her hair an electric cloud under her crown. 'Got it!'

Grace stopped the timer and reset it. 'Ninety seconds on the clock, guys.' She set the timer down on the table next to the clown package and trotted back inside.

The cake was shaped like a pumpkin, deflated on one side where it had fallen in the oven. She yanked open cabinets, looking for candles. Her life was chopped into the smallest, bite-sized pieces. Her memory was jumbled, too, as if all those bits had been heaved into the nearest box, willy-nilly, tossed like a salad mixer, and thrust under the bed. She was sure she had candles. At least she thought she did. Maybe that was an old birthday.

'Candles?' Marcie pulled a pack out of her pocket and Grace yelped her thanks. They worked silently, counting out five candles and one more for luck.

Grace marched the cake through the sliding glass door and set it on the picnic table. Jeanne's gravelly voice was reading the clue out loud for Katie's team:

'It used to have red little bulbs that we ate
We washed them and sliced them and got

out a plate
But now it is fall and the message is clear:
Find the vine that is dying; you'll find a clue
here.'

'Radishes,' Benjy said. He lifted the eye patch on his pirate costume.

He was Marcie and Frank's boy, a year older than the girls. His sister was in Katie's class. He'd be tall like his mother, with shots at basketball scholarships, which was a lucky thing, considering what he had in the brains department.

Katie shook her head and bolted with her team around the side of the house toward a graveyard of tomatoes. They returned in a flash, Benjy gripping a desiccated tomato vine while his sister, Elsa, dressed as a cat, waved the clue.

'Reset it! Reset it!'

Grace reset the timer as Jeanne read the clue out loud:

'Congratulations! You've come to the end!
Gold glinting bounty to share with a friend!
It's tucked in a corner but still is in view
Climb up to the plate. It's waiting for you!'

'A plate, a plate. Something in the kitchen?' Amanda, a sweet-faced Raggedy Ann, looked at Katie.

'Or a baseball diamond,' Benjy offered. 'You have one of those here?'

Katie shook her head, thinking, and Grace could see the gears shifting as she coolly evaluated the backyard. *Climb up to the plate.*

'Up there.' Katie pointed into the dim cavern of the tree house that sat in a notch of a pepper tree. 'It's got to be something to eat and it's on a plate, I bet. Come on, Amanda, I'll help you up. You want to be first?'

Amanda beamed and Grace felt a small glow of parental pride that her daughter was playing nice. Amanda lifted her striped skirt, gripped the bottom wooden slat, and one by one they climbed up the tree, where chocolate coins glinted in shadow.

Katie leaned over the edge, holding on to her crown, and grinned upside down before settling next to her friends. Empty gold wrappers rained down from the tree house.

'Sorry to interrupt, Grace.' Jeanne stood tensely. 'But you need to see this. Alone.'

Jeanne had taken it off the picnic table to make room for the cake, only the wrapping paper felt damp. She went into the kitchen and put it in the sink.

A wise choice, considering the blood.

It was a doll, chest split. Blood welled in the cavity, sloshed over the side, oozing from the doll's small marble eyes, spilling out of its dainty mouth, staining its tiny porcelain teeth, and even without touching it, Grace could see it came from flesh stuffed into the cavity.

A heart.

Had to be pig, she told herself. Part of one.

Twine bound the doll's wrists over the bloody hole, bending the arm sockets so that blood poured out the armholes onto the wrapping

154

paper. A small slip of paper curled next to one wrist, attached with a paper clip and rubber band. Grace used the tine of a fork to unfold it. It was handwritten in ink, a jaunty jingle:

She's five years old! And soon you'll see
The game she gets to play with me!
All Hallows' Eve you'll play a part.
Ere midnight tolls, I cut your heart.

16

Saturday, 1:15 p.m.

'Katie, how you doing in there?' Grace couldn't keep the anxiety out of her voice as she waited outside the bathroom door.

'Fine. You don't have to wait for me.'

Grace checked her watch. 'It's getting late, honey. I want to get on the road.'

'Why are we leaving again?'

'It's an adventure, that's all.'

'But where are we going to go trick-or-treating?'

'I bet the hotel has something nice.'

'Mommy, I want to be *here* tomorrow on Halloween.'

'I know, honey, but this is going to be great, too. Different, that's all, but still great.'

'I want to still wear my costume.'

'You mean in the car? Okay.'

She'd agree to anything if it got Katie moving.

After opening the package, Grace had called her crime lab boss and insisted he stop by after the party. Frank had herded Katie and his two kids into the backyard to pick up trash. Jeanne supervised from a lawn chair while Marcie waited inside with Grace. Their boss, Sid Felcher, took one look at the doll, the note, the paper, and sniffed.

'Grace, you really need counseling,' he said finally.

156

Grace shot Marcie a look of disbelief. Marcie shook her head as if to clear it of a slight ringing noise.

'Are you insinuating that Grace planted this doll? Is that what you're saying?'

Sid studied his fingernails as if noticing for the first time he bit them. He became aware they were watching and he slid his hands into the pockets of his high-rise pants. He was wearing a shirt with koala bears on it, and the round, chubby faces accentuated his own.

'I'm not suggesting anything,' he said in a bored voice, 'I just think — '

'But you're not,' Grace snapped. 'That's exactly your problem, Sid, the thinking part.'

Marcie shot out her hand and gently squeezed Grace's arm. 'I'll take them in and analyze them.'

'You have plenty to do.' Sid's finger stole to his mouth and he gnawed.

'I'll do it on my own time,' Marcie said.

'With company supplies?' He put his hand in his pocket again.

'I'll pay for it.'

Sid breathed through his nose, his gaze flicking from one to the other. 'Fine,' he said abruptly. 'But I'm serious, Grace, if you think this little stunt — '

'Stunt?'

' — is going to make anybody forget you shot an emotionally fragile kid — '

Grace pushed him toward the door. 'Get out of here. Out. I mean it. Now.'

Marcie stared stone-faced at the door as it

closed on Sid. 'I'll do it today. I'll have Frank drive me home and I'll pick up my car and go in.'

'Thanks.' Grace smashed her fist into the door and leaned her forehead against it.

That was less than an hour ago. Grace had called all Warren's numbers but couldn't reach him. Marcie and Frank had pleaded with Grace to come with Katie to their house, and Jeanne had made the same offer, but Grace didn't want to involve her friends in whatever darkness had come for her.

She only knew she couldn't spend the night at home. She ran through a list of possibles, ruling out places that were far away or too remote, and deciding finally to treat her daughter to an overnight stay at a fancy hotel in Laguna Beach overlooking the water, two hours away and surrounded by the luxury of capable hotel security and locked doors.

Grace heard the front door open and she moved to the head of the stairs and looked down. Jeanne came into view. 'I've got both suitcases in your car and Helix loaded into mine.'

'She's dawdling.' Grace glanced back at the closed door.

'You want me to gas up your car? One less stop.'

'That would be great, thanks. Take my purse, it's on the sofa. Try my Visa. I don't think that one's maxed.'

'I'll take Helix along. Get him used to riding shotgun with me.'

Grace nodded her thanks and took up her post again at the bathroom door. Far off, she heard the sound of her car start and pull out of the driveway. She rapped softly on the door.

'You okay?'

'I'm drinking lemonade,' Katie said through the door. 'Can I take my bike?' It was Grace's big present to her this year, a Barbie bike with training wheels, exactly what Katie had wanted. Grace hesitated.

'Please, Mommy?'

'Sure.'

'And the other stuff? All the new stuff I just got? The Pretty Ponys and the beads and — '

'Sure, okay. I'll get everything together. Just push it along in there, honey, okay?'

Grace went downstairs past the wall of photos on the stairwell. Their lives were tracked in frozen images, everything she held dear. Katie swinging a bat. Katie, a chubby three-year-old ballerina in a pink tulle tutu, looking faintly like a joyous hippo in *Fantasia*. The bike was on the back patio, next to the barbecue grill. The party seemed a lifetime ago.

Grace wheeled it inside, relocking the sliding glass door. The presents had been stacked on the sofa in the family room and Grace made several trips through the house, depositing them at the front door in the darkened living room. The blinds were shut on the leaded windows flanking the window seat, bathing the room in a gloomy stillness. She wheeled the bike through the house and stood it up next to the presents.

There had been silence upstairs, not even a

159

toilet flushing, and Grace felt a small flick of unease dart up her spine.

'Katie?' No answer. Grace moved to the stairs and called up. 'Katie?'

She climbed the first stair, listening. Silence.

'Katie Marie. This isn't a good time to play a game. You need to answer me.'

Still the silence.

'Katie?' She gripped the newel post. Adrenaline surged through her body. She started climbing, taking the stairs two at a time, her heart banging. The bathroom door was locked.

She leaned on the door and pounded, twisting the knob. 'Honey?'

Fear tightened in a band across her chest and she ran into her daughter's room; there was another access to the bathroom that way.

'Katie!' Grace slammed into the door, trying to open it and failing. She rammed harder and felt the old lock give way, bursting into the small bright bathroom.

She wasn't there.

The bathroom had white tiles and an ornate sink. The toilet paper had unrolled slightly, the end on the tiles, fluttering lazily. The seat was up. Katie's hairbrush lay on the counter, along with a glass that had held the lemonade.

She couldn't breathe. She literally couldn't take a breath. The window was open.

The window looked out over the service alley separating Grace's house from the osteopath's next door. That side of his house contained no windows, only skylights.

A ladder leaned under the bathroom window,

the open bathroom window. In the hedge separating her house from the doctor's, Grace saw a bright slash of pink tulle.

Grace had sewn that tulle onto the sleeves of Katie's costume not more than two days before. Next to the tulle was a footprint. It was large, heavy, a man's print.

Fear shot up her body and she gripped the side of the sink to keep herself from falling. She leaned out the window and screamed her daughter's name. Silence.

Somebody had taken her daughter out the bathroom window, down the ladder in a split second. And gone where?

Grace whirled and ran. Boats in back. Or the street in front.

One or the other.

She hadn't heard a car start up in front. So the back.

She ran down the hall into her bedroom and tore back the blinds, unlocking the sliding glass door and racing onto the balcony that looked down over the boats.

A family was rowing by in a dinghy, the father good-naturedly paddling as his two daughters trailed their fingers through the water. Nothing out of the ordinary.

'Katie!' she cried shrilly, and the family glanced up, puzzled. 'Have you seen a little girl? A five-year-old girl in a princess costume? Pink. She was just . . . '

The father shook his head, bewildered, and Grace retreated, racing down the hall, pelting down the stairs, flinging open the front door, running into the street, looking wildly back and forth. She was panting, taking great, deep gulps of air, not able to catch her breath.

A quiet, peaceful day. Nobody out.

She ran into the house again, up the stairs, checking, rechecking, blindly ripping back curtains in Katie's room, her face numb, turning, hoping to see her, find her. The quilt lay bunched on her bed.

'I'm back,' Jeanne called from the front door.

'Jeanne, was there anybody outside? Anybody driving by when you came back?'

'What's going on?'

'Anybody driving anything?'

'Grace?' Jeanne climbed the stairs.

'She's gone, Jeanne. Somebody took her.'

'What are you talking about?'

'I don't know what to do. Call the police. I have to call the police.'

'Oh, my God.' Jeanne pointed toward Katie's bed. The quilt bunched at an awkward angle and Grace ripped it back.

A single sheet of paper lay spiked to the bedsheet.

It was a real spike. It pierced the sheet and impaled the thin sheet of paper, holding a typewritten message.

Grace knew then. The Spikeman and whoever had taken Katie were the same. The paths converged here, in a peppy jingle pierced by a spike.

She's gone! So try this on for size.
Alert the cops, and Katie dies.

I'm watching. You must track the clues.
A playful round of subterfuge.

'I'm calling the police.' Jeanne started down the hall for Grace's bedroom.

'No!' Grace screamed. 'God, no.'

Clue one: a fragrant posy in her glove
Will lead you to the one you love
But don't delay. Your daughter's gone!
The timer's tripped. The game is on.

Grace thrust her hands through the quilt, searching. She felt it, a small, almost invisible wire leading off the bed and against the wall. She yanked. A timer flipped onto the bed.

It was a kitchen timer, white, with a small rounded face. Twenty minutes marked, the rest of the timer painted enamel red. Blood red.

Ticking.

Oh, God. Twenty minutes. Someone had taken Katie and now Grace had twenty minutes to figure it out. To save her.

17

Saturday, 1:24 p.m.

Katie was gone.

In one instant, Grace had dropped into a spiraling free-fall that blasted apart her contained world, her schedules, her sense of order.

Katie was gone. Her mind was fighting it. It was too big.

Twenty minutes. *Fragrant posy in her glove.*

Grace looked around the bedroom, dazed. A current rippled up her body, suddenly shocking her into moving. She yanked open Katie's closet, pawing through clothes.

'What are you looking for?' Jeanne cried. 'Katie? You think maybe she's here in the — '

'Her T-ball glove. That's the only glove that's hers. Check the family room.'

Jeanne started down the stairs, her cane clanging on the steps, while Grace checked under Katie's bed, the clothes hamper, her bookshelf, sweeping aside the Beanie Bears, scattering books, displacing trophies, sifting through shoes and puzzles and dolls. Where had she seen it last? The glove was everywhere, nowhere.

She could hear Jeanne moving through the family room, tearing apart cushions and pushing aside books, but the sounds were far away, unreal.

'It isn't here,' Jeanne called.

'Look everywhere, every room. And the trunk, the car trunk. Her T-ball bag's there.'

Grace moved into the hallway and shoved her hands under the sheets and towels in the linen closet. Nothing. Panic flooded her on the heels of shock, and she ran down the hall to her bedroom and checked under the bed, between the sheets, in the closet. She pushed her hands through folded sweaters but found only the familiar enamel box. She moved into her own small bathroom and yanked back the shower curtain, checking the cabinet under the sink. The small of her back trickled with sweat.

How many minutes had gone by? There was another room upstairs, a bedroom crammed with boxes she'd never managed to unpack, wrapping paper, projects started and stopped — a room fit for *Clean Sweep*, Marcie always joked. She inched between the canyons of boxes and made it all the way to the small window, finding only dead flies and a spiderweb. No glove.

She rechecked the timer in Katie's room. Seven and a half minutes had slid by and now her hands were starting to shake. She made herself slow her thinking. Where else upstairs hadn't she checked?

Katie's bathroom. She opened the cabinet under the sink. A stray barrette and an abandoned Barbie town house were squeezed into the space, along with cleaning products, extra rolls of toilet paper. Grace ripped aside the shower curtain and there it was.

Katie's softball glove sat on the porcelain

curve of the tub under the faucet, and nestled in the socket, a sweet-smelling bright yellow flower with five petals. There was nothing else.

She snatched up the glove and flower and ran back into Katie's bedroom, picking up the timer. 'I found it.' Her voice was still shaky and she cleared her throat and tried again, shouting it.

She carried it carefully down the stairs, balancing against the wall so she wouldn't fall. The trembling had spread down her legs now and she made her way carefully into the kitchen, where Jeanne sat doubled over in a chair, a hand to her face.

Eight minutes gone. Twelve minutes left. Until what? What would happen to Katie if Grace couldn't figure this out? Jeanne stared at her, dazed. Grace put the glove and timer on the table.

'You know flowers,' Grace spoke slowly. 'What kind of flower is this?'

Jeanne frowned. It was clear she wasn't tracking and Grace felt her panic rise.

No time. 'Come on, Jeanne, you took that night class. I've seen your garden. Buttercups, daffodils, daisies — the middle parts. What else is yellow?'

'Yellow,' Jeanne repeated. Grace wanted to scream. The timer clicked. Eleven minutes left. 'Flower.'

'Yes. Flower. It means something. Is there anything about this one — how many petals it has — five, Jeanne, it has five petals, or the color, bright, bright yellow, not pale . . . '

Grace was reaching and she knew it.

Jeanne flicked a glance at the flower Grace held in front of her. 'I don't have this one in my garden.' Jeanne's voice was detached, polite, and Grace knew she had slipped into shock.

'Yes. But maybe you've seen it before or — just what else is yellow, Jeanne? Maybe something you've only heard about.'

A long moment went by and Grace wondered if she should get in the car and race to a nursery. The closest one was Walter Anderson's on Midway. With the traffic, would she get there in time? And if she didn't, what would happen to Katie?

'It could be woodbine.' Jeanne's voice was strained.

'Good, good, Jeanne. What else? What can you tell me about woodbine?'

Jeanne licked her lips. Her eyes looked glassy. 'I can't believe she's gone.'

'Woodbine,' Grace said again, her voice steady. She crouched down and clamped her hands on Jeanne's arms. Jeanne shook as if she'd been hotwired. Grace searched her eyes. 'What can you tell me about woodbine?'

'Carolina wild woodbine,' Jeanne said softly, her eyes locking on to Grace's.

'That's right. What about it?'

It was as if Jeanne were on a tape delay, as if the shock of finding Katie missing had seriously jarred the fragile mechanism that received messages, and now Jeanne had to decode them and translate them back before speaking.

'Grows naturally in the South, all the way into Mexico down into Guatemala.' Jeanne sucked in her cheeks with the effort of remembering.

'It grows in the South,' Grace repeated, unable to keep the pressure out of her voice. 'How about here? Does it grow here in San Diego?'

Jeanne nodded, voice almost inaudible. 'Not usually, but it can. Needs good water, soil. A climber.'

A climber. What did climbing have to do with Katie? Katie climbed like every kid. Across jungle bars. Into forts. Up trees. Was it the tree in their backyard? She had climbed that tree up to the fort just a few hours earlier. Grabbed the prize, the chocolate coins.

'I'll be right back.' Grace dropped the flower on the table. She'd relocked the sliding glass door after getting the bike and now she unlocked it and climbed up the pepper tree.

Dust motes spiraled in a lazy pattern through open wooden slats. Nothing there but stray crumpled gold wrappers left behind from the party.

And then Grace knew time was running out and the air left her body, and into the stillness, terror galloped on metal hooves.

'It's poison, I just remembered.' Jeanne stood at the bottom of the pepper tree, leaning on her cane.

'How much time do we have left?' Grace was climbing down, tearing a hole in her pants as she scraped her knee on a sharp branch. Jeanne shook her head. Grace ran past her into the house. Five minutes left, that was it.

'It's a powerful spinal depressant. It slows the respiration. It can kill you.' Jeanne stood in the kitchen archway, her eyes staring and wide.

Grace snapped a look at her, shocked. Was this what had happened to Katie?

'Where's the phone?' She was going to have to call the police. Jeanne had upturned the cookbooks on the kitchen counter and Grace pawed through them, following the phone cord.

'It's like paralysis,' Jeanne said, adding abruptly, 'And, and, it has another name.'

'What other name?' Grace shoved aside books and found the phone.

Jeanne blinked, the word slow, forming her lips around it, expelling breath, as if all those steps were suddenly painfully complex, out of reach.

Grace dialed 911.

Jeanne's eyes cleared. She smiled expectantly, the good pupil with the winning answer. 'Jasmine.'

'Jasmine.'

'Yes. Another name for Carolina woodbine is jasmine.'

Grace put down the phone.

18

'Could you look it up, Mr. Esguio, in your records?'

Grace shifted the phone to her other ear and changed lanes. Saturday-afternoon traffic stalled her at a light on Scott Street. She could lose Katie because of a light.

'For you, Grace, anything.'

Green. She willed the car in front of her to move forward through the intersection. A crosswalk of kids stopped her. She could hear Esguio snuffling, shifting papers. On the car seat next to her, the timer clicked toward the red line. Three minutes left, that was all.

'They're losing the priest over at Saint Agnes, best one we ever had. A real shame. He brought up the numbers and the place was packed, and not just on feast days, either, and you know what it boils down to, Grace? Politics.'

He sighed. In the background, she heard the whine of his fax machine. When the last of the kids reached the curb, Grace tapped the gas and the car shot forward.

'They figure, let's put him into some parish that's hurting, watch him work miracles. Oh, here we go. Yeah, it's Jasmine, like the flower. I always thought it was Jazz, that's what everybody called her, but her given name's Jasmine. Is it important?'

'Yeah. Thanks.' She started to click off.

'Wait. Wait. Hold it. Grace?'

'Still here.'

'Just got a fax, strangest thing. Only has your name, a smiley face, a picture of a — I don't know, looks like a nail or something.'

A spike. The Spikeman was trying to tell her she'd passed the first deadline.

'Anything else?'

'A clock, looks like. Give me a minute here.'

'Is there a fax number showing where it originated?'

'What? Oh. Looks like one of those mailbox places. Over in Hillcrest, Office on the Go. Want the phone number there?'

She scribbled it on a gas receipt as she waited to turn left onto Nimitz and then right onto Rosecrans. The new subdivision rose in sandstone-colored blocks, with porches and balconies and neat lawns, but it created enormous traffic jams and now she was going to pay for it. She missed the light and groaned.

'Oh, yeah, had it sideways. Hands set at three.'

Grace glanced at the dash: 1:47. Just over an hour to figure out the next step.

'Grace, whatever you're doing, confession will clear it right up.'

She had the urge to laugh. 'I'll remember that.'

She clicked off. She needed backup. Now. *Alert the cops, and Katie dies.* Paul wasn't a cop. He was a nonsworn. Worked the crime lab. Would the Spikeman get that as a legitimate distinction? She had to act fast if she was going to find Katie. The more time that went by, the longer the odds of ever seeing her daughter alive again. She tried Paul's cell.

Pick up pick up pick up alert the cops, and —

'Collins.' He sounded out of breath.

'Paul, I don't have much time. Katie's in trouble.'

'Trouble. What kind of trouble?'

His voice dropped out. She had a call coming in. 'Hold on, Paul. Have to get rid of this.' She clicked over. 'Hello?' Her voice was cautious.

The voice was mechanically distorted but there was no mistaking the rage. 'Do you think I'm stupid? Don't ever try that again. She's nothing to me, understand? Nothing. If you try that again, she's dead.'

He clicked off before she could speak.

'Hello?' It was Paul's voice. 'Hello?'

She felt sucker punched, kicked so hard the breath left her body. The Spikeman knew somehow what she was doing. Who she called.

She folded her phone off, changed lanes, and sped up.

★   ★   ★

Grace yanked open the door to the halfway house without knocking. A startled group of clients looked up from the kitchen table where they were preparing sandwiches. There were four of them, all marked with the unmistakable stamp of suffering. The women shrank back in alarm but the man waved his peanut butter knife and took a step toward her menacingly. He had concave cheeks and a hunted look in his hazel eyes.

'Back!' he cried. 'Stay back.'

'Do you know where Jazz is? Jasmine? Is she upstairs? I need to find her.'

She had to pass them to get to the stairs and the man took a step forward, barring her way. 'Not here,' he said distinctly. 'Not here.'

Next to the stairs there was an open door that led down into the basement. A bright yellow light spilled up the stairs. A door opened in the basement and the familiar figure of the caretaker came into view. She glared up the stairs at Grace. Grace stepped back into the living room and held her ground.

'You. Get the hell out of here.' Opal pounded up the stairs and slammed the door shut behind her. 'Who in the hell do you think you are? Coming in here again after what you did. This is a law-abiding place. With clients who want to be left alone.'

Grace raised her voice. 'Anybody know where Jazz is? It's important.'

'Don't talk to them,' Opal commanded. 'Don't talk to her, people.'

A thin-haired woman looked timidly at Grace, and then at Opal. She closed her mouth.

'I'm calling the cops.' Opal moved toward the phone. The clients huddled together, alarmed. Afraid, Grace realized. Just like she was.

Alert the cops, and Katie dies. 'God, no, please, leave the cops out of it. I don't want any trouble. I need your help. My little girl is missing.' Something in her voice must have communicated the desperation she was feeling.

The clients stirred uneasily. 'She sure the hell isn't here,' Opal said.

The man put the knife down. 'Jazz left. Last night late.'

'Do you know where she went?'

'Stan.' Opal's voice held a warning.

Stan raised his chin and spoke clearly. 'She got a phone call and she ran out that door. Only took what she could carry. I know my rights. I studied that in school before I got sick. The right to free speech.'

'And the right to remain silent,' Opal barked.

Stan snapped his head down, his hands squeezing his sides and his chest heaving.

'See what you made him remember? Get out and don't come back.'

'It's my kid!' Grace cried. 'Don't any of you have kids you love? Sisters or nieces or kids of your own? Somebody must know where Jazz is. Please, my kid's life depends on it.'

Concern and alarm creased their faces. 'We can't tell you anything else,' a woman mumbled. She wrung her hands.

Opal pushed Grace out the door. 'If I ever see you here again, I'm going to press charges. Is that clear?' She closed the door in Grace's face.

She stood helplessly, trying to figure out her next move. Jazz had left the night before; she could be anywhere. She'd have to check beaches, under viaducts, the seedy part of Midway, the approach to Old Town where the trolleys came, even Shelter Island wasn't out of reach.

It was overwhelming. She couldn't possibly

find Jazz by three. Katie could already be out of the country by now. She checked her watch. Ten more minutes had gone by.

She didn't know where to start. She made herself think through what Stan had blurted out. Jazz had only taken what she could carry. So she'd been walking. But was she met somewhere? Was she picked up?

And that was last night. A lifetime ago. A shape moved in the window and a curtain fluttered. It was the wispy-haired woman. Slowly she raised a stuffed lion. Made it wave a paw at Grace. The lion Eddie had won for Jazz at Belmont Park.

She was trying to tell Grace where Jazz had gone. Grace nodded and ran for her car.

19

Belmont Park in Mission Beach was seven acres of concrete, wooden rides, and concessions built near the promenade that fronted the beach. When she ran from the halfway house, Jazz might have dragged her meager possessions to somewhere in the canyons of the park. It was a distance on foot, but she could have taken the bike path next to the floodplain to reach it. Providing she was still medicated and nothing had altered her course. She'd left at night, plunging into the dark, a helpless, mentally ill woman fleeing with nothing to protect her from the demons she'd encounter in the world, more terrifying even than the ones she carried with her.

Grace parked on the street and ran under the arched entrance. Overhead, the Giant Dipper roller coaster shivered down the track. Straight ahead the carousel twirled, the wooden horses and ostrich and giant rabbit moving in a ponderous circle, the patina on their necks faded and rubbed satiny by hundreds of thousands of tiny hands.

Costume. Everybody was in costume.

Grace felt her heart skid. She'd been hoping the park would be empty.

It was crowded with disguises.

The hard thing was keeping herself steady.

176

Concentrating on the next thing. It was after two now. She had until three. Where would Jazz go? What would she do? Grace doubted she'd have money to ride anything, but she could still be anywhere in the park. *If* she was there.

Impulsively, Grace trotted over to the ticket booth next to the museum and slid the photo of Jazz across the counter, raising her voice over the cacophony of clanging machinery, tinny music, shrieks from the coaster riders.

'Have you seen this woman?'

The ticket taker was in a Winnie the Poo costume with two fuzzy ears poking up like miniature tombstones. His eyes were bright and resigned. He studied the photo.

'I need to find her,' Grace repeated.

'Good luck.'

He shoved the photo back and Grace stopped it with her hand.

'You haven't seen her?'

He half laughed. 'In this crowd? It's half-price carnival day. You buying ride tickets? 'Cause I've got paying customers.' He looked past her to a man waiting behind her wearing a Zorro cape and clutching the hand of a toddler dressed as a dinosaur.

Grace pointed at the stuffed lion in the photo. 'This. Where would they have gotten it?'

'Past the Coconut Climb there's a basketball throw.' He raised his voice. 'Next.'

Grace hurried past the carousel and the blur of hand-painted images, Lindbergh and the Hotel Del and Shamu and all the squealing children bobbing up and down on the historic wooden animals, their mothers close at hand, no missing children there, that was for sure.

At the Coconut Climb, two plastic palm trees rose like a cartoon into the blue sky, and a man climbed the pole as casually as if he worked for the phone company. She threaded through a group of teens dressed in black, raced past a ride called Chaos that tipped its riders in a twisted spiral. A water plunge, and eateries, ice cream, a Fat Boyz, a video place.

At the basketball shoot, she spotted the familiar stuffed lions offered as prizes.

A middle-aged man steadied the ball and took a shot. It banged off the rim and Grace moved in, shoving the photo of Jazz at the attendant. 'Have you seen her?'

The attendant frowned, studied the photo. 'Not recently.'

'Not recently today or not recently?'

'It's still my turn,' the man interrupted. The attendant scooped up the ball and gave it to him. The sun glanced off the metal hoop as the man rolled the ball off his fingers and it shot through the basket.

'Have you seen her today?' Grace pressed.

'I already told you, no,' the attendant said. His smile was mechanical as he detached a lion from the hanging stack and held it out to the man. 'You can take this size with you, or try again and go up a size. Bigger's better, right? Only five bucks.'

Grace pressed on through the crowd, hunting. Panic thumped up her chest and her face felt hot. If Jazz had left the park already, then Grace didn't think she could find her in the time she had left, but if she was still there somewhere, then Grace had a shot. But what if she was wrong? What if Jazz had never made it there at all?

'Prepare for total Chaos,' a mechanical voice intoned, and the ride lifted skyward and the riders shrieked. She made one complete pass through the park, checking faces, hair colors. Across from an arrow pointing to Henna Tattoos, a police substation was tucked into the wall, and Grace resisted the impulse to open the door, sit down at the desk, spill everything.

She turned and looked back toward the center of the park. The Beach Blaster shuddered skyward, shaped like two giant claws holding fistfuls of riders in a metal King Kong grip.

A little girl dressed in pink stood staring up at it, her head tipped back.

She was wearing a pink princess costume. It was modified; somebody had ripped off the organza and ribbons Grace had added, but it was the costume and it was Katie.

Her hair rose in two ponytails of sparkling caramel-colored curls.

Grace took a step. 'Katie?'

She must have screamed it because the little girl jerked around at the sound of her name.

A sparkly pink mask covered her face, but it was Katie. The golden-colored skin, the small, sturdy body. Relief surged up her body like a hot wire, and she closed the distance between them in a few short strides and scooped up her daughter and ripped off the mask.

The little girl had blue eyes and freckles.

She stared at Grace, her eyes blank with shock.

Her body stiffened. She opened her mouth and screamed.

'What are you doing? What do you think you're doing with my child?' A muscular woman in a polo shirt and jeans ripped the child away. 'Becky, honey, it's okay.'

The woman had dropped her purse and the ice cream cones she was carrying, and the cones had fractured on the pavement, the ice cream slippery mounds already melting.

The little girl wailed and wrapped her arms around her mother's neck, burrowing her face, her cheeks already slick with saliva and tears.

'I'm sorry,' Grace stammered.

It wasn't Katie. The enormity of that took her breath away. She stared helplessly at the little girl.

'Get out of here before I call the police.' The woman gripped her daughter tightly and swung her away from Grace.

Grace turned and ran. She ran past the rides, the police substation, ran until she reached the cement retaining wall that looked out over the sand. She doubled over, heaving, staring blankly out to sea. A ship on the horizon stood motionless as if cut out of paper in some pirate book. Desolation swept over her and she fought to keep from crying and then she fought to keep from throwing up. Her daughter was still out there somewhere.

Two college-age students gamboled on the

180

beach, tossing a soccer ball, but the sand looked cold and nobody was in the water. Along the water's edge, a shirtless man jogged, a T-shirt binding his head, and behind her on the promenade, an endless surge of people passed by, their voices masked by the pounding of the surf.

She swallowed hard and pressed her fingers into the pebbly cement retaining wall, trying to get her bearings.

A man on a heavy Schwinn pedaled past in lazy arcs, a Hefty bag of aluminum cans slung over a shoulder. He wore red shorts and combat boots. He braked to a stop and checked the trash can near Grace.

'Excuse me. Do you know where anybody homeless might go around here during the day?'

He sorted trash and extracted a can, sliding it into his bag.

She raised her voice. 'Excuse me.'

'I'm not homeless,' he interrupted. He stared at her belligerently. A scar cut down a cheek. Whatever had happened had narrowly missed an eye. A front tooth was broken.

'No,' she said. 'Of course not. Not you. Her.'

She extended the photo, and he took it. The waves crashed. A gull screamed. He nodded and passed the photo back. He spiraled a finger, and at first, Grace thought he was giving her the universal symbol for crazy, but then his finger slowed and he pointed down the beach, away from the lifeguard tower.

'I'd check out there. Sometimes they like to hang out there.'

'Where?' she cried.

But he was on his bike and gone.

Grace took off her shoes and went onto the beach, looking. People dozed and slept but none of them was Jazz. Grace made herself slow down, checking every mound, every hollow in the sand, every shadow.

Against the retaining wall near a public bathroom she spotted a figure.

A figure with long black hair.

Grace ran.

* * *

Jazz's beautiful black hair was snarled in clumps and tangled with sand. She lay limp, hands clasped, covered in a filthy ski jacket. Next to her was a battered Safeway cart stuffed with junk. A toaster and cord dangled over the handle.

Grace shook her shoulder. 'Jazz?'

The young woman's eyes snapped open and she reared up, gripping a filled Hefty bag she used as a pillow. She was trembling. She had wide, vacant eyes and chapped lips and her bony hands were reddened from sleeping outdoors. One night without shelter had done this. A week from now, she'd be unrecognizable.

'It's fine, it's fine. I'm not going to hurt you.'

Jazz scrubbed a hand across her mouth. 'Sad day, sad, sad day.'

'I won't hurt you, I promise. Jazz, do you know where my daughter is? Katie. Do you know where she is?'

Jazz gripped the Hefty bag and rocked. 'I've

been waiting. I'm the keeper and you have come.'

She couldn't do this anymore and she grabbed Jazz and shook her hard. 'Where's my daughter?'

Jazz wailed, the sound a pure cry of keening grief, and Grace snapped her hands away and took a step back. Katie wasn't there. Katie had never been there. Terrorizing Jazz wouldn't bring her back.

'I'm sorry,' she stammered. 'I didn't mean to scare you.'

Jazz covered her face with a thin arm, her shoulders shaking. Grace lowered her voice and fought for control.

'What are you keeping for me?'

'It's the Bad Thing, but it's my job.' Jazz's voice was muffled by her arm and Grace squatted so she was at eye level.

'Give it to me, Jazz. Now.'

Jazz gripped Grace's wrist with surprising strength and dragged her close, until Grace smelled the reek of sour breath. Her eyes slid to the palm trees behind Grace.

'Can't take a bath, it's acid, eats right through.' She shuddered and her bony shoulders shook. Jazz must be off her meds by now, her thinking disorganized, seeing things.

Grace clenched Jazz's shoulders and spoke slowly. 'Jazz. The thing you have for me. I need that, whatever it is. I came to get it. Here I am. Let me look, okay? In your things.'

Jazz sucked in a breath and moaned. 'Things things rings sings pings I took them I took them I confess. Mess, oh God what a mess the patroness of mess, the protector of complector. The goddess of fire and ruin. Runes. Run. Better run. Have to run.'

She swatted Grace's hands away as if warding off bats.

'What are you protecting, Jazz? What does the Spikeman want me to have?'

Jazz reared her head and gnashed her teeth. Saliva flew. She scrabbled to her knees and rocked. 'I have a gargoyle in my left ear, hurts hurts bite.'

'Give it to me, Jazz.' Grace's voice was soothing. 'Give me whatever he gave you to guard. I'll take it now and you'll be free.'

Jazz lunged at Grace, her fists thrashing, and Grace grabbed her arms to contain her. Jazz writhed and moaned. A strong, spastic kick upset the cart and a Hefty bag spilled to the ground.

Jazz's dark eyes glittered. She bit her cracked lip and a bright bead of blood appeared. 'The Bad Thing's in the bag. In the bag in the bag in the bag.'

Grace knelt and ripped it open.

'I did my job.'

'Yes, honey. Yes, you did.'

'It was hard. I did my job.'

'Yes. Yes.' Grace ripped open the bag. Papers. Charts. Marked with THE CENTER FOR BIOCHIMERA on the tags. She blew out a breath. 'Good work, Jazz. I'll take you home now. Come on.'

'No.' Jazz tightened into a ball. 'Not there.'

'Jazz, it's not safe here.'

Jazz recoiled. 'Not safe with you,' she hissed. 'You're the keeper now.'

In the moldering pile of rags a cell phone rang in the shopping cart.

'Oh, no, no, no,' Jazz moaned. 'He left it here for you. Told me not to touch it! If I touch it, he'll disembowel me, put me in a soup, use it to soften my bones! Only you! The new keeper. It's ringing for you.'

Grace reached into her wallet and extracted a twenty-dollar bill, sliding it into Jazz's icy hand. 'I'm sending somebody for you,' she said, feeling helpless.

'Answer, then go away!' Jasmine shrieked over the sound of the phone.

Grace plunged her hand deep into the cart and pulled out the phone, clicked it on.

'According to my calculations, you have four and a half minutes before time's up.' The voice was distorted, tinny.

'I found the charts.'

'Now find the timer.'

'Wait.'

'Four minutes, Grace.'

Grace upended the shopping cart, ignoring the wail that erupted from Jazz, and plowed through the bits of Jazz's life. This timer was Art Deco, shaped like a palm tree, with fronds that swiveled as the time evaporated. Along the base of the palm tree were enameled coconuts, and Grace realized they counted out hours and minutes.

The biggest frond was pointed at two hours. A hundred and twenty minutes. Her watch said 2:59, so she had until almost five that afternoon.

'Found it,' she barked into the cell.

'Congratulations. You've just bought your

daughter two hours.'

'But — '

'Leave this cell phone with Jazz. Go home, Grace. You have work to do.'

He clicked off.

'He wants you to have it now, it's yours.' Grace put the phone down next to Jazz's head. 'Jazz?'

'Go. Go,' Jazz moaned, her eyes radiant with insanity.

'I'll get somebody here for you,' Grace promised. 'I will.'

She left Jazz motionless, breathing shallowly, and when she turned to look back at her, Jazz was asleep. Grace wondered if she'd been awake all night and all that day, waiting.

Two hours.

Was he watching her? Is that how he knew she'd picked up the charts?

If so, then who was watching Katie? She felt tears come and she blinked them away as she drove out of the parking lot. She hadn't realized until that moment how much she'd been hoping she'd find her daughter with Jazz.

The car in front of her slammed on its brakes and Grace leaned on her horn and changed lanes. She'd scribbled the number of the halfway house on a grocery receipt, and she pawed through her purse until she found it.

At the halfway house, an answering machine picked up, the message recorded by the same impatient caretaker, Opal, who bullied clients. Grace left anonymous, explicit directions on where to find Jazz. It was three-fifteen when she pulled into her driveway.

Jeanne and Helix met her at the front door. Grace shook her head and walked into the kitchen. She dumped the charts on the table and placed the palm tree timer next to them.

'Shouldn't we call the police?' Jeanne's face was chalky white, every line deep.

'Tried that. Jeanne, he's serious. He's going to kill her if we contact the police. He's listening.' She looked around the quiet kitchen. 'He could be listening here. For all I know, he's planted bugs in this house. Jeanne, I have less than two hours and work to do.'

'What's going on?'

'He's playing the Timer Game, Jeanne. Katie's favorite game. I have to play the Timer Game to get her back.' Grace banged the timer down on the table. The frond had turned slightly. She had one hour and forty-three minutes left.

Jeanne closed her eyes. 'How can I help?'

'I don't know if I'll be leaving suddenly or how long I'll be gone. Take Helix and go to your house. Wait for my call.'

Jeanne locked eyes with her for a long, measured beat. 'Call me if there's — '

'Of course.'

Grace opened the first file, and after a moment heard the sound of the front door closing. It was quiet then and she sorted charts on the table.

There were five medical charts.

One of them was Katie's.

20

Saturday, 3:22 p.m.

Grace found Warren's card and ran outside, crossing the street to the side that didn't have the view. She rang the doorbell on a house with a faded paint job and waited as she heard a woman's quavering voice. 'Yes?'

'Mrs. Montgomery. It's Grace. From down the street.'

'Grace?'

'Down the street. Remember, Katie and I brought you cookies last Christmas?'

The door unlocked. 'Goodness, is it Christmas already?' Mrs. Montgomery blinked in the sudden light. She had beautiful thick white hair and dark brown eyes and still perfect teeth in a face seamed with age. She was wearing a stained bathrobe that was missing a button and Grace felt a stab of guilt that she hadn't thought to stop by in almost a year.

'My telephone is broken. I was wondering if I could use yours for a brief call?'

'My phone?'

'Your telephone.'

'I think it works fine, dear.'

'Good, that's good. I need to use it. Just for a minute. May I come in?'

'Of course, come in. Come in. I'll fix tea.'

'Oh, no, I'm sorry. I'm so sorry. If I could just use the phone.'

'Of course. But I think it works fine.'

She ushered Grace into the small kitchen. Remnants of several meals still lay on the counters and Grace darted a look at the burners. All off. The phone was a rotary dial and it took her a moment to get used to how slowly it clicked around the face.

Mrs. Montgomery shuffled to the stove, a pan in her hand. 'Would you like some tea?'

'Oh. Thank you, but I can't.'

'Of course. Some other time.' The old woman went to the table and put the pan down next to a pillbox and a bowl of aging fruit.

She tried his home first and got a recording and tried his office. Warren lived and breathed the Center; if she could reach him anywhere, it would be there. He picked up on the fourth ring, his voice cautious. 'Yes.'

'Warren. It's Grace. Katie's gone.'

'What do you mean, gone?'

Tears sprang to her eyes. 'Please, can you just come over right away?'

Mrs. Montgomery picked up the pan, a bright smile on her face. 'I'm going to make us some tea. Isn't that a good idea?'

Grace covered the phone. 'Mrs. Montgomery, your program's on and it's really good.'

'Oh. My program.' She wandered into the living room, still clutching her pan.

'Grace, tell me everything. What do you mean, she's gone?'

Grace told him the rest. On the way out, she stopped in Mrs. Montgomery's living room. The old woman was dozing in front of the television, mouth open. Grace locked the door.

At home, she searched the house and found two stray balloons, bagging them in the trash. She washed her hands and changed clothes, then brought a legal yellow pad into the kitchen and sat down, forcing herself to pick up the stack of charts.

Touching them made her feel slightly sick. She got up and poured a glass of water, staring out the kitchen window across the boats bobbing gently with weekend passengers. Her hands trembled. She drained her glass and went back to her seat.

She worked with charts in the lab, but before a moment ago, she hadn't held a medical chart in over five years. She braced herself and picked up the top one. It had a small row of gold stars pasted to the tag. A quick shuffle revealed gold stars on all of them. That explained one thing: why Jazz had gone straight for those charts when she'd created such a mess in Deep Six. Grace remembered the row of gold stars on the outside of the metal filing cabinet that Rosemary Melzer said housed the pediatric files that went back years. Somebody must have put those stars on the filing cabinet, making it easy for Jazz to find them.

Four charts were similar and Grace stacked those together and put them aside.

She skimmed Katie's chart. The chart was for ear surgery when Katie was eleven months old. Grace frowned, taking down names and details, wondering what she was supposed to find.

She closed the chart and reached for the other

pile. She knew what waited for her. This was a special hell she was entering, a door she'd locked and barred years ago. A specialized world she'd spent years of training to enter, and minutes to leave.

She wiped her mouth with the flat of her hand. Black-and-white grainy prints, sonograms. Four pregnancies. Each baby with a serious heart defect revealed by ultrasound in utero. Developing hearts that needed repair. Or worse.

Her specialty. Navigating the fragile world of reconstructing damaged hearts for kids born with constricted valves. Or missing chambers. Or faulty pumping. And when that failed, for those who'd lost all hope, sometimes transplants. Taking away shredded hearts and putting alien ones in their place, donor hearts that beat at a cost, beating only as long as the savage mix of lethal cocktails — prednisone, cortisone — kept rejection at bay and opportunistic diseases, cancer, fungal pneumonia, osteoporosis — in a five-year-old! she'd marveled the first time she'd seen it — from invading the already breached immunity wall.

So many ways to die.

She'd soldiered on. Soldiered. That was an image she didn't want in her head.

Okay, she'd gone on, stitching, healing, transplanting, working with hearts sometimes as small and soft as figs. A pediatric heart surgeon.

Almost. She quit right after Guatemala, before she'd taken the boards. But almost.

She'd been so proud of that. She picked up the two charts on the top of the stack and placed them side by side, turning to the face sheets, copying facts onto two yellow lined pages: names, addresses, phone numbers:

DeeDee and Fred Winger Terry and Bob Frieze

She didn't recognize the Winger name, but Bob Frieze's name was familiar. She scanned down the page, checked his occupation. Of course. Robert Harling Frieze.

He was an internationally acclaimed artist based in L.A, using found objects combined with acrylics and photos to create disturbing and savage-looking works of art. She'd seen his name recently in the paper, hosting an art auction benefiting kids with genetic anomalies. But five years before, being rich and famous didn't stop Frieze and his wife from the pain of knowing their unborn child had a heart defect that killed a third of its victims before they were ten. Without a transplant, it was a death sentence.

Neither chart went past birth. They were only charts identifying heart anomalies.

One hour seven minutes left. Where in the hell was Warren?

She massaged her temples. These kids were being typed for transplants before they were even born. She reached for the third chart. Four years ago, a poor and frightened native couple, Maria and Arturo Miasonkopna, had listed as their address Mile 36, Dry Arroyo Creekbed, Old Pascua Village, Arizona. They'd used Medicare to pay for a sonogram that revealed their unborn daughter's withered left ventricle. The chart ended two days after delivery, with an infant named Hekka.

Hekka. A shock ran up her. Hekka. That was the name of the Indian girl in Mac's report, the one going into the Center to wait for her heart-in-a-box.

The palm tree frond on the timer swiveled over a notch and she stole a quick look. An hour and three minutes left. That was all. She reached for the next chart.

Richard and Adrian Bettles. Bettles. Eric Bettles. She was looking at the chart of the boy who had later gone on to make history. The first heart-in-a-box. Two out of the four charts dealt with kids getting lab-created hearts. Perfect matches.

She jerked her head up. A banging, a muffled voice. She eased the chart down and crept to the door. Through the viewfinder, Warren looked rumpled, his white hair sticking up. He wasn't alone. Three men stood silently behind him, a squat older man and two workmen carrying boxes of equipment.

Grace stepped outside and closed the door. 'I told you to come alone.'

'How much time do we have?'

She glanced at her watch, disbelieving. 'Fifty-nine minutes. Did you hear what I said?'

'Hustle, people.' Warren reached around her and opened the door and the workmen took the boxes into the house.

'Who are these people? Didn't you hear what I said? What are they doing?'

'Checking for bugs.' He nodded at the man standing next to him. 'This is Bill. A PI specializing in finding missing kids.'

Bill had an old man's bulbous nose and hearing aids wedged into mottled ears. He held himself proudly and carried a CSI kit in an age-freckled hand.

She remembered the voice on the phone. The warning. *If you try that again, she's dead.*

Warren said quietly, 'Bill's the man who found Sara for me, Grace.' He looked away.

Grace exhaled and nodded. It was terrible, this choice, risky as hell, but maybe this was her best chance at finding Katie. Her only chance.

'Come inside.'

She told Bill everything she could remember about the doll and Katie disappearing and finding Jazz and the charts. He took careful notes and asked few questions.

A workman wearing a Bartman T-shirt poked his head into the room. 'Found one in the phone. I disabled it, but he won't know that.'

'Thanks, Stu.' Warren settled in his chair. Stu nodded and went back to work in the family room.

'They're wiring your house, Grace. This goon has got to be contacting you, right? We'll be able to put a trace on the phone and find out where he's got her.'

'You could do that?' She almost wept.

'It's already happening. These are the charts?'

She nodded.

He took out a pair of reading glasses. A muscle in his jaw clenched as he picked them up. He looked up briefly and there was bitter anger in his eyes. 'My charts. My Center. My credibility. I'm pissed.' He raised his voice. 'Stu?'

Stu trotted in, holding a cable wrapped around his wrist like a thick snake. 'Sir?'

'Before the day is out, I want an extra dozen working security at the Center.'

'All shifts?'

'All of them.'

Stu nodded and Warren turned back to Grace, his voice still hard. 'You take Bill and show him where this happened.'

They went upstairs, first to the bathroom, where she pointed out the footprint next to the ladder, and then on to Katie's room. Bill grunted as he stared at the spike impaling the note and reached into his brown shiny jacket, pulling out a pair of latex gloves.

'I'll print these here.'

He squatted next to the bed and snapped on a glove.

'No.'

'I know it's your territory, CSI and all, but I thought you'd want to be downstairs with Warren. My degree's in criminology, I won't screw this up.'

He pulled on the second glove and flexed his fingers.

She shook her head. 'That's not it. Warren's allergic to latex.'

'Say what?' He clicked on a small flashlight and examined the spike in close light.

'Your gloves. Give me those and bag them and then wash your hands and the outside of the bag.

Use my sink, not Katie's. Warren's allergic to latex,' she repeated. 'Even airborne particles can cause a severe allergic reaction.'

'I never heard of such a thing.'

She was getting impatient. 'You could kill him, close off his airway. I saw it happen to him once, when I was working at the Center. Scared the hell out of me.'

'No kidding.'

'My bathroom's down the hall.' She pointed as she started down the stairs. 'When you're done, leave the baggie in the wastebasket. Wait right there. I'll get you a different set.'

She ran down the stairs and through the kitchen out into the laundry room. Warren sat hunched over the charts, a look of tense concentration on his lined face.

She found the box of nitrile gloves on the laundry room shelf and when she carried them back through the kitchen, comprehension and horror flicked across Warren's face.

'I didn't even think about that. Bill brought latex?'

She nodded. 'Keep reading. I'll be right back.'

She went upstairs and there she left a chastened Bill, then joined Warren at the kitchen table.

'It's the damnest thing.' He rubbed the bridge of his nose. 'One of the keys to this mess is Jazz. She has to know more than she's telling.' Warren called into the family room, 'Stuart. You almost done in there?'

Stu came in carrying a length of cable, the front of his shirt smudged so it looked as if Bart sported a mustache. 'About another five minutes.'

'Good. I've got a job for you. I need you to find a mentally ill woman named — '

'Jasmine,' Grace supplied. 'Jazz Studio.' She told him where she'd last seen her and where she lived and Stuart took notes on a small pad he pulled from his hip pocket.

'What does she look like?'

'I've got a picture. I just remembered.' She ran to her shoulder bag and found it. Stu studied it and tucked it in his wallet. 'Okay, boss. Where do you want her, when I find her?'

'Bring her to the Center. I don't want her scared, Stu. So keep that in mind. She's off her meds and definitely unstable so move carefully.'

Grace's relief at knowing they'd find Jazz and that maybe she could supply information that would help them find Katie was cut short when she glanced at the timer.

'Thirty-nine minutes. What are we looking at?'

Warren shook his head. 'So strange. These four charts.' He splayed a heavy, manicured hand across the top of them. 'And then Katie's.'

'Let's start with Katie's.' It was back again, that frantic thing in her that was saying they were running out of time and maybe calling him in was too costly, too time-consuming.

'What do we have here?' She positioned the chart so they both could read it and shoved the others out of the way. 'Her ear surgery at the Center,' Warren said. His voice was staccato, the tempo speeding up. 'That's all this is.'

'Exactly.' She flipped the page to the face

197

sheet. 'A short admit, a 23:59, meaning Katie was released less than twenty-four hours from her admission time.'

'And you knew the doctor, right?' Warren peered at the name. 'Dr. Calderon.'

'Family doctor, dead now.'

'So he's not a bad guy, at least not on the page.'

Warren glanced at the timer and Grace followed his gaze. Her stomach tightened. Thirty-five minutes.

'We're okay.' He put a calming hand on her arm. His fingers were ice. The stress was taking its toll on him, too.

'Think, Warren,' Warren said, talking out loud, 'you've written down the names of the scrub nurse, circulatory tech, anesthesiologist.'

'Yes, yes,' Grace said impatiently. 'Routine.'

Routine but agonizing. Being with Katie, holding her hand while the anesthetic glided like an eel down the IV, had taxed all Grace's resources and left her soaked in sweat, sending her into a full-blown attack. She'd thrown up when Katie was safely in surgery.

'Can you remember anything out of the ordinary?'

Grace squeezed her eyes shut. 'No, nothing.' She snapped her eyes open. 'Yes, yes! Remember? Katie disappeared.' She grabbed Warren's arm. 'Oh, my God, remember, they'd moved her after surgery during a shift change. Stuck her on another floor and nobody knew where she was.'

His face clouded. 'You're right. I fired the nurse over it, too. I couldn't believe the incompetence. Never got to the bottom of it, either. How she'd been wheeled out of recovery and stuck on another floor.'

It had been terrifying. It had taken two frantic hours of searching before they located Katie on the surgical floor looking dazed, skin damp and buttery, wailing when she recognized Grace. Grace scooped her up with such force Katie had shrieked in pain, and later Grace found a bruise the size of a bullet on her toddler's back, where she'd inadvertently banged Katie against the metal crib bar in her haste to pick her up.

She and Dr. Calderon had each called Warren; he'd been livid, insisted he'd get to the bottom of it. Pilot error is what he called it later. Simple pilot error. Never happen again.

It never had with her. Grace never let it. All it did was reinforce that Warren was spread too thin to monitor the hospital side. She vowed never to use the hospital again. She threw down her pen and glanced at the timer. Twenty-nine minutes.

'What are we missing? We're missing something,' Warren muttered. She could see his anxiety growing as he tapped a pen sharply against the pages.

'Charts are always supposed to follow the patient,' Grace offered. 'Track exactly where they went and what was done.'

'You're right.' Warren scanned the pages at the end of the ear surgery. 'An ID number's supposed to track every test, every room transfer.'

'Katie was moved to a hall, Warren, and left

there.' After four years, it still rankled.

His gaze snapped up and held. 'I'm sorry,' he said quietly.

Grace closed Katie's chart. 'Okay, the others, this is the weird thing, Warren.'

She pulled out the Bettles and Miasonkopna charts. 'This first one is the boy who got the heart-in-a-box last year, Lee's first patient.' She tapped the second chart. 'And this chart belongs to the girl who will get the heart I just saw growing in the lab.'

'We have twenty-one minutes left, Grace.'

'Yeah, I just think it's a little — '

She was interrupted by a sharp pounding on the door.

The men laying cable immediately sprang to their feet and joined Bill as he stealthily crept down the stairs into the living room. They were all holding guns. Bill motioned to Warren and Grace to keep their heads down. Warren pulled Grace down to the floor.

'You expecting anybody?' he whispered.

She shook her head. The pounding increased and Bill inched toward the door. He was carrying a five shot .500 Smith & Wesson magnum, a big gun that would leave a big hole.

'If you're there, Mrs. Descanso, can you open up? I'm Arlen, down the street.' Grace scrambled to her feet.

Bill stepped away from the door as Grace peered through the viewfinder. Arlen stared up, nose flared, wearing a baseball cap, hardware glinting in his teeth. She opened the door. He was fourteen, in baggy red shorts and a Chargers jersey. His shoes were boats.

'I got your paper.' He held up the *Union-Tribune*. She checked her watch: 4:41.

'I already got the Saturday paper you delivered this morning, Arlen.'

He shook his head. 'All I know is, somebody paid me fifty bucks to put this one into your hands. Come on, please, Mrs. Descanso, I got to do the right thing. I got an algebra test first thing Monday, that's bad enough.' He looked ready to cry. On the street, his mother waited in the car, motor running. He handed her the paper and raced down the steps.

'Arlen?'

He turned. Pimples flecked his cheeks and his jaw looked suddenly too angular.

'Was it some guy?'

'What do you mean?'

'Gave you the fifty dollars.'

Arlen shook his head. 'Some skater. Seen him around but I don't know him. I go to St. Charles, so I'm not sure of the Correia kids.' The horn tooted. 'Just a kid, okay?'

He turned and darted into the car, and Arlen's mother gave a half wave as she drove off. Grace waved back cheerily, pretending her life still had meaning and order. Still had Katie in it.

The paper felt like lead in her hands. She closed the door and locked it.

21

'Okay, we're in business,' Bill barked. He was dividing the paper into sections and thrusting them into various hands. 'Let's get this thing laid out and see what it has for us. Stu, you take this section, Brian, you start with these. Lay them on the floor page by page. Grace, Warren, you take these. I'll check out the classifieds. We're looking for cutouts, anything marked up, underlined, or any headlines with the following words.'

He turned to Warren and Grace.

'*Timer, game, kidnapping, missing medical files,*' Grace shouted.

'*Spike,*' Warren suggested. 'Look for *spike,* too.'

'Or *Katie,*' Grace added.

They worked feverishly, laying out pages across the floor until it was covered in islands of newsprint. The only sounds were the rustle of pages, breathing, and the labored repositioning of their knees in front of fresh pages.

'Eight minutes, guys,' Warren said.

Grace looked at the paper helplessly. Two hours had incinerated into eight minutes.

A despair was beginning to burrow into her heart. She was falling into some black maelstrom where nothing was as it seemed, and Katie was always just one tantalizing step away.

'Found it,' Bill said abruptly. He snatched up a

page of classifieds and the group crowded around as he punched a square finger at an ad in personals:

THE TIMER GAME

The rules are simple, clean and dry
You beat the timer; she won't die
At least not yet, and that's the key.
What box unlocks? Move fast, and see.

Underneath, there was a tagline: *Their job is making you look good. Oh, and take the timer with you.*

Grace paced. 'She's going to die in seven minutes if we can't figure this out.'

'Box, you have a safety deposit box?' Bill snapped.

She shook her head. 'Clean and dry, clean and dry.'

'Laundry,' Warren said. 'Doesn't that sound like a laundry slogan? Where do you go?'

She was already snatching up her purse, the charts, and the timer and racing for her car.

'Wait, I'm coming with you.' Bill labored after her.

'No, you can't! He's going to be watching! He sees you and that's it. He'll kill her.'

'I'll take a different car. I'll park a ways away. Don't worry. He's not going to see. But I'm going to see him,' Bill said grimly. 'We're going to nail this asshole.'

The laundry was two blocks away on a side street. Bill pulled to the curb and Grace drove past him and skidded into the strip mall. She ran into the laundry and banged on the bell. Past the hanging racks she glimpsed a young Asian woman bending over a steam table, pressing clothes. Grace dinged the bell over and over until the woman trotted around the racks, wiping her hands on a towel and smiling.

'Do you have anything for me? Grace Descanso.' She dug into her shoulder bag and found her wallet, spilling cards and money onto the counter. The timer dropped out onto the counter and the frond clicked over another notch. Less than three minutes left.

The young woman frowned in confusion. 'Do you have the ticket?'

'No, no. Grace Descanso. You must have something for me. Here.' She found her driver's license and held it up. 'Please.'

Time stopped. There was only the sound of churning washing machines and the imperceptible quiver of the enamel frond as it slid again.

Two minutes left.

The woman's face cleared. 'Ah. Yes. I remember now.' She went to the rack directly behind her and ran her fingers lightly along the hangers. She was a tiny woman, with long glossy hair and a short skirt that bagged over her small rump. Her fingers slowed and she detached the hanger, and Grace felt her knees buckle.

It was a single item, bagged in plastic, the wrapper printed with the phrase: *Our job is making you look good.*

In the plastic was Katie's jacket. Blue, a zipper. Katie's warm-up jacket, soft flannel on the inside. Last week they'd torn the house apart, trying to find it, Grace sure Katie must have left it at school — *check Lost and Found!* He must have taken it out of Katie's closet. Stood there in the dark, breathing, running his hands obscenely over Katie's things. His boldness stunned Grace. He'd been in the house. He'd taken the jacket. He'd planned this out.

'When was this brought in?' Grace was ripping off the plastic wrapper, checking the cuffs, the pockets of the jacket. Nothing. The palm tree itself was beginning a slow twirl, counting down the seconds. A minute thirty. Twenty-nine. The woman frowned and checked the tag. 'That's odd. It doesn't say.'

'How much? How much money?' Grace's fingers checked the seams. Nothing.

'No, no. Already done. Ah, this. Is this what you need? For your mailbox?' The woman turned back the jacket tag and Grace saw the outline of a small key, attached with a strip of masking tape.

'God.' Grace swept everything into her shoulder bag. She ran.

The strip mall was a small L, and Grace ran past the Christian Science reading room, past the insurance brokers. She caught a blur of Bill's stolid body, propped against his car across the street, pretending to read a newspaper. There was a UPS store that sold cards and bubble wrap, with a Xerox copy machine and notary.

And along one wall, small brass mailboxes.

Grace slammed her shoulder bag down on the

sorting table people used to wrap packages. She spilled the timer out and picked it up and felt a surge of terror. It was whirring in a circle now.

Forty-five seconds. Forty-four.

She snatched up the jacket and ripped off the tape. The key fell into her hand. It was a small, fat key engraved with the number 1227. It had to work. Had to. She ran along the rows of boxes, searching.

A doughy woman with pale eyes shot out from behind the counter. 'Help you?'

It was the second row from the top. Grace's hand shook. She inserted the key. It turned. She yanked open the door. The timer must have been electronically calibrated to the lock turning in the post office box; the instant she inserted the key, turned the lock, yanked open the door, the timer shuddered and went still, the fronds frozen in her hand. She stared at the numbers, fascinated. Her breath came in unsteady gusts. Two seconds.

Two seconds left on the timer.

Grace moaned and collapsed against the flat metal wall of post office boxes. The woman darted to her side, eyes wide with concern. 'You okay? Need a doctor?'

Grace shook her head. She opened her fingers and looked at it again, still not believing how close she'd come to not making it.

It was hot inside, October heat trapped in the space, and the cashier had opened the back door for cross ventilation. A UPS man came in the back way and stopped in front of a high stack of boxes waiting to be picked up. He was in his midtwenties, with good muscles under his short-sleeved shirt, styled brown hair, and a pen tucked behind an ear. He leaned over the stack of boxes and used leg muscles to lift, and Grace saw the firm flex of haunch as he transferred boxes onto his dolly. He piled them easily and wheeled them out the back door to his truck.

Grace unclenched her fingers and set the timer down. Two seconds. It took a moment to see the open mail door, key still in the lock. Something glowed inside the box. She didn't want to do this. She really didn't. She lifted it out.

A yellow cartoon hand — just a couple of fat fingers, really, like the kind she'd seen in ToonTown in Disneyland or a Chargers game — free-standing in poster board and Styrofoam, pointed toward the counter. Around the base of the hand someone had used a black marker to write the letters *s d n*.

'This is cool.' The cashier had picked up the palm tree timer, examining it closely. 'What is this? A timer? Can I buy it from you?'

'Sorry.' She didn't know if she was supposed to keep it. She took the timer back and dropped it into her bag, pointing at the initials on the hand.

'These your initials? SDN?'

The woman shook her head, losing interest. Grace numbly shoved everything back into her purse. A cyclist trotted into the shop, carrying a package under an oiled arm. The woman brightened and touched her hair, heading behind the counter. 'Mel. Just in time. I was about to close things up.'

SDN. SDN. Through the back door, Grace saw the UPS guy slamming down the hatch on his truck. He went around to the front of the cab and got in.

A finger pointing toward the counter. What was she missing? Something. She scanned the boxes of small objects for sale on the counter: gag items, travel puzzles, key chains with tiny balls that rolled into sockets, truncated plush animals. Nothing with SDN.

The cyclist thumped his package down on the counter and bumped into Grace, knocking the cutout from her grasp. It fell to the floor. The biker had a high-tech pair of Speedos, black and cobalt blue, and they both bent in unison to retrieve it. He was younger and faster and appeared — from this view — to shave his legs. Tanned and hairless. He snapped the cut-out back into Grace's hand, full of apologies and good cheer. He'd given it to her upside down, the finger pointing out the back door now, toward the UPS van waiting to back up. It was a small back lot, and the van was moving carefully. Upside down, the lettering — she'd been so sure of that lettering, when she'd seen *s d n* — became *u p s*.

Grace dropped the hand, scooped up her leather shoulder bag, and ran through the back of the shop into the alley.

He was backing up now, the UPS guy, music cranked up, windows vibrating to the bass, lipsynching, his eyes on the rearview mirror, foot heavy on the pedal. Grace lunged. She banged onto the front window and he swerved and braked, startled. They stared at each other through the glass. She'd caught him by surprise and his first instinct was fear. It roiled up his face like a tidal wave, taking away his competency and training and leaving behind a kid. She smiled reassuringly and clambered off the front of his van. He switched off the ignition and opened his door, his face blankly neutral now, waiting for whatever came next.

'Do you have something for me? Grace Descanso.'

He frowned, shifted his weight, checked the seat next to him, glanced over his shoulder at the stacks of boxes. He was frowning, but nicely, as if he really wanted to be of help but couldn't, and was starting to shake his head when he swiveled forward in his seat and his hand fell on something between the seats. He pulled it out.

It was a UPS packet, slim cardboard. 'That's weird. It wasn't here when I — ' He scanned the name and stopped. 'Descanso. Is that what you said?'

She nodded and he extended the packet. He had a slight lisp but his voice was strong and deep. He held out a clipboard and pen. 'Sign here, please.'

'I don't understand.' She scribbled her name on the line.

'Makes two of us.' He shrugged. He had an affable smile, all business. He checked his watch and scribbled his initials, already switching on the ignition.

'Where did you get this?'

'Beats me. Funny, it doesn't have an address on it, just your name. And this. Says to open immediately.'

Grace stared at the package. It was cardboard, the size of a manila envelope, but lumpy. A thought whispered, steady and calm. If she hadn't figured this out, the package would have gone back with the UPS man.

Game over.

She ripped open the envelope as the UPS truck rumbled away.

Inside was a typed note: *Drop your cell phone and the timer on the ground. Dump the PI and his pals or she dies.*

Along with the note there was a set of keys to a car. A tag dangled from it with an address three blocks away, taking her even farther from where Bill waited and watched. She turned off her cell phone, crouched down, and left it and the timer in a patch of weeds.

A pain spiked her chest. Her body pinged with falling stars, dying sparks of energy. She was alone again; the only hope her daughter had of rescue was pinned on her and it seemed too small a save. She was physically not capable of holding it together much longer without a break. Was that part of it, the Spikeman planning to exhaust her until every resource was depleted? And then what? Trying to save Katie when she could no longer think or move or hope?

She started walking and then she broke into a run.

22

She found the Acura parked at a curb two blocks up from Blockbuster. Her mind had ceased sorting; she was numb, moving forward with no expectation. Inside the car, a cell phone rang. She couldn't seem to grasp the rental car key correctly. It kept slipping. The phone continued ringing. She unlocked the car and slid onto the seat. Whoever had dropped it off had much longer legs. 'Yes?'

The voice was tinny, distorted. 'Very good, Grace. Nice save.'

'Where is she? Where's my daughter?'

'It was inventive. Getting the detective involved. I'll give you that much. That's why I didn't off your daughter immediately, even though you deserved it. I'd hate to end the game so soon. But really, what does it take, her finger in a box? Don't try that again.'

Grace looked around the silent street. She was parked in front of a stucco apartment complex, ringed with a black steel fence. An elderly woman with hair as soft as dandelion fluff thumped down the steps, trailing a small poodle on a rhinestone leash.

'The game,' Grace repeated.

'What do you call it?'

She closed her eyes. 'What do you want?'

'I'm not a monster.'

211

'Let my daughter go. You want me, right? Take me.'

'Oh, how touching. The mommy card, and so early. Very sweet.'

'How do I know she's even alive?'

'You don't.'

'God, please — '

'It's not going to hurt. What happens.' He sounded petulant.

Grace blinked. A woman driving an SUV barreled past her and pulled into a driveway down the street. She hopped out and started hauling grocery bags out of the backseat.

'I'll do whatever you want.'

That made him laugh. 'Don't worry about that, Grace. You will.' He clicked off.

She stared blankly at the phone. There had to be a timer somewhere. Numbly, she checked the storage area between the seats and the pockets on either door. She found it in the glove compartment under an AAA map of Los Angeles. It was a stopwatch, set to go off in forty-five minutes. But where was she supposed to go? Someplace in Los Angeles? She'd never make it in time. The way she drove, L.A. was at least two and a half hours away, with traffic. This was early evening on Saturday. And nothing was marked on the map, either. No circles, red marks.

The only thing she knew for sure was that she couldn't go home again. She realized in that instant how very glad she'd been to see Warren, how safe she'd felt with Bill and the competency of the men wiring her house. She was alone again and afraid.

The setting sun cut a blinding beam through the windshield and Grace flipped down the visor. Clipped to the visor was a flyer. Only it wasn't a flyer.

It was a color picture of Katie, swinging upside down in the tree fort in their backyard, holding on to her crown. Her hair had caught the light, and it almost blinded Grace, glints of red and spun gold and caramel, an explosion of curls. Katie looked dizzy with happiness.

He'd been there that morning, at Katie's party. From the angle, he'd been on a boat. He'd shot a candid of her daughter on the day everything changed.

So. Grace had been within a boat's length of the man who had stolen her daughter. Was Katie on a boat? Or underground. Grace had read cases of kids taken, trapped in coffin-sized spaces. She couldn't think about that. She'd die if she thought about that. She took a steadying breath and turned the photo over.

The back, the side that had been slapped down onto the windshield, held an address and the name of a shop: Art Cry Galleria.

★   ★   ★

It turned out to be a small gallery in Hillcrest specializing in sadomasochistic art. Grace had tucked the stopwatch into her pocket. She'd run into bad traffic on Washington and the usual parking congestion in Hillcrest, but she finally pulled into a spot at a curb three blocks from the shop. Her legs weren't working properly. She

213

stumbled a lot and she made her way carefully over the uneven sidewalks to the heavy chrome and glass door and pulled it open.

There was less than half an hour left to find the next clue.

The gallery was small, walls painted black and red. Hip-hop music throbbed from every speaker. A sweet-faced kid studded with piercings and dressed like a snake trotted over and asked if she could help. It came out as a lisp and Grace realized her tongue had been forked.

'I'm not sure,' Grace said, her eyes scanning exhibits. 'Do you have anything for a Grace Descanso?'

The girl went away and asked the cashier as Grace went painstakingly around the room, going over every piece of sculpture, every painting on the wall, and each black-and-white photograph, a monotonous blur of knives and pincers and handcuffs, hunting for anything that could lead her to Katie. She hesitated at an exhibit consisting of nothing but blood spatters, as if a criminalist had slapped court exhibits between flats of acrylic. Was the Spikeman trying to tell her he'd hurt Katie?

The salesgirl came back. 'He says no,' she said.

Grace nodded. 'Thanks.' She glanced at the salesman. He had dead white skin and black hair and was thinner than healthy people usually were. He never looked at her.

Fourteen minutes left.

Two men in tank tops and earrings came in and browsed. Grace studied them carefully. Were

214

they there to deliver a message? An elderly woman spilling out of a girdle came in and Grace pressed closer, listening. Picking up a birthday present for her son.

A present. Was that a code? It was Katie's birthday. This terrible day.

Eleven minutes left.

There was a thick stack of Mapplethorpe prints and S & M posters, and Grace started at one end and methodically went through them. Nothing that remotely suggested Katie. Only images that planted disturbing pictures in her mind of what could be happening to her daughter at that moment.

Seven minutes.

The only thing she hadn't checked yet was a rack of coming events that hung behind the counter. The salesman was ringing up a zucchini-sword acrylic statue for the woman. She stood at the counter and tugged violently on her girdle when she thought no one was looking. The zucchini was short and muscular and the sword was only nicked an inch toward the top, almost as if it were a circumcised zucchini, except that didn't explain the straight pins. The woman buying it for her son liked it, that was clear. Grace stood off to the side as the platinum card went through, poring over the pamphlets, art exhibits, announcements for shows, advertisements for auctions, personal appearances by artists, bios. Her eyes went back and reread the third one from the bottom. Robert Harling Frieze.

She knew that name. She'd seen it on the

medical chart. The salesclerk glanced at her for the first time and she gestured at the brochures. 'Could you hand me that one for the Robert Harling Frieze exhibit, please? The one that's tonight?'

He passed it to her silently. She was almost to the door when he looked up from the cash register and said, 'Excuse me. Miss?' He was frowning, the unsigned sales receipt still in his hand. 'Is your name Grace?'

Grace grew very still. 'Do you have something for me?'

The woman he was helping shifted impatiently.

'Actually, you have something for me.'

'I do?'

'A stopwatch?'

Grace pulled it out of her pocket. He took it from her and turned it off. Four minutes left. A lifetime. He carried it with him back behind the counter.

'Wait. I do have something for you now.'

He ducked and came up with a copy of *Art Digest* and a square box the size of a pack of playing cards.

'And you have no idea who left this here, or what he looked like.'

'Excuse me.' The woman's voice was heavy with impatience. 'I've got a flight to catch.'

The clerk cut her a sympathetic look. 'I'm so sorry, ma'am.' To Grace he said, 'All I know is, a man in black face paint came in here about an hour or so ago, said you might be by. Said not to give you anything, even if you came up and identified yourself, unless you picked up the Frieze brochure. That was the signal.'

Grace looked at him.

'And then I was supposed to take the stopwatch. That's my payment. For helping out. It was a game,' the cashier said. 'That's what he said. You'd be playing a game.'

Masking tape secured the box and Grace snicked a fingernail across the edge as she walked outside, ripping the tape off. Inside was an electronic hourglass. Digital grains of sand floated from the top down through a compressed neck and settled in drifts along the bottom. She had no idea how much time she had left. She stood on the street and watched the sand moving, getting a sense of it. There was still a good 75 percent of it left to be filled in. If the Spikeman had come into the shop an hour ago, that meant she still had three hours to go.

More than enough time to drive to Robert Harling Frieze's gallery opening in Los Angeles. Providing she was reading the timer correctly. She bit her lip and surveyed the street. The mailbox annex Office on the Go was only a few blocks past where she'd parked the car.

Maybe the Spikeman had gotten careless and left her a clue when he'd sent the fax with the smiley face to the taco van owner, Mr. Esguio.

But that wouldn't give her any margin for error heading north. On the other hand, this might be the only chance she'd have to ask questions. She dropped the timer into her bag and cut through an empty lot, passing Corvette's

217

and a gregarious crowd of dinner celebrants.

Office on the Go was decorated in red, white, and blue bunting, a small mailbox way station wedged between shops of an acupuncturist and a fortune teller, both closed. Grace flashed her crime lab badge and got the clerk to pull information about the fax. She had a beak nose, beautiful shoulders, and toned arms. She was tall for a woman and wore a knit suit more suitable for afternoon lunch, and her ring finger held the faint outline of a missing band.

'Now I remember.' She brightened. 'He paid cash to send the fax.'

'You were here?' Grace leaned in. 'Ma'am, this is important. What did he look like?'

'Well, that's just it, I don't know.' The clerk sounded apologetic and slightly embarrassed. 'He was wearing a clown suit. Blue. Said he was on his way to Children's Hospital for a benefit. I'd been in the Junior League for years, so we started talking.'

'Anything that jumps out at you?'

'You mean, besides the clown suit? Yeah. He said he was with the police auxiliary, and well . . . ' She shrugged, hesitating, and Grace realized she was feeling foolish.

'Even if it's little, something you think doesn't really matter.' Grace edged closer.

'He didn't know what the Junior League was. We work at Children's all the time, at least I did, and with the police auxiliary, too, and so, I don't know, it just made me think maybe he wasn't with the auxiliary after all, you know?'

A clown suit. In blue. To match the wrapping

paper covering the bloody doll. He was toying with her. Playing a deadly game, with Katie's safe return as the ultimate prize.

Grace walked numbly through the crowded street. Everywhere she looked, there were eyes.

23

Saturday, 8:53 p.m.
It was in Westwood not far from the botanical gardens on Hilgard Avenue, painted cobalt blue and lit with pink neon, three stories high with a crate elevator latched to the side. Grace got there at close to nine. A clump of emaciated women, all in black, spilled onto the sidewalk, holding plastic champagne glasses and smoking.

It was disorienting, racing through traffic, taking the smallest of breaks, rushing into L.A., and seeing how relaxed and casual those women were, chatting about inconsequential things. Her bones ached from the long drive, her heart from the pain of missing Katie. It felt that the farther away she drove, the less chance she'd have of ever seeing her daughter alive again. And yet this is where he was sending her. Directing her.

She checked the digital hourglass as she walked through the door into the bright light. Everything but the top six rows were filled in and her stomach fluttered. Inside, there was someone who would take the timer from her and tell her what she had to do next. But she had to hurry; she was running out of time, and if she ran out of time — *no, she wouldn't think about that.*

It was a warehouse-sized room, with lighting and winter white walls. Neon pink stairs led to a loft on the second floor. Huge violent canvases in hot, electric colors adorned the walls of the gallery on the first floor, fractured photos thick with paint, glass shards, and broken pottery. In the middle of the room sat Plexiglas cubes with what looked like disembodied body parts. There was a car wreck and a train wreck and an underwater sea wreck — that one with a green-haired girl trapped inside a window, a hidden pump swirling her hair and making her silicon lips tremble. She looked just alive enough that Grace caught a breath and looked again.

About fifty people stood shouting over the noise, the decibel level so high it seemed to bang off the walls. There was a bar set up on the other side of the room and Grace made her way over, trailing behind a hollow-eyed woman and a tall man carrying a scythe. A bleached, aging bodybuilder manned the drink table. Grace ordered a Coke, yelling to be heard.

'What do you think?' the bartender shouted as he slid her drink across.

'About this?' She shrugged a look at the paintings and put the timer on the counter.

'That's four bucks.' His eyes flicked to the timer.

'For a Coke?'

'You actually think somebody's going to buy this effluvia?'

She fished money out of her shoulder bag and dropped an extra buck into his tip jar, glancing at a painting hanging behind him. Five feet high, a cheerleader screaming, inside of her mouth glossed in green, her tongue a blue snake, her perfect teeth the color of bad cheese. One breast hung out of her torn uniform, cruelly bisected with tattooed words: *sex. have some. Candy High. feel my . . . pain.*

'I have enough bad dreams.'

He nodded, satisfied. 'I'm not crazy about it, either.'

'It's not a matter of not liking it. I think this Robert Harling Frieze guy is brilliant. I mean, one of them sold in New York for what? Close to half a mil?'

His eyes turned cold. 'You done? I have customers.' He poured two white wines and took a twenty from a man.

Grace yelled over the thumping music and voices, 'I'm actually interested specifically in his blue period.'

The bartender looked at her sharply and she swallowed in spite of herself.

'His most productive period, I've heard. Never seen a blue one, he apparently hoards them or something, and the value of one of those — '

'I don't know anything about that.'

She nodded, let it pass.

'Why the blue period?' He rubbed a nonexistent spot on the counter.

She shrugged, her thoughts churning. *Why? Because that's what you were creating when you discovered your baby would be born with a bad heart.*

Instead she said, 'It's about loss. Grief. Over and over, eyes coming at you. Something unformed. A promise broken. Not broken so much as ruptured, I guess. Shredded apart.'

She'd memorized that driving up, the article spread on the seat next to her. She hoped if he

222

read his own press, he waited a long time between reads. 'See him here?'

Robert Harling Frieze stared at her coldly. 'No.'

'Well, if you see him, you tell him he has a fan.' She stuffed a second buck into his tip jar.

'Upstairs.' His chest looked damp under his black silk shirt.

'Say what?'

'I think that blue stuff, saw it on the third floor.' He picked up the timer, and the pixeled sand particles blew in a sparkling cloud.

The walls of the loft on the second floor were hung with simple pen and inks, mounted in Plexiglas, depicting the end of the world. A sunburned guard sat on a folding chair, reading *Guns & Ammo*. He looked up, his eyes spaced close together so that his nose looked pinched. Grace studied a sketch hanging next to the stairs leading up to third. Bugs devoured humans in this one, only some of the bugs carried guns and briefcases. The steps were narrow, lit only by a dim bulb. She started climbing.

'Hey.' The guard tossed down his magazine. His voice was adenoidal and his ears were chapped and peeling. 'It's off limits, third floor. No can do.'

Over the noise, she heard the groan of the freight elevator. 'I was told — '

He stood up. He carried weight in his thighs and they bulged under his uniform. He flexed his fists casually and she stepped past him down the stairs.

'Fine.' She moved toward the neon staircase

leading down to the main floor.

A couple arguing in German pushed past. The woman was bulky and short, wearing a thick tweed suit that made her hairy calves look enormous. The man gesticulated with his hands, flinging them out and stabbing the air. He had dark hollows under his eyes and his suit smelled like he'd worn it too long this trip. His hand flew out and clipped the woman — inadvertently, it seemed to Grace — and she reeled back toward the steel bars of the pony wall overlooking the main room. The guard lunged for her and caught her in a backward dip that looked like he was heavy-lifting a discus thrower. Grace used the distraction to dart up the stairs to the third floor. Locked.

Not locked, warped. She pushed gently. It burst open and she lost her balance and fell forward into darkness. Into a body. Into a man. Fear juiced through her. She screamed. He grappled a hand over her mouth and yanked her to him. His other arm clamped around her and spun her against the door, slamming it shut. He pressed against her, his body huge, tight.

'You speak, you die.'

She didn't move.

'Hear me? Try that again and I kill you. Understand?'

She nodded, his hand choking her airway. He pinned her tighter to the door and snapped on the light. Robert Harling Frieze on steroids. Bulked up, angry. A vein in his neck throbbed. Spidery lines bloomed across his nostrils. His hair was cropped, and up this close, it looked gray, not blond. He had sculpted lips a little too pink for Grace's taste and pretty, almost girlish ears tucked close to his scalp. Graying chest hair tufted in the V of his black silk shirt, and he wore a gold necklace that made him look strangely out of date. All he needed was the hip jut and finger twirls and he could have been in the background behind Travolta in *Saturday Night Fever*.

'What do you think you're doing?'

He hadn't let go. His fingers pressed her carotid. Lights popped in her eyes. She kept eye contact but she really couldn't breathe now, getting to be a problem here. 'Choking.'

For an instant he stared at her, puzzled. He dropped his hand. She doubled over, gulping air. Nausea roared up and she fought the impulse to vomit.

'Try anything — '

'Bathroom?'

He jerked his head and she rushed through a jumble of art crates and stacked canvases, suddenly sure she wasn't going to get there in time. She leaned over the filthy bowl, her legs trembly, scalp wet with sweat. Long after her stomach emptied she kept throwing up.

She wiped her mouth and gargled with water she cupped in her palm.

'Here.' Robert shoved a shot glass at her filled with amber liquid. 'Drink.'

She gripped the glass and tossed it down, not thinking. *Oh no oh God oh no oh God.* Scotch. *Warm*, golden scotch malt, 80 proof, had to be, burning gold in her mouth.

She spat it into the sink, furiously gargling

over and over. That taste, that warm beautiful taste going down, she'd find a bar, buy one, just one . . .

'You're starting to anger me,' he said. A muscle near his eye twitched.

She patted her way to the window and stared at the street. A couple were climbing into a limo at the curb. She could still taste the scotch. It made her knees weak. She didn't know which side he was on, that was the problem, and until she did, she wasn't going to risk bringing up Katie.

'You owe me answers.' He pressed in a little too close and she shifted backward.

She glanced around the room. Did he have Katie? Was Katie there somewhere? Her eyes roved over the crates of canvases, taking in an easel with a half-finished painting that looked like one of those kids with the big eyes, only this kid had Legos for arms and stood over a land mine. Dusty filing cabinets. Mailers. Crates. Too many places. All without Katie.

'I told you,' she said. 'The blue period, something about the eyes — '

'Eyes, you think I don't know my own press? Who are you and what do you want?'

He held his hands loosely, fingers taut, shoulders massive. A sharp pain galloped through her intestines and she ran for the bathroom again, shutting the door. He followed her; she could feel him breathing, listening, and she felt stripped and afraid. Had he done something to Katie?

'Going to the bathroom. Mind?'

He said something she couldn't hear and his shoes scraped against the cement as he moved away. She looked around. There had to be something there she could use. Against a two-hundred-pound man who pumped iron? She only had another minute before it would be obvious to Robert what she was doing. Besides what she was doing. A small, cramped space with a toilet and sink. Prisons had better bathrooms. She could clang on the pipes. Maybe somebody downstairs. Over the noise? Not likely. Nothing. Where was picture wire when she needed it? A box cutter? Or glass for matting photos? She could break a piece, slip a shard into her pocket. He was an artist; he should have more stuff.

Only there was no wire, no razor, no glass, no nothing, except fear jangling her body and flooding her with primitive chemicals that all spelled death; she was going to die there, in a dirty space with a maniac artist who didn't even have the decency to stock his bathroom for emergency hacking, and Katie gone, so gone, with no one left to save her.

She'd dropped her bag on the floor when he grappled her. The keys. They were still in her pants pocket. She could rush the freight elevator —

Robert banged on the door and she jumped. 'You expired in there?'

'Not yet.' She finished, washed her hands, dried them on her top. She opened the door.

He stood in the middle of the room, arms folded over washboard abs. She'd have to get around him to the elevator. She picked up her

227

bag and her hand stole to her pocket and touched the keys. Distract him long enough to leap into the elevator, drag the gate locked. She'd bean him. She'd bean him with the keys and —

'What does the silicone queen want now?'

'Excuse me?'

Frieze scowled. 'Don't give me that.'

'Honestly, I have no idea what you're talking about.'

'Think I'm some rube off a turnip truck? You give her a message from me.' Frieze flexed his fingers and she backed away.

A lie came bubbling up, born of the hours she'd spent poring over medical charts. The Spikeman had left her the charts, placed them, like bodies arranged — *God, no, don't think about bodies* — he wanted her to use the charts. 'I'm pregnant. Something's wrong with my baby's heart. I researched, tried to learn everything. Five years ago, your wife was pregnant and you went to the Center for BioChimera. What happened there? Nobody tells me anything; I thought, maybe if I came here, I could save my child.'

Grace stopped.

Dumb surprise washed across his face. His mouth gaped. 'This isn't about alimony?'

Alimony. He thought Grace was a spy for his wife. Ex-wife.

'This isn't about hiking up the already criminal amount I pay that shellacked leech every month to get her nails done?'

She swallowed laughter. No wonder Robert

Harling Frieze bartended his own opening. Downplayed how well things sold. There was probably a Robert Harling Frieze sales rep working the crowd, discreetly closing deals far from attorneys and an ex wanting still meatier chunks of artist Bob, the industry.

'No. No. It's about what happened to you and your wife at the Center for BioChimera in La Jolla. She was pregnant and had a sonogram and I need to know — '

'Let me get this straight. Terry didn't send you.'

Grace shook her head. He studied her sharply and nodded finally, believing her.

'Now please repeat everything, I didn't get any of it.'

She felt weak. She looked around for a place to sit and settled onto a packing crate.

'Remember that sonogram five years ago at the Center for BioChimera? Where you found out the baby your wife was carrying had heart problems?'

'You're not a reporter?'

'No, no,' Grace said. 'I — my child is at stake.' The air went out of her and she felt close to tears.

'You want to know what they did.' His voice was flat.

Something fluttered inside, some warning. She lifted her head, alert. 'What they did,' she repeated.

'That's why you came, right? To find out about the second sonogram.'

'I want to save my child,' she said, her voice low.

He looked at her. Grief convulsed his features. 'Your baby will die horribly if you do this, no matter what they promise you. What have they told you so far?'

'Nothing.'

'They make you sign the form, says they're not liable, it's experimental? Injecting the mother with this unknown substance. What was I thinking?'

She grew still. Slowly, she straightened. 'What are you talking about, injecting?'

'I'm talking about the second sonogram, lady. The one they don't record, or if they do, it's in some code only they can read.'

She stared, not comprehending.

'They took you back in there — late at night for us — rigged up the machine again so they could look at him, and injected something.'

'Who did this?'

He barked a laugh. 'You actually think they'd use their right names? Ter and I tried to find them later — spent thousands — it was all hush-hush.'

'What did they look like?'

'People, okay? The woman was middle-aged, sort of faded. Didn't look like much. The guy — I only met him when he set things up and that was all. This is weird, but being an artist, I remember he had great cheekbones but kind of wild eyes.'

'Did you meet them through the doctor?'

He shook his head. 'We'd made it back as far as the lobby and Ter needed a minute, that's what she said, to catch her breath. We'd had the sonogram and the doctor had told us the news about our baby's heart. We collapsed on a sofa and I was doing my best to comfort her, when suddenly, on either side of us, there they were. At first, we thought, Jeez, give us some room, and then we realized they were there because of us. To this day, I don't know where they came from. They were lurking, waiting for us. That's how it felt later, when I thought about it.'

'What did they inject? Do you know?'

Robert sighed, scraped a meaty hand through his hair. 'We knew Trey — that's what we named him — would need a transplant early. That's why Ter was so upset.'

Voices on the stairwell and laughter, silenced by the guard, calling them away.

'They cover themselves, say it could kill the baby, have you sign a release — but who believes that part, when you know if you don't do something, your kid is as good as dead? They told us, we did this, there'd be a heart for sure for him, when the time came.'

'For sure.'

Robert nodded. 'And that it would be a perfect match. That's impossible, you know? But we were desperate, willing to try anything.'

'So you came back late at night.'

'They'd told us where to go. It wasn't the hospital side. It was the research side. There was another couple down there first. Like they were running us through an assembly line.'

'What did they look like?'

'The other couple? Scared, I remember. That should have been our first clue to run like hell,

231

but I didn't put it together until later that they were probably there for the same thing. They came out of the examining room. She was young. Maybe still in her teens. I just remember she looked like she was in shock. Like she'd been hurt. Her husband was a little older, maybe early twenties. We were willing to do anything to save our son. Even did the vitamin booster.'

'Booster. Who did that?'

He shrugged. 'Same lady. Just after he'd been born. She came to our house instead of us going there and then I never saw her again. God, we were stupid.'

'What happened?'

His scowl deepened. Fists shot up and for a terrible moment, Grace was certain he was going to hit her. 'Want it? Fine, lady, whoever you really are. Here it is, be my guest.'

Robert Harling Frieze ripped a loose bedsheet off a large Plexiglas frame and held it up.

The blue period. Los Angeles.

A boy. A baby.

Half baby.

Half monster.

Robert Harling Frieze had perfected hybrid art, taking found photos and attaching — *attacking*, Grace thought, was more like it — bits that assaulted the senses.

Whatever anxiety the twenty-first century held, he'd stuck his thumb into the current of dread that defined the age. It was brilliant. It was hideous.

He'd taken photos of Trey from different angles and merged them together. A beautiful toddler stared back, maybe two years old, soft smile, dimples, eyes.

Eyes. Too many eyes. Pained. Beseeching. Baby fingers spread. Knobbed.

Gray slime molds sucked at the canvas face, the neck, the back.

Living mold encased in Plexiglas.

Tumors eating the photo. The baby.

'We were willing to try anything,' Robert said again. 'This is what started the end for us, right here. They stuck him with something. Stuck her. My wife.'

'What happened?'

He shook the painting. 'This is what happened. No, Trey didn't get a transplant. He got tumors. Hundreds of them, shunting his optic nerve, crowding his cortex, lumping his skin, twisting his spine. Making this.'

He smiled savagely. His eyes filled with tears.

24

She stopped at a late-night Target and bought toiletries and a change of clothes. As an afterthought, she cruised the Halloween aisle. Everything was picked over, but she found a Cleopatra wig wiry with electricity, and added it to her purchases.

Ever since Katie had vanished, Grace felt as if she'd abandoned her old life, perhaps for good. All she had was what she could carry with her, and the burning need to find her daughter. That meant playing the game. His game. Wherever it led.

After Robert Harling Frieze showed her the canvas, he collapsed in huge, barking sobs that brought the second-floor guard running up the stairs two at a time. In his hands, he carried a manila envelope with her name on it.

It was getting familiar now, the low-level minion delivering her marching orders, what she was supposed to do next.

'Who gave this to you?' She was scanning the thinning crowd from the second-story balcony that looked over the viewing room.

The guard shrugged. 'Some guy with a scythe and pancake makeup.'

She remembered him from earlier and realized wearily she didn't see him on the floor now. 'And he's long gone.'

'Looks that way.'

She walked back to the car before opening the envelope. In it was a registration form for the Century Plaza Hotel. She drove in silence. Katie was usually in bed by eight o'clock, and she'd gotten up early, excited about the party. Grace blinked back tears.

The desk clerk wore a badge with AMELIA in black letters, and red devil horns that sparkled in a nest of white-blond hair. She asked if Grace was going to use the same credit card, and Grace checked the registration form in her hands. It was her Visa. Somehow he'd accessed her Visa.

'Let's put it on this one.' She dug an American Express out of her purse, a small act of resistance. Amelia's fingers clicked across the keys, entering the new data.

'How long will you be staying with us?'

All Hallows' Eve you'll play a part. Ere midnight tolls, I cut your heart.

'Overnight.'

'We have a king-sized bed, nonsmoking, with valet parking, the way you asked.'

Grace thought of something. 'Did my request for a specific room make it into the computer?'

The clerk scanned the information and shook her head. 'I'm sorry, I don't see that here. Which room did you have in mind?'

Grace let her shoulders relax. At least her room wasn't bugged. 'Something high that can't be accessed by an adjoining room.'

From somewhere in the hotel came the grinding beat of a live band. She remembered passing a sign advertising an accountants' convention. Next to the lobby an escalator rose, bearing a doughy woman dressed as Bo Beep talking with a man in a sheepskin jacket. A Halloween minimalist, that one. The Spikeman could be there, watching. He could be the sheepskin guy, glancing her way as the escalator carried him out of view.

The clerk slid the key card across the counter and pointed with a lacquered fingertip at a tower. 'You're on floor twenty-three. Need help with your bags?'

Grace shook her head. 'Traveling light. Business office. What time does that open?'

'Not until eight.' Grace had already started walking away when the clerk called, 'Oh, yeah, I forgot. There's this.'

Amelia put on the counter a wooden pyramid made of mahogany and inlaid with cherry.

'This is for me?' Grace didn't want to touch it.

'You know what it is, right?'

Grace shook her head.

Amelia smiled. 'It's really cool. It's a meditation timer.' She picked it up and studied the bottom and frowned. 'Huh. Looks like it's already been set.'

'Any idea for how long?'

'Looks like six. I'd be happy to reset it.' She reached for a knob on the bottom.

Grace snapped out her hand and stopped her. 'No, no. I'll take it just the way it is.'

She yanked it out of the clerk's hands. She could feel the wood faintly thrumming as she walked to the elevator.

She'd be up well before six. Exhaustion seeped

through every pore, but she feared sleep even more, and the dreams that would come.

Her room looked out over Avenue of the Stars. Traffic droned in a constant stream. There was a movie complex across the street and a busy night crowd of people in costume lined the sidewalk. She wondered if *The Rocky Horror Picture Show* was about to start. She'd gone with friends once at midnight to see it the night before Halloween. They were all in med school and what she remembered most was how cold the sidewalk was in Baltimore that time of year.

She needed a drink. She needed to calm down and figure this out.

She took a shower and curled into a ball. She willed herself to slow down, empty her mind. The Spikeman had led her directly to Robert Harling Frieze and his revelation about experiments done on his son in utero, experiments Robert was sure had later cost his son his life.

The Spikeman was orchestrating what she found.

Parceling out facts, tantalizing bits, horrifying truths. The reality was that incrementally, fact by fact, hour by hour, the Spikeman was forging a relationship with Grace, an intimacy of horrifying intensity. He expected her to discover the truth.

But only in his time. His rules. His truth.

And what would be forged in that moment of comprehension between the two of them? Even in the best-case-scenario — and there couldn't be any other, she wouldn't permit it — even when she swept Katie into her arms and held her and all the Bad Things were gone, would the last Bad Thing still be there, lodged deep, leaking poison?

Would it always be there? Would he?

It was the dark dance of accommodation for survival. She was letting him in. Because she had no choice. And in that humiliating immediacy she was showing him more, baring more of herself, drawing closer to him than she'd ever been to anyone.

Grace had always understood the mechanics of fear, every woman did: the darkened parking garage, the click of a lock in an empty hall, the moment on a street when the energy shifted and a woman knew with certainty things had slid irrevocably from safe to not safe.

They were fragile, those walls, easily breached, and the Spikeman had found the perfect way in. He had stolen Katie, and Grace raised her arms above her head and walked to him willingly. Endured his games. Played along.

She felt like a whore. She felt like a mother.

The only thing worse than what he was doing with her was what he could be doing to Katie. She felt overwhelmed with tiredness and fear.

Where was Katie, this night? Had her daughter slipped into exhausted sleep? And who would hold Katie when she cried?

Grace closed the window sheers and spread the charts and a legal pad out on the table. She started a pot of coffee and thought about it. Robert Harling Frieze's story was one of four. Was she supposed to track the others?

She felt hollowed out. She hadn't eaten all day

except for a bite of toast midmorning. She wondered if there were any messages on her home phone, but if she called and used her code to hear them, Warren's team would track her right to the Century Plaza.

Dump the PI and his pals or she dies.

She called Jeanne. It was after eleven at night but her AA sponsor picked up on the second ring, her voice strained.

'It's me.'

'Have you found her?'

'No.' She explained what she needed and got off the line. The coffee was ready and she poured a cup and stared sightlessly at the sheers. The streetlights were soft blotches of red and blue against the fabric. She waited five minutes and called back.

'Six messages from reporters, all wanting to rehash the shooting. Want their names?'

'Was one of them named Mac?'

Jeanne checked the list. 'Mac. Mac. There's a Mallory,' she said finally. 'That's about the closest.'

'Anything else?'

'Your buddy in the crime lab, Paul Collins. Wants to know what in the hell you meant when you said, 'Katie's in trouble.' Also he found a palm print on the taco van.' She recited the rest of the message and Grace wrote down: *Print doesn't match AFIS files; going to have to search the old way, one palm print at a time.*

'Anything else?' The sharp sound of Helix barking came through the phone line.

'Helix, hush. A couple more things. Marcie

called, said to call her on her private line at work or on her cell, she has news about the wrapping paper that doll came in and — *Hush! Helix! I mean it.* Sorry, and let's see, oh, yeah, and a call from somebody who identified himself as Oscar, Dusty's dad. It's about that drawing Katie sent. He sounded really broken up, but didn't want to leave a message on the phone, just wants you to call him when you can.'

Except I can't, Grace thought tiredly. Annie and Oscar's number was in her address book at home and she couldn't go back there now, it was too risky. She had no idea if Warren had left somebody there when she'd disappeared. She'd forgotten all about the pen pal letter Katie had written to Dusty. It all seemed pointless and far away and infinitely valuable. She wished she could see the drawing again, the smudges and erasions, Katie's scrawling signature, hold it close.

The barking continued and Jeanne said, 'Shit. Gotta go. Somebody's pounding on the door.' Her footsteps retreated and returned almost immediately.

'Grace.' It was a rumbly, pissed-off male voice she recognized immediately.

'Bill. My favorite PI.' Of course they'd tracked Jeanne immediately after Jeanne had called Grace's line and retrieved her phone messages. Grace hadn't thought that through.

'Where in the hell are you?'

'I can't tell you that.' Her hand tightened around the phone.

'You never came out of the postal annex so I went in. You were gone.'

'Put on Jeanne again, okay?'

'I'm not done with you.'

'Just please — '

He passed the phone to Jeanne. She sounded subdued.

'Don't tell them anything, understand?'

'I don't know anything!'

That was true. Grace realized she hadn't told Jeanne where she was. 'This is important. Click off and dial a number.'

'Which?'

'Any number! It doesn't matter! I don't want them star sixty-nineing your phone and tracking me down. If I need to reach you, I'll call your cell. Do it now!'

Jeanne took a ragged breath and hung up. Grace looked around the room.

Safe to not safe.

Any PI worth his license could find her. She had to leave. Now. Before Bill drove up from San Diego, or worse, hired some Los Angeles PI she'd never met to sit in the lobby behind a magazine and track the spoor of her fear when she left. She'd been so relieved to get Warren Pendrell involved, but he'd looped in the private investigator, and now that involvement could cost her Katie.

She scrabbled up her things, remembering right before the door slammed shut that she'd left the timer on the nightstand, and raced back for it, her throat dry. Back in the lobby a pianist sat at the baby grand piano, playing something moody with one hand and drinking from a tumbler with the other. A relaxed group of revelers all dressed as Elvira, Mistress of the Dark, clumped around the bar, their lips slashed in purple, and she could feel eyes on her as she crossed the lobby.

Her teeth were chattering by the time she reached the door.

A fog had floated in and the moist air chilled her to the bone. The valets looked perfectly right on this night before Halloween, dressed in uniforms that reminded her of guests at Alice's tea party, glided and braided in knickers and rounded hats. She sat on the stone bench as they brought the car around, the cold seeping through her pants.

She had no doubt the Spikeman would find her. Her only goal was to let him know she'd followed the rules. She drove aimlessly and found a hotel on Fairfax across from CBS called Farmer's Daughter. Her room was on the third floor, small and clean with a silhouette on the door that looked like Barbie with braids, jauntily holding a watering can.

She made another pot of coffee and worked on her notes for almost an hour. She rubbed her forehead. A tight knot banded her back, right under her left shoulder blade, from tensing over the desk, hunching over the wheel of the car, pushing on to the next thing, hoping against hope the next clue would lead her to Katie.

The legal pad was covered with scribbled notes and she smoothed the top page, as if her hand could somehow free the words and send them skittering briskly into some recognizable solution. Something she'd missed. Exhaustion tugged her down into a cottony wave and she knew she'd soon be yanked hard into sleep, despite her efforts to stay awake.

'Did you ever do anything wrong, Mommy?' The voice was so pure, so clear in her mind, it was as if Katie were still there, next to her. Katie had asked her that a few nights before, when Grace was tucking her in.

It had caught Grace by surprise and then she realized what Katie needed. 'A million things, Katie, but the rightest thing I ever did was having you.'

She stroked her daughter's hair. Katie stared back, eyes grave, waiting for the rest, the set piece, the thing they always did, reestablishing connection.

'Because you, Katie.' It was a whisper. 'You are my — '

'Heart,' Katie finished.

Grace knew then what the note meant.

All Hallows' Eve you'll play a part.

Ere midnight tolls, I cut your heart.

It was Katie. It was all about Katie.

Katie *was* her heart, and if Grace couldn't save her, it would core Grace's heart as cleanly as if the Spikeman had used a knife.

She stared at her notes sightlessly. She couldn't do this anymore. Not by herself. Her mind roiled with images and a wave of helplessness washed over her. She felt utterly unable to act. She wanted decisions to be taken out of her hands, she wanted it not to be up to her to determine what happened, to save Katie.

She was going to have to make that call.

25

All Hallows' Eve, 12:08 a.m.
She wouldn't use the phone in the room or the cell phone in her bag the Spikeman had provided. She waited until after midnight to take the elevator down. She'd slid past exhaustion into a shattered sense of floating. There was a pay phone in an alcove near the lobby but it wouldn't give her the privacy she needed, and she kept moving.

Across the street from the hotel, a ghostly line had formed in front of the CBS building, everybody in costume. A game show, she suddenly thought. They're lined up for *The Price Is Right*. That small, homely desire for fame, however fleeting, cheered her like a faint message from a cooling planet. There was life somewhere else, no matter how distant and foreign, and she would find it again.

Light and laughter spilled from the Tart Restaurant next door but she turned away from it, toward Beverly Boulevard. She shifted her bag. The charts were too important to leave in the room but they were bulky companions on a walk.

She stopped walking. It didn't matter what phone she used. He could track her. He knew exactly where she was that instant because he'd planted something.

It was either in the charts or in the cell phone.

244

Audio bugs, an activated GPS, something. Charts were the easiest; he must have known she'd take them everywhere she went, they were the only clear link she had to Katie. She was going to have to look at everything, the rental car, the phone. He had to be tracking her right that minute, a green pulsing dot of energy.

What had Paul Collins said when she'd inspected the taco van? *Loud was wired . . . a video cam attached to his shirt button.* Put there by the Spikeman. The Spikeman knew electronics.

An all-night diner on Beverly was tucked into a row of darkened shops, and she hurried toward it. She found a booth at the back, ordered vegetable soup and milk, and took out the charts and yellow notepad. The dislocating thing, the thing that unnerved her the most, was that she worked in an environment where everything that was happening to her was absolutely credible, where creepy sociopaths were real, and where it was abundantly clear that bad people targeted good ones, sometimes just for the sheer kick of causing pain.

She hadn't had time to figure out who was after her and why, and now she thought back over her career in the crime lab and wondered about the doers she'd helped convict and what had happened to them. It seemed a long line of foul-smelling, crumbly-toothed meth addicts, interspersed with murderous boyfriends wielding knives and clubs and guns, avaricious employees fearing discovery, furious ex-wives and greedy girlfriends. Nobody popped out.

She shook her head and flung down her pencil, frustrated. It rolled against the charts and caught the edge of the metal clasp on Katie's chart, and Grace examined it as carefully as if she were blind.

A dot no bigger than a pencil point had been attached to the underside of the clasp. Grace remembered a gag gift Paul Collins had given her last birthday, and she rooted through her bag, hoping she still had it. She found it tucked in a zippered pocket, a magnifying glass, and she wiped it clean on the hem of her shirt and studied the dot. Under the magnifying glass, a world of microscopic coils leaped out at her. A GPS device, embedded in the one chart the Spikeman knew she'd never leave behind.

She checked the rest of Katie's chart and found nothing. The waitress came with food and Grace pushed everything out of the way.

'You a lawyer?' The waitress glanced at the charts as she put down the steaming bowl of minestrone and placed two packets of Saltines and a glass of milk on the table. ''Cause I got this custody thing.'

Grace shook her head.

The waitress shot her a long, measured look of suffering, her eyes flinty.

'Sorry,' Grace said. She meant it.

The waitress whirled and fled back to the kitchen. Grace ate the soup and crackers and ordered coffee. It took her another hour, going page by page, before she found it. The metal clasp on the Wingers' chart was slightly thicker and a different color, a deeper silver. Under the magnifying glass, she discovered the thin veneer of plastic coated a delicate tracery of wires. She studied it, knowing she'd seen one like it somewhere before. She drank a second cup of coffee and rechecked the charts and found nothing else. If the first thing she'd found — the dot on the underside of the clasp on Katie's chart — was a GPS, and she was pretty certain it was, then maybe the second thing was an audio bug.

Tracking her. Listening. If he'd gone to that amount of trouble to hear her and track her movements on a grid, it had to mean he wasn't visually spying on her. Not in person. There'd be no need. It gave her a small crack of opportunity, if she could figure out how to use it.

By the time she'd paid her bill she'd thought of the first step.

26

All Hallows' Eve, 2:44 a.m.
There was a pay phone at the Chevron gas
station on the corner of Beverly and Fairfax,
and she pulled coins out of her pocket and
dialed the number from memory. She'd gone
back to the room and put on the Cleopatra wig
and heavy makeup, joining a boisterous group
of partiers as they stumbled down the stairs
singing college fight songs. She couldn't risk the
night clerk identifying her. She needed to be
safely upstairs in her room, tucked in for the
night.

It was close to three in the morning. The line
in front of the CBS building was longer now,
people in lawn chairs and lying on blankets,
eerily replicating the scattered surge of homeless
people she'd seen grouped along the boardwalk
in San Diego.

A solitary car sailed silently past her and she
hesitated, her hand frozen at the coin slot, until
the car picked up speed and made the light.

Marcie answered right before the voice mail
kicked in, her voice thick with sleep.

'It's me.' Grace started crying.

Marcie came instantly awake. 'Oh, my God.
Where are you? What's happened?'

Alert the cops, and Katie dies.

Like Paul, Marcie was a nonsworn, a tech in
the crime lab, not a cop, but it was clear the

248

Spikeman wasn't making that distinction, and what could Marcie do if she got her involved? He'd find out, somehow. She wasn't going to take any chances.

'I've only got a minute.' She wiped her nose with the back of her hand. 'Marcie, what did you find with the birthday paper?'

'You need to tell me what's going on.'

'Please. Don't ask questions and tell no one that I've called. I mean it.' Her voice cracked. 'Katie's life could depend on it.'

'What's happened to Katie?' Marcie cried.

Grace was silent.

'Grace?'

'I can't,' Grace said heavily. A long moment went by. She could almost feel Marcie nod on the line, trusting her, even though she didn't understand, and it filled Grace with blank gratitude.

'First the heart. It was a pig's, from the blood sample, just the way you thought. I gave the clown paper to Paul but he didn't find any prints.'

'How'd you explain it?'

'Don't worry, I didn't tell him. The ink used to write the message was part of a shipment of four million Bic pens sent to supply stores across six different states. The string was something you can get anyplace, but the actual paper itself was gold. I took it to Tracy in Fibers and — get this — it's cotton.'

'Okay, so it's handmade.'

A couple in bunny ears wandered past, hand in hand, chattering animatedly. Grace shifted the receiver to her other ear and leaned into the phone, shielding it with her hand.

'Yeah, but most handmade paper isn't organically grown. There's no trace of bollworm.'

'I give up. What does it mean?'

'It means the San Joaquin Valley. The California Institute for Rural Studies cultivates about ten thousand acres of organically grown cotton, caterpillar free, by imposing a strict ninety-day ban every year.'

'But the paper's blue,' Grace remembered. 'So it was dyed.'

'The fibers are dyed, yeah, and stained the paper a faint blue. Those blue fibers were added to the cotton, by the way; turns out they come from recycled uniforms. Also there's the distinctive stippling of trace metals, the kind found in license plates. I looked it up in Tracy's little book. Seems there's a successful print operation there, where they manufacture survey marking tape, binders, custom files. They tried handmade paper for a while, too, a couple of years back.'

'I'm not getting it, help me out here.'

'License plates. Uniforms,' Marcie said. 'The wrapping paper around the bloody doll and notepaper — both were handmade three years ago in a small manufacturing plant at Folsom Prison.'

Grace shifted the phone.

'Grace? Are you still there?'

'Folsom.'

'Yeah.'

'I'm going to need you to get me in there later

today, say around six or so.'

'It's a Sunday, Grace. And Halloween, in case you're interested. They're not going to do that. That's totally against policy. These things take time.'

'I don't have that.'

'Grace, look, whatever's going on — '

'Marcie.'

There was silence on the line. Marcie said, 'How do I explain it?'

Grace thought about it. 'There's an AW I know. He might come in. He likes working weekends.'

She'd met him through AA. He'd attended some meetings at the group Grace frequented when he was in San Diego on prison business. On a couple of late nights over cups of coffee, they'd shared war stories from work and their last names. Alcoholism had cost him his family, and he'd confided to Grace that he worked all the time because he hated going back to an empty apartment, but Marcie didn't need to know that.

She searched her memory for his name and found it. 'Syzmanski. First name Thornton, but he likes to be called Thor.'

She dug through her wallet and came up with a card and read his home number off it.

Marcie copied it down. 'What do I tell him?'

What could she say that wouldn't circle back to Katie? 'Tell him I'm working a case involving a serious threat against a prominent business-man. We tested the postcard in the lab.'

'Postcard?'

251

'Yeah, there was a postcard, Marcie, but I can't tell you more than that.'

'If he asks?'

'Then I'm in trouble,' Grace said simply. 'No, tell him it's a prominent bioresearcher.'

'Shit. Was it?'

'Who wants this handled quietly.'

'Damn, Grace. This wasn't tested in the lab. You want me to lie for you.' Marcie sounded tired.

'Yeah, I guess I do.'

'My integrity's more important than what?' Pissed, needing to hear Grace's answer.

Than my kid dying. Than my kid gone forever. 'Look, Marcie. Katie's been — ' She stopped, her throat thick. She tried again. 'Somebody — ' She cleared her throat.

Marcie took a breath and blew it out slowly. Grace could hear her start to write, her voice subdued. 'Okay. We tested the postcard in the lab and what? It was made out of the same stock paper as the wrapping paper?'

Grace was silent.

'Are you serious? It was made out of the same paper?'

'It had the same blue thread, that's all I know. Remember this case we worked when I first started five years ago?'

'We worked a lot of cases, sweetie.'

'Closer to five and a half is how long I've been there. The one with the clasp on the file that turned out to be an audio bug that the research assistant carried into top-level meetings to steal biotech secrets for her boss. She'd cut herself on

252

the underside of the clasp and that's how we nailed her.'

'Vaguely. What do you need?'

'Names, the case, how it came out, everything you can get for me.'

'Where can I send it?'

'Can't. I'll call you when I can. Take your cell with you if you go out.'

'I suppose it's too late to tell you to be careful.'

'A little.'

'Still.'

'I will. And don't tell anybody what I said. About Katie.'

Marcie made a sound. 'I can keep secrets.'

Grace hung up, shaken. It was someone at Folsom. Someone who'd worked in a print shop. Who was out of prison now. Or still incarcerated, passing that peculiarly distinctive paper to someone outside. Okay, that was a place to start.

She checked her watch and realized the window of time she felt she could safely be out of the room was rapidly vanishing. She dug into her pocket and pulled out more coins and dialed Jeanne's number, rousing her out of bed and telling her what she needed.

Afterward, she stacked the last of the coins on the narrow shelf under the phone. She was stalling and she knew it. She rearranged the coins. She'd given herself an hour. Any longer and he could find out she'd gotten away.

She'd done everything she could think of to make it seem she was still in her room at the Farmer's Daughter watching TV. She'd called downstairs: hold her calls, she was in for the night. She'd turned off the cell phone and left it and the charts behind, positioning them on the bed next to the TV so the audio would pick up the channel tuned to an old Reagan movie, eased open the door and made certain the hall was clear before slipping into the stairwell, later joining a group of revelers coming into the lobby. This close to Halloween, nobody gave her costume a second look.

Almost half an hour gone. She found the scrap of paper in her purse and punched in the numbers, fed in the coins required, and waited. She could hear him pick up and pat around, as if trying to remember where he was. Asleep, for starters.

Or had been. 'H'lo.'

She'd heard his voice on television. Impossible not to. But this was intimate, deeply personal, and she felt the years slip away, the walls disintegrate.

Her mouth felt clumsy. She said her name and he came wide awake.

'Where are you?'

'I'm only going to say this once. Go to a secure line. Nothing inside the building where you are. Nothing in your car. Secure. Call me back at this number.' She read the number off the phone. 'Have it?'

'What is this?'

'If I don't hear from you in ten minutes, it'll ring into space, Mac. That'll be it.'

'Grace, is that you?'

'Nine and a half.' She hung up and rubbed her arms, trying to warm them. Time stopped.

Bits of memories shot through her mind. The warm lump of Katie's small body heavy against her chest, and there she was, stunned with fatigue, scared and weeping into the downy scalp of this sleeping infant who depended solely on her to survive and she couldn't even remember to buy baby shampoo. A soccer ball hurtling toward the goal and Katie snapping up her skinny arms and diving for it, a look of terror and triumph blazing across her face as she skidded hard across the dirt, reaching up, catching it. Grace standing over the kitchen sink, still jet-lagged and nauseous after three days rattling in claptrap buses and transferring to sputtering small planes and winding up in a jumbo jet lifting into the blue Guatemalan sky like a magic trick, standing there at the sink and squinting at the bright pink square blooming in front of her in the pregnancy test kit, blooming like a rose, and still not getting it, not believing, needing to go back and buy a second kit just to be sure.

The phone startled her. 'Yes?'

'What did the inside of the room look like?'

She checked her watch. 'Look, Mac, I don't have time.'

'What did it look like?'

She exhaled. He made a sound. 'Yeah, that's what I thought.'

He was hanging up. He couldn't.

'Wait!' she shouted, and across the street, a person in line turned and stared at her blankly.

'Where we worked?' Her voice low now, intense. 'Or where you said good-bye?'

She could tell by his silence he was startled. Yeah, asshole, you said good-bye, remember?

'Where we stayed. Location. Description. How it smelled.'

She closed her eyes. 'The walls were bamboo. We slept on a straw mat. We'd left the window open so we could feel the rain. Warm rain. Hot breeze. Not an unusual combination for the Guatemalan highlands.'

He drew a ragged breath. 'God, it is you. I'm so sorry. My business attracts these women who . . . ' He stopped. 'That's not important. What I want to say is, you wouldn't believe how hard I looked for you.'

'You're right,' she said. 'I wouldn't.'

The silence grew.

'You were looking for the story that would get you onto CNN. Looks like you found it.'

That stopped him. His voice changed. 'So the question is, after all this time.'

'I need something, that's all.' She tried to keep her voice even and failed. Her mouth worked and she felt close to tears. She couldn't cry.

'Grace?'

Tears stung her eyes. 'Mac, I'm in bad trouble, and I don't know who else to trust.'

'Oh, honey.'

His voice real now. Not his broadcast voice, plumper, richer, but the remembered voice of the man whose calloused hand had gently caressed her hip and told her he loved her, now and always, forever and ever. The voice of the man who had rocked her in his arms night after night, and buried his face in her hair, groaning as she wrapped herself around him and they melted into each other, sweat and tears and time fusing so that even now, all this time later, it still burned like a chipped star in her heart.

'Talk to me.'

27

All Hallows' Eve, 6:01 a.m.

She was up until almost four in the morning working everything out, and then sleep yanked her into a drugged undertow.

The meditation timer woke her up slowly a couple hours later. First she was aware of a mellow, insistent sound and then it occurred to her she'd been hearing it for some time. She patted her nightstand and finally found the off switch buried in the top wooden inset. Every bone ached and her mouth felt gritty. She lay quietly staring at the ceiling, and then it came rushing in. Katie was gone. She pushed herself out of bed and made a pot of coffee.

If she let herself think about Katie and where she'd spent the night, it would derail her. She stood in the shower under stinging hot water, brushed her teeth, and changed into the clothes she'd purchased at Target: underwear, a dark green T-shirt, and cotton pants.

She was living two lives now and she had to keep them straight. Katie's life depended on it. In the one life, she followed the clues set out by the Spikeman, clues that were leading her to interviews with Robert Harling Frieze and maybe the others. In her other life, she was secretly pursuing avenues he knew nothing about. Leads that might take her to Katie.

She pulled back the curtains. Pale light

washed into the room. This early, the street was empty. She sat at the desk and opened the charts, positioning her legal pad and reviewing what she knew. Five charts all from the Center, one for Katie's simple surgery, four for ultrasounds revealing fetal heart anomalies. Two of those kids got lucky: Eric Bettles last year and Hekka Miasonkopna sometime soon, each getting hearts-in-a-box built out of their own cells by Lee Ann Bentley.

That left two. Robert Harling Frieze lost his son to tumors when the toddler was two. Tumors the grieving artist was certain were caused by an experimental injection his infant son had gotten at the Center when he was still in utero. Is that what happened to the Wingers' baby?

She reached for the Winger chart. Five years ago, Fred and DeeDee Winger lived in Fallbrook, a rural community east of San Diego. Twenty-two-year-old grad student Fred worked as a TA at San Diego State, while his young pregnant wife, DeeDee, typed and filed in a law firm.

She tried the Fallbrook number first; it was disconnected. Then she called San Diego information and got the alumni office number for San Diego State. She dialed, wondering uneasily why she hadn't heard from the Spikeman. She'd been given until six. It was already almost seven. Why the silence?

'You're lucky I picked up,' the woman at the SDSU alumni desk said into the phone. She spoke in a Southern drawl in one run-on sentence, not breaking for air. 'But it's

259

homecoming week, alums piling in. We're trolling, hoping to snag them, which is why I'm here on a Sunday morning early. We're not supposed to give this out.'

'It's his wife I'm trying to reach. Went to high school together, a reunion's coming up.'

Grace could hear her fingers clicking. 'Okay, I'll bite. You tell me the name of the high school, and I'll tell you their last known address.'

Grace skimmed the chart, hoping to find the name of Dee Dee's high school. Nothing. She'd messed up and she knew it. She hung up, frustrated. She tried the law firm where DeeDee had worked. Nobody picked up. Hardly surprising on Halloween and a Sunday. Grace read through the chart again and called the history department where Fred had been a TA. An automated voice told her to call back Monday.

She massaged her neck, wondering what else she could try. Hekka was probably at the Center by now, judging by Mac's report. If Grace was there in person and had time, she might be able to gain the parents' trust, but not over the phone. That left the Bettles family in Poway. Their son had received the first heart-in-a-box a year ago. Maybe they could tell her something.

She got their number from Information and dialed. A woman answered on the second ring. Grace's voice was ragged and close to the edge.

'Mrs. Bettles?' What Grace wanted sounded freakish now, a crank call.

'This is her sister, Margaret. They're gone

until Monday. I can take a message.' Her voice was sleepy.

'This is Grace Descanso. I'm calling from San Diego. I'm a civilian working in the police crime lab.'

'Good Lord. What's happened? Are they okay?'

'Of course, I'm so sorry. I — no. Everything's fine. They're fine.'

'What's this about?' Margaret's voice had hardened slightly.

'No big deal. Fund-raising actually. Sorry to have bothered you.' She hung up slowly.

She checked her watch: seven-eighteen. Time was melting again. She had to hurry. Grace's eyes went to the phone face and for the first time she saw the blinking red light.

Her heart skidded. She pressed the message button and was mechanically connected to a voice that told her the call had come in at 6:07. She'd forgotten to tell the desk to let calls through. How could she have forgotten? She licked her lips, waiting.

'Mommy. Mommy.' That was it, the entire message, those two words.

A sad little voice, a cry. It dissolved her, brought her to her knees.

She was here and she'd missed the call. Missed talking to Katie.

Tears rolled down her face. She called the front desk. 'I'll take calls now.'

'Of course, Ms. Descanso. Are you all right?'

'Just connect my calls.'

'Of course.'

261

Her plans were flimsy, a house of cards smashed by a monster. She felt small and alone and too tired to do this. This wasn't going to work. She wasn't going to get her back.

She's alive. The thought darted across her consciousness as fast as a green bird. There and gone. *Katie's alive.* She was still alive at six that morning.

Grace's system flooded with adrenaline so hot she doubled over, panting, wondering if this was how a heart attack felt, or a stroke. Her scalp prickled with sweat.

It didn't help Katie if she fell apart. The only chance her daughter had was here. With her. She had a sudden flash of Katie warbling country-western songs in the car, curly head thrown back, legs golden, lashes curling on her flushed cheeks: *dance! I hope you dance!*

The phone rang. Her throat closed. She picked it up. There was static on the line, a sound that could have been a dog barking. Or a child's cry.

'Don't you want to know what she's doing right now?'

'I want to talk to her. Put her on the phone.'

'You missed her, Grace. That wasn't nice.'

Grace squeezed her eyes shut. 'Put her on.'

'Too late. Can you imagine how that made her feel?'

'I'd rather imagine how you're going to feel when I find you and kill you.'

His sharp intake of breath made her realize she'd caught him by surprise.

'You think that's funny? You think that's wise?

You can't go around hurting people, Grace. This is what happens when you hurt people. People you love get hurt.'

She tried to find her face with her hand and missed. 'Tell me what I did,' she whispered. 'Maybe I can fix it. Let me fix it.'

He sucked in a savage gulp of air and blew it out softly. 'This is the only freebie you get. The only time you can miss a deadline.'

The click was a dead sound in her ear. Grace rolled into a trembling wet ball, hugging her knees and moaning. No. No. She was going to breathe in and out. She stayed that way, knees jammed against her chest, until she felt her heart slow.

There was a knock on the door. She sat up and wiped her face. 'Yes?'

'Delivery from CVS Pharmacy over on Fairfax and Third.' An Asian accent.

She rolled cautiously off the bed. 'I didn't order anything from the drugstore.'

'Package, ma'am.'

She hesitated and opened the door. A middle-aged Asian stood holding a package wrapped in brown paper, sealed with masking tape. He handed it to her and turned to go.

'Wait.' Maybe he knew something. 'Let me pay you.'

She darted into the room for her bag and ran back out. The blue hallway was empty. She heard the sound of the elevator starting. Slowly she closed the door and relocked it.

This timer was shaped like a bullet with a computerized face and was about the size of her palm. Across the top in computerized pixels pulsed the notation:

4 0 5 N 5 N S R 5 8 SUPER 8 PUNCH.

Underneath it was the number 240.

28

All Hallows' Eve, 8:04 a.m.

Grace checked out of the Farmer's Daughter and parked a block away, the timer beside her on the front seat as she dismantled the cell phone. It was clean. Feverishly, she combed the car with the magnifying glass and discovered an audio bug. That made two. One on DeeDee Winger's chart, and one under the dash. But no video. At least none she could find.

He could have hidden one. She had no real way of knowing and that scared her. If he'd hidden a camera she hadn't found, then it was the worst news, news that could get her daughter killed. The number on the timer had changed to 229, so that must be minutes.

She looked at the message in the timer again: 4 0 5 N 5 N S R 5 8 SUPER 8 PUNCH. A combination, maybe to a safe, but where? Until she heard from him, or figured out what he wanted her to do, she'd go forward in her secret life. Praying she didn't screw up.

Traffic was light on Fairfax Boulevard. Ten minutes later, she pulled into the drive-through lane at a Taco Bell and gave her order. Afterward she drove into the parking lot and spotted the silver rental parked at the rear with a space next to it. All the saliva in her mouth dried up.

He'd parked the way she'd asked. He was silhouetted behind the wheel and even at a distance, she recognized him. He must have been looking for her in his rearview mirror because he got out of his car then and took away the orange cones he'd used to save her spot. She parked as he climbed into his car and reached across to open his passenger door. She focused on the tricky part, taking the food and the cell phone with her, leaving the charts on the seat, but quiet with the food bag so the Spikeman would think she'd left it there. She shut her car door hard, turned, and slid into Mac's car, closing his door gently before she let herself look at him.

'Hello, Mac.'

'Grace.' His voice was unsteady.

The years had etched deep grooves, but he still had the same searching eyes and thick gold hair, laced with brown and a little gray. He smelled good, soap and fresh laundry, and wore a long-sleeved cotton shirt in a soft blue-green the exact shade of his eyes, a color that made his skin look like honey. The optimism in his eyes had died. He looked older. Weary. He'd cut himself shaving. A nick by the jawline. Grace had the sudden sense of spiraling into space, everything sliding away: years, jobs, the life she'd built. He kept staring. She swallowed.

'God. You look like hell.'

She felt her face warm. She offered the bag. 'A burrito or a couple of soft tacos.'

He hesitated and reached down into the bag, still looking at her. He came up with a soft taco and stared at it dumbly before unwrapping it.

'You still have it.' She reached over and touched the Swiss Army knife attached to his key

266

chain. She'd given him that the last day they'd been together. Now it was worn and polished to a satiny pewter. He locked eyes with her and looked away.

She knew she needed to eat. The exhaustion and panic had churned up an acid soup in her stomach and the thought of food made her sick, but she picked up the burrito and opened it. She tore off a small piece of tortilla and chewed. It tasted like cardboard.

'Your cell phone's off, and you brought them?' Her eyes roved over the leather seats and settled on a leather satchel in the backseat.

'I use a BlackBerry; it's off, and yes, I brought them. Three cuts on each CD, both CD's exactly the same, although it doesn't make sense. Aaron's been up since you called, getting them ready.'

'Thank him for me.' She checked her watch. 'We'll need them in about ten minutes.'

He finished the taco and balled up the wrapping. He reached for the second taco and unwrapped it. 'You said somebody close to you was kidnapped but you couldn't get the police involved. What's that about?'

She cracked open the carton of milk and drank, alternating sips of milk with a bite of burrito. It seemed the only way to keep it down. They ate in silence.

'Are you involved with anybody?'

He looked at her. 'Come on, Grace. I drive up from San Diego so you can ask me — '

'This is hard enough,' Grace said.

Mac stared out the window. 'Was. Someone in

San Diego, most recently. I'm not anymore.'

He turned and regarded her and she knew she needed to say it before she lost her nerve. 'My daughter,' she said. 'It's my daughter who's been kidnapped.'

He sat in silence. It was a long silence. 'You have a daughter?'

She read the carton. It was 2 percent, fattier than she liked, but she needed the calcium.

'How old is your kid?' His voice was strained.

'Young.' She drained the carton.

'How old?' It hung there in the air, and Grace could see him doing the math, figuring out when he'd seen her in Guatemala, how many years that would make a kid, if it was his. 'Grace?'

'Her name is Katie Marie and she just turned five.' She couldn't finish the burrito. She rewrapped it and put it away. The silence went on so long Grace wondered if he'd heard.

'Five. You're sure.'

'Sure what? Sure that she's five? Sure that she's yours? Come on, Mac. Even you.'

'It's a reasonable question. A lot can happen.'

'A lot did,' she said quietly.

He scraped a hand through his hair. 'I can't believe it. I have a kid. A daughter. Five. Why the hell didn't you tell me? It's not like you had no idea where to find me.'

That much was true. A couple high-profile romances, one with a television colleague, had been splashed across the pages of *People*. Not the covers, Grace reminded herself sourly. Just a couple of inside pages, but still. And she could always find him on CNN if she needed a fix. 'We need to get things ready.'

He reached into his leather satchel and pulled out two Sony Walkmans with burned discs.

'Where do they start?' She looked at her watch. She had three minutes maybe.

'What do you mean?'

'The sound. What's the first sound? And do they match exactly?'

'Ten seconds of dead air at the top, followed by six minutes of ambient sound. Exactly what you asked for, and yes, they're calibrated so they exactly match.'

'Eating? Bag rustling?'

'Exactly what you asked for,' he repeated. 'Starts with the sound of a person sitting down. What does she look like? I want to see her.'

Grace had expected that and she slid a photo from her wallet toward him. Mac studied it and looked up, his eyes silvery with tears.

'She's beautiful.'

'Yes. You can keep it.' It cost her to say that and she looked away.

'She's got your curly hair.'

'It's your color hair, though. That kind of caramel blond. She tans, too.' Grace knew her voice held pride and love and a kind of wistfulness.

'Your eyes,' he said. 'That dark brown with the black lashes. And your dimple. The high cheekbones. And your smile, look at that.'

'Think so? I think it's yours. I always thought — ' She stopped. It hurt talking this way.

'What position does she play?'

It was a soccer picture taken when the season started. Katie held the ball casually gripped against her. The sun glinted, turning her curly pigtails bright gold. She still had her baby teeth and she was grinning, her face wide and hopeful.

'Mostly D. The coach puts her in as goalie second half, when everything's fallen apart and he needs a kid with courage. She plays T-ball softball, too. First base, usually. A little rec basketball. If there's a trophy involved, she's in.'

'They give out trophies to five-year-olds?'

'Oh, yeah. For everything but ballet, that's why she quit dance.'

He smiled. 'Goalie. She's going to be a heart-breaker.'

'She's already broken mine,' Grace whispered.

He looked across the car at her and their eyes locked; for a single instant, they were parents. Only she'd kept him away. For the first time, she understood she'd done something terrible to Katie she'd never intended.

Something terrible to him. To them all.

'What? Having a dad isn't important? You of all people know that's not true.'

That stung and she looked away. 'Can we do this later? We don't have time.'

He wasn't ready to let it go. 'How did you explain it? All the birthdays I never sent anything. Christmas. She must have been miserable.'

'I told her you were dead.'

'What?'

'I couldn't deal with it.'

'You couldn't? It's always about you.'

Something low and venomous came into her voice. 'They stoned her to death. Did you know that? Sister Mary Clare.'

She would not cry. She would not let him see her cry. She could see the shock on his face. He hadn't known. All these years, she'd been so sure.

'Oh, my God.'

'Mac.' Pain in her voice. And caution.

'I came back late, it's true, but I came back, just the way I said. The clinic had been burned to the ground. Nobody would talk to me and when I got death threats, I pulled out. I went stateside, looking for you. You'd disappeared. You never showed up at Cedars-Sinai. I got so I checked death notices and finally I had to believe that you'd died there in the village.'

'I didn't want you to find me. My phone's in my maternal grandmother's last name.' She added, 'It took everything I had just to get through it.'

'Through what, Grace? What happened there?'

She shook her head and turned away. Two kids on bikes barreled into the parking lot.

'That's supposed to work? A head shake, looking out the window?'

'I can't, Mac.'

'You're going to have to.'

'No! I don't!' she lashed out. 'If we don't get her back, he will kill her, Mac, by midnight tonight. These damn timers, these clues. I don't know where he's taking me except north away from San Diego and I don't know why.'

Her voice cracked and she yanked her hand

back when he tried to touch it.

She checked her watch again. She opened the car door and scooped up the Walkmans, positioning her cell on the seat. 'If my cell rings, don't answer.'

'I can help, Grace. You have to let me help.'

'I'll be right back.' She snatched up the Walkmans and unlocked her car door noisily, and this was the tricky part, she pressed *Play* on both Walkmans simultaneously. She realized she was holding her breath. She waited until both Walkmans kicked in: stereo sounds of somebody sliding into a car, sitting down. She left one Walkman on her seat in her car, slammed the door closed, and sat again in Mac's car closing the door, the second Walkman in her lap.

Paper bag rustling sounds filled the car. As far as the Spikeman knew, Grace had come back into her car, slammed the door shut, and was starting to eat. In Mac's car, the cell phone the Spikeman had given her started to ring.

'Quiet. Don't say a word. Don't even breathe.'

Mac nodded. She picked up her phone, clicked it on. 'Yes.' The car was filled with a symphony of eating sounds, lips smacking, bags ripping.

'Drive-through and then stopping for a potty break? Terror give you the squitters?'

She could feel Mac start to shift in his seat and she held up a warning finger.

On the CD, somebody chewed noisily. 'I'm having breakfast in the car,' Grace said into the phone. 'You mind?'

'I can hear.' His voice was biting.

Relief shot through her. It was working. Grace said, 'How's Katie?'

The Spikeman hesitated a beat too long. 'Sleeping. You're running behind, Grace, and that's not acceptable. There's a schedule to keep and you're ruining it. You don't want to do that.'

She closed her eyes. 'I got the timer. I need help understanding.'

'Very true. Many things happen on journeys.'

Journeys. Okay, so it was directions. Had to be. She examined the timer. She was to drive north on 405. North on the 5. 'They're directions, right?'

He was silent.

'I want to know she's okay. My daughter.' She'd almost slipped. Almost said *our*. Mac was looking at her, face strained. 'Put her on.'

He broke the connection. Grace put the cell down slowly. The sounds of eating coming from the Walkman were obscenely loud in the silent car, but it marked the time they had left. A little under a minute.

'He's got audio bugs,' Mac said. 'And a GPS. That's why you had us park together.'

She nodded. 'So it would look like I'm still in my car when I'm sitting here in yours. Could you Google someone on your BlackBerry?'

'You can have it.' He pulled it out and handed to her. She shook her head.

'Your BlackBerry's got a GPS in it; it emits a pulse. We can't risk having him pick that up and figure out we're working together. I think the most we can do is use it for a quick

273

fifteen-second search. Before I forget . . . '

She pulled a wad of yellow-lined pages from her pocket.

'It's all there. What I need you to do. Right now can you turn on your BlackBerry and Google Fred and DeeDee Winger? Where he's working. Where they live.'

She checked her watch. She had maybe thirty seconds left.

His fingers clicked across the BlackBerry keypad. 'Too many Wingers. Nothing.' He turned it off.

'It's okay, I'll find them. Any idea what SR is?' She was looking at the timer.

He studied it. 'State route. Should be marked on the highway. How will I contact you?'

'Can't. I'll call you when I can.' She scooped up her cell and the Walkman.

He looked at her, his eyes sad. 'For God's sake, Grace, tell me what happened.'

She pushed open the door. 'It's all written down. Everything I need.'

'Damn it, Grace, if I'm going to be blamed for something, at least tell me what the hell I did. You told me to go, remember? You told me to chase the story.'

'Would it have made any difference if I'd asked you to stay?'

It hung there, the question. The answer.

She started to get out and he reached for her and pulled her into his arms, a hard hand on her back, one in her hair, his breath sweet and warm. She smelled his familiar scent, a deep male scent of loam and musk, emanating from some private solitary place deep inside. 'We'll get her back,' he said.

There was a moment when they almost kissed, and then the moment passed and he released her and she fled into the hot California air.

29

All Hallows' Eve, 8:47 a.m.
She was crying as she pulled out of the lot and she had to be very careful on the road, trying to find the 405 to take her north. Her shoulders shook silently, but occasionally a great braying sob would escape and she'd clamp her fist in her mouth and bite down hard.

On her shelf in the box in the closet was a yellowed news article, the creases white with age. It didn't matter; she knew the article cold.

DOCTOR OF THE HEART
Dateline: *San Quetzalda Verapaz,*
Guatemala
by *Mac McGuire*, AP WIRE SERVICE

She'd been there two weeks performing surgery under the most primitive of circumstances, overwhelmed with the need and the poverty and the sheer numbers lining up for aid, some having walked for days carrying loved ones too ill to be moved, trying in her spare moments to train some of the older orphans who lived in a single room at the clinic.

Tired, and happier than she'd ever been in her life.

Then a bus with a piano incongruously strapped to its roof like a dead horse rumbled into the square and braked to a dusty stop.

It's a four-hour bus ride from Guatemala City, past roadside stands with paint-blistered signs selling Pepsi and Orange Crush, but a lifetime away for one 27-year-old American pediatric heart surgeon.

The bus had climbed through an explosion of green coffee fields and pine forests. Mist fogged the air; the locals called it *chipichipi*, a pulsing dew that made the bus seem as if it were suspended in a fevered dream.

That's how it had felt, when she'd seen him.

There was a lake near the clinic on the edge of the village and Grace was wading through reeds, holding her skirt bunched around her hips. It was melting hot and she'd piled her black hair high, not realizing she was being observed as passengers piled out in a torrent of good-natured sweaty shoving. Grace lifted her gauze skirt in two wings, her high bottom cupped. She sank into the lake.

The water bubbled. She rose, smoothing back her hair, and turned. And out he stepped, tall and rumpled blond amid the dark-skinned small Indians, a pack on his shoulder and a hungry gleam in his eye. In that instant, Cristina, the doe-eyed teenage assistant, began screaming in the clinic and Grace ran from the water, dripping wet, and darted into the tin-roofed building.

Dr. Grace Descanso completed a joint residency in pediatrics and thoracic surgery in December.

And celebrated by coming here. A sweat-soaked, mosquito-netted, dilapidated shed, where she's spending two months working with some of the world's most needy.

He told her he'd flown into Guatemala City and had climbed into the first bus that was leaving, not concerned about where it was headed, just happy to be on the road, and she envied his spontaneity, and how he'd always known he'd wanted to be a writer, was a writer, could go anywhere and be anything, reinvent himself at will in a million different ways.

Disappear, if that's what it took.

And come back to life whenever he wanted.

That's what she wanted, yearned for, that kind of spontaneity. She'd had to be so controlled her entire life; it was her only defense against the chaos of living with Lottie and trying to protect her younger brother, Andy. And now here was a man, loose, funny, his mind greedy for information, wanting everything, wanting her. Two hours into the ride, he'd heard about Sister Mary Clare and the miracle doctor helping her. And yes, he'd added, tilting his head back and narrowing his green eyes. He'd heard she was gorgeous.

Looking almost as young as some of her patients, with expressive intelligence in her brown eyes and glossy black hair to her shoulders, Descanso looked over the makeshift OR with its IV lines and sparkling surgical instruments sterilized in water pumped by hand.

'Come on, don't make me sound like some saint,' Dr. Descanso said. 'Sister Mary Clare's the one who's here. I'm just helping out.'

The nun shook her gray head. 'I do simple things, test for malaria and TB, teach basic hygiene, but Grace . . . ' She stopped and shook her head again.

Sister Mary Clare runs the basic first aid station here, along with an orphanage for kids whose parents have been killed in the aftermath of a decades-old civil war, still bursting into flame in remote villages far from the watchful eye of organized government. The aging nun sent a request back to her home parish in San Diego for Band-Aids and simple medicines.

And got Grace.

Mac had followed her into the clinic and threaded his way through a waiting room crammed with suffering. They watched him go down the hall toward the sounds of a child screaming, their eyes dark and silent. Nobody spoke.

In the two weeks she's been here, Dr. Descanso has saved a 30-year-old woman from bleeding to death after the stillbirth of her fourteenth child; repaired a hernia the size of a watermelon in a man bent over from a lifetime of heavy lifting; and helped a five-year-old boy take his first steps after resetting a bone from an old break that had permanently twisted the boy's ankle so it pointed backward.

The air inside the makeshift OR was hazy in the heat. A mother was holding down a child shivering in shock, her right arm almost severed from an accidental machete wound. The child had been running, the mother was explaining in Potomki, when she tripped and fell, extending her small arms to break the fall. Grace was moving fluidly, washing up over a makeshift sink, listening as Sister stood in jeans and a wimple and translated, coaxing her young assistant Cristina to apply pressure to staunch the bleeding, and rapidly assembling everything she'd need.

Grace glanced up and they locked eyes. Mac looked a little pale. 'If you're going to stand there, help,' she snapped. 'Wash up first.'

He was unreliable, he told her that right from the start. Couldn't be counted on. His work drew him, even as he slid into doctoring that week, working next to her, sleeves rolled up. At night, they wandered streets and she felt a faint rustling of dark suspicion directed at foreigners — especially those who drew blood and comforted children. They were outsiders, and everyone knew it.

It made her afraid, not only for herself, but for him. Afraid for the times he'd disappear, telling her it was best for her if she didn't know where he'd gone, or whom he was seeing. She'd spotted him once in the town's only café, hunched over a guttering candle, talking earnestly to a dark-skinned man she didn't recognize.

There were stories everywhere, and he actively sought them, making plans to join scientists doing DNA testing on the bone shards of *desaparecidos*, plotting a trek through the Cerro Cahui reserve to study endangered wetland Peten crocodiles, and the darkest, most violent story of them all, whispered reports of organs snatched from children and sold on the black market.

But the things he didn't talk about were balanced by the things he shared, stories she sensed he'd told no one, stories he'd saved up, stories for her.

He'd grown up in the mountains of Colorado in a place called Bergen Park, five miles from Evergreen, and had ridden a bus to school every day of his life until he could finally afford his first rattletrap car. He'd had the perfect childhood, he'd told her, until the day his younger sister fell through the ice in Evergreen Lake and drowned.

And then things had pretty much gone to hell, but he was okay. His dad had left and then come back, and his mother was dazed with grief and lost to him and his brother, but he played football and his dad still came to all his games. His mother, too, both of them sitting together on the cold, windy bench, crowding in on his younger brother as if they were emperor penguins protecting their chick, as the Cubs dashed onto the field to the roaring cheers of the crowd. So. University of Colorado at Boulder and some lost years writing a novel that never went anywhere, a stint embedded in Afghanistan, a graduate degree from Columbia School of Journalism, and no despair, really, except for that thing about his sister.

He'd told Grace that as they scrubbed down the simple room she used for OR. From outside came the faint sounds of the orphans' childish laughter, and the wet slap of laundry as Sister Mary Clare hung the wash. Grace looked at him searchingly.

And damned if his eyes didn't fill. He turned away, embarrassed.

She came up suddenly on the balls of her feet and kissed him. His shirt was open and small beads of sweat glistened in the warm hollow of his throat. His hair was tousled gold and his eyes were wide, and in that instant, she'd seen a new life for herself, stretching out through the decades, babies growing up, having babies of their own, years spilling like puppies one on top of the other, a life full of buoyant opportunity, because Mac was in it.

The simple but life-changing surgeries are a far cry from the sophisticated procedures she's spent her residency learning how to perform, heart transplants for kids.

In less than seven weeks, Grace Descanso goes back to her old life stateside, forever changed.

Her kiss was direct. His body radiated heat and more than that, substance. He was the most present man she'd ever met, and when he kissed her back, she felt a current sing up her spine. She exhaled and her lips parted and he pulled her to him, and they kissed with an intensity that thrilled and alarmed her. He sunk his hands into her hair and she closed her eyes and moved her hands over him as if she'd been doing it all her life.

A week later, he had found his way to her bed. It had been the most natural thing in the world, having him there standing in her room, next to the open window. Moonlight had slanted across the simple wooden table. A hot breeze from the Guatemalan highlands brought the rich scent of tropical rain, moon lilies, and pine. They'd taken turns washing in a tin basin and she still wore a gauze shift, naked underneath.

He reached for her hand. She took his and guided it under the nightgown. Her breast was warm and heavy in his hand. He grazed the nipple with his palm and she made a sound, eyes half open, glazed. He kissed her mouth, her naked shoulder, her breast, and she took a step back and lifted the nightie over her head, shaking her hair free. She dropped the nightie to the ground.

She exhaled. She wasn't tethered anymore. There was nothing holding her except the substance of the man standing in front of her. He found her mouth and kissed her. Her arms went around him and tightened. He sank his tongue into her mouth. There was desperation and hunger and a yearning to come home. He pulled back the sheet and laid her down, looking at her. She reached for him.

He dropped his shirt and came to bed. She could feel his heart beat in the flat of her hand. His hands moving, too, electrifying, hot. Their mouths. She shifted and took a breath. She was drowning.

He groaned and opened his mouth and she dug her hands into his back, and when he entered her, she trembled and cried out and she tasted sweat and the salt of her own tears. She wanted him to know every corner, every dark place. The sadness, the constraints melted, and left behind the truest part, messy and enthusiastic, bubbling with laughter, staring in squint-eyed wonder at the world. He believed in her, and that belief fueled her own and made her careful with him, wanting to know everything he'd held back, his weakness, imperfection, the things that brought him joy. She wanted to be the carrier of that kind of joy, glad and alive.

'They call me *doctora de la corazón*.' Doctor of the heart. And she smiled.

'And she smiled,' she repeated softly. She scrubbed away tears.

Twenty minutes out of Los Angeles, she stopped at a Unocal station where she borrowed a key for the women's bathroom. She carried her cell phone and charts with her and left them on the dirty sink while she started the second cuts on the Walkmans. She locked one of them inside the restroom. There was a pay phone next to the self-serve island and she closed the booth door and put the second Walkman down on the ledge as she called his cell. On the Walkman, there were the simple sounds of somebody using a toilet.

Mac picked up on the second ring and she said, 'I'm going to tell you a story. It's short, because we don't have much time. It started the morning you you were due back at the clinic.'

She'd awakened to the sound of men with machetes hacking a space big enough for a landing strip. Those same men barred Grace's path when she tried to leave the building. That's when she and Sister Mary Clare discovered that Miguel and José, the two youths they'd been training as assistants along with Cristina, had vanished during the night into the mountains. But first the boys had drawn blood from all nine of the younger orphans.

'Sister Mary Clare put in a call for help to the diocese in Guatemala City, but the signal kept breaking up.' Grace kept her voice steady. 'Outside, there was a banging sound against the building. The men were stacking dried vines against the side of the clinic. A funeral pyre. The kids were terrified. And so were we.'

At the Unocal station, a carload of teens pulled up to the gas pump and a boy got out, his pants dragging. He slouched into the office to pay. Grace closed her eyes, remembering.

Besides the suffocating heat, the thing she remembered most was the smell. Nine orphans, the oldest ten, with sour diapers and sickly sweet ointments covering raw skin, harsh disinfectants steaming the washroom; the dusty odor of wood crumbled by termites, and outside, the smell of vines bleeding sap.

'We heard a noise from the sky. Thunder, we thought at first, though the sky was a blazing blue. It was a military helicopter.' She leaned her forehead into the glass of the booth. On the CD, the sound effects had moved to the washing-up stage and Grace knew time was running out. Maybe four minutes, tops, while the person on the CD brushed her teeth and put on makeup.

'Guerrillas. Two men in fatigues and boots carrying Uzis stepped out, backs to the helicopter, protecting the man who emerged next. Deputy General Tito Velasquez. I'd never heard that name before that day. And after him, two men in white lifted out a stretcher and ran toward the clinic with their patient.'

'A wounded guerrilla,' Mac offered, his voice steady.

'It was a girl on the stretcher, Mac. A little girl.' She pressed her hands against the glass to steady herself. 'Deputy General Velasquez's daughter. She was six. Close to death. Sister Mary Clare and I launched into triage, stabilizing her, getting in an IV, taking her temperature, the basics. The girl we'd been training to help, Cristina, was useless. Wandering in circles, whimpering. All the time, an Uzi was trained on us. And then we saw why. Velasquez had gathered up all the little kids, the orphans, and lined them up against the wall.'

It came shooting toward her past the barriers of time, every detail clear. The paint flaking off the walls. Heat beading the girl's stretcher, the back of her gray hand where they'd punched in the IV. Cristina twisting her hands into her dress, a sturdy girl of eighteen with bad teeth, shaking, on the edge of hysteria.

'*¿Esteban? ¿Quién es Esteban?*'

Velasquez's voice pulsed with urgency, staring at the wide-eyed kids pressed against the wall as far away from him as they could get. Nobody breathed. Velasquez's mouth twisted into a terrifying caricature of a smile and Grace was suddenly very afraid.

'*Tengo dulces para Esteban. Y tambien para el niño que me diga dónde está.*' Treats for Esteban and the kid who points him out.

Velasquez pulled out taffy pieces, and every hand along the wall shot up. Ten-year-old Esteban himself, dark-eyed and solemn, stepped forward confidently, his hand out.

'*Yo soy.*'

'*¿Esteban?*'

'*Sí. Soy yo.*'

Velasquez signaled, and the two men in white stepped forward and clamped their hands around Esteban.

'*Oye,*' Esteban protested. '*Mi dulce.*'

'*Me olvidé.*' Velasquez whacked his head and grinned, like that old V8 commercial. *I forgot! I coulda had a V8!* And he gave each of the kids along the wall a piece of candy.

He saved the biggest piece for Esteban. A golden caramel with a creamy white center, all wrapped in cellophane. Esteban grinned, unwrapped it, and popped it greedily into his mouth as he trotted off between the two big men in white. One of them carried a bag. They took him to the office at the end of the hall and closed the door.

It was a small sound, awful in import.

A crack. A sigh. The sudden smell assaulted their senses, the scent of urine and feces and raw meat. Grace made a move and the Uzi came closer. Sister Mary Clare dropped to her knees and prayed.

'What is this? What do you want?' Grace cried, voice rough with terror.

Velasquez reached in his jacket pocket and Grace stumbled back, certain it was a gun.

It was a clipping. The AP wire story by Mac McGuire. About the bright young heart surgeon, working miracles.

Capable of anything.

'*Mi hija necesita un corazón.*' My kid needs a heart. His voice was matter-of-fact. A to-go order at Pizza Hut. Grace stared uncomprehendingly.

From the other room came the sound of blade cracking bone.

Cristina burst into tears and a toddler clutched her knees, moaning. The kids looked apprehensively toward the sound and huddled close. A preschooler wailed and was shushed by her brother.

They carried it back into the room in a cooler, exactly like the ones they used stateside after a harvest.

Grace knew then what was in the other room. What was left.

'No. I won't do this. I can't.'

'You can and you will.' He had a faint American accent. 'We did tests.'

The blood tests, she realized in horror. The blood Miguel and José had drawn.

'And Esteban is the best match.'

'You could have gone to a hospital. There were other ways.'

Velasquez exchanged looks with the others. He smiled. 'Let us just say, I am a person of interest. Hospitals are out of the question.'

'I don't have the right equipment. The ventilator doesn't work. You'd have to bag her the entire time.'

An eye flick at the man with the Uzi. He lifted it and leveled it at Grace. 'Sister will bag her.'

Sister Mary Clare, with arthritis in both hands. It was painful for her to do simple sutures anymore, and now she was expected to manually inflate a child's lungs for several hours? Sister Mary Clare struggled up from her spot against the paint-peeled wall and stared wonderingly at her twisted fingers. Next to her, a child whimpered and buried her face in the nun's waist.

'You don't understand. There's no way this would work. I'd need a team. There's no cardiac monitor. All I have is a pulse oximetry, no automated blood pressure cuff — I couldn't regulate her vitals and without that — It's doomed, understand? It's crazy even suggesting it.'

'You will not call me crazy,' Velasquez screamed, the cords in his neck extended.

Nobody breathed. A soldier banged through the door carrying a cardboard box and slammed it down. The children jumped. The soldier peeled back the lid. Inside were syringes, latex gloves, drapes, IV's. All opened. Unsterile. The soldier looked impassively at Grace.

General Velasquez shrugged toward the man holding the cooler. He was short, dumpy-looking, with hooded eyes and balding black hair. 'I brought an anesthesiologist and a nurse to assist.'

She felt tears rise. 'Then let them do this, not me.'

'No, you're the heart surgeon, *you*,' he said sharply. 'You will do this.' He pressed his lips together angrily. 'He's already dead, Grace. All you can do is save yourself.' He touched his daughter's hair. 'And her. You must save her.'

'And if I don't?'

'I kill one child in this room for every minute you delay.' He glanced at his wrist. A Rolex knockoff. 'Starting . . . *now*.'

They'd been teaching the kids English. They'd been so proud of their English.

Along the wall, the kids froze, and she could see helpless, beseeching understanding in their eyes.

'I need to sterilize. And scrub. Everything has to be cleaned, we have to boil water.'

Cristina collapsed wailing down the wall and the children dived after her, burrowing for comfort.

'Get them out of here.' Grace's voice came from some other place, autopilot, and her medical training kicked in, those labs, the thoracic surgical rotations at the Center.

It had all led to this, the dismemberment of a little boy she would feed to a little girl.

To save the others. To save herself.

There was no air-conditioning and sweat poured down her body, blinding her vision. Next to her, Sister Clare struggled to bag the lifeless girl, pressing her heel into the bag, finally, when her fingers gave out. Every muscle in Grace's body ached. It felt like hours, but in reality, the fast part was putting the heart in. There was simply no way this would work and she knew it. She was closing the dome of the atrium when it occurred to her to ask what would happen if she failed. When, was more like it. If she did the best she could and the patient still died.

'But you won't let that happen.'

'Not on purpose but — '

'You will not let that happen,' Velasquez repeated more sharply.

She took a slow breath. Nodded. 'No. I won't.' She kept her voice calm, steady. 'But if she dies — she won't, but if she dies. For any reason — '

Velasquez jerked his head toward the window covered in a sheet to keep prying eyes from looking in. 'You know what they think out there. What the rumor is.'

She kept working. Sweat coated her body under her gown and dripped down the inside of her gloves.

'The rumor's always been, the *americanos* steal the children, chop them up for body parts, for organ transplants. You've heard, yes?'

Her fingers slipped and she steadied herself and kept suturing. The man with the Uzi nudged her.

'Yes.' Her voice was faint. 'Yes, I've heard.'

291

'And do not think that man will save you, that man who writes so beautifully.' He crumpled the newspaper article and shoved it back into olive green pants. 'Did you not wonder why he came so far on a bus?'

She blinked back sweat. Her vision blurred.

'He did not come to write this. You were, *cómo se dice*, a cover, *una distracción*. He used you, Grace, you were nothing to him. He had to meet a dangerous man here, a man who promised to take him to the place where they steal children and cut out their organs. He needed a reason to be here, and when he saw you that first day, he picked you.'

He made a small, savage gesture of dismissal.

'Out of a hat.'

Desolation swept over Grace, the kind that's the result of hearing a terrible truth. Mac had lied to her, from the beginning.

'Grace,' Mac said into the phone, his voice anguished.

'Let me finish, Mac, there's only a little left.'

She squeezed her eyes shut, and saw again the general, the small, still body of his child on the table in front of her. And the cost of the lie.

The general's eyes flicked back and forth from Grace to the table, to the gray body, already slipping away.

'If she dies. If my Maria dies, we will tell the villagers we interrupted a ring of organ thieves. Stopped you. Too late to save Esteban, *pobrecito*, but the rest. You've seen the dried vines piled against the clinic walls.' His voice was conversational.

She used the back of her wrist to wipe away the sweat.

'It will burn. The clinic. You will burn. Or be stoned. Or torn apart.' He shrugged. 'One match. A well-aimed rock. One has so little control over the masses.'

At the Unocal station, the kid had finished pumping gas and the car pulled away, and Grace jerked up her head and looked blindly around. Her heart rang in her ears.

'Grace.'

'She died. The girl died.'

On the phone, Mac made a small sound.

Grace blinked.

'Sister Mary Clare was stoned to death. Two kids and Cristina died in flames.' Grace's voice was almost inaudible. 'And I gave up medicine.'

'Oh,' he said. His voice was tired. 'Oh.'

The sounds on the CD ended. 'Story's over, Mac. Time's up.'

30

All Hallows' Eve, 10:34 a.m.
Grace crested the low brown hills out of Castaic
into the Angeles National Forest, part of her not
believing she'd told Mac, part of her knowing
that telling him was the best chance they had of
finding Katie, and the only chance she had of
coming back to life.

Even at meetings, she'd only told part of that
story. It was too hard. It made her feel tender
inside, fragile.

She drove carefully, staying just over the speed
limit, keeping the windows down and the air
blowing hard across her face. There were dark
shadows in the green parts of the forest, but
most of it was winter brown. She needed to get
into Folsom later, and as long as the Spikeman
was sending her north, maybe she could still pull
it off.

It was better, almost, being exhausted. The
edges of pain were softer. How sharp would that
loss be days from now, completely rested, if
Katie was still gone?

She picked up the timer. SR 58. State route
58, she translated. And then Super 8 Punch.

Ninety minutes left. *This is the only freebie
you get. The only time you can miss a deadline.*
She picked up speed. Driving. Spending this day
driving was a terrible thing. Unless Katie was
there, and she was moving toward her. She

294

thought of Mac again and the pressure of his hand on her back, the sweet smell of his breath, and after a while, she turned on the radio and let it carry her the rest of the way, but time was speeding by past her window.

An acrid taste filled her mouth, the smell of an old forest fire, or maybe the smell of fear.

Dust clouds obscured the road and out of the dust, a sign appeared: BUTTONWILLOW 58. She sailed past a field of sugar beets. On the periphery of her vision, a motel sign hung over the freeway. SUPER 8.

58 Super 8.

It registered a beat too late and she swerved to make the exit, barely missing a van. She corrected the wheel, sliding wide, and slammed on the brakes to stop from hitting the car in front of her, her stomach heaving in a mix of acid and alarm.

She thrust her head out the window and took gulps of air to steady the nausea. A gasoline tanker truck was swinging wide into a Mobil station and she inched around it, searching for the yellow and black motel sign jutting up on metal stilts. It stood at the end of a line of fast food outlets — a building faintly encrusted with the chalk that came from desiccated air.

She pulled into the parking lot and burst out of the car, going into the lobby past a small kidney-shaped pool. Nausea rushed up her body and she shot into the bathroom, quivering over the toilet, her face damp. She wet a paper towel and sponged off her face, composing herself before she looked at the timer. Fourteen minutes left.

A broad-faced young woman was poring over a Sudoku puzzle at the counter and looked up in concern when she saw Grace. 'You okay?'

Grace nodded, trying to think of the best approach and feeling the press of time. Across the parking lot, workmen carried racks of folding chairs toward a small stamp of grass between the hotel buildings. Grace put the timer on the counter and smiled.

'Sudoku. I love that game. I'm always getting right to the end and finding two sevens in the same square or something. Frustrating. I'm so happy to see you — ' She stared at the name on the badge. 'Lizzie.'

Lizzie grinned back. 'Do I know you?'

'Probably not. Here's the deal. I'm playing this game. It's like a scavenger hunt. I was supposed to come here. This motel. At least I think I was. And ask for Punch.'

'Punch? I don't know anybody by that name.' Lizzie frowned nicely and put down her pencil. 'Show me the clue exactly. Maybe I can help.'

Grace put the timer on the counter. The numbers had slid down, melting to twelve.

'High-tech.' Lizzie turned the timer over. 'Pretty cool coming up with a game like this.'

Grace nodded faintly. She pointed at the number along the bottom. 'That number? That means I have less than twelve minutes left to get this thing solved.'

Lizzie's eyes widened. 'Oh. My. Okay. Well, then. Let's see. Punch punch punch. I use a hole punch. Could that be it? Are you supposed to take it someplace? I don't mind.'

Grace shook her head. 'You wouldn't lie to me, right?'

'About what?' Lizzie sounded deeply offended.

'Earlier, there was this clue, but I couldn't get to it unless I did all this stuff. So even though the guy was supposed to give me the clue, he couldn't even tell me he had it, unless I came up with — '

'Oh, oh, I get what you're saying. No, no. I'm on your side.' Lizzie looked around the lobby and cocked her head, studying the breakfast room, now silent and empty.

'There's punch in the machine outside,' she said finally. 'One of the choices.'

'Show me.'

Lizzie abandoned her post and raced outside toward a pop dispenser, her sandals slapping the tiles as Grace followed.

She crouched down and examined it. Nothing behind the rubber flap, in the coin dispenser, or jammed into the dollar slot. She stooped down and looked underneath. Nothing.

She dug a dollar out of her wallet and fed it into the machine, on the off chance when the punch thundered down behind the flap, it would dislodge a note with it.

Punch. Nothing else. Now Lizzie was looking worried, her pale blue eyes clouding.

'God. I don't know what to suggest. I really don't. Can I see the timer again?'

Grace held out the timer. Seven minutes. That was all. Lizzie smiled reassuringly. 'Well, it's not like somebody's going to die if you can't figure this out. It's just a game, right?'

Grace's heart stalled.

Behind them in the grassy enclosure, the chairs had been set up in rows facing a low wooden platform. A workman said, 'Hey, Lizzie. Where's the curtain?'

'Inside, Jimmy. I'll get it.' She turned to Grace. 'Sorry. I gotta go. Good luck, okay?'

Grace stood frozen. Three and a half minutes. *The only freebie you get.* Punch. There had to be something she was missing. Something obvious. Jimmy was sunburned in a white shirt and jeans, and a time card lipped from his back pocket.

Punch. 'What are you setting up?' Grace fell into step with Lizzie and Jimmy.

'Oh, it's this thing we do for the kids Sundays. Most of the time it's reading. It's a puppet show today. You should stick around. It's going to be cool.'

Grace stopped. 'Puppets. Punch and Judy?'

Lizzie sucked in a breath. 'Damn. That's right. Punch and Judy. There you go.'

Grace turned urgently to Jimmy. 'Do you have something for me? I'm Grace. Grace Descanso.'

31

'I have to get the key.' He patted his pockets. 'Where'd I put it? Here somewhere.'

Two minutes left. 'What do you need?' Grace's voice was harsh. 'The timer?'

'Yeah, I'm going to need it when — oh, yeah, I remember.' Jimmy pulled a small brass key from his wallet. Grace thrust the timer into his calloused palm.

The numbers at the bottom of the screen whirred in a dizzying blur. He turned the timer over, examining it. They were standing amid rows of folding chairs near the makeshift stage.

'You have . . . thirty seconds.' The voice came from the timer, clear, female, and as toneless as if it had been calibrated by machine.

Grace gripped the top of a folding chair, squeezing her eyes shut, and behind her eyes was Katie. If this failed, there would be nothing left holding her to this earth, no reason to stay.

'You have . . . ten seconds,' the voice said.

'Okay, okay,' Jimmy muttered. 'Found it. Oh, shit.'

Grace snapped her eyes open. Jimmy's large hands clumsily tried to fit the key into a tiny slot in a crease of the timer. He dropped the key.

Grace snatched it up.

'Five . . . four . . . three . . . ,' the voice counted.

'I'll do it.' She grabbed the timer out of his hands and slid the key into the lock.

'Two . . . one . . . '

She twisted it. The timer pulsed in radiant bursts of blue and violet, as if she'd come to the end of a computer game and was rewarded with a miniature light show, a rainbow of light.

'Con . . . grat . . . ulations. Write . . . this . . . down.'

She stared at Jimmy, stunned, trying to regroup. Jimmy pulled a pen from his pocket and positioned it over the back of his time card as the voice intoned ten numbers.

Jimmy pressed hard, making the numbers big. A moment of silence, punctuated only by a sigh from Jimmy as he slid the pen back into his pocket.

'Good . . . bye.'

The screen went dark. Grace bent over and took a long breath.

Jimmy whistled. 'Wow.'

'Double wow,' Lizzie said admiringly. 'Nothing like this ever happens here. Pretty cool.' She offered the Sudoku page. 'You want to use this to copy the number?'

Grace nodded her thanks and copied the number Jimmy had written down. She tucked it carefully away in her wallet.

'You have something for me, Jimmy.' Grace needed to keep moving. The dark end of this terrible game was drawing near; the monster with the teeth stood on the hill with its weapons raised and she was riding to meet it.

'It's in my truck.'

She followed him silently to the parking lot. Jimmy pulled a small bubble-wrapped package out of the glove compartment and handed it to her.

'It was this Internet site. They wanted somebody who lived in Buttonwillow and was a gamer. Random posting. I wrote back and before long, it came in the mail.'

Grace unwrapped the package. The timer was as slim as a compact and the size of Jimmy's time card, indented slightly on one end, as if it fit into something. Bits of colored pixels floated to the surface, a conjurer's trick. She expected the familiar numbers, she was counting on them, actually, to shore herself up, but the numbers were gone now. Across the top of this timer a single word coalesced and pulsed: TONIGHT.

It was scarier, not having numbers, not knowing how much time she really had.

Ere midnight tolls, I cut your heart.

But that didn't tell her anything. It just meant that by midnight, it would be over. It was 12:40, by her watch. Eleven hours and some change, the outer limit of time left before Katie was killed.

As she stared at the pulsing word, the random-colored pixels began forming a shape.

A shape she knew well. It was a picture of her daughter, smiling up at her, under the word TONIGHT. Katie was smiling straight at the camera, eyes bright with trust, curls cascading. Jimmy bent to the asphalt, wet his finger and dabbed it to the ground, picking up something.

'Any return address on the package?'

'Nope. There was a postmark, but it was blurred. Someplace back east.'

'Were you supposed to call anyone when I showed up? Or leave word on that site?'

'That's the thing. It crashed a few days ago. You know how these things go. This fell out when you opened it.' On his finger were two small shiny letters, the kind she'd seen sometimes when she opened birthday cards that spilled confetti.

Both the letter *D*. *D D*. DeeDee.

DeeDee Winger. At the end of the last timer, after the pixeled light show, a voice had intoned ten numbers. That had to be DeeDee Winger's phone number. She slid the new timer into her bag. 'I have to leave. Thank you,' she called over her shoulder. She ran for the car, passing parents shepherding children in costume.

32

All Hallows' Eve, 3:08 p.m.
It was DeeDee Winger's work number at a farm community called Lodi, not far from Sacramento. It was farm country, and as she drove past miles of irrigated crops, the sky itself seemed drained of color, a milky blue that shimmered in the heat and made her feel curiously short of breath. Exhaustion and unreality twisted in a tight knot behind her eyes.

She had the timer right beside her on the seat, so she could see Katie's face. She first noticed it about half an hour away from DeeDee's farm, and she gave a small cry and pulled over to the side of the road.

Part of Katie's shirt had been eaten away. The pixels chewed.

It was after three when she pulled into a gas station in Lodi and bought a Snickers and a pack of Camels from a cashier dressed as Oscar the Grouch. The can she was wearing clanked as she pointed Grace in the direction of the Wingers' farm. Green miles of cotton, pistachio, and garlic stretched to the horizon, punctuated by toiling laborers and huge machinery.

Grace drove slowly down a dirt road surrounded by vast groves of almond trees bristling with gray-green hulls. A shaker moved through the shivering trees, gripping trunks with hydraulic vises that rattled the almonds into blitzing sheets. Not far from the parking lot she spotted the administration building, and a security guard pointed her toward a beige corrugated building that vibrated with sound.

She found DeeDee Winger wearing a trim jumpsuit and clear goggles, standing on a viewing platform in a room the size of a hangar. The medical chart put her current age at twenty-four. Almonds roared down an angled path of belts in front of her.

'Cattle padding,' DeeDee yelled over the noise. She gestured at thin paper shells, hurtling down into a compactor that pressed them into a soft, grayish block. 'Livestock bedding. Nothing's wasted.'

'Could we go someplace a little less noisy?'

DeeDee checked her watch. 'I can break in five.'

★ ★ ★

The company lunchroom was a low, Spanish-tiled building, air-conditioned and clean. Grace followed DeeDee to an empty table near a window as they put down their trays. At a long table by the window, farmworkers hunkered over trays, speaking Spanish. Out of uniform, DeeDee was plumper, wearing peach-colored shorts and a flowered shirt, sleeves rolled up.

'Know much about almonds?' DeeDee cracked open a milk carton and poured.

'Just that an Almond Joy wouldn't be much without one.'

DeeDee grinned briefly and closed her lips

over a crooked front tooth. 'The Central Valley, we move more than 600 million pounds a year.'

Grace made the appropriate noises as she dug into a chicken salad.

'Know who's snapping them up right now? China. We send out twenty-five million pounds just to them. Amazing, considering the almond probably originated in China.'

Grace kept eating and she could feel DeeDee rein back her enthusiasm. 'You didn't come to talk almonds. Tell me again, I couldn't hear much over the sorters. Of course, at this point, I can't hear much at all. We've been at this twenty-four-seven since August. Thank God harvest ends today on Halloween. So what do you need?'

DeeDee looked at her, her face trusting and open. Grace took a long swallow of her drink. 'I'm getting a master's at San Diego State — '

'No kidding, that's where my husband went.'

Grace nodded. 'Well. I'm getting a psych MA, focusing on neonatal issues. Exploring the lengths to which expectant parents will go, in order to save the baby's life. My prof unearthed names of patients who'd had troubling sono-grams that fit in that category. You're just the first one I'm contacting.'

'Oh.' DeeDee took a delicate bite of tomato. 'I'm confused. How did you find me?'

Grace nodded, prepared. 'Your husband's TA job. They update their former employee records.' She shrugged. 'Probably find my shoe size on the Web, look in the right place.'

'That explanation doesn't make sense.'

'It would if you Googled yourself. You'd be amazed.'

'Medical records are sealed.'

'You signed a release at the Center for BioChimera.' Gambling that if the Frieze couple had signed one, so had the Wingers. 'It allowed your record to be shared for medical teaching purposes.'

DeeDee ate in silence. A flush crept up her neck. She put down her fork.

'My whole record?'

Grace shook her head. 'A very narrow document. Your name. The troubling sonogram. A notation that you'd signed a release form. That's it. But the release was signed shortly after the sonogram and the Center is a prominent research facility, so my guess was, you'd signed it to try something experimental. Something you hoped would save your baby's life.'

'Fred didn't want us doing it, but I felt like we didn't have any choice.' Her eyes suddenly brimmed with tears. 'I'm sorry, I didn't expect that, it's been so long.'

Grace reached for her hand and DeeDee grabbed hold. Her hand was hot.

'Okay. What do you need to know?'

'I guess basics first.' Grace took out her notepad and opened it to a fresh page. 'Kids?'

DeeDee slid her hand away. 'Two. Freddy's only six months, and Diane's almost three. They stay with Mom the days I work.'

The oldest was almost three. So the fetus DeeDee Winger was carrying five years ago didn't make it. 'Forgive me for taking this into a painful area. Five years ago, you were pregnant.' Grace's voice was gentle. 'And your sonogram revealed a heart anomaly. I'm curious. What happened at the Center after you signed the release?'

A long moment went by.

DeeDee ducked her head. 'This is confidential. Don't use it with my name, okay?'

'Absolutely.'

DeeDee glanced around the room and lowered her voice. 'I have epilepsy. The ob-gyn told me later maybe the drugs I take to control it, maybe that caused it. Epstein's anomaly.'

Grace nodded.

DeeDee swallowed, looked away. 'Both my kids are adopted. I never wanted to risk — '

'You miscarried,' Grace said quietly.

'Not right away. They explained it. How drugs that today are routinely prescribed to save lives, once were experimental. How if we agreed to go forward, it was free.' She looked at Grace, her eyes shot with pink. 'I never would have agreed, if I'd thought there was any chance — '

'They told you it was free. You were trying to do the right thing to save your baby.'

DeeDee nodded miserably. 'We knew she'd need a transplant. That's why we were at the Center. It was a girl. We found out that much.' She plucked at her paper napkin, ripping it.

'What was the doctor's name?'

'Dr. Michael Yura. Gave us his card. That's how I remember.' She spelled it. 'The nurse called him Mike and she told us her name but I didn't write it down.' She swallowed hard.

'We were young and so afraid, and we'd just gotten such terrible news about our baby's heart.'

'You still have the card?'

'Not anymore. After we adopted, I tossed it. Didn't see the point in keeping it anymore.'

'Where did you meet them?'

'They followed us out to our car. They said they could do something that would radically increase our baby's chances of being matched to a donor without hurting her. All we had to do was come back later that night for a second sonogram. Said we'd be working through the research side of the facility, not the hospital side, and that most assuredly our ob-gyn would not approve, so if we decided to return, we needed to know that it was experimental, not accepted procedure, and to keep it quiet. That was the main thing we agreed to. Not to tell.'

Her voice caught. The tissue was a small pile of snow next to her untouched plate.

'Some warning went off; I mean, why late at night? But I was too afraid to ask. Fred and I were going through a hard time. He was stressed; we were kids, broke, all I heard was the part about how maybe they could do something that would help save our baby.'

'Do you remember what they looked like?'

'That's just it, we never saw them again. And I was crying so hard I don't really remember. When we came back that night, somebody different met us in the lobby. A young woman in a white lab coat. Knew our names. I thought at first she was just a little kid. Couldn't be old enough, and she told us she wasn't, she was just the messenger.'

The messenger. That's what Jasmine called herself. 'Remember what she looked like?'

'Really beautiful black hair, I remember that. Looked almost Indian.'

She had to be describing Jasmine. A schizophrenic woman in her teens, that's how old Jazz was five years ago, involved in something sinister at the Center. Warren's business had become too complex for him to properly oversee, and now it could cost him everything.

But the cost to Grace was much greater.

'They kept saying it would be safe. They stressed that part. That's the only reason why we did it. We thought it was like — '

'A second opinion.'

'Yes. We followed her to the research side and down to the basement. It was a small examining room, almost thrown together. God! I hear myself saying this and I can't believe it.'

'People do desperate things to save their kids,' Grace said. She took a long drink of water and finally looked up. 'You met the doctor downstairs. What did he look like?'

'It was a woman. Solid. Older than me, so that covered a lot of ground. Her hair was kind of, I don't know, bland, like she didn't take care of it.' She swallowed again. 'Said her name was Dr. Margaret Moyerson. Not a medical doctor, she stressed. A bioresearcher dealing specifically with transplant issues in neonatals.'

DeeDee gazed into the distance and Grace waited.

'She had a sonogram table right there and she had a gown waiting, and I changed and lay down, and she put the gel on me and hooked me up. Fred held my hand. I saw my baby's heart beating, tripping like a little bird.' She choked and went on. 'It was so big, the needle. She acted surprised that Dr. Yura hadn't told me there'd be an injection.'

A bell blasted. Workers shuffled to their feet, depositing trays and moving outside.

'Wait, Dr. Moyerson injected something?'

DeeDee nodded. 'Directly through the uterine wall.'

'What did it look like? The injection?'

'Cloudy pink. I remember thinking, a girl color for my little girl. I felt it immediately, this sharp pain. I could see it on her face, a kind of alarm. It didn't happen for another week. Cramps. Fever. Nausea. I wasn't even sure it was connected to the injection, you know? It took me a month or so before I put things together in my mind, and by then, it was too late.'

'What do you mean?'

'We checked the AMA directory after I miscarried. Dr. Yura wasn't listed.'

'And the Center didn't have a researcher listed named Dr. Moyerson.'

'That's just it. They did. Only it was a woman in her late sixties, grouchy and upset that somebody had stolen her identity. As soon as we saw and talked to her, I gave up even trying to explain what we had done. By then, I just wanted to get out of there and put it behind me. But finding that out, that's what made me think that maybe it wasn't my body, with all its problems, that made me lose the baby. Maybe the injection had something to do with it.'

DeeDee stood and scooped the napkin onto the plate of untouched food, scattering the napkin bits like snow.

'When you were leaving the examining room, do you remember if there was another couple, waiting to come in?'

Dee Dee frowned. 'What does that have to do with anything?'

Grace shrugged. 'I'm just wondering if they were doing the same thing to other couples.'

Dee turned even paler. 'You mean experimenting? God, I hope not. We almost divorced over it, it was so bad. It's safe with you, right? I mean, you won't use my name?'

'It's safe.' They cleared the trays and walked outside.

'I'm just wondering how the researcher — Dr. Yura? Was that his name? Figured out your baby had a heart defect in utero.'

'I asked myself the same thing, when I thought about it. They just appeared, you know? Followed us right out of the Center. They were both in hospital whites. It was a research hospital,' Dee Dee said again. 'World-renowned. We thought she'd be safe.'

33

All Hallows' Eve, 3:42 p.m.
Grace took the timer from her bag as she raced to the parking lot, the sour taste of anxiety in her mouth. Katie's shirt was gone. The tips of her caramel-colored pigtails were shifting, the pixels swarming as if alive. Bit by bit the face she loved the most was disappearing.

Ere midnight tolls, I cut your heart. It was already almost quarter of four.

Central Valley spread out in long shadows of neat green fields, the heat of the day hanging heavily in the air. Plumes of dust roiled in localized spots, marking areas in the fields where heavy equipment was in use. The car was where she'd left it, parked at the edge of the lot.

Where was the next clue? Where did he want her to go? He always had the next clue waiting. There was nothing stuck under the windshield wiper. Nothing under the tires. How could she save Katie if she didn't have the next clue?

Two workers trudged down the road speaking quietly in Spanish, and Grace waited until they passed, until she was sure they weren't delivering the next stage of the game. His silence was unnerving, but even worse was the timer. She kept compulsively looking at it, and every time, it seemed that a small part of Katie had been erased. She'd burned up so much time, driving away from San Diego. Was she only burning up time? Would she watch helplessly as Katie vanished before her eyes? She stole a look. The tips of her pigtails were gone.

She rechecked her watch. Jeanne would be at the gas station now, waiting for her. She slid the timer resolutely into her bag as she drove by a group of day laborers on the side of the road, waiting for their ride out.

One of them held a ball hammer carelessly in his hands, and he squatted in the dirt and idly smacked apart stones. Attached to the wooden rail fence on the right side of the road hung a series of painted signs, bearing a homely ad in a jingle rhyme, the kind she remembered seeing in a Walker Evans photo for Burma Shave, signs spaced just far enough apart to whet the interest of everyone driving by. She slowed down and read:

TO TRACK A MONSTER YOU MUST ASK

She slammed on the brakes and veered off the road. Her heart banged against her breast pan. These signs were for her. She waited as a battered truck barreled past her down the road, dust boiling in its wake. She eased her car back onto the road. There were three more signs spaced a distance apart:

THE QUESTIONS THAT RIP OFF THE MASK.
HEAD SOUTH AGAIN. IT'S TIME YOU KNEW

313

THE WRONGS YOU'VE DONE COME BACK ON YOU.

Grace made a U-turn into oncoming traffic and gunned the car amid a cacophony of furious fists and horns. There was less traffic going that direction. A battered school bus had pulled into the parking lot, and the last of the day laborers was climbing on board. She pulled to a stop and ran, banging on the bus door as it clanged shut. The driver opened it, the snarl on his lips fading when he realized it wasn't a day laborer he could bully.

He still made his body look as formidable as possible. 'What?'

She ran past him up the steps and searched aisle by aisle until she spotted him. She grabbed his shirt collar and yanked him straight up out of his seat. It was so unexpected that the ball hammer clanged to the floor.

'Who hired you?'

'¿Qué?' The man's eyes darted. He was in his early thirties, with a skinny face mottled with patches of adult acne.

'Trabajo. ¿Quién es su jefe?'

The driver had lumbered from his seat. 'Lady, are you on or off?'

'Policía,' she said. Immediately the bus began emptying, men running down the aisle in a crush, fighting to get off. She tightened her grip on the migrant's collar.

'Thanks, thanks a heap,' the bus driver roared.

'I'll go after I talk to him, but I have to talk to him.'

314

The driver glared and stomped off the bus. The men clumped under the shade of a wisteria and watched what she'd do. It was just the two of them now.

'¿Quién?' she repeated.

'No sé.' He looked scared and said in halting English, 'I look, I want work, no work. Work!' He mimed banging a sign into a fence. 'Veinte dólares.' He pulled a grimy twenty out of his pocket. 'Es para mi familia. Necesitamos a comer.'

And then she did let him go, feeling lousy. He'd spent all day looking for work, and finally had found it at the end of the day, a chance to hammer up a couple of signs along the road and get a measly twenty bucks to feed his family.

'Here. You take,' he said, almost crying as he extended the limp bill.

'No. No, lo siento.' She meant it; she was sorry.

She left him huddled on the bus, feeling his shame and humiliation and pride and wishing she didn't have so much at stake. Kindness had been the first casualty in this terrible war.

When she got to her car, the cell phone was ringing. She picked it up, watching through her windshield as the day workers scuttled past her and climbed back on board.

She started driving and clicked it on. 'You bastard. Where is she?'

'Mommy?'

Grace slammed on the brakes. She'd ridden a roller coaster once that had later bucked somebody off and killed him, and it was like that, her insides hurtling down a long chute, the velocity knocking her head back, her brain slamming against the skull, the friction rolfing the planes of her face, melting her. She was falling.

The shock made her voice calm, her everyday Mommy voice, loving and matter-of-fact. She clenched the phone, sending all the love she could muster shooting across the phone line. 'Katie, Mommy's so glad to hear you. What do you see?'

'Mommy, where are you?' Her voice was strained, little. 'I'm scared.'

'I know, honey. I love you and I'm going to find you, I promise. I'm looking hard for you but you have to help me. Do you know where you are?'

'No.' She started to cry and the sound broke Grace in two.

'Are you far away from home or close?'

'I don't know.' Her voice trembled, rising.

'It's okay, honey, it's okay. You're doing great. Are there cars around where you are?'

'Uh-huh.' Katie sniffed and Grace could hear her wiping her face.

'How about people? Any people?'

'A lady.'

'What does she look like?'

'I don't know.' Fretful now, anxious.

'You're doing fine. What do you see?'

'It's all black.' Snuffling sound. 'An', an' it feels like it's shaking. Moving.'

The bastard. He had her somewhere in darkness with an accomplice.

'Honey, put the phone down, hide it if you can, but don't hang up, sweetie, just — '

'Mommy!' She screamed. The line went dead.

Grace sat staring blindly out the windshield, panting shallowly through her mouth. Her lips felt numb. She put the car in gear and drove.

The gas station was attached to a curio shop and café. Both bays in the garage had cars up on blocks. Grace saw Jeanne immediately, standing at the rear of her blue Taurus rental car, her flaming red hair tied up with a green scarf. She was leaning on her walking stick. She'd parked in front of the café, and Grace pulled in next to her, got out of the car, and burst into tears. 'Thank you for flying up, renting a car . . . '

Jeanne let go of the stick and lurched into Grace's arms, patting her, smoothing her hair as if she were a child, murmuring over and over, 'It's okay, honey. It's okay. It's okay.'

Grace blindly accepted a tissue and honked into it, allowing Jeanne to take it from her and lead her to the Taurus.

'There's some fruit in the car. I didn't know when you'd last eaten. And something to drink. And my cell. It's yours as long as you need it.'

'I have to make a call on your phone,' Grace said. 'And then we'll talk.'

Jeanne handed her the keys and Grace slid into the Taurus, feeling the relief that came from knowing she was in a space she was certain hadn't been bugged. She'd had to be so careful for so long. She called Mac.

'Are you okay?' His voice sounded strained.

317

'I talked to her, Mac. Not more than five minutes ago.'

'Katie?' His voice was thick with emotion. 'Oh, my God.'

A station wagon was pulling up to the self-serve bay and a Marine in uniform was getting out. His wife opened the other side and helped the kids out. Three little girls in matching kitty costumes headed with their mother toward the café as their father started gassing up.

'Okay. This is good news. This is good. She's still alive. Good. Thank God. Okay. That makes sense. She's in San Diego then,' he said, thinking out loud.

'How do you know that?'

'My contact at the phone company keyed your cell off that last call. The Spikeman's using a cloned cell to talk to you. Stolen.'

'He's got an accomplice.' She told him what Katie had said about a woman.

'My contact's getting a bead using transformer towers.'

'So Katie's still in San Diego.' It seemed as far away as the moon.

'They're on the move. My contact's tracking them directionally.'

'You're saying Katie is in a car?'

'Some sort of a vehicle, yeah.'

'Where?'

'Driving into La Jolla on 5. I've got somebody at the San Diego/Tijuana border, Grace, monitoring that so at least by car, they can't take her out of the country.'

'It's not the police? They're not involved, right?'

'Someone I worked with,' he repeated. 'He's got the cloned cell on a computer grid so if the Spikeman gets in line to take her over the border, he can do a pretty invasive search.'

'Why can't he just stop a car now?'

'Doesn't work that way. It's not that sophisticated. But at least we know she's still alive. When you get a call again, we'll get a better read on what's happening. Try to keep the line open longer, Grace. That's the important thing.'

'I won't be using that phone. Or that car. I'm driving Jeanne's car into Folsom. That's what I'm using cut three to cover. Even without it, they can still track that cell, right?'

The station wagon was gassed up now, and the Marine got in and drove it to a parking space before going inside and joining his family.

'You mean, can he see the stolen cell on the screen? Yeah, it's just not as tight a directional radius as it would be otherwise. Look, don't worry, they won't take her by car over the border.' Papers rustled. 'You asked me to check if Eric Bettles is using any immune-suppressant drugs. That doesn't make any sense, Grace. We both know he doesn't need them, since it's a heart built from his own cells.'

'Did you check it out anyway?'

'I did. I felt like an idiot, but I did. He absolutely is not taking any drugs to prevent rejection of his heart. Got it confirmed by his cardiac doc and his pediatric nurse. Plus, he doesn't have any of the hallmarks of taking the meds. No tremors, weight gain, need to pee constantly, bleeding gums, brittle bones, fragile

319

skin, or body hair. He's good,' he repeated.

'And Hekka?'

'Your notes said it looked like she'd gone back for a second procedure that next night but I can't confirm that. She might have, I don't know.'

'You didn't ask?'

'She's taken a turn, Grace. She might not make it. Even the surgery's iffy. It just didn't seem the right thing — '

'You're getting ready to tape it.'

'Grace, I've been doing *this*. I've been a little busy.' His voice was short. 'Someday we're going to have to talk. About what the general said to you in Guatemala. I was meeting someone there, it's true. But I wasn't using you as a cover. You have to believe me, Grace.'

'Anything else?'

He made a small sound and when he spoke his voice was even. 'The global positioning system triangulates the signal and picks up the audio bugs. That means he can hear you as long as you're carrying the charts or have them in the car where the second audio bug is.'

'You're saying somebody doesn't have to be right next to me to pick up sound.'

'Yeah, you were right about that. Whoever it is, they're here in San Diego, not where you are. They don't need to be, to track and hear exactly what you're doing. Just be careful what you say. As long as you're in the car he gave you, or within range of the audio bug in the Wingers' chart, he can hear you. Another thing. I talked to Marcie the way you asked me to.'

'And?'

'Marcie said the case that involved the audio bug embedded in the metal brad of a file, it resulted in a hung jury so the defendant walked. Pretty messy, from the sound of things. The defendant was a researcher at Scripps and got fired, tried to countersue but it was tossed out.'

'Have a name?'

'Cecilia O. Perkins. Ring any bells?'

'Not yet.'

'Grace, the minicam found in Eddie Loud's shirt lapel came from a shipment that was stolen and ended up in a warehouse in Brazil.'

'Brazil. I'm not tracking.'

'The serial number is part of a series of cameras and editing equipment found in the raid of a child abduction ring. They cybertrack the flow of online child pornography and — '

She sat up straighter. 'What are you trying to tell me?'

'I've been working this story undercover for almost six months.'

'What are you telling me?'

'Thailand. Brazil. The Philippines. They steal children, Grace. And use them — '

'*What are you telling me?*'

He exhaled. 'I promise you.' His voice was heavy. 'Grace, I promise.'

A panicky fear surged up her body and she felt her skin wash in sweat. Katie was alive, and with every primitive cell in her body she needed to get back to San Diego, to save her.

'Get me home, Mac. I want to come home.'

'Where are you?'

'Less than an hour out of Folsom. The Spikeman expects me to drive home but there's no time. I don't think I'd even get home if I started now, and I'm meeting a warden at Folsom who's going to tell me about the wrapping paper that covered that bloody doll, maybe give me a lead on who this guy is. But then, oh, God, Mac, you just have to help me get home.'

'That's not too far from Mather Field,' Mac said. 'When can you be ready?'

Grace peered out the window at Jeanne, leaning heavily on her stick. She did the mental calculations. 'A little before nine.'

'Mather Field. Got that? I'll have somebody there. Ask for Jeb Shattuck. Okay?'

'Jeb Shattuck,' she repeated.

'And if I can't get Jeb, ask for him anyway, and they'll direct you to whoever's waiting. Check in at the FBO desk.'

'Got it. Thanks. Is that it?'

He hesitated. 'I got a phone call,' Mac said. 'Nobody I knew. Just a voice, a woman on my cell, telling me she knew about Katie, and if I called in the cops or the FBI, they'd kill her.'

Grace was having trouble taking a breath. 'They know about you? How do they know about you?'

'I don't know. But I do believe they mean what they say, Grace. Be careful when you're inside Folsom. What you say. Who you say it to.'

She clicked off slowly. She called Marcie and got her voice mail, and she left Jeanne's cell number as a call-back. She got out of Jeanne's

322

car. Fifteen minutes had passed. On the timer, Katie's pigtails had vanished up to her chin. Jeanne waited on an iron bench in front of the café.

'You okay?'

'Oh, Jeanne.' Grace knew she didn't expect an answer.

Jeanne reached over and gave her knee a brisk squeeze. 'What do you need me to do?'

Grace pulled out a yellow legal sheet covered in writing.

'I've written everything down but let's go over it, too. I'm not sure you can read this.'

Jeanne put on her glasses and studied the page. 'Okay. In five minutes, I get into your rental and start to drive.'

'Right. The first thing you do when you go to the car, turn off the cell phone the Spikeman gave me. He made me leave mine in a post office parking lot and gave me this one to carry. He doesn't like it if the cell rings and I don't pick up, so turn it off.'

Jeanne nodded and glanced at her watch. 'At five o'clock exactly I get in the car, turn off your cell, and drive. Any particular place?'

'As if I was starting back to San Diego, heading toward the freeway, but don't get on it. This is the tricky part. You get in the car, get settled, at five-oh-six you press *Play*. The Sony's cued to cut three. You'll hear the sound of a tire exploding. You must immediately turn the car around and come back slowly, weaving if you can. Park as near to the mechanics' bay as possible. You leave the charts and cell phone on the seat, along with the Sony, get out, and slam the door closed. Go into the café and wait for me. We'll be in a hurry when I come back.'

'That's it?'

'That's it. Except for this.' She leaned in. 'Under no circumstances, none, utter one sound while you're in that car. He can hear you. He can't know I'm gone. And of course don't use that cell.'

'We're tricking him.'

'Big-time. The sounds he'll hear on the CD are the sounds of mechanics fixing a bad tire. Replacing it, along with the damaged rim. It will sound as if the car is being lifted up, so they can get underneath. It will take a long time. Three and a half hours of time exactly.'

'So you'll be back by eight-thirty-six.' She reached for Grace's hand.

Her eyes filled.

'Maybe it's too late.'

'Too late?'

'Maybe this one won't have a happy ending.'

Grace looked away.

'Don't say that. Don't ever say that. We'll find her.'

'Yeah,' Grace said. 'Sure.'

34

All Hallows' Eve, 5:39 p.m.
The CD on the seat next to her emitted sounds of squealing tires and a car braking to a stop, followed by the grinding slap of a car on a bad tire. She was listening so she'd know what Jeanne was hearing. And the Spikeman. Before that cut ended, she'd have to be safely back.

She called Mather Field and got directions as she drove into Folsom on her way to the prison. Dusk was softening the ivy-covered brick buildings along Main Street, and a trail of trick-or-treaters floated in the silvery light, clutching bags of candy and their parents' hands.

She pulled the timer out of her bag, shot a hard look at it and flinched. Dark pixels had gnawed away the pigtails and part of Katie's chin. Her bright eyes and trusting smile filled the screen, made more shockingly present by the dark blanks around it. TONIGHT still pulsed along the top. Grace shoved the timer back into her bag.

She took River Way past the American River, a silver band bordered by orange and gold canyons of foliage so intense in color, they looked tweaked on a computer.

She was trying hard to keep her exhaustion and terror at bay, but over and over she kept hearing in her mind her daughter's little voice, and the scream that abruptly cut short her cry for help, and for the first time, she had to let in the idea that had been pressing so hard against her heart that she couldn't breathe, that maybe Katie was already dead.

Maybe she'd been killed the instant the phone connection had been cut. Maybe his final act of cruelty was forcing Grace to listen as her child was murdered.

She'd been so stupid. The Spikeman had never intended for the clues to lead her to Katie. She'd been playing the game banking that underneath the madness lay a kind of order, and if she played well, it might just win her the points she needed to save her daughter's life. Now it occurred to her that she'd gambled everything expecting fair play from a madman.

There was no order. Only the jumbled, angry chaos of a killer.

Prison Road cut through bright orange oak and yellow prairie grass. A buck blurred by and shot into the trees. The road curved and she turned onto New Folsom Road and drove until she reached a granite slab statue constructed on piles of rock under an enormous sign: CALIFORNIA STATE PRISON, SACRAMENTO. She remembered hearing that the statue represented the new Folsom rising from the old, a stark and somber sentinel at the gates of hell.

Here the road divided. She hesitated, took the fork that went past the sign, and rounded a corner. Folsom stood silhouetted against the hill behind it, like a city of the damned, scratched with barbwire and glistening with spikes and broken glass topping high stone walls. But she was going to the newer complex, the one holding the worst offenders. Somewhere inside those walls was a man who knew something important about what had happened to Katie.

She backed up and turned around and took the other fork. Mac's warning rang in her mind. *Be careful when you're inside Folsom. What you say. Who you say it to.* She followed the road to the newer facility, parked in visitors' parking, and made the approach on foot. Ahead of her, the road cut under a granite and concrete building. Huge American and California state flags hung limply from poles against a twilight sky. A wooden arm, the kind used in parking garages, barred the road as it cut under the building. Only employees could park inside.

The guard stepped out of the guard shack holding a clipboard. He was middle-aged and matter-of-fact, wearing a shade of green that reminded her of a park ranger. The white lettering on his black nametag read S. FELLEAU. She tried to relax the muscles in her face to look less alarming, but the truth was, she was a wreck and she knew it.

He must have seen it, too. He narrowed his eyes and studied her thoughtfully. The inside of his nostrils were pink, as if he was recovering from a cold, and when he spoke, he carried it in his head, so that it sounded foggy. 'It's Sunday,' he said. 'We're closed.'

'I know. But I'm expected.' At least she hoped she was. It occurred to her that she hadn't called Marcie back to check on whether she'd had any luck getting her in. She could have just driven

327

fifty-five minutes for nothing. The idea made her feel faint.

'Name?'

'Descanso.' Her voice held a quaver she didn't like and she put more authority into it for the rest. 'Grace, first name, Emily, middle. I'm with the San Diego Police Crime Lab Unit.'

'Business?'

'To see Associate Warden Thorton Syzmanski.'

'ID, please.'

She pulled her ID out and handed it over and waited. He checked it against his board.

'Are you carrying? You have to check it here if you are.'

'No.'

He went inside the guard shack, picked up a phone, and talked, looking at her through the window. She turned resolutely and faced the parking lot and her solitary car. A dusky light was softening the hills of oak. A wild turkey darted into view and melted into the foliage. She looked at her watch. 6:09. She hadn't factored in waiting. It gave her less time inside. Less time to make it safely back.

After a few moments she heard the door of the guard shack open and he came out.

'Somebody will be along to escort you in.' He held out his clipboard and pointed. 'Sign the registry log, please.'

He'd already written in her name, the time and date. She scribbled her signature and he took the clipboard and gave her a visitor's pass that she clipped onto her shirt. He stood next to her, as if part of the deal were making sure she

328

wouldn't bolt under the parking garage arm and make a run for it inside, although why anybody would want to run *into* a prison was beyond her.

Footsteps echoed on the cement. Thor Syzmanski strode through the underpass toward them, his graying head gleaming in the ceiling lights of the underpass. He was wearing a navy blue suit and tie, and he carried the weight of his struggle with alcoholism in the fierce lines around his eyes and mouth. He had thin lips and they were compressed in a tight line.

Felleau nodded. 'Sir.'

'Thanks, Sean, I'll take her from here.' Syzmanski turned to go and stopped. 'We might need a van. I'll let you know.'

Felleau nodded again and stepped inside the guard shack. She hurried to keep pace. Syzmanski was a tall man and he didn't shorten his stride as they walked through the underpass.

'What the hell are you doing?' He kept his voice even, gazing at the prison complex ahead of them.

She stopped walking. 'Hello to you, too, Thor. So nice to see you.'

'Do you have any idea the position you've put me in? No, of course not.'

He made a sound of disgust and walked around the corner of the concrete building and strode through the sliding glass doors, waiting as she meekly followed him in. They were alone in the silent lobby and he punched the button for the elevator that would take them upstairs.

They were facing a row of framed photos of the current prison administration, and as he spoke, he directed his comments to the wall, talking to the photos of the plant manager, the captains, the associate wardens, the deputy warden, and finally to the warden himself, a strong-faced man with shaggy eyebrows and great slabs of ears.

'Sunday, for starters. That's a flag right there. Ever hear about professional courtesy? Putting in a written request? Or hell, Grace, just giving me a call, letting me know when you want to come up. See if it works for me. But no. I get a call at home on a Sunday from some lab colleague of yours — flag number two, by the way. Investigators travel in twos. That's the way it's done. I assume you want to talk to somebody inside.'

She nodded.

'Any idea who?' The elevator dinged and his hand slammed out and held the door open as she walked through.

She shook her head.

'Why does that not surprise me?' He stepped in after her and the elevator door slid closed. He punched in the top button and the elevator rose.

'And I'm going to catch holy hell from the police agency. Somebody from the ISU staff is supposed to escort you around, or the public information guy — he's nice, you'd like him — but not me. There are going to be questions and I need answers.'

'Why did you do it then?'

He looked at her. 'Because I'm worried about you.'

The elevator opened and he waited as she

walked into the silent hall. She followed him down the corridor. He opened the door to his office. The window faced out over the prison complex in the distance, a group of concrete buildings surrounded by fence. The lights were on and they burned through the twilight. He motioned her into a seat.

He took the one behind his walnut-veneer desk. 'I heard what happened.'

She looked at him warily and then realized he was talking about how she shot Eddie Loud. She should have expected it had made news there: Senator Loud's home was Modesto.

'You're on leave, Grace. Your supervisor thinks you're . . . ' He glanced down at a small notepad on his desk and read aloud, 'Unstable, in need of counseling, and resistant to getting help. Oh yeah, and he didn't know squat about this postcard that was supposedly tested for fibers in your lab. Doesn't seem to have a tracking number attached to a case, either.'

He snapped the notebook shut. 'Did I miss anything?' He was studying her and she felt curiously close to tears, vulnerable, as if she'd been called into the principal's office.

'I'm not drinking, if that's what you think.'

'How many meetings have you taken since it happened?'

She hesitated. 'None.'

'None?'

'Look, I've been a little busy — '

'*None?*'

'I'll go, okay? But I just can't go now.'

'Then when, Grace?'

331

'I just saw my AA sponsor, if that counts.'

He frowned. 'You mean up here?'

'At five o'clock in Lodi. I left her at a corner café and when I leave here, I'm meeting up with her again.' She shifted in her chair. 'I wouldn't lie about that.'

'You shouldn't lie about anything, Grace. That's the ticket to hell and we both know it.' He'd been toying with a pencil and he threw it down. 'Then what is this? Why are you here?'

She exhaled. On his shelf above a row of prison regulation documents sat a framed photo of his three kids. They shared his coloring, a ruddy cast to the skin and mousy-colored hair, and were smiling into the camera in a tentative way, as if they couldn't quite trust it.

'I'm not representing the San Diego Police,' she said. 'You're right, I'm on leave right now. I'm here at the request of a prominent businessman, Warren Pendrell. He received a threatening postcard. Marcie already told you. She tested it in our lab at my request, on her own time, and if anybody gets in trouble for that, it needs to be me, not her.'

She was remembering the earlier CSI case that had led to her being sidelined at the lab after the accusation of slopped samples, and how she'd dragged Marcie into that one, too. How it had led to Marcie sharing Grace's fate: six months of no field work as all the cases they'd touched were reanalyzed and cleared. How Marcie's involvement had cost her overtime money that her family needed. Her mother had health problems and Frank had just lost his job. Things were better now for them, but Grace owed Marcie a lot, and she knew it.

'Dr. Pendrell wants me to take care of this quietly. Find out who's after him. And why.'

'And this couldn't wait until regular visiting hours? A regular business day?'

'Warren's on a tight timeline. He's selling the company to a Swiss research and development group, but after Eddie Loud's death, the buyer is nervous.'

'How does his death factor in?'

'Eddie Loud was a patient at his facility and the publicity's bad for business. Warren — Dr. Pendrell — needs to find out if this postcard is a viable threat. The sale's imminent and the buyer's goosy about the publicity surrounding Eddie Loud's meltdown. This postcard could be enough to kill the sale if it becomes public. Warren's a mentor of mine so . . . ' She trailed off.

'I should throw you out right now and be done with it.'

She swallowed. Tears welled and spilled silently down her face. She made no move to wipe them away. If he threw her out, he was throwing out her best hope of finding Katie.

He studied her, his voice neutral. 'You're crying over a personal favor that has nothing to do with you. If ever I was on the fence about believing Sid's evaluation of your mental state, this would swing it for me, this right here.'

He swiveled his chair and looked out the window. He took his time. The tears were bright cold tracks down her face. Syzmanski blew a gust of air and turned his chair toward the desk, grabbing a cube of Kleenex and smacking it down in front of her. Grace realized she'd been holding her breath. She made a small sound and dug out a tissue, wiping her face as he spoke. His demeanor now was all business and she was grateful for that. It gave her back a small measure of dignity.

'Your lab buddy, Marcie. When she called, she said the postcard came back as having components of metal from license plates, and the blue thread cotton from the prison uniforms.'

Grace nodded. It was a lie. All they'd tested was the wrapping paper, but he couldn't know that.

'Have the postcard?'

She shook her head.

'What did it say?'

'It had his photo — Warren Pendrell's — shot as he was leaving the multimillion-dollar business he founded. The angle looked like it was taken in the parking lot. A knife was embedded in his chest, drawn in ink with spattered blood drops.'

'Any leads on the ink?'

She thought of what Marcie had said about the ink used in the note attached to the bloody doll. 'Part of a shipment that went into four million pens sold in six Western states.'

He was taking notes now. 'Any words?'

This part, at least, was true. ''He's coming for you, the Spikeman.' The same message that Eddie Loud had given her right before she killed him.

'So you think it's somebody inside? We haven't made handmade paper in three years. We only tried it for six months. Besides, they sold it in the prison gift shop. Somebody could have come in, paid cash for it, walked out the door and never left a trace.'

'Maybe it's somebody with a grudge who's out now. Who thinks he's been ripped off in some way by this sale.'

Syzmanski swiveled in his chair and stared out the window. The sky was darkening and a velvet canopy of lights outlined the prison.

'Spikeman. It's not a name I remember hearing. I share a secretary with another AW and she won't be in until tomorrow. I'm not equipped to do a full-out computerized search of AKA's until tomorrow, but I did pull a list of inmates who'd worked at the print shop on that paper detail during the six months of time it was in operation. You can see if anything pops out.'

He opened his desk drawer and pulled out a computerized printout and slid it across to her. There were eight names on the list. She recognized two names, both infamous killers, but none of them, she was almost certain, had passed through her lab on their way to life sentences.

'You keep checking your watch. You late?'

'I'm flying back to San Diego with my sponsor in an hour or so, out of Mather Field.' She rechecked the list so he wouldn't see the shock on her face when she'd checked the time. She needed to be back in the car in less than an hour. Where did her life and Warren's intersect? That was the key. She wasn't seeing it. 'It's — I don't know.'

Syzmanski pushed his chair back. 'I don't know how else to help you.'

She thought of something. 'Is anybody on this list a scientist or researcher?'

He shook his head. 'Don't think so.' He took the list back and scanned it standing up.

'Or doctor. Maybe a medical doctor.'

He stopped reading. 'That narrows it down.'

He punched the intercom on his desk and leaned in. 'Yeah, Sean. Could you send the van around, and alert B facility to take Benny Jingelston out of his cell and have him waiting upstairs in an interview room?' He listened to a garbled response. 'I copy. Thanks.'

He walked around the desk and opened the door. 'He'll be there in ten minutes.'

'Thank you,' she said simply.

He nodded and turned off the light, locking the door as they stepped into the hallway.

'Who's this guy again? Benny? What's he in for?'

Syzmanski looked away. 'Kidnapping, distribution of pornography, and murder.' His eyes were flat. 'Benny ran a child porn ring.'

35

All Hallows' Eve, 7:03 p.m.
Benny Jingelston stared up at her as the door opened and his eyes went carefully down the length of her before settling back on her chest. She fought the urge to cover herself with her arms as she took the seat across the table from him.

He had a doughy face mottled with scars. His feet were small in blue canvas shoes. He was wearing blue pants and a blue chambray shirt. His fingernails were neat and he smelled sweet, like talcum powder. He gel-combed his sparse hair over a pink scalp.

She and Syzmanski had ridden a bright blue van over to the B facility, and come in through a sally port, two secure electronic doors, neither opened at the same time. The guard was watching their progress on banks of video monitors as they climbed the metal stairs to a locked door at the top. They waited as the guard upstairs electronically buzzed them through.

Now Syzmanski stood outside the interview room, glancing through the glass window occasionally to make sure she was okay. Two guards paced in the hall, ready to escort Benny to his cell. Benny clasped his small hands on the table. Leg shackles clanked as he shifted.

'Do you know who I am?' According to her watch, she had exactly forty-two minutes.

Forty-two minutes to get what she needed, and be back in the car.

He shook his head and smiled. 'A pretty lady in a hurry. What's your hurry?'

'Answer the question.'

He hesitated and then shrugged. 'Grace. Grace Descanso. Guard told me on the way over. The name who's calling me out. That's the last freebie, by the way.'

'Does it mean anything to you?'

'Should it? Do you know who *I* am?' His dentures clicked.

'A killer. A child killer.'

He rolled his eyes and looked away. 'So harsh. I was in the business of marketing children, yes,' he said matter-of-factly. 'And sometimes things went awry.'

His eyes found her again, his gaze cold and unblinking. 'Why are you here?'

'You worked in the paper-making shop. Did you keep paper for your own use? Give it to special people on the outside?'

'You can do better than that. Ask me a specific question.'

'What kind of doctor?'

'Did you bring anything?' He held out a small, moist palm.

'Anything.' Her mind blanked.

'Barter. Did you bring anything?'

She pulled from her bag the mashed Snickers bar she'd purchased at the convenience store where she'd gotten directions to DeeDee's almond farm. Benny snatched the candy bar up and sniffed it, taking his time.

'Smells like, well. You know what it smells like.' He closed his eyes a long moment, inhaling. He exhaled, opened his eyes, and smiled. 'I've been in here over three years but you never forget. Children, now, have a smell all their own. Like sweet grass.'

Her heart skidded. He carefully ripped the wrapper off and set it aside.

He looked at her and smiled, his lips loose and rubbery. 'There's a lot of pain in your face. You know that?' He said it conversationally.

She was silent. He slid a finger along the length of the candy bar and licked the digit. He kept eye contact. She held it. He was testing her, she knew, on some primitive gamesmanship level. She didn't react. Finally, he picked up the candy bar and took a generous bite.

'Thoracic surgeon. I did heart transplants. On kids.'

Her stomach felt sudsy. She was certain she'd never worked with him or seen his name but she had to be sure. 'Did you ever work at the Center?'

He pursed his lips and chewed. It took a long time swallowing. 'The Center.'

'The Center for BioChimera.' She thought back further. 'Or back east at Johns Hopkins. Did you ever work there?' A humming started in her ears.

He shook his head and took another bite, tilting his head and biting delicately, avoiding his front teeth. 'L.A. Their parents loved me. Loved me. I found ways of moving their darlings up the lists. Ways of providing the right heart at the

339

right time for the right price. You can phony up transplant forms. On the Internet, you can download just about anything.'

The humming was getting louder now, a thin whine reverberating through her head, up her neck. 'Did you know Warren Pendrell?'

'I don't know why you're bothering. Wasting my time. This is simple information you can download off of any computer.'

Except she didn't have time. No access. No time.

He finished the candy bar and sucked his fingers clean, wiping the saliva on his pants. 'The simple answer's no. What else do you have to trade?'

She pulled out the pack of Camels and ripped off the cellophane, pulling one out. She slapped it onto the table, out of reach. 'Kids you targeted for the pornography. How did you find them?'

Benny eyed the cigarette. 'The usual. Single mothers. Distracted. Irritable. Kids not well supervised. Needing a male role model.'

She stared at him. He motioned impatiently for her to release the cigarette. She rolled it over to him.

He tamped the cigarette and stuck it in his mouth. 'Light?'

'You can't smoke in here, Benny, you know that.'

'What are they gonna do? Arrest me?' He took the cigarette out. The paper was damp on the end that he sucked.

She took the matches out and put them on the table out of reach. 'How did it work?'

'I can tell you what the ideal combination is. Not that I did it this way.' He stared at a stain on the wall. 'You snatch the kid. Have somebody who can do the video part, and somebody else to — recycle the product when it no longer serves a useful function.'

Grace looked at him. She wanted to kill him. Snap his neck. Smash his windpipe. Do a fraction to him of the harm he'd done to others, except then she'd never find Katie.

'Is your operation still viable?'

He motioned for a cigarette and she took another one out and flicked it across the table at him with such force it bounced into the air and sailed off the table.

'Easy,' he said mildly, catching it midair and pocketing it in his shirt. 'Viable. I don't run things from the inside, but I hear things.'

'What kind of things?' She tossed him another and he stowed it behind his ear.

'About how easy it is in San Diego to grab a kid, drug her, dye her hair. Matches.'

He waited as she slid the matches across. There was something, right on the edge of consciousness, if she could find it. He tore off a match.

'Things about people — bad people, oh, so bad — taking pictures of kids in — shall we say *awkward* positions? And then there are those children who are simply not as — *tractable* as one would wish and so they're — sent on to perform a more useful function.'

She grew very still. A numbness was closing her throat, making it difficult to breathe. 'Who? I need a name.'

He looked at her and for the first time laughed. Syzmanski's face appeared in the glass viewing window and she waved him away. It was stronger now, the knowing. Something was off, something just out of reach. He struck the match and held it to a cigarette, inhaling deeply.

'Do you honestly think a candy bar and a couple of smokes can buy you that?'

She stared across the table at him and it clicked, the thing right on the edge of awareness. 'San Diego.'

'What's that?' The pungent smell of smoke filled the air.

'You said San Diego. You knew where I was from before I told you.'

Benny took a long drag on his cigarette and tamped it out on the candy bar wrapper, not looking at her. 'I heard from the AW.'

'Bullshit.' She lunged across the table at him. His arms were surprisingly hard under his shirt. 'He was with me the whole time.'

Benny yanked his arms back and banged on the table. The door burst open. Syzmanski stood with the guards.

'I'm done.' Benny clambered to his feet. 'I want to go back to my cell.'

'You know something,' she cried. 'What is it?'

The two guards grabbed his arms and he shuffled out the door and down the hall.

'He's not going to tell you anything else,' Syzmanski said quietly.

The sally port opened and the electronic gate clanged shut.

'Who has access to him?'

'You mean outside?' Syzmanski stepped into the interview room and picked up what Benny had left behind, the candy wrapper and the burned match, and stowed them in his pocket. 'His lawyer. The ACLU's getting involved. Just their kind of pond scum, a doer of kids. How are you, timewise?'

She glanced at her watch. 'I have to be in the car in twelve minutes.'

He relocked the interview door and they walked toward the guard station at the far end of the hall, both of them picking up their pace.

'He has to call collect, right? You have a log or what?'

'We record everything,' Syzmanski said. 'But it's recycled. It depends on how far back the call was made as to whether or not we still have it.'

'I need that information. I need it now.'

'I can't, Grace. Not today. There's a limit to what I can accomplish here.'

She waited as the upstairs sally port guard surveyed the bank of video monitors showing the two guards hustling Benny toward a cell block across the yard.

'I have to know who he's been in contact with.'

The guard nodded to Syzmanski and pressed the electronic buzzer, opening the upstairs sally port. The door slid closed behind them and the stairwell opened. Grace and Syzmanski kept talking as they made their way downstairs, their footsteps clanging on the metal steps.

'Tell you what, tomorrow I can have somebody go through the tapes and see if he made a recent call.' Syzmanski's voice was placating.

'You don't understand.' Her voice rose. 'By tomorrow, it's too late.'

Syzmanski stopped walking. 'You're right, I don't understand.'

They were being watched on all the video monitors. She stopped talking and waited as they were electronically buzzed through into the sally port downstairs.

'The list,' she said quietly, as they stepped outside into the night air. 'Can you get me the list of people approved to see him? The visitors' list.'

She was already walking toward the Admin building. She wasn't going to wait for the van to return. The temperature had dropped while they'd been inside. A cold wind bit her neck.

'Any name in particular?'

'The whole list, but particularly any San Diego connection.'

'I thought you were in a hurry.'

'I am.'

He left her at the guardhouse outside the prison and went back to his office. The guard gave her a cup of coffee and disappeared into the warmth of the guard shack. The carton warmed the tips of her fingers but it did nothing to take the chill out of her heart. She braced herself and reached deep into her bag and pulled out the timer.

Katie's smile was almost gone. The eyes still beamed at the camera, wide and trusting.

She pressed her hand against the face. She

sighed. She took her time putting it away, lingering over how she placed it in the bag, adjusting it, making sure it was secure, as if — as if, she suddenly thought, she were preparing a body for last rites.

Benny Jingelston had been ready. He'd known she was coming, even before she did.

The Spikeman had set it up. Even this. He'd wanted her to come to Folsom, or at least he'd been prepared if she did. Knowing that if she was able to secretly investigate the paper-making, it would lead her here, to Benny. Was Benny's story a lie? A false trail? Trying to get her off course. Wasting time. Somebody who could do video, Benny had said. Anybody could do video, with the ease of technology and the Internet.

She checked her watch. 7:35. She walked over to the wooden arm of the gate and looked through the underpass, as if by staring long enough, Associate Warden Thor Syzmanski would materialize. The guard opened the door and stuck his head out. 'Help you?'

She shook her head. She leaned against the guard shack and pulled out her notepad. Dr. Mike Yura, DeeDee had said. He was the younger doctor — *(fake?)*, she wrote next to his name — who'd talked them into coming back for the second sonogram. Maybe it was an anagram. The Spikeman liked to play games. Playing the Timer Game for the highest stakes she'd ever known was the clearest manifestation of that, but it was even there in his use of clown wrapping paper.

She played with the name in her mind, rewriting it on the pad: Mike U. Ray. Muray Kie. Maury Eik. Ike Mayru. May Rukie. She rubbed her eyes. None of those rang even slightly. Yura. Yura. Yura sucker, yes? She played with the first name again. Kiem. Kiem Yura.

Kiem. Yura. Say it fast ten times. Her mind raced, repeating the name over and over like Yin scrabbling inside the exercise wheel. *Keemura keemura KEEMura.* She straightened. Change the accent and there it was. Chimera.

A mythical beast. Part goat and lion and dragon. The name of a multibillion-dollar enterprise. The Center for BioChimera. And another, less familiar definition: an intermingling of cells that normally don't belong together. He was good.

Footsteps crunched aross the cement in the underpass. Syzmanski had a list in his hand.

'I can't access until tomorrow the complete list of people cleared to see him, but here's the ones who showed up last visiting day on Thursday.' Syzmanski pointed to the third name on the list. 'Two attorneys and this one.'

A woman. Cecilia O. Perkins. The same woman Mac said had been fired as a researcher from Scripps for trying to steal biotech secrets after she'd planted an audio bug in a chart.

'It's Benny's sister, if that's any help. You can take the list with you.'

'Thanks.' She tucked the list under her arm.

Syzmanski smiled briefly. 'Whenever you're ready to tell me the truth, I'll listen.'

'Thanks for that, too.'

He turned and said over his shoulder, 'Oh, and she goes by her middle name. Opal.'

Grace jerked her head around, stunned. 'What did you say? Opal?'

'You know her?'

'The Opal I know's a caretaker for mentally ill clients in a halfway house.'

'Have a last name?'

'Not yet.' She turned and started to run.

36

All Hallows' Eve, 7:44 p.m.
She let herself look at the timer again as she slid into the car. The smile was completely gone and it appeared that pixels were starting at the top of Katie's forehead and working down so that the last thing to disappear would be her eyes. Locked on Grace.

She realized suddenly she wasn't hearing the CD, and her heart skidded, and then she heard the murmur of voices, garage mechanics talking, and the clang of tools. She did the mental calculation. It was 7:44. The CD would run out at 8:36. It would take longer than that to get back. Once the CD ended, there was a chance her absence would be discovered. She had to move faster, and even then she feared it wouldn't be fast enough to save Katie. At the rate Katie's image was being erased, it would disappear before they reached San Diego.

She drove carefully until she hit the interstate and picked up speed, allowing herself finally to think about what she'd learned inside. It had to be the same Opal. That would explain Eddie Loud targeting Grace. Opal would have set it up. Eddie lived at the halfway house so Opal had easy access to him. It was all part of some elaborate puzzle carefully orchestrated before Katie's birthday party, long before Eddie Loud warned her about the Spikeman.

But why? What had she ever done that had set this in motion?

A lady, Katie had said, her voice small. Maybe the main player was female. Maybe if a synthesizer could alter voices, it could alter gender.

For years Grace had balanced the pieces of her life with Katie like some exotic high-wire dancer, juggling car pools and play dates and whispered confidences late at night, knowing that the slightest misstep would send it crashing down. And now somebody named Opal had wormed into the middle of her world and plucked out the only thing that mattered: Katie.

She was driving too fast toward Lodi, a sick feeling in her gut. A high wind fence stitched across a brown dusty hill in the beam of her headlights, and a power plant winked by in a blur of gleaming metal. She dialed Warren's numbers. Nobody picked up. She tried Mac next.

'Mac.' His voice was short.

'Benny Jingelston's as creepy as they come, Mac. He was a surgeon. A heart guy, working on kids. He had a child porn ring.'

'Wait a minute, I know that name. Benny Jingelston. I ran across his name working on this series. He was the source at Folsom for that clown wrapping paper around the bloody doll?'

'I think so, yeah. He has a sister in San Diego, Mac. Opal Perkins. *Cecilia* Opal Perkins, the Scripps bioresearcher. Listen. I think she could be the same woman who's the caretaker at the halfway house where Eddie Loud and Jazz

349

Studio lived. I need you to check that out. She and Benny could be working together.'

'Which means this Opal could have Katie.'

'I don't even know if she's the right Opal. Call Warren Pendrell. Keep calling him. He's not picking up right now. Sometimes he's in the lab, but he always checks messages.'

She didn't want to get her hopes up that they were getting close. She sorted through her purse and found the address and number to the halfway house, along with Warren's numbers. She recited them into the phone.

'Warren can give you the caretaker's last name. If it is her, don't go in by yourself. Go in with the police.'

'If Katie's there, I'm getting her out.'

'We don't know what we're up against, Mac. At least go in with Warren. He can send somebody in with you. He's got good security.'

'If there's a chance she's in there,' Mac said, his voice thick, 'I'm going in.'

She folded the cell closed. What she'd learned inside Folsom terrified her. Next to her on the seat, the CD ended. Panic flushed up her body in a wave and she drove faster.

It was after eight thirty-six when she took the exit leading to the café and curio shop. The gas station was lit up; a man in shorts was putting gas into a camper.

The red Acura wasn't near the mechanics' bay. She slowed the car and coasted the length of the garage, slowing further near the parking slots in front of the curio shop.

Her rental car. The red Acura. It wasn't there.

350

Jeanne was supposed to meet her inside the café, but the car should be there, unless Jeanne had driven it off somewhere.

She circled around the back of the building and found it parked next to a black sedan under a streetlight. The driver's door hung open.

Fear squeezed through her as she ran over to look. The keys were gone. The charts were gone. The cell phone lay on the seat next to the Walkman, its cover up.

The burned CD was gone.

Grace's breath gusted. She slid into Jeanne's Taurus and drove toward the café. In the front window was a red-haired woman.

She was sitting between two men. They were big men. Men Grace had never seen before, and even from the angle of the window, driving by, Grace could see the gun bulging under the vest of the man leaning into Jeanne, see Jeanne's wide eyes, her face white.

See her fear.

37

All Hallows' Eve, 8:36 p.m.
Grace kept driving. She parked in the back next to the Acura. Light spilled out the door of the restaurant, open to the cool night air, and she got out and heard the sounds of a busy kitchen. She opened the screen door and went in, walking briskly through the kitchen and catching out of the corner of her eye a busy trio working the grill and another cook chopping vegetables.

The kitchen had a long steel counter with warming lights and a row of metal clothespins where the orders were stuck. A waitress wearing a white and pink apron was collecting a set of dinners, positioning them up her arm. Grace found the employee bathroom and on the hook next to it, an apron that matched one the waitress was wearing. She put it on and pushed open the door leading to the restaurant.

It was cooler and quieter on that side of the café. It was a busy Halloween night and most of the tables and booths were filled with people in costume. Grace spotted Jeanne's red hair. They had moved her over toward the cashier and one of the men had gone ahead to pay the bill. Jeanne looked gray, leaning on her cane. Her purse bulged and Grace knew she must have the charts tucked inside.

The bigger guy stayed close to Jeanne, one hand clamping her elbow. Anybody casually looking at it would think he was helping, but Grace knew he was applying pressure to a point in her elbow that would incapacitate her with the slightest touch.

Jeanne saw her in that instant and Grace nodded toward the kitchen door. Jeanne blinked and kept her face blank.

The man holding Jeanne's arm must have sensed her presence and he craned his massive neck to get a better look. Grace turned and pushed through the swinging door into the kitchen, her heart pounding. She smiled at a sweaty-faced cook as he transferred three plates onto the warming counter. She picked up a plate with meatloaf and peas and a second one of chicken Parmesan.

'I'll take these.'

'Wait,' he snapped. She kept moving. 'You,' he said again more loudly.

The dishwasher looked up curiously from a soapy sink and put his head back down. It didn't concern him, whatever it was. But the cook was attracting attention and Grace stopped walking, the plates burning hot indents into her arms. She turned and looked at him.

'Yes?'

He snapped down a ticket and handed it across the counter. 'Don't forget the check.'

'Right, right.' She smiled and took it and banged through the swinging door.

The man who had paid was going through the door, and the other guy was taking up the rear, pushing Jeanne along. It wouldn't be long before they had her outside in their car.

Jeanne slowed down, protesting that she needed to use the bathroom before they went, but the man holding her arm wouldn't hear of it.

'What are you trying to do, kidnap her?' Grace said in a loud voice, drawing stares from nearby diners. When he turned and frowned at her, Grace knocked into him with the hot plates of food. He turned instinctively to block the momentum of congealed mashed potatoes, lava gravy, peas as hot as steel pellets, and the loaf of burning hot meat flying dead-on into his flat, surprised face, and in that instant, Jeanne raised her cane and smashed him in the testicles with Willa. He went down like an ox.

Grace dropped the second plate of food with a crash, and the red marinara sauce and chicken slicked across the floor. Hearing the commotion inside, the first man ran through the door, slipped on the sauce, and bucked headfirst over his partner. Grace yanked the stick from Jeanne and cracked him in the head with Willa, and his eyes rolled back.

Grace cried, 'Somebody call nine-one-one. These are very bad men. Very bad.'

She fumbled for her CSI badge and pulled it out. 'CSI San Diego. On a case in Lodi. Hold these guys for the police. I repeat, do not let these men out of your sight.'

She turned to Jeanne and thrust out the stick. 'This way. Now.'

Jeanne grabbed Willa and lurched after Grace through the swinging doors into the kitchen. A butcher knife lay on a cutting board and Grace grabbed it and went through the kitchen out into the damp night. Nobody had moved. Nobody said a word.

'Which car are they driving?'

Jeanne pointed to the sedan.

'Wait in the Taurus for me. I'll do the driving. I'll be right back.'

Grace trotted over and drove the butcher knife into a tire, yanking out the blade and moving to the next one. After she'd slashed all four, she ran to the Acura and did the same thing. She left the knife at the screen door and ran back to Jeanne.

'Fuck,' Jeanne said.

Grace's hands shook. She couldn't seem to get the key into the ignition.

'Damn.' Jeanne rolled her palms across her knees and wiped her mouth.

The key slid in and Grace cranked the gas, careened around the corner, and shot out into the intersection. She coasted through a four-way stop.

She pulled from a side pocket the directions she'd scribbled earlier and passed them to Jeanne. 'Where am I going?'

'Left here. Toward Dead Cat Alley.'

'You gotta be kidding me.'

'That's what you wrote. Then left on Main Street and merge onto 1-5 south.'

They rode in silence through the middle of town on Main Street. A bar spilled Halloween revelers onto the sidewalk, the costumes strange and hard-edged, full of chainmail and studs. The car joined the traffic heading south on the freeway. Jeanne abruptly started shivering, her teeth chattering, and after a while, she rolled down the window and took giant gulps of air. 'Pull over,' she cried. 'I'm going to be sick.'

Grace swerved into the emergency lane and stopped the car. Jeanne rolled out her side and crouched down over the embankment, heaving. Grace remembered the brads and slid the charts out of Jeanne's purse. She unfastened the brad on Katie's chart, wondering if even then the Spikeman was sending someone after them.

She'd had Jeanne read the directions out loud. Even over the sound of the engine, the Spikeman would have heard. It wouldn't take him long to figure out where they were going.

Flying out was the only thing that made sense, if they were to make it back in time.

Jeanne clambered up to the open door. 'Oh God, do you have anything to drink?' Passing traffic illuminated her face. It was white and pinched.

'Just the end of what you brought me.' The watered-down cola was still sitting in the drink holder, and Grace passed it to her and went back to work, slipping the brad free.

Jeanne eased back into the car and sucked the can dry. 'God, I feel so sick.' She carefully stowed the can, her movements deliberate to offset the slight trembling in her fingers.

'Just rest, honey. I've got to get these out before they find us. I should have asked you to do this right after the CD ended.'

Jeanne leaned her head back and closed her eyes. 'They were already there before the CD stopped, Grace. They pulled up about twenty minutes after you left.'

Grace worked on the audio bug in the Wingers' chart until it came loose in her hand. She scrambled out of the car.

Jeanne watched her through the open window. 'What are you doing?'

Grace trotted over to the damp stew of vomit and dropped the brads. They drove in silence for several miles, Grace checking the rearview mirror. 'Did they tell you anything?'

Jeanne's eyes clouded. 'I asked them about Katie. They pretended not to know who I was talking about. They did say they wouldn't hurt me. They just needed to — how did they put it — derail your efforts overnight. That was all.'

So the Spikeman was trying to stop her from getting home. They wanted her to head home. And have the dislocating pain of not getting there in time. Another game. A Timer Game she'd lose. When she'd seen the HEAD SOUTH signs posted along the side of the road, that had been the first thought that had flashed through her mind. She'd never make it in time, driving.

It must mean Katie was still alive. Whatever they were planning, they hadn't done it yet.

But that was before the Spikeman had realized she'd talked to Katie.

'Who were those men?'

'Hired hands. That's all.'

Grace gunned the gas. 'We have to hurry.'

38

Clouds obscured the sliver of moon and left the
highway a silvery trail in the dark. She sped
down Mather Field Boulevard. The field was an
old air force base, and the architecture was
square and boxy, tan with brown roofs. In the
median strip new construction gleamed, punctuated by palm trees. The field was lit like a
stadium and the ramps were massive enough to
lift old B52's into the air. Grace skidded to a
stop, and stuffed the charts into her shoulder
bag, already half out the door.

'I'm going ahead and getting us checked in.'

She raced into the building, past a blur of
white walls adorned with photos of helicopters,
instrument panels, cargo loaders. A clerk
manned a counter, under a sign with the word
TONIGHT. Grace stole a glance at the timer. A
bright spark of light in a thin band. A spark of
light in Katie's eyes. She waited as the clerk
assisted a middle-aged couple, her panic rising.

Her only hope was that Mac had already
found Katie at the halfway house. *It's a lady.* She
wanted so much for it to work like that. She
turned on Jeanne's cell. There was a mailbox
icon and she pressed *Play*, willing it to be Mac.

Assistant Warden Thor Syzmanski cleared his
throat and said, 'Grace, hell, I don't have to lie to
you. It's not my weekend with the kids; I got

nothing else on my plate. I looked back through some tapes and found what I think you might want. Got a pencil?'

Grace took down the number Thor Syzmanski dictated. 'Benny got this call yesterday from his sister, Opal. It's a little scratchy but I think you can make out the words.'

A beat of silence. Grace heard the familiar voice from the halfway house, and her stomach plummeted. 'Everything's in place,' Opal said. 'Just do what we planned.'

'Doesn't help me much,' Benny said.

'Doesn't hurt you either,' Opal snapped. A long silence. 'Not my fault you're where you are. You know what to do, just do it.'

The line went dead. Thor's voice came on. 'Grace, you get that? Anyway, hope that helps.' He hesitated. 'Stay sober, kid. Next time.'

She closed her cell phone and took her place at the counter. 'Jeb Shattuck.'

'Shattuck, okay.' The counterman had curly sideburns that matted around the frames of his glasses. He moved slowly as he checked the roster.

'I'm in a hurry,' Grace pressed. 'I'm Grace Descanso.' She pulled out her ID.

'Jeb's through there.' The counterman pointed to a side door. 'I'll buzz you through.'

Grace glanced up and saw Jeanne crossing the lobby, leaning heavily on her cane.

'I'm going to need a cart or something for my friend.'

'No problem.' The counterman picked up the phone as Grace pulled the timer out of her purse. TONIGHT. The word pulsed across the screen. A bright spark from Katie's eye was all that was left. A blot of perspiration formed in the small of her back.

TONIGHT.

She took a step back, away from the counter, and stared up past the clerk to the word above his head. It was the same typeface as on the timer.

TONIGHT.

'Oh, my God. Do you know how to stop this?'

He held up his hand. 'Sorry, couldn't hear. Yes, a cart, thanks.' He hung up. 'You were asking something?'

'This timer. Do you know how to turn it off?'

The light on the screen was dimming.

'I have no idea.'

'You don't understand, you do, you just don't know it.'

A man driving a golf cart rolled to a stop in front of Jeanne and the counterman raised his voice. 'Ben, you haven't punched in yet.'

Grace's head snapped. Time. Time cards. Punch. Punch and Judy. Punch a time card. Along the base of the timer was a small indentation.

'Time cards. Where do they punch in?'

He pointed. A metal slot had been cut into the counter and it was here that the time cards were inserted and automatically stamped.

Grace shoved the timer into the slot as the last light in the pixels cooled.

A burst of exploding colored pixeled fireworks lit the screen.

'What the hell?'

She yanked the timer free and shoved it across the counter at him. 'Here. Take it. I don't need it. Grace,' she said, her voice uneven. 'Grace Descanso. Do you have something for me?'

The counterman shook his head. He turned the timer over in his hands. 'How does this work?'

'A packet. Something.'

'I guess I could check the vault. See if anything's been turned in.'

The fireworks evaporated. The screen was blank. He put the timer down reluctantly and pulled a set of keys out of his pocket. The golf cart bearing Jeanne moved out the side door onto the tarmac as the clerk checked under the counter.

'Well, this is interesting. Grace Descanso, right?'

He placed a packet the size of a plane ticket on the counter. A slip of paper fell out. A faint stripe of blue threaded through the weave. He bent down and retrieved it.

'Sorry. It's not a secure packet. Let me make sure nothing else fell out.'

Grace stared at the paper, knowing what she'd find, feeling the familiar skid of her heart, the click of recognition:

It's finally here, with one last clue!
A dusty prize is pointing you.
Inside the past, inside a cell
The answer lies, a living hell.
I haven't killed her, no, not yet.

It's you I want, and you I'll get.
Flesh on flesh, two souls consume.
The alternative: a fiery tomb.

Work fast. The meter's running.

The man at the counter said, 'And this. I think this was part of it.' He held up what he'd found. 'A timer.'

39

All Hallows' Eve, 9:23 p.m.
The Cirrus sat on the side of the runway
under bright lights, its white, sleek body
dwarfed by a fuel truck parked next to it. A
gas nozzle lipped into the wing of the plane,
held by a man with a bristly brown ponytail
hanging to his waist. Grease saturated the
pores of his skin and his fingernails were
almost black. He was wearing an orange
jumpsuit covered in stains.

It was cold now and Jeanne shivered as she
read the clue. 'She's alive.'

'If we can trust a madman.'

'I don't see what choice we have, Grace.'

Grace was looking at the timer. White numeric
face, industrial and homely. Written in bold
black it said: 2 HRS, 37 MIN. It reminded her
uneasily of the clocks in every operating room
she'd ever been in. She put it back into her bag
and took the clue Jeanne offered.

'Okay, ladies, rock-and-roll time.' Jeb stood on
the wing and extended a hand down, helping
Jeanne climb up.

She took a seat in back and Grace joined Jeb
up front. The leather seats smelled new, and
sitting up high in the small, enclosed space, she
could see runway lights winking below in the
darkness like a carpet of stars.

'How long before we're airborne?'

'Soon.' He reached over and secured Grace's door.

'How long before we're there?'

'You're worse than a kid.' He saw her face and added, 'Two hours twenty minutes.'

'We'll be landing seventeen minutes before midnight?'

He nodded. 'Close. The harness attaches here.' He positioned it over her shoulder and she snapped it together. He handed her a headset attached to a small mike, and she put it on.

'The mikes are voice-activated,' Jeb said, his voice tinny in her ears. 'Play with them to get them positioned right. You can talk to each other for a while if you want to get used to them. There's a tank of oxygen in the back, too.'

The fuel truck was backing up, clearing the plane. Jeb punched buttons on his console and listened to the Automated Terminal Information System recording in his headset.

To Grace and Jeanne he said, 'We'll be flying to eleven thousand feet. Colors start to drop out at that altitude. There are nasal cannulas that attach if you need them. The tank's inside that leather bag between the backseats. Oh, yeah,' he added, 'when I hold up my hand it means stop talking. I need to hear what's going on.'

He held up his hand almost immediately and spoke into his microphone, 'Mather Cirrus three twenty-one Bravo Golf at FBO. IFR to Montgomery Field, San Diego, ready to taxi.'

All she could think about was calling Mac again, hoping to find out out how things had gone at the halfway house. If he'd found Katie.

A voice crackled in the headphones, repeating what Jeb had said and adding, 'Cleared to taxi to twenty-two left. We have your IFR flight plan. Advise when ready to copy.'

Jeb answered. A voice in the headphones cleared him and gave him climbing instructions and a departure frequency. In the flicker of green lights on screen, Jeb checked altitude and heading indicators, and readings on winds, temperature, and dew point.

'Okay, ladies, here we go.'

'Do you have a satellite phone, and can I use it when we're airborne?'

'Yes and yes.' They taxied to the end of the runway. Jeb did a final check, the tower cleared them for takeoff, and within moments the plane gathered speed and lifted into the air.

Airborne, Jeb turned off the landing light, a headlamp under the nose of the plane that illuminated the center line of the runway. The airfield lights sparkled in a bright stamp below.

Jeb spoke to the tower, adjusting the plane's flying altitude. On the wings, flashing white strobe lights whirred. Behind them, the airfield grew smaller until it disappeared.

Grace pulled the charts out. 'Can we have some light? I'm going to make a call.'

Jeb passed her the satellite phone and punched on reading lights. The phone was heavy in her hand, with a long spoke of a receiver that stuck up. A cross between an early version of a cell phone and a walkie-talkie.

'Press *Power*, then *Talk*. I'm cutting your mike so you have some privacy. It'll take a while to get a signal, but it'll come.'

Grace did what he said. She dialed Mac's number. He picked up on the second ring.

'Did you find her?'

'Short answer, no.'

'Did you go there? To the halfway house?'

They were still climbing. On a green screen in front of Jeb, the altitude of the landscape shifted as they rose, the outlines of mountains appearing on the grid.

'I couldn't get ahold of Warren. I thought about calling the cops, but I didn't want to have to slow things down by explaining.'

'You went in alone?'

He hesitated. 'Not exactly.'

She was confused and then comprehension flooded her, followed by angry disbelief. 'You took a film crew in. You filmed it.'

'Tape,' Mac said. 'They use tape.'

'You taped it,' she repeated, her voice rising. 'How could you tape it? That's what this was to you, a story? That's all this is?'

'No. Grace, it's not like that.'

'How could you do that?' She cut him off as he started to speak. 'Wait, I don't care. Katie's all I care about.'

His voice was angry. 'It's not what you think.'

'It's *exactly* what I think, Mac. It's what it's always been with you. The story. Doesn't matter what it costs — '

'Look.' His voice rose. 'Our daughter needs both of us — '

'You're lecturing me?' she shouted. Jeb glanced at her and Grace stared out her window.

366

Far below, a tracing of lights scattered like glitter across the landscape. 'You're telling me how to behave when it comes to my daughter?'

'Ours,' he roared. 'Grace, I don't carry a gun. I can't go blasting into some dangerous place and expect to blow away the bad guy. All I have is the power of that camera, and by God, I'll use it for this. I'll use every scrap of every single thing I know if it helps to get her home.'

Grace closed her eyes. 'Opal? Was she there?' Her voice was toneless.

He took a breath to compose himself and when he spoke, his voice was civil. 'One of the clients said they thought she'd pulled out earlier today. They'd seen her taking two suitcases with her. Nobody saw a little girl there. I want you to know that. Nobody saw her,' he stressed. 'I want you to remember that when I tell you the rest of it.'

She was digging her fingers into the phone so hard the nails turned pink. 'Go ahead.'

'Grace, in the basement, there was a room.'

She went cold. She focused on details: the way the leather seat felt, the generous expanse of leg room, the dark, silent night, and the sliver of moon emerging from clouds, details so she wouldn't have to hear the sound of his voice.

'It had big photo lights in it, Grace. The room. There was a bed in there, too. It looked like it had been used recently.'

She closed her eyes. *I haven't killed her, no, not yet.*

But there were so many ways to kill the soul of a child.

She let out a breath. 'I have a number for you. Maybe a lead on where Opal is now. She called her brother, Benny, in prison from this line. Get your contact at the phone company to track down the address.'

She recited the phone number that Thor had left on voice mail.

'Grace. Are you sure?' He sounded strained.

'What is it?'

'I know that number.'

At first she was certain she had misheard him. 'Say again?'

'I know that number,' Mac repeated. 'I used to call it all the time. It's Lee Bentley's private lab number. You asked me if I was serious about anybody lately? Yeah, it was Lee.'

40

On some level she expected it. She'd never pictured Mac alone: he was too public a figure, the women he dated too high-profile. Still, knowing that he'd been involved with someone she despised stung. But that was a tiny matter compared with the rest.

'Let me understand this,' Grace said carefully. 'Opal called her brother in prison, using the phone in Lee's lab. Do you realize what this means? Lee's involved. Has to be.'

'You don't know her the way I do.'

'Clearly.'

'That was a cheap shot,' Mac said. 'Grace, Lee's a researcher who after tonight is going to be rich beyond her wildest imaginings. She's probably going to win a Nobel prize.'

'What do you mean, after tonight?'

'Hekka's losing ground. They've speeded things up. She gets her heart-in-a-box tonight.'

'And let me guess. You're right there, taping it.'

He hesitated. 'Look, my crew's put in a lot of — '

'You're taping it?' Until that second, she hadn't believed he would.

'Grace.' His voice was tired.

'I don't even want to hear from you, unless you're calling to say you've found Katie.'

She clicked off and tried Warren's numbers but he wasn't picking up. She left the plane's

369

callback number on his cell and at his house, but when his office voice mail kicked in, she spoke loudly, trying to offset the roar of the engine.

'Warren. This is critical. It's Grace. Do you know of any connection between Lee Bentley and the caretaker at Eddie Loud's halfway house? I know her first name is Opal. Her brother, Benny Jingelston, is at Folsom, and I think he could be our guy. I think he sent the postcard to you. Or he knows who did. Anyway, Lee's involved in this mess.'

Grace thought of the retina scanner. How it protected him from everybody but Lee. And himself. It was Warren's greed and ego that made him vulnerable. She wasn't above using it.

'Lee let Opal call Benny from her lab phone. She's been putting at risk everything you've worked so hard for. Protect yourself. And for God's sake, keep looking for Katie.'

She hesitated, not knowing what else to say. 'You've got this number. Call.'

Grace touched Jeb's arm and mimed reconnecting the mike. He flicked a switch.

'What was that?' Jeanne said into the mike. 'You looked like you were shouting.'

'I'm going to shut off my mike from your conversation,' Jeb said. 'Give you girls some privacy again the rest of the way. Let me know again if you want me reconnected.'

He shut off his mike again. Grace didn't want to talk to Jeanne about Mac; it was too complicated. Instead, she said, 'I told you on the ride to Mather about Robert Harling Frieze and the tumors he thinks were caused when his son got a prenatal injection. And how DeeDee miscarried from what was probably the same kind of injection. So that leaves Benny.'

The child pornographer, heart surgeon. She told Jeanne everything that had transpired in the prison and Jeanne made a small sound of disgust into the mike.

'The handmade paper came from him, I think that's clear. It went to his sister, Opal. She sent the postcard to Warren. And wrapped up the bloody doll with the note for me. It would have been easy yesterday to stick it on the table. She could have jogged by or waded in from a dinghy and dropped it off,' Grace said. 'Be gone in seconds. Remember how everybody was inside for a minute, starting the Timer Game? It could have happened then.'

Jeanne was thinking. 'Opal directs Eddie Loud, and he warns you about the Spikeman.'

'Right,' Grace said. 'That puts the game in play. But things started a long time ago.'

'Exactly,' Jeanne said. 'DeeDee Winger said she met up with Jasmine five years ago in the lobby, as a go-between for couples needing that second injection. Maybe that's why Opal's trying to derail the sale. Maybe she's still doing dangerous research at the Center, and if it changes hands, she wouldn't have as much freedom to keep doing it.'

'Warren is pretty distracted,' Grace admitted. 'I've never thought he had a handle on what everybody was doing there. He's preoccupied with empire building.'

371

'Do you think Opal was the one experimenting on those pregnant women?'

'Could be.' Grace checked her notes. 'Middle-aged, faded, hair kind of limp. Doesn't match Lee Bentley's description, I'll say that.'

'Let me have a crack at the charts again.'

Grace passed them over the seat. 'Oh,' she said suddenly. 'I just figured out why those thugs showed up. You carried the charts into the café with you, didn't you?'

'Yeah. I thought maybe I could find something while you were at Folsom.'

'The charts were bugged. Remember?'

Jeanne looked up. 'God, I forgot. So they knew right away you'd gotten away. Sorry.'

'I'm just glad we got you out of there.'

'Me, too.' They lapsed into silence, Jeanne studying the charts, Grace studying the clue.

'Son of a bitch was experimenting,' Jeanne said from the backseat. 'I found a notation in the charts that could be that second sonogram. Dated September third. Oh. Wow. On all three of these charts, there's the same notation on the side, Grace. September third.'

She passed DeeDee's chart over the seat.

Grace saw the scribbled notation: *Sept 3 Cm complt, chk pre tpcht*. 'That backs up what Robert Harling Frieze said about seeing another couple coming out of the examining room right before they went in. Second sonograms done on DeeDee Winger, Terry Frieze, and Adrian Bettles. Performed the same night five years ago at the Center.'

In the headphones, Jeanne's voice popped.

'Middle-of-the-night injections. Back-to-back on scared pregnant women. Whatever Opal was injecting, it killed the Wingers' baby before it was born. Gave the Frieze toddler tumors. But Eric Bettles later gets the first heart-in-a-box. We need to figure out what was injected. And why. It's just that . . . '

Her voice trailed and Grace sat up. 'What are you thinking?'

'Building that checkerboard fur coat on the back of a gerbil was tough enough to keep an entire section of scientists working around the clock for about ten years. Grace, building a heart in a lab just doesn't sound credible. Sorry, but there it is.'

In Grace's mind, Yin skittered in his exercise wheel, his checkerboard back a blur of brown and white. Through the window, an outpost of homes appeared in darkness and receded.

'Okay. Let's say, for our purposes, there aren't any hearts-in-a-box.' Grace adjusted her microphone. 'Let's assume that Eric Bettles last year got a regular transplant, and in a couple of hours, Hekka gets a regular transplant, not a second heart-in-a-box.'

'Devil's advocate,' Jeanne said. 'Eric would have to be on immune-suppressant drugs the rest of his life, and you told me that Mac rechecked that. Eric's not on any antirejection drugs, Grace. So it has to mean he has a heart-in-a-box. There's no other explanation.'

'Unless his donor heart was engineered in some way to be a perfect match. Engineered so he'd never need antirejection meds.'

Jeanne made a small sound. 'You can't engineer something after it's dead, Grace. Donor hearts are dead. Kaput. End of story. Until they're hot-wired inside a new body. You're talking about changing something at the cellular level, making it not just compatible, but the same. And that kind of cellular reorientation means life. You can't inject engineered cells into a dead donor heart like India ink and change the cells. You'd be adding something in addition. Not comingling. There's no way a donor heart could be engineered after it's harvested. It doesn't make sense.'

The lights of Bakersfield stretched beneath them. Grace stared out blankly, trying to calm her thoughts long enough to find whatever thread was tantalizingly just out of reach.

'Almost forgot,' Jeanne said from the backseat. 'Dusty's dad called again. He left a phone number this time. Science is the only god I worship, Grace, but it definitely has its limits, and taking somebody's dead heart and making it a spot-on match for somebody else just isn't — '

Grace sat up. 'Say that again,' she interrupted.

'Science is the only god — '

'The part about Dusty. Dusty's dad. He called again. I need the number.'

Jeanne rummaged through her bag and handed it over the seat. 'What is it? What did you find?'

Dusty. A dusty prize is pointing you . . .

'Oh, my God.'

41

Dusty. Dusty prize. *A dusty prize is pointing you
. . . Inside the past.*

A foggy male voice picked up on the third
ring. 'H'lo?'

'Oscar, it's Grace. You called and left a
message on my machine.'

She pictured Anne's husband, a broad-faced
farmer, sunburned and steady. In Iowa, snow
would be falling, blanking out the flat expanse of
brown fields, the wind-bare trees.

'Katie sent that pen pal assignment she
wanted Dusty to answer.'

. . . inside a cell, the answer lies, a living hell.

'I'm sorry. Who is this again?'

'Grace.' She tightened her grip on the satellite
phone. 'Annie's friend. Katie's mother.'

Below them was an inky black expanse. She
glanced at a screen on the control panel and saw
the outline of mountains. Jeb pulled back on the
throttle slightly and the plane adjusted course.

'Grace Descanso. My daughter, Katie, sent
that pen pal letter to Dusty and you called me
back. I was wondering — well, is everything
okay?'

There was a sound on the phone; a small
choked sound of a man crying.

'I should have called and told you.'

She squeezed her eyes shut, willing the sound
to stop, his voice to become normal, instead of

the ragged gulps of air and tears.

'Anne fell apart, she's been in and out of hospitals, it's been bad, Grace. I've had my hands full, trying to keep the girls going. I meant to call, or write, at least, but how can you put something like that in a note?'

She was filled with dread. 'Something like what, Oscar? What aren't you telling me?'

'When Katie sent that drawing, wanting Dusty to be a pen pal — ahhh. Just a minute.' She heard the sound of him blowing his nose. 'I'm back.'

'What happened?'

'A year ago last Sunday. I can't believe — I didn't think we'd ever get through this year. Dusty was riding his bike, throwing these flyers for a food drive — going for a Cub Scout patch in service. It was early in the morning. Cold. Anne was waiting for him at the end of the road. With a cup of hot cocoa in a thermos. Only he never made it.'

They were flying over the L.A. basin now, a sparkling mantle of twinkly lights against the black wash of ocean, glinting with silver.

'They found him later that next night. They looked into cults, especially after Columbine — ' He broke down. 'They'd taken his heart, Grace. Cut it right out of his chest. Look, I'm sorry, I can't — ' He was gone.

She hung up and put her head in her hands. In the seat next to her, Jeb adjusted a switch. 'You okay?'

'I need a car. Can you have a car waiting for me at the airport? It's important.'

His voice in the mike popped. 'Forgot to tell you. Mac has a ride waiting for you.'

She nodded her thanks. She wanted to lean her seat back and do nothing, stare at the ceiling of the Cirrus and close her eyes. She wanted to go to sleep and when she woke up, Katie would be flying in the door to their house, sweaty and talkative and covered with grass stains and dirt. Her back hurt. Her legs. Her heart. Dusty dead. She remembered the day Anne had called to say she was pregnant and now Dusty was dead. Through the seats, Jeanne touched her arm. Grace hugged herself and rocked.

Dusty, killed. She remembered a small active boy clambering over the rocks at the Children's Pool in La Jolla, sliding, falling, trying to get a better look at the seals that had taken over the beach. His heart cut out.

All Hallows' Eve you'll play a part.
Ere midnight tolls, I cut your heart.

She'd been so certain about that part; that it was a metaphor for the bond she and Katie shared, but now a darker meaning emerged.

He meant it.

He was going to cut Katie's heart. Cut *out* Katie's heart. Panic surged, coupled with a cold fury at what he'd done and what he meant to do.

'What did he say?'

Grace told her.

'I can't . . . ' Jeanne faltered.

'We're cracking this thing.' Grace forced

herself to come back from the edge. 'It's terrible but we're cracking it. Stay with me, honey, okay?'

Doing for Jeanne what Jeanne had done a million times for Grace, making her voice be matter-of-fact and reassuring, a voice of strength and competence. Only she had nowhere to go, no avenue to explore. Dead ends. Dead ends and death.

She pulled out the last clue and read out loud: ''A dusty prize is pointing you.' Clearly Dusty. And what we learned. 'Inside the past, inside a cell.''

She put down the clue. 'Folsom? Do you think it's about that? The interview with Benny Jingelston?' She was trying to pull Jeanne back from the dark place and was relieved when she heard her adjust her mike in the backseat.

'Cell. Maybe a cell phone,' Jeanne offered. 'Or it could be that injection that Robert Harling Frieze talked about.'

'And DeeDee Winger. Pass me the charts, okay?'

Jeanne handed them over the seat. The route was following the coastline now, and the beach communities were bright patches of sparkles along the black expanse of water. LAX was off to the right, a string of plane lights coming in, red and green lights on wings.

You can't engineer something after it's dead.

The moon suddenly loomed in front of them, thin and curved, floating over a vast, inky ocean. Jeb cut his voice off again, so he could talk to whatever tower was close.

You're talking about changing something at

the cellular level, making it not just compatible, but the same.

Grace thought about Yin's back, twitching in brown and white squares.

She was rocked by a small, stunning thought. 'Jeanne, tell me again what you did in that lab where you worked. How you got the brown fur to accept a transplant from a white-furred gerbil.'

Jeanne cleared her throat. 'Well, when the body's developing, there's that tiny window of time when the fetus is figuring out what's *self*. So we injected bone marrow from the white gerbil into the developing fetus of the brown gerbil and waited, and then Yin was born with an immunity system that recognized cells from Yang as *self*, instead of foreign cells to fight. So later, when we transplanted fur — ' She stopped. 'Where are you going with this?'

A shelf slid into place in Grace's mind; the door locked. She felt a burst of adrenaline, followed by calm. 'Human fetuses develop along a timetable, don't they? Where the thymus is figuring out what's *self*, what isn't.'

Jeanne stared straight ahead at the back of Jeb's head, a horrified look dawning on her face. 'Oh, no. You don't think . . . '

Grace looked at her. 'I don't know what to think.' She redialed Oscar's number.

He answered on the first ring, voice weary. 'Oscar.'

'Oscar, it's me again, Grace. The accident he had.'

'What?'

379

'When Dusty was four. She'd come out to see me, right after I started working CSI. We were at Children's Beach in La Jolla that day, looking at the seals. And he slipped on the rocks and broke his arm. He had to have surgery at the Center and get pins in it. Do you remember when that was exactly?'

'What? Oh, Grace.' He sounded resigned. 'Grace, Anne's sick, she doesn't need questions.'

'This could be important, Oscar.'

'How?'

She closed her eyes. 'I was pregnant, I remember that. So it was probably late summer, early fall.'

'Wait a minute, you think this could have something to do with — '

'I don't know what to think, Oscar. But, yeah. I don't know. Maybe it has something to do with what happened to Dusty.'

The silence grew. Finally he said, 'They're in the garage. His medical files.'

She clicked off. The interior of the plane felt cold and she rubbed her hands together trying to warm them.

'Want to tell me what this is?' Jeanne asked.

Grace shook her head, unable to speak. She began ordering the charts just so, lining up the notes she wanted to review:

DeeDee and Fred Winger (miscarried)
Robert Harling Frieze and Terry Frieze
    (toddler lost to tumors)
Adrian and Richard Bettles (Eric gets
    successful transplant, perfect match?)

380

Something bleated and Grace jumped. Jeb flipped a switch and said into his mike, 'That's the cell. Pick it up and press *Talk*.'

She did what he said. 'Yes?' Grace said into the phone.

'September third,' Oscar said without pre-amble. 'Five years ago, September third, Dusty broke his arm and had it set at the Center for BioChimera. Anything else?'

'Yeah. This is even weirder, but do you remember when Dusty came home from San Diego, seeing a bruise on his back? Or maybe his hip?'

'A bruise.' Oscar grew quiet. 'I remember something like that. Yeah, yeah, I do. Annie thought he banged himself when he tumbled down the rocks. Is it important?'

'Yeah.' Grace felt faint. 'Yeah, actually, it is.'

She clicked off and stared blankly out the window.

It was easy to see it then, how it worked.

Vacationing four-year-old Dusty Rhodes slipped off some wet rocks while watching seals play in La Jolla, and for the first time, Grace wondered if the fall itself had been orchestrated. No matter.

He fell and broke his arm and had surgery at the Center for BioChimera. His insurance was good there at the hospital and they were only minutes away from the Center when the accident occurred, so it made sense to have him treated there. That was five years ago.

It turned out to be hugely important, where he went. Because that same night, three pregnant women came to the Center. There they were

381

injected with an unknown substance.

Not unknown anymore.

It was bone marrow.

Taken out of Dusty. Bone marrow injected into the developing fetuses of three women, injected as an experiment, so the developing fetuses would forever recognize Dusty Rhodes's cells as *self*. One miscarriage. One toddler died of tumors.

But one kid, Eric Bettles, grew up to be a sickly boy who won the Lotto of medicine: a heart so perfectly matched, he'd never need meds. Perfectly matched because it had been engineered for him. Engineered out of another boy's cells.

All the time Dusty Rhodes was growing up, riding a bike, learning to play the harmonica, another kid's frail body was being groomed to accept Dusty's heart as a perfect match, accept it because their cells had been intermingled in utero.

She stared. Her throat closed. She was falling.

The plane shifted and she realized they were beginning their descent into Montgomery Field. Grace fumbled for her checkbook; looked at the calendar, what the date was, a year ago Sunday. The date Dusty Rhodes went down a road in Iowa, flinging papers on his bike. And never came back alive.

October 23.

Her breath made a rattling sound as she wrote it down. Lining it up, knowing what she'd find.

October 23, one year ago — Dusty Rhodes was kidnapped/killed.

October 23, one year ago — Eric Bettles got a heart-in-a-box.

Not a heart-in-a-box. A heart taken from the chest of a boy.

Her pen clattered to the floor. Nausea rushed over her and she closed her eyes, willing her stomach to calm down.

'Grace?' It was Jeb, in the headphones.

If it was true, then she'd find the same thing one more time.

'Grace, you okay?'

Katie's ear surgery. The bruise on Katie's back, after her ear surgery. Right after Katie had disappeared from the room and nobody could find her. Katie's fussiness and irritability. How she screamed when Grace tried to hold her.

It wasn't the ear surgery; it was the pain in her back.

Where she'd just had marrow removed.

They'd taken Katie, wheeled her away from post op, punctured her bone marrow, sucked out what was needed.

'They pulled marrow out of healthy children and injected it into developing fetuses, so later, there'd be a perfect match.'

'Excuse me?' Jeb said.

'The neonatal window,' Jeanne cried from the backseat. 'Where everything is accepted.'

Not possible. An evil beyond imagining.

This wasn't the way it looked. It couldn't be. There had to be an explanation for what she saw. *That's good,* the voice inside said, *because Hekka Miasonkopna's got a chart, too.* Grace pawed through the papers and found Katie's sheet for the day she went into surgery.

She already knew what she'd find. Katie's ear surgery had been four years before, September 16.

The same day a small, terrified Indian woman named Maria Miasonkopna came to the Center late at night for a second sonogram. A sonogram never recorded on the chart except for a brief notation on the side. A secret sonogram in a secret room.

Grace knew where to look for Katie now.

At the Center for BioChimera, on the pediatric transplant floor, the floor nurse picked up on the fifth ring, her voice out of breath.

'Hekka Miasonkopna's room? Sorry. Nobody there.'

'Is she in surgery?'

'I can't tell you that.'

'Wait. This is important — '

The connection broke.

42

All Hallows' Eve, 11:41 p.m.

Jeb made the approach into Montgomery Field and brought the plane down smoothly as Grace stuffed the charts and loose pages back into her bag. He took off his headphones and motioned for her to do the same.

'You okay?' His eyes were kind and searching under the baseball cap.

She shrugged, unable to speak. 'Thanks for the ride. What time do you have?'

He checked his watch. 'Exactly nineteen of.' He reached over her and unlatched the door. He glanced back at Jeanne. 'I'll make sure your friend gets home. Take care of yourself, Grace.'

She ran for the car. It was a black sedan waiting out front. Her driver had soft pink cheeks and thick eyelids that made him look sleepy.

He nosed the car into traffic and climbed the familiar road leading to the Center for BioChimera as she dialed Mac's number. He wasn't picking up. She tried Warren's number at the Center. Nothing. On impulse, she dug out the number that Thor had given her, the number Opal had used to call her brother. Lee's private line.

It was disconnected. Fear seized her. She leaned closer. 'Can you go any faster?'

'Hold on.' He stomped on the gas as she tried

385

the Center's main number.

A recorded voice said, 'You've reached the Center for BioChimera. If you've reached this number during normal business hours, the desk attendant has momentarily stepped away . . . '

No, no. She clicked off, thought better of it, let it ring through, listening to the message, punching zero, praying for connection to a real voice.

'Security,' a nasal male voice grunted.

The driver was speeding down Torrey Pines Road now, past the gray blank walls of biotech buildings. 'Yes, this is Grace Descanso and — '

'Spell it.'

'Look, this is an emergency and — '

'Dial nine-one-one.'

'I don't need nine-one-one. I have to talk to Warren Pendrell. Dr. Warren Pendrell. He's the CEO, the director of the center — '

'Ma'am, if this is an emergency, hang up the phone and dial — '

Grace cut the connection. The car bumped into the parking lot.

'Which side?' the driver asked.

'Hospital.'

He headed for the Emergency entrance. She unsnapped her seat belt and was out the door the instant the car came to a stop. Bedlam greeted her inside the ER: an entire girls' basketball team still in uniform, crying and bleeding after what looked like a bus accident; an inert boy dressed as Robin Hood, his mother pressing a towel to a mangled arm; and an elderly man in a Batman mask experiencing

386

what looked like cardiac arrest.

It would take forever to make someone understand, and by that time, Katie would be dead. She pushed through the double doors, flew by a scrub nurse before she could do more than launch a startled protest, and found the elevator. It was stalled on three. She sprinted down the hall to the stairwell and climbed.

It was two more flights up and she pushed herself to move faster, knowing she was physically close to the end of what she had left.

She burst into the bright hall on three, her legs trembling. The first OR was dark. She checked the clipboard on the door. Not Hekka. She raced down the hall and glanced through the octagonal window of the second OR, pulling back as the surgeon flicked a glance her way. The draped patient was a toddler, not a kid Hekka's age. Maybe they'd hidden her. Maybe Hekka wasn't in OR at all. She had to be.

Grace slammed through another set of doors. A small desk spilled with charts. A harried intern sat in front of a computer entering data, rising in surprise as she ran past. To her left, a room opened onto a row of cotton curtains surrounding gurneys of patients preparing for surgery.

One curtain had been pushed back, revealing a drowsy teen murmuring to his mother. An IV snaked into a pole, the fluid bag almost full. Was Hekka swaddled inside a dim cell in prep? She considered racing down the row, ripping curtains open. She'd do it if it came to that.

A lab coat hung on a hook, next to a red metal crash cart. She slipped on the coat and pushed the cart into the hall, past a nurse and the intern excitedly describing the flash of Grace's green top as she'd darted past. Grace kept her head down, pushing the cart past a waiting room.

An old man with braids sat inside, whittling a block of wood, a knife in a gnarled fist. He was carving a small figure. An old man. An Indian. He didn't look at her, his knife taking small nips out of the wood. A small figure of a dancing man glowed in his twisted hands.

Grace retraced her steps. The waiting room was empty except for the old man. She knelt in front of him. 'Hekka.'

He stared, eyes cloudy with cataracts.

'She's yours, isn't she? A granddaughter, maybe? Where is she?'

How much English did he know? He blinked impassively.

'Understand? I need to find her. This isn't a heart built for Hekka in the lab. This is a heart they are stealing from another child to put in your Hekka. A child still alive. My child.' Her voice broke.

He glanced at the figure and kept carving. Too late. She wasn't getting through. No help here. Grace scrambled to her feet and pushed the crash cart on, passing a surgical locker room.

Where was Mac? Light gleamed from the OR window at the end of the hall. She ran to the window and looked down.

The OR was below her. A dark-haired girl lay on the table, Swan-Ganz line in her neck, EKG suctions clamped to her thin arms and chest. A nurse swabbed her chest with yellow antiseptic.

They were just starting, still casual. An anesthesiologist tweaked dials. The perfusion tech manned the bypass machine. A skinny man with bleached hair tips held up a white card in front of a burly cameraman calibrating a color bar, both in OR gowns and wearing surgical booties. They were joking casually.

It had to be Mac's team. That was Hekka down there.

It meant they were still taping. Mac was going forward with the taping, he wasn't even trying to find her.

That was the girl who was going to get Katie's heart, unless she could find a way to stop it. She banged on the window and the man with the dyed tips jerked his head up, trying to locate the source of the noise. The operating lights made it difficult.

She banged along each window, harder and harder, her desperation mounting. She had to make them understand. Had to stop it. She couldn't find the way in.

How could Mac still tape with his daughter missing?

You're wrong about one thing, Mommy. He's not dead. He visits me sometimes.

That was crazy. She'd been driven to the edge and had fallen over it and the ground was speeding up, coming right at her.

Why wasn't he doing more to save her? Why hadn't he canceled that shoot?

She pounded on the window. She wasn't sure they could hear the words, but there was no mistaking the desperation on her face. 'You have to help me. Stop this operation!'

From the angle above the OR, she could see the intern who had tried to stop her, racing up to a security guard, see the guard slant a look at her. He nodded as the intern gestured wildly and the guard reached for his walkie-talkie. Grace ducked away from the window and ran.

She raced back down the hall the way she'd come. She couldn't be found. They'd think she was some nut. They'd contain her.

And Katie would die.

From the stairwell came the stealthy sound of feet scraping up metal stairs.

Coming fast. The security guard.

Heavy footsteps, no attempt now to hide. Grace backtracked toward Hekka's OR. The crash cart stood in front of the surgical scrub room and Grace yanked it in after her and closed the swinging door. From the hall came the sound of the stairwell door bursting open and the ragged sound of panting.

She looked around wildly. Lockers gaped open, the floor was littered with discarded gowns. She darted into a shower stall and closed the curtain. Her heart raced.

The scrub room door opened. In her shoulder bag, Jeanne's cell rang. She clicked it to *Vibrate* and shut her eyes, praying he hadn't heard.

She could hear breathing coming closer. The stall curtain ripped aside.

It was Mac.

'God, Grace. My sound guy said he spotted you through the viewing window. What were you doing, banging on the window?'

'Thank God, Mac. They'll believe you. Come on, let's go.' She was dragging him toward the door.

'Where are we going?'

'Into OR first. We have to stop Hekka's operation.'

He stopped walking now. 'Look, Grace, I know you're not thrilled with the work I do but — '

'You know what they're doing down there? They're going to put Katie's heart in that girl's chest.'

Even as she said it, it sounded hysterical. Not believable, and she could see his eyes shift, a hardness creep in. He raised his hands, placating her.

'Grace, you've been through a lot, and I know you've got to be right on the edge of losing it. Maybe you have.'

Mac looked strained. He'd been up almost as many hours as she had, she reminded herself. She'd called him shortly after three in the morning, and he'd spent the rest of the night building the CD audio pieces she'd used to break away from the Spikeman. He'd driven to L.A. and back. Looked for Katie at the halfway house.

He dated Lee, a small voice said.

He defended Lee. He'd taken a crew to Opal's place. To tape. Not to save. To tape. He was still having his crew tape Hekka. So which was more important?

Whose side was he on?

'Grace, I don't have time to argue news with you.'

'You're right. We don't have time. I know where she is, Mac. I know where Katie is. Lee's got her.'

He made a small sound of impatience.

'Lee never created a heart-in-a-box, Mac. That scientist you got to rebut her on camera — '

'Newt Poundstone?'

'Whoever he is, he was right.'

'And you know this because?'

She thought of the best way to explain it. 'Remember that CNN piece you did on the hand transplant? And then the woman in Paris who had part of her face transplanted?'

He nodded, frowning, trying to figure out where she was going with it. Grace's phone vibrated. She ignored it.

'Remember how doctors found both times that by infusing the patient with donor marrow cells, it increased the chances of the donor part being accepted? The patient not rejecting?'

'What are you saying?'

'That's the work I did at the Center, Mac, making transplants compatible. Lee figured out she could inject bone marrow cells into a *fetus*, Mac. And have that fetus forever recognize that donor as *self*. That's what she did. Lee's the ringleader, has to be. She had a helper. Opal Perkins took our daughter's marrow and injected it into Hekka when Hekka was still in utero.'

'Wait a minute. Opal's involved. Lee's involved. You could do conspiracy theories for networks, Grace. You're good.'

'That's what Lee did, Mac. She's getting ready

392

to kill our daughter, harvest her heart, and use it in Hekka.'

The phone started vibrating again and she pawed through her bag, tumbling the timer out onto the floor. Mac retrieved it; even before he handed it back, she could see that the face of it had changed. Four minutes, six seconds before the timer went off.

Ere midnight tolls, I cut your heart.

It was here, finally. The worst. She dumped the timer back into her bag and clicked on the cell, her eyes on Mac. 'Yes?'

'I think it's time you slowed things down, Grace.' Mac shifted closer.

In the phone, Marcie was saying, 'Listen very carefully.' Mac grasped Grace's elbow and she moved away, out of reach, backing up against the scrub sinks. He seemed too close, his face watchful, tense.

'What's up?' She covered the phone. 'I'll be there in a second, Mac.'

'Grace, you said Mac. Are you with Mac McGuire? Don't say his name. Just yes or no.'

Mac shifted his weight. Blocking the door.

'Yes.' Her heart was hammering so fast she could barely hear.

Mac stepped closer and Grace felt the air shift. From safe to not safe.

'Grace, get away. Understand? Whatever it takes, get away. Tell me where you are.'

In the hallway, a muted voice was paging a doctor. Grace pressed her finger to her ear and glanced at Mac. She shrugged.

'Could you speak up? I'm at the Center on the

hospital side and it's hard to hear.'

Her heart was racing now; a high, singing noise pounded in her ears that made it hard to hear what Marcie was saying, and harder still to understand.

'You're there already,' Marcie said. 'Okay. I'm going to count floors, and you'll say 'uh-huh' when I get to the right one.' Marcie counted slowly and when she got to three, Grace said 'uh-huh.' Eyes on Mac. 'The cops are on their way. Understand? Be there soon. Got that?'

'We're trying to find her,' Grace said, looking at Mac.

Mac was studying her face carefully. Something clicked beneath his eyes.

On the phone, Marcie said, 'Paul Collins ID'd the palm print in the taco van Eddie Loud was driving.'

'Yeah, I'm really worried.'

Another silence and then Marcie said, 'Remember that awful case with David Wester-field, killing that little girl in his RV? How we found Danielle van Dam's handprint in his RV?' Her voice was heavy. 'Paul ID'd the palm print in the taco van and it belongs to Mac McGuire, Grace.'

Grace was skidding, the way it felt when she was in an elevator and it dropped twenty floors fast.

'Did you hear me? The palm print is Mac's.'

Grace sighed, some part of her already knowing the rest, not believing, but knowing.

'The worst thing. God, I wish to God I wasn't having to tell you this. The worst thing. The print wasn't in the van itself. It was inside a small cabinet in the van. Paul found three other handprints there, too, Grace. All different. All belonging to kids. All of them missing.'

Grace closed her eyes. Time was imploding, events colliding, her mind on fire.

I've been working on this piece for six months, Grace. Lies.

Benny Jingelston across the table from her at Folsom. *I can tell you what the ideal combination is . . . somebody who can do the video part, and somebody else to — recycle the product when it no longer serves a useful function.*

On the phone Marcie was saying, 'He's extremely dangerous. Do you understand? Do not, repeat, do not allow him to take you anywhere, Grace. We have a team on the way. They're bringing a warrant for his arrest. One other thing you need to know. There's a marriage license in Carmel for a Mac McGuire and a Lee Ann Bentley. They're married, Grace. Whatever they're doing, they're in it together.'

Marcie clicked off.

What does Daddy say?

Just private stuff. He's coming back for me.

Grace had been so sure it had been Katie's need for a father that had created one. But now it turned out her instincts had been right after all. Hide from him. Hide her child. Hide them both. She'd hidden from Mac. But Lee Bentley knew exactly where they were and she'd told Mac. How long ago? No way of knowing. But long enough for them to plan it out together. His wife.

He'd visited Katie in her room.

No wonder Katie had disappeared without a trace. Without a sound. In the blink of an eye. She hadn't gone with a stranger, somebody unknown to be feared.

She'd gone straight into the arms of Daddy. Straight into hell.

'Where's Katie?'

'What?' Mac took a step toward her. There was a wary coldness in his eyes.

She backed away, stepping on dirty scrubs littering the floor.

'What have you done with her? You and Lee.' Her hip touched the crash cart she'd pushed. A wheel jammed. She couldn't back up anymore. He kept coming. She could smell his skin, a man's scent laced with sour sweat. She wondered if there was anything in the narrow metal drawers that could stop him. The side with the drawers was angled away from her. She let her hand dangle, moving her body in front, eyes on him.

'What are you talking about?' He shrugged, boyishly mystified, but she wasn't buying it.

'I know what you did to those other kids,' she interrupted. 'Your palm print, Mac. It was in the van.'

'I have no idea what you're talking about.' His voice was harder now.

'You've known for years Katie was yours. And you hated me enough — I got away! You hated me for that. And you planned it out perfectly, how you'd take her. What? Lee didn't want anybody else's kid along for the ride? Is that it?'

'That's not funny, Grace.'

Grace shifted her weight and inched her hand along the drawer behind her until she found the handle and slid the drawer open. Gauze rolls, from the feel of it.

'Only a couple of little snags,' she went on. 'Minor, really. Warren was going to sell this place. And you'd both lose the perfect place to do what you had to do. Is that why Warren isn't answering? Did you get him, too?'

Mac shifted his gaze to the crash cart and back and she knew he could see she'd opened a drawer behind her. He wasn't smiling anymore.

'Hold it. You think I took Katie.'

'The cops are on the way. You're done, Mac. This is it for you.'

Her fingers moved to the second drawer and inched it open. She felt metal and slid her fingers along it. A hemostat. Not sharp enough. She kept going. More metal. Her hand closed.

He wet his lips. 'Grace, I think this whole thing — ' He took a step and lunged.

It was a retractor she brought up, a blade on one end. He knocked her hand away but the blade slashed his arm and he grunted and lost his balance as a bright line of red appeared. She yanked free an empty metal tray and banged it down on him and he fell badly, his hands splaying out. There was a muffled *whump* as he hit the floor. She was making gagging sounds, trying to stop herself from throwing up. Adrenaline shot through her.

She stooped cautiously and listened. His breath whistled. A lump welted his forehead.

Blood streaked his arm, and she wrapped a towel around it and dragged him to an oversized locker. The first one held clothes, but the next was empty, and she scrambled behind him and half lifted, half dragged him in, shoving his knees up to his chest, folding his arms on top, resting his head. She closed the door and jammed a wad of gauze into the hole where a lock would go. She'd alert security he was in there. Wounded, angry, and dangerous.

But first she had to save her daughter. She ran into the hall, pounded across the sky bridge, and headed for the door guarded by a retina scanner, the steel door guarding Lee's lab.

43

Grace ran. Lee's lab was on the other end of the winged V across the sky bridge. She was certain now where she'd find Katie. Lee would use her private lab as a killing ground, and take Katie's heart from there, pretending it was the second heart-in-a-box. She'd do it right at midnight.

Grace reached the heavy glass doors leading to the private lobby Lee shared with Warren. Locked. She banged her shoulder into the glass, trying to break it.

'Warren, it's me, open up. It's Grace. Hurry!' She crashed harder into the glass with her shoulder. A crack spidered across the frosted glass.

Inside the door, a shadow appeared.

'Drop your hands and get away from that door.' Behind her in the hall, the gunman's voice was flat and he carried his weight on the balls of his feet, coiled and tense.

Grace took her hands away from the glass and stared in the direction of the voice. There were two men, both with weapons drawn and pointed at her.

In unison they said, 'Grace.'

They lowered their weapons and she did a double-take, recognizing Stuart and the shorter man who had been in her house the day before, wiring it.

'I've got to find Lee before the timer goes off. Please.'

'You're not making any sense.'

'Can you open the door?'

'That I can do.' Stuart put his revolver back in his shoulder holster. They came down the hall as he was taking keys out of his pocket. 'You remember Brian.'

Brian nodded curtly at her, his gun still drawn.

'He has to stay out here, guard the hall.' Stuart unlocked the doors. 'There's shit going on right now, we have to protect Dr. Pendrell. Where in the hell have you been? We tracked you to the Century Plaza and then zip. Dr. Pendrell's been worried sick about you.'

She ignored the question and pushed open the doors with such violence she fell into Warren's arms.

'Hey,' he said in surprise.

The steel door was closed, the lobby empty. He was dressed in a trench coat and the lines in his face seemed deeper.

'Did you get my message? Come on, I need you to open the door.' She pulled him toward the retina scanner.

'Let me take off my coat, okay?' His movements were weary. He looked exhausted.

'There's no time.' She pushed him forward.

He allowed the red light to spark his retina. He blinked and Grace sped around him into the lab hallway as the steel door opened.

'I'm coming with you.' Stuart slid through at the last moment. The lab hallway was silent and their footsteps echoed as Grace raced past Warren's open office and tried the door to Lee's lab. Locked.

'What's going on?' Warren said again. He had taken off his trench coat and he gave it to Stuart to hold.

'I was right. Lee's got Katie stashed someplace, and, Warren, she's going to kill her.'

'Wait a minute, stop. Grace, slow down. You're not making any sense.'

'There's no time to slow down!' Grace pounded on the door and twisted the handle. 'Katie! Honey? Can you hear me?' She twisted the handle again. 'Where's the key, give it to me.'

Warren clamped his hands gently on her shoulders and turned her toward him, forcing her to look at him. 'Grace. Take a breath. Now.'

She forced herself to slow her breathing.

'First of all, I have no idea what you're talking about.'

'You didn't get my message?'

Warren looked at Stuart. He shook his head. 'Grace, I just walked back in here not more than five minutes ago. We're closing escrow within minutes. Remember? I have to be back for the wire transfer. That's why I'm here. I want to get that handled and then I swear I'm yours. However you need me.'

He glanced back at his open office door, and she sensed his troubled preoccupation with business. It made her feel even more frantic.

'I left you a message,' she repeated. 'Where have you been?'

Again, he looked at Stuart. Stuart looked pained. Warren said quietly, 'Grace, we just came from the police.'

It was one of those moments that seemed to

hang. Time was suspended. In that instant, all the life surging through her froze, waiting for the rest of it. Adrenaline rushed up her body in a volcanic swell. She was disoriented and calm. So calm. That's because it wasn't happening.

'No,' she said. 'No.'

'I had to identify — '

'No,' she said more loudly. It was rude of him, continuing to speak. When she'd made it so clear she couldn't hear this. Wasn't going to hear this.

'They found her in an alley off of Midway.'

Grace blindly reached a hand out and missed the wall. She was falling.

'She was shot, Grace. I'm so sorry to have to tell you this way.'

She couldn't breathe. The floor was rushing toward her. Warren caught her and held her. She took a ragged breath.

Dimly, she heard him say, 'I can't believe I lost her. Jasmine's dead, Grace. She's dead.'

She looked at him blankly. 'What did you say?'

'I tried to find her and I failed. I *failed*.'

She righted herself. 'Wait. What did you say? You said Jasmine. It's not Katie?'

He looked confused. 'No.'

His eyes cleared.

'Oh, dear God. Katie's still gone. Oh, Grace, you thought — ' His voice sharpened. 'No. Grace, what's happened since yesterday? Where did you go?'

He hadn't heard her before. Hadn't understood.

'Katie's here somewhere. At the Center. I'm sure of it. Lee's heart-in-a-box never worked,

Warren. It's a lie. We have to find Katie and stop this.'

'Stop what?'

'Lee's going to kill Katie and use her heart.' Grace wrenched the key out of his hand and opened the door. 'Katie?'

The lab had been stripped. Counters wiped clean, no vats.

'What happened here? Where is everything?' Grace ran down the aisles, yanking open cabinets. Where was her daughter? Was it too late?

Warren cut her off rounding a corner and clamped a hand on her arm. 'Remember, I said the sale was going through? Lee's cleaned out her lab, she hasn't run off, Grace.'

Grace wrenched her arm free. 'Warren, listen to me. Lee Bentley is the one who sent you the postcard. She and Mac McGuire are in this together. They're married. Did you know that?'

Warren's eyes snapped open in confusion.

'Mac's wounded, I stuffed him into a scrub locker in the cardiac OR wing on three, across the sky bridge.'

'I'm not tracking any of this.'

'Listen carefully to me, Warren. Mac and Lee have been in this together, along with a woman named Opal. She runs the halfway house Jasmine and Eddie were in. Lee has Katie somewhere here, and we have to find her before she's killed. Understand? Stop Hekka's operation, that second heart-in-a-box. It's not a heart-in-a-box. It's Katie's heart Lee plans on harvesting and using in Hekka.'

Warren took a stumbling step. She reached out and he pushed her hands away, and in that simple gesture was the stunned humiliation of an old man.

'I'm okay,' he said abruptly. 'Stuart. You and Brian find Lee. Contain her discreetly, but I want her stopped, got that? And brought to me. Until this mess is sorted out, nobody operates on Hekka.'

'Sir,' Stuart spoke in a short burst, his words clipped and urgent, 'all due respect, what about guarding you? Until the sale goes through you're — '

'Nobody's back here, we've checked. Nobody can get through that retinal scanner without me. I'll be fine. The important thing is finding Lee. And stopping her. Hurry. I'll reach you by cell if necessary.'

Stuart nodded. He raced down the corridor and pushed the button to open the steel door. It whispered shut behind him. Warren took his cell phone out of his jacket pocket.

'Now tell me what this is and what I can do.'

'There aren't lab-built hearts, it's all an elaborate fraud.'

'Lee showed them to me, in the lab. Wait. Let me take care of this.' He spoke curtly into his cell phone. 'Dr. Frederickson. Anesthesiology. I don't care. No. Patch me through.'

'Lee knew you wanted to sell, right? She knew if she came up with a heart-in-a-box, her cut would be millions.'

She could see Warren processing it, not liking

what he found. 'There never was a heart-in-a-box, is that it?'

'Lee extracted marrow from specific healthy kids and injected that marrow into developing fetuses with bad hearts.'

'The neonatal window,' Warren whispered. 'When all matter is considered self.'

Grace nodded. 'Exactly. While the fetus is developing there's that small, brief time when it's sorting out what's self and what isn't.'

'So you're saying, she took this bone marrow from healthy kids and injected it into the developing fetus during the neonatal window so — '

'So there'd be perfectly matched hearts ready and waiting when the time came. Total compatibility. Hearts perfectly matched, because the injected marrow was treated as self.'

Into the phone Warren said, 'Phil, how far are you? No. You're not going to get that heart. We'll try another donor, if one comes available — No, that heart's not coming.'

Warren grimaced and shouted into the phone, 'I'll explain later. Security's on its way to enforce it. No, that's it. It's going to *have* to be. Fine.' He clicked his cell, got a new line, and placed a quick call to security, describing Mac's location, but his mind was on Lee and the damage she had done.

'Is there any other place Katie could be? Anyplace else in the Center that's security-monitored and sealed?'

'Lee lied to me. The sale's a fraud. Jesus. I've got to call — '

Grace clamped her hands on the old man's

405

arms and felt his muscles tense. '*Where could she have put Katie?*'

His eyes refocused. 'She has a second lab down the hall but there's nothing there.'

They ran down the silent hall and Warren unlocked the second lab. He was right. There was nothing. She could see Warren's growing desperation. He unlocked the door to his private lab, roving the immaculate aisles, pace speeding up, already knowing the futility of their search. Nothing but gleaming counters, wide empty spaces. Where was Katie?

'Empty because of the sale, but I thought maybe — '

'There's got to be someplace else,' Grace cried. 'Think.'

Warren closed his eyes. 'We have a supply room tucked around the corner. We've used it as a staging area for things we're taking with us. Believe me, there's not enough room in there to move around, let alone — '

They heard it the same instant. Faint, thready, coming from down the hall. '*Mommy.*'

Tears blinded her eyes. She ran toward the sound, toward her daughter, her terror melting into relief. A single padlocked door stood in the cramped hall.

'I'm *here*, honey. Hang on. Mommy's here.'

Warren twisted the key in the lock. Grace yanked open the door. A dim cave. 'Katie, honey? It's Mommy. Warren, could you turn on — ' She stopped.

Mommy. The same sound. The same intonation.

Plexiglas cubes glowed in Day-Glo colors: lemon, lime green, pink, purple, the cubes hanging in the darkened room like props on a set. In the corner, something wheezed.

Katie's doll hung in a vise, tipped, its tiny chest pressed by a metal screw.

Mommy. There were sixteen squares on the wall, flickering with images.

She backed away. Four wide screens across, four down, each of the sixteen danced with different videos, black-and-white, color, some in extreme close-up, and one shot as if it had been sighted along the ridge of a gun. The images capturing the moments of Grace's life. Katie taking toddling steps, crowing with delight. Katie wearing soccer pads eating an ice cream cone. Katie getting into the car at Albertson's, talking to Grace, both of them laughing.

Behind her, the door closed and locked.

Warren smiled. In the half-light of flickering monitors, his mouth twisted in a nasty grin.

From her bag came the sound of a bell, tolling. It was a rich, deep sound that lingered in the air and faded into silence, and in that moment, Grace felt as if her soul itself hung suspended. It tolled again.

Warren extended his hand and Grace pulled the timer from the bag and gave it to him. He turned it off.

'Welcome to my world, Grace. Welcome back.'

44

Midnight

Grace backed away and banged into something behind her. A shrunken body of a girl stood in a Plexiglas case, her eyes permanently wide and staring, her tiny feet planted a distance apart. She was wearing pink shorts and carrying a puppy she held frozen against her chest.

No. A statue, so lifelike it looked miniaturized. Grace recognized Warren's daughter at about age six. Wearing anklets with scallops and Buster Brown shoes and a T-shirt hiked up on one side. She wore her straight brown hair in bangs, and a small yellow plastic barrette pushed the hair away from an ear.

The daughter who'd grown up and run away. Grace's eyes were adjusting to the dim light and she looked past the statue and saw a heavy chair with arm clamps. A chain lay on the floor next to it, bolted to the wall of screens, and the flickering images played along its length, culminating in a set of ankle cuffs. Somewhere a bellows sounded, air wheezing like a manic fun-house distortion. Something made of cloth fluttered on a frame like a torn flag.

It was a small room, and a console rose in the middle of it. It was from here that Warren could regulate the video on the screens. He watched her taking it all in, a smile playing across his face. She gauged how far the door was, and how fast she'd have to move to get there. What she'd have to do to disable him.

He reached into his suit pocket and lifted out a small, snub-nosed revolver and pointed it at her. She took another step back and heard the sound again, more distinctly, the throaty rasp of bellows pushing air through a contained space.

'In a few moments that phone will ring, and when it does, I'll put in my access code and my part of the deal will be wired to the Caymans. Within five minutes, a helicopter will be landing on the roof to take me to an undisclosed location, a location which is sympathetic to *americanos* with large bank accounts and a need for privacy.'

'What about Katie?' Her fingertips were turning numb. It was spreading up her arms.

'There will be no Katie by then.' His voice was matter-of-fact. 'You'll have a choice. Come with me. And live. Or stay. And be killed.' He motioned toward a door. 'This leads to an anteroom. Strictly off-limits, but you're welcome to look.'

He prodded her with the gun, and she stumbled and righted herself and walked down a small set of stairs leading to the side room. 'Go on. Poke your head in. Take a look. That way you won't entertain any fantasies about where it leads.'

It was an anteroom facing a steel door. The door had no knob so it must slide open and shut, she thought. She wondered if it opened by retina scanner, the way the steel door leading to his and Lee's labs did. If there was a door, it meant something was behind it.

She pressed her palm against the door.

'Katie.' Her voice trembled. 'Honey, can you hear me? I'm right here.'

She felt the cold metal against the small of her back. 'She can't hear you, I'm afraid. Move away from the door now. This is the last time you'll be permitted in this space.'

So Katie must be on the other side of that door. Her legs gave way and she caught herself. He prodded her with his gun and she stepped out of the anteroom, up the stairs, back into the main room, every step a brutal reminder of the distance that kept her from Katie.

Her mind raced; she needed to get him talking, find a chink.

'You're just leaving your office, your paintings, your books?'

He made a small sound. 'The Degas and the first editions? Copies. I sold the originals years ago. I've been leaching the bones of this company for decades, Grace. But we're talking about you.'

He was guiding her toward an upright Plexiglas coffin. They drew closer and Grace saw that it contained a stained wrinkled lab jacket, a pack of cigarettes, and a drinking glass smudged with coral lipstick. Scattered on the floor of the exhibit were clippings of curly hair. Her color. All encased in the Plexiglas, as if it were sports memorabilia from the big game. The exhibit was lit with blue light and it made the lab jacket and lipstick glow eerily white.

'What? You don't remember? I'll never forget.

The first day we spent discussing your future plans, Grace. How you were going to save the world, one small, damaged child at a time. You informed me of this while smoking a cigarette and cutting your hair with surgical scissors. And rushing back into the pediatric wing when necessary. Oh, how I admired your dedication!'

He was crazed, standing silhouetted against the screens, leveling his pistol at her heart.

'I see you don't remember this at all.' His voice tightened and she was afraid.

'We did a lot of things together,' she started.

'Shut up.' He waved the pistol in the direction he wanted her to go. 'Keep moving.'

They were coming up on the sound now. She stopped walking. 'I remember this one,' she said quietly. 'I wore it the day you told me you'd recommended me at the parish for work in Guatemala.' She glanced at him. He nodded.

It was a dress, cotton with a wide skirt in a small print with buttons down the front and capped sleeves. It hung on a frame. Bellows pushed air through a nozzle positioned inside it, so the air expanded the dress and flapped the hem, as if it were inhabited by an invisible Grace, breathing and shifting, with cartoon gargantuan breasts, the whooshing punctuated by the faint cries of the Katie doll saying, *Mommy, Mommy!*

'You saved these things? All these years?'

'Mementos, Grace. Mementos. They can fuel love. Or hate. Hate is actually more difficult to keep alive than love. It has to be fed.'

Again Warren pressed the gun into the small of

411

her back and reached for her elbow. They moved sedately around the dress. Grace's mouth went dry. Trapped in Plexiglas was a yellowed flyer wrapped around a tightly rolled paper bag, held together by a rubber band.

'You don't know about this one.'

But she did. Dusty's dad had just told her about his son throwing those flyers for his Cub Scout badge. 'You killed him, didn't you?'

'I wanted to see if it worked, yes. And it did, brilliantly.'

Grace looked away, remembering Dusty. Seeing in her mind's eye Eric Bettles bouncing the basketball in the driveway with his dad.

'Perhaps you're bored? Perhaps you'd like to speed things up?'

She tensed. On the multiplex screen Katie was in her T-ball uniform, running to home, safe. Balancing on a beam, jumping off. Dragging her feet through leaves after school.

Warren smiled. 'I thought not. Well, don't worry. I truly saved the best for last.'

He moved her along, past the pedestal holding the flyer. She trembled. Her legs gave way. He looped an arm around her.

They were standing in front of a new pedestal. It was a small exhibit. A terrible one.

He'd taken a photo of Katie's face and blown it up, mounted it on springboard. The wind was blowing and it fanned her hair out in radiant concentric circles of light. Her eyes were closed, the lashes long and curly, and her mouth open, wide with laughter. He'd attached the photo with a spike to a crude rack. The spike protruded

412

from Katie's forehead.

On the rack hung Katie's princess costume. The sparkly crown. What she'd been wearing when she'd disappeared. He'd looped the laces of the Air Walkers together and hung them on the rack, and they twisted in the air, pink socks stuffed and rolled into the shoes.

'Why 'Spikeman'?'

'Why not? It's catchy. Has kind of a snap. Even the excess of the Timer Game can be justified. I did it for my own amusement. Look at any of the games on TV. *Survivor. The Amazing Race.* Enormous planning, but oh, the fun! I had the time, the resources, the energy. I enjoyed it. And the science. Bringing you along step by step until you understood. The problem with being brilliant is that there are so few who understand. But you! You would see!'

'If I'd missed a deadline?'

'Katie would have died.' His voice was matter-of-fact. 'Let me clarify that. She would have died *sooner.* That's all. Sooner. It heartened me to see the effort you expended. It made you a worthy competitor. That's the only reason I'm even offering you a chance to go along on my great adventure. You amuse me, Grace. There are few women who do.'

'So Mac wasn't — '

'Mac was the best source of help. So I set out to discredit and disable him.'

'They weren't married? Mac and Lee?' Part of her lifted, part of her sang.

He laughed. 'God, no. They dated a few months, until he figured out what she was.'

'And that is?'

'A monster. A beautiful, amoral, cold-blooded, lovely-to-look-at monster.' He shrugged. 'She amuses me, too. She'll be joining us in our little ménage à trois.'

'But the palm print. Mac's palm print was found in the taco van.'

'Let's just say Marcie wasn't above a few well-placed lies in return for a million dollars cash.'

Marcie was in on it. Grace hadn't expected that.

'But you called security. He'll be rescued.'

'Oh, no, Grace, I didn't. Mac's going to bleed to death.'

'Why are you doing this?'

Warren Pendrell came closer until she could feel the soft whuff of his breath. He spoke quietly, almost in her ear, an intimate act that terrified and repulsed her.

'Money. Pure and simple. Hundreds of millions of dollars are at stake here, Grace. This place has been a money pit since day one. Do you know how hard it is to bring any drug onto the market? Thousands of biotechs go under every year, banking on the wrong horse. I'd had a couple of expensive disasters in a row. I wasn't going to lose everything, not after what I'd poured into this place. I needed a hit. Something huge.'

Onscreen, images of Katie as a toddler eating birthday cake, two fists at a time.

'And then it turns out Lee Bentley had the answer all along. She came to me one day and explained how the heart-in-a-box could be made to look real, how we could make all this money. We could use what you'd learned — about infusing patients with donor cells when they got a heart transplant — and expand on it. Infuse bone marrow cells into a fetus while it was developing. And make it one hundred percent compatible. Fake people into thinking the heart-in-a-box was real. And I knew my prayers had been answered.'

On the screen, Katie was searching for clues, laughing at somebody just off camera. Playing the Timer Game, the footage grainy and uneven, shot through the windows, the game played at the party Saturday, every Monday. So many games on the screen, Katie laughing in every version, tall and shorter again, stretching and compressing like Alice.

'What was in the bioreactor if it wasn't a heart?'

'Oh, it was a heart created on a collagen form and seeded with cells, just exactly the way it looked, and maybe in another ten years, they'll get the damn thing to work properly, but I don't have ten years, and for now it's too fragile to survive any kind of pressure, let alone the pressure exerted when blood pumps through. No, that's for show. For Belikond.'

Warren gazed out over his domain, one hand on his hip, the lord of a ruined castle.

'And I realized I could — take care of a few nagging loose ends of my own. And then little Dusty came to visit and had his — accident, and we realized we could use him, too. Take his

415

marrow. Experiment on those three couples. See if it worked, so we'd have the advantage of working through the kinks before harvesting the one we truly were interested in. Opal was quite skilled by the time she drew Katie's marrow to use in Hekka's body.'

Onscreen, a blurry image came into focus and Grace saw herself again as a new mother, holding her baby in her arms, a look of light on her face.

'Why me? What did I ever do except leave medicine?'

Warren's face tightened. The images of Katie, her small fists weaving, flicked across his face as he stepped in front of the screen.

'It was my granddaughter who came off that stretcher. My granddaughter who needed a heart. My granddaughter you killed through your own ineptness.'

'Guatemala?' She was confused. 'You're talking about Guatemala? I didn't kill — '

'Silence.' In the flickering images, his face looked demented. 'I depended on you, Grace. When you told me the nun from your parish was going to Guatemala, I went to the parish myself, on your behalf, remember? Told them what an asset you'd be to Sister Mary Clare. I set up everything. Got word to my daughter. Her husband.'

'The general.'

'The general. They were looking for him everywhere. He couldn't bring her in for treatment to a regular hospital but I'd been working with you for months. I'd seen what you could do, the miracles you wrought. I arranged everything. And you failed.'

His voice rose in a staccato lash of fury. 'You dropped the ball. You didn't come through. *You killed her! You!* After I'd guaranteed my granddaughter's safety! You made a mockery of me, Grace. And you canceled any chance I had of bringing my daughter home. He disappeared, afterwards, and took my daughter with him. And then to find out you were expecting. You were going to get the gift that had been taken from me! No, I was delighted to use Katie. It was fitting.' He took a shaky breath.

'We knew before you did, Grace. Who the daddy was. We've known all along. Do you know what it's like, losing all you hold dear? You do now, don't you? You have a taste of what that's like. That endless loss of hope.'

Grace licked her lip. 'I want to see her. Katie. Where is she?'

Warren raised the clicker and aimed it at the screen. The screen melted away. And in its place, lights blazed. Grace found herself staring down into a cement operating room.

Katie lay strapped to a gurney.

45

Mac came to with a start in the pitch black of the locker and fought nausea, and then remembered where he was and fought panic. He was crouched in a fetal position, legs locked under him, wounded, the space so small he had to squeeze his shoulders to fit. His feet stung and he furiously moved the balls of his feet, flexed his ankles, trying to get back circulation.

The air was close and hot. His lungs burned and he wondered how much longer before he ran out of air. Pricks of light came through the sliver of vents. He forced his breathing to slow. Searing pain shot up his left arm. He slid his good hand over and pressed the wound. Renewed pain raked his arm and he dug his forehead into the metal door to keep from passing out. His arm was slippery with blood. Bad news. He was still bleeding.

If he didn't suffocate, he'd bleed to death.

He remembered his key ring, and he squeezed his good hand around his chest and slid the ring out of his pocket. He breathed shallowly and he could feel his back slick with sweat.

He found the Swiss Army knife and detached the tiny penlight and trained it on his arm. A gash slippery with blood. He opened the knife. It was dull and flimsy, and he hacked at his shirt, ripping a piece he fashioned into a clumsy tourniquet.

He aimed his penlight at the crack between the door and locker. Keys were stronger than a knife blade and he tried them all: cars, trunks, house in Atlanta, all the keys to all the newsrooms in his life. Too thick. None slid into the crack.

Credit cards were useless against whatever Grace had wedged into the locker to hold it. He slid the blade into the crack and leaned hard against the door, the top of his head banging against a hook. The blade snapped off in his hand. He wiped his mouth, beamed the light on the blade. It had snapped neatly across, leaving a straight edge protruding a half inch from the handle. Just right to slit his wrists and be done.

He flashed the penlight up. Three flat prongs flared off a hook from a metal base screwed into the top of the locker. He held the penlight in his teeth, keeping the hook in view, and inched up his good hand, using the sheared-off blade like a screwdriver. The screws dropped like metal hail onto his face, and he yanked the hook free and shoved it into the crack, leaning all his weight into the door. Blood rushed to his face and he strained, cramming the hook into the wedge and using it as a lever to pry the door.

A sliver of light appeared. He gasped, relaxed, panted against the door, and tried again, pressing the hook deeper into the crack and leaning his shoulder into it as if it were a brand he was gouging into his flesh. The top of the door bent and he leveraged that into a bigger opening, still not big enough to climb out of, and then suddenly the door burst open and he fell out, blinded by the sudden light.

What had they done to his daughter? How could he find her? *Katie, Katie.*

He patted for his keys. Nausea surged up his throat and he took vast gulps of air. He rolled to his knees and gripped the buckled door, steadying himself before he tried standing. Pain shot down his arm and he fought the urge to pass out.

A roll of gauze lay on the ground and he bent painfully down, the pressure in his bleeding arm slowing his progress to a trembly set of lurches, and retrieved it. He remembered his keys then and found them inside the open locker.

It was too hard to stand right away, and he eased into a sitting position and rested his back against a closed locker and looked at his arm. The tourniquet had bled through. He pressed the gauze against the wound. The crash cart still sat with a drawer open, the way Grace had left it.

He was in a hospital. He could crawl into the hall and yell. Somebody would find him. Help him. No time. He had to stop the bleeding and find Katie. Not get stalled in ER explaining himself.

He planted his feet and took deep breaths, and when he was ready, he used his good arm to pull himself up. His legs shook from the effort. He shuffled to the crash cart and found suturing thread and a needle and a sharp blade he used to saw the tourniquet free. He rolled up what was left of his shredded sleeve and pressed fresh gauze into the wound, forcing his panic down.

She'd only nicked him a good inch or so, not severed a vein. It was messy but it wasn't lethal. He mopped the blood and stitched the damage, remembering the slippery feel to the arm of the soldier in Kabul, how he'd stitched him up, how he'd helped Grace those weeks with everything she needed in the clinic. Sewing people up sometimes. Old men. Little kids.

Where in the hell was Katie?

He finished and cut the thread and wrapped a piece of gauze around the stitches. He was shaky then, but okay. He looked up.

Lee was watching him from the doorway, a smile playing across her perfect features. She was wearing fresh scrubs. In one hand she held a gun. In the other, a cooler.

'This what you're looking for?'

It was small, an Igloo that could hold a six-pack of beer and a couple of sandwiches.

'What did you do?' He grasped his bandaged arm and shuffled toward her, voice hoarse.

'I think you already know the answer to that.'

'You did this to Katie?'

'Oh. You know about Katie.' Lee swung the cooler gently in her hand.

Some cold dark thing moved in his solar plexus; he'd never felt as close to killing anyone as he did in this moment, facing this woman staring calmly back, one small hand grasping the cooler. He wondered if it already carried his daughter's heart, a heart slack in a bubble of saline, resting on a bed of shaved ice. 'Where is she?'

'Gone, Mac.'

He shot forward and his hand closed on her throat.

Lee pressed the gun against his head. 'Don't. Do. Not. Step back. Away.'

Lee held his gaze and he felt her blood surge through his fingers, how easy it would be to squeeze her throat, press harder. He dropped his hand and took a step back.

'It was a lie, all of it.'

'The lab-built hearts. Yes. It's not possible, at least not with the technology we have now.'

Mac weighed the chances of knocking the gun free, smashing a fist through her face, and yanking the cooler out of her manicured hands. The revolver was a Bodyguard Airweight, a Smith & Wesson five-shot, specially altered with a silencer so it wouldn't snag silk when she ripped it out of her pocket and aimed it, like she was now, at somebody's face.

'Where is she? Where's Katie?'

'What do you care where she is?'

He forced himself to think logically. If the heart was just the first harvest, it meant Katie was still vented on a heart-lung machine. 'That's what you do in your lab, you and Warren carve up kids.'

'Only two,' she said mildly.

'Two.' If she was vented, maybe he could still save her.

'How do you think Eric Bettles got a perfect heart-in-a-box a year ago? Thanks for your part in it. You played it perfectly.'

She stared at him quietly, a mocking smile on her face.

'We're not monsters, Mac. Just greedy. Belikond wants to buy the Center and its assets, and the big one is the heart-in-a-box. So we had to make it look real.'

'And then you take the money and leave.'

'We take the money and leave,' she repeated. 'The transfer is complete in exactly — ' She glanced at her watch. 'Ten minutes. And then we — '

'Disappear,' he finished.

'Yes.' She smiled briefly. 'Clearly, I'm going to kill you, that's the only reason I'm telling you all of this.'

The pain made him dizzy and he shifted his weight, trying to stay balanced. His knees felt soft. His fingers moved in his pocket, and he found what he needed. The blade was broken where he'd snapped it off, but it still had a good inch on it, straight across.

'Did you target Katie in particular?'

'Of course, she was yours and Grace's child.'

That knocked the air out. 'You knew.' He felt along the edge.

'Katie had to die. When we realized how you'd leeched onto Hekka, we needed to know what you knew. Nothing, as it turned out. That's why I came on to you, to find that out.'

Mac kept silent, his fingers moving. He found the handle. 'So when you came on to me you were just . . . '

She laughed. 'You are such a guy. What a guy thing to say.'

She raised the gun.

'Good-bye, Mac. It's been fun.'

46

Katie lay draped in sterile sheets, curls limp. It was the stillness, the quiet of her small body that made Grace's heart seize.

Her bare chest glowed under the harsh light. EKG leads had been pasted to her arms and a trach tube burrowed down her slack throat. She was vented. A machine was breathing for her, but she was still alive.

Grace's mind raced, running down paths, sorting. Every path led straight to this, staring into an operating arena where her five-year-old daughter lay poised like a sacrifice on the altar of a psychotic god.

'I haven't killed her — not in the technical sense. She's not brain dead. I did that to prolong your exquisite suffering. We'll be doing multiple harvests with this donor. Normally, the kidneys go first, but Hekka coded, so we're taking the heart first.'

Warren leaned over Grace, casually using the clicker as a pointer, pointing out the less flamboyant aspects of harvesting.

'We'll be harvesting the liver, lungs, corneas, kidneys. We've dummied paperwork for the transplant coordinator, so you have the comfort of knowing that every scrap of Katie will be used. But the heart, well, that one needs no transplant papers. That's the one perfect match in the bunch, the heart-in-a-box.' He laughed.

Her mind was slow, numb. All she could see was her daughter and how defenseless she looked. 'Is she on a neuromuscular blocker?' Her voice had a quaver in it.

Warren's mouth twisted in a smile. 'That would be rich. Awake and paralyzed. She's on a blocker, but she's out cold, Grace. Has been since we mixed chloral hydrate into a glass of lemonade and left it in her bathroom. She's on desflurene and a new neuromuscular blocker, succinylcholine. The old one caused liver damage and since we'll be harvesting her liver . . . ' He shrugged.

The words were slow, not understandable.

'What about her voice? Calling me?'

He went to a console near the screens and leaned into a microphone and said, 'It's all black. An', an' it feels like it's shaking. Moving.' He punched a button, adjusted dials, and the voice morphed, getting higher and higher until chillingly, the voice coming from the console was Katie's, with just the right timbre, pitched with anxiety.

It's all black. An', an' it feels like it's shaking. Moving.

'We had her doll. So we could match the voice and build what we needed.'

'You told the anesthesiologist that Hekka wasn't getting a heart.'

'You think somebody was on the phone when I said that? No, they're expecting it. They probably have Hekka's heart removed by now, the procedure taped by Mac's crew. Isn't that rich? Taping the operation where his own

425

daughter's heart is implanted in the chest of another kid. Titus Andronicus has nothing on us. Hekka's waiting. Won't have to wait much longer.'

Grace looked down at her daughter and thought of the transplants she'd done at the Center, the seamless preparation with an experienced anesthesiologist, OR techs opening the instrument trays and setting them up, the circulatory nurse, the main surgeon, the assistants.

The room was empty, except for Katie.

She couldn't imagine an entire medical team participating in this evil.

'There should be at least ten people in the room. You're not doing the transplants there.'

'No, Grace, just the killing.'

Grace couldn't breathe.

'She's under deep sedation, a barbiturate coma. All we have to do is take her off the respirator long enough to affect her brain. It won't take long. We'll monitor it closely and when her heart rate starts slowing, we'll put her back on the vent, but of course, by then, she'll be brain dead. Then she'll be wheeled into an OR where a team will perform the transplants. You don't need accomplices, Grace. Just coordination and good paperwork. And of course, a killer.'

From the cement scrub room, a woman emerged dressed in scrubs and a hospital mask, a pager attached to her lab coat. She raised her face curiously and stared at the wall as if she could see them, and Grace recognized Opal.

'It's dangerous, the line of work you're in,' Warren said. 'You make so many enemies with time on their hands. Opal Perkins, trying to help out a boss by getting what he needed from a competitor. Using that audio bug on a chart. Costly, her arrest and trial. The unpleasantness cost her a career at Scripps. She was happy to walk across the street to the Center for BioChimera. Happy to groom damaged adults into playing their parts. The nurse and Dr. Mike Yura. Those were mentally ill clients, five years ago, who lived at the halfway house. Conveniently gone now. Opal groomed them into following DeeDee Winger and her husband into the parking lot, following Robert Harling Frieze and his wife. Talking them into coming back later that night. The advantage to using the mentally ill is that they *believe*.'

'Jasmine.' Grace remembered what DeeDee Winger had said about the woman who'd met them that night at the Center and taken them down into the basement. *Really beautiful black hair . . . Looked almost Indian.*

Warren nodded. 'Jasmine had a bit part but Opal was a star. Happy to come back at odd hours and extract bone marrow she later injected into the wombs of women carrying children with malformed hearts. Happy, so happy to be here tonight, Grace. For the final act.'

Warren prodded Grace with the pistol and she felt the cold metal press into the small of her back.

'Come on, take a seat.'

Below her in OR, Opal peered up at Warren,

427

waiting, only her eyes visible under the mask, eyes bright with malice. Warren shook his head slightly. He pushed a button so his voice could be heard through the speakerphone in OR. 'Patience, Opal.'

Opal nodded and crossed her meaty arms, staring at Katie with a look of such hatred it made Grace's blood cold.

'Well, shall we?' Warren pointed at the viewing chair. It was bolted to the ground and had armbands of steel. Next to it lay the heavy chain attached to the wall, the chain with ankle cuffs.

'Wait. What about Eddie?'

'What about him?' Warren's voice was bored.

'You picked him on purpose? Sent him in the taco van to deliver a message to me. A warning. You'd scrambled his thinking; you knew he'd kill the drug agents because they were in Tyvek suits, and the patrolman out back because he was a threat. You knew I'd have to kill him before he killed me.'

'Of course.'

'You wanted him to die.'

'I was counting on it. Senator Loud was trying to shepherd through legislation which would have impacted the dollar value of my assets, allowed generics to be marketed more easily. I warned the senator, discreetly, of course, that if he continued, I'd harm what he held most dear. He continued. It was business, Grace. That's all.'

He shifted his gun. 'Ready?'

'Wait. Wait.' A plan came into Grace's mind. Not a plan, an act of desperation. Her last, if it failed. 'I'd like to hold something of hers in my hands.'

She kept all hope out of her face. Katie lay in the half-light, draped and prepped, her small face pale. Warren shrugged.

'Fine.' He flicked a glance at his wristwatch. 'Thirty seconds on the clock, Grace. Remember the door's locked and I won't hesitate to shoot you in the back if you try to run. Ready. Go.'

She raced to the exhibit of Katie's things, passing the odd exhibit of the dress billowing over bellows. The dress continued to balloon as if a phantom Grace were inside, gasping.

She reached for the Air Walkers, her back to him.

'Fifteen, Grace. You have to be back in your seat by then. Show's about to start.'

She ripped open the shoes' tiny pockets, the little cubbies, praying it was still there. A dime. Bubble gum.

A latex balloon.

47

Mac dodged to the right and snapped the blunt blade out of his pocket. He hurled it straight at Lee, putting his good arm and shoulder into it. It glanced off her scrubs and clattered uselessly to the ground.

It was just enough to make her shoot wild. It was a shocking pop, a small sound. A bright hole slivered a locker behind him. She steadied the gun and aimed, her lovely yellow-green eyes wide, the gun hot in her hand.

It wobbled.

She looked confused for a moment, and then her hand went to her throat, and Mac could see an ivory handle, wedged into the hollow. She opened her mouth and closed it, making little sucking noises. The gun banged to the ground and she pulled the bloody shaft of the knife out of her throat and stared at it, her eyes puzzled, as if still trying to figure out what it was.

A wash of blood bibbed down through the slice in her neck, soaking her scrubs red. She toppled and fell. Mac stared at her. He felt numb. He snatched up the cooler and opened it.

There was only ice in it and Mac let out a low sound of pain and relief. Katie's heart hadn't been harvested yet. Maybe he could still save her.

Don Jose stood hunched in the doorway.

Mac swallowed, putting down the empty cooler. 'Don Jose.'

The old man raised a yellowed hand corded with veins. 'Acceptance of the natural order of things. That is the Yaqui way.'

This from an eighty-year-old man who had just hefted his knife and sailed it into the throat of a woman brandishing a gun, slicing her throat and killing her.

Don Jose smiled slightly, as if reading Mac's thoughts. 'Sometimes the natural order needs assistance from unnatural quarters.'

He cocked his head as if listening to a sound only he could hear. His old eyes stared across the shower stalls and sinks, the damaged locker gaping open, and settled his gaze on the still body of the beautiful woman dead at Mac's feet.

'It has begun.' He shuffled over to Lee's body, crouched down, and retrieved his knife.

And still Mac needed to be sure. 'You know there's no heart for your granddaughter.'

'Yes.'

'And you know that by not getting one, she's probably going to die.'

'It comes for us all, Mac McGuire. Go swiftly. Or it may today find you.'

'Thank you,' Mac whispered.

He bent and clumsily lifted Lee to his shoulder. He ran.

★   ★   ★

'Five, Grace. Don't make me clamp you in these ankle cuffs. The arm restraints should be sufficient. I want you in this seat now.'

He turned slightly to emphasize his point, *this*

431

chair, and *now means now*, and in that brief moment, Grace saw her chance and turned toward the dress. It gusted and she shoved her hand into the gap left by the neck hole, found the metal nozzle expelling hot breaths of air. It was a small balloon, pink, curled in the Velcro pocket for days. She couldn't mess up; couldn't poke a hole. She lipped it over the nozzle and slid it down, anchoring it. It bubbled with air.

A sleight of hand. Look this way. While I do this. She stepped in front and reached for the zipper on her pants. Her mouth curved into a gargoyle smile. The sound of the bellows changed; blowing into a contained space.

A contained latex space.

'What are you doing?'

She leaned against the rack for support. Her legs trembled. Inside the dress, the pink balloon expanded.

'Isn't this what you want? What you've always wanted?'

Anger darkened his features. He bridged the distance between them in three steps and grabbed her arms. 'I don't know what kind of game you're playing, but you're done.'

He was dragging her toward the chair. The balloon bulged under the dress, and suddenly there was one huge breast and one sagging one, and Warren flicked a glance toward the dress and frowned. He pushed her aside and ripped the dress open. It was big now, a pink balloon unnaturally expanded past breaking point, air wheezing and inflating it with each push. A small bubble filmed the balloon, milky white, the weak spot.

Warren's eyes changed. 'No. You didn't.'

He jumped backward trying to get away, tripped, and toppled the Katie exhibit, losing his grip on the gun. Grace kicked it out of reach as he grabbed his throat, eyes wild.

He was wheezing. 'My shot. My epinephrine. On the console. Next to the phone.'

Grace retrieved the gun and pointed it at him. On the console, the phone rang.

'That's going to be Belikond,' she said calmly. The gun shivered in her hands and she clamped her hands around it and it stopped moving.

The balloon exploded.

A loud, muffled *whump*.

Latex shredded the air.

'No!' He dropped to his knees, his face bright red. Tears streamed. He was making choking sounds now, scrabbling away from the dress, trying to get away back toward the window, back toward the chair and the awful chain bolted to the wall.

The phone rang and rang and then it stopped ringing as his screams took on a hoarse edge. He had rolled himself next to the window. A cockroach, she thought in wonder. A scuttling bug. She put the gun down, and yanked him back, rage fueling her, rage at what he'd put her through, at what he'd done to Katie. She dragged him a few inches until he was within range and clamped the cuff around his ankle.

Above him the tattered balloon gently streamered out with each gust of forced air.

433

Grace punched the speaker button and suddenly Warren's high-pitched wheezing, his thrashing struggle to breathe, filled the OR arena, the terrifying sound of a man on the edge of insanity whose airway had closed. His legs started to jerk.

In the OR, Opal went to the window and looked up in confusion and the beginning of alarm, sensing something was wrong. She ripped off her lab coat, the pager a wink of gray plastic as she left it behind and rushed for the door.

Grace scooped up the revolver and darted into the anteroom and pressed against the wall. She heard clicks, an electronic beep signaling the door was being unlocked. It snicked open.

Opal stood blinking in the half-light. Grace came down hard with the butt of the revolver, and Opal rocked back on her heels and sent a fist slamming into Grace's arm, catching her by surprise and sending the gun flying.

The steel door was sliding shut.

Grace pushed past Opal and vaulted into the room. There was the sensation of air rushing and then silence as the door sealed shut.

She stumbled and regained her footing. Katie lay in stillness, her mouth open around the trach tube, her small, defenseless hands palms up, a drape over the bottom half of her body. Grace let out a breath, words tumbling in an incoherent rush of love and relief and alarm as she went to her and slid her arms underneath her body, holding her gently, a precious weighted cargo. 'I'm here, honey. Mommy's here. Everything's okay now.'

Katie was cold. So cold.

Somewhere near Opal's abandoned lab coat an alarm bleated. It wasn't the same sound as the door opening, so Opal wasn't coming back. The vent machine looked standard. It registered twelve breaths a minute, average for a sedated child, with a tidal volume of 200 cc's of air. She'd need to get somebody there to run tests. Her daughter's lungs were paralyzed from the neuromuscular blocker. Katie would have to stay on the vent until the potent drug could be washed from her system and her own lungs could take over, and then she'd have to be brought up slowly and carefully.

It sounded like a microwave oven, Grace thought. But it was coming from the lab coat. The speakerphone was still on and she heard Opal's exclamations, and the sounds of her scrambling through the room, and of Warren's labored breathing.

An alarm sounded in some other part of the building, and a rumbling undertow gathered momentum, like a giant sea swell. As if a massive herd of people were moving at the same time.

Grace smoothed a clammy curl off Katie's forehead. 'Okay, sweetie, I'm going to have to figure out how to get us out of here.' Talking out loud to her daughter shored her up, and made her feel braver than she felt.

She studied the viewing window. It hung a good twelve feet above the sunken operating room. And the panes of glass were threaded with steel bolts. Even if she could stack everything in the room together and somehow break through the glass, the panes were too small for her to wriggle through, let alone safely transport a small inert body attached to a vent machine.

R2-D2, Grace thought. Or was it C-3PO? One of them talked in those little beeps.

Suddenly in the viewing window, Opal stared down at her, a gloating hatred animating her features. Warren wobbled against her, his head lolling.

'Fool,' Opal hissed, her voice reverberating through the OR room. 'Don't you know what you've done? There's a bomb in the room, Grace. A bomb. You'll never get out. Neither of you.'

The beeping was coming from the crash cart. Grace's gaze went to the lab jacket Opal had torn off and left behind.

'It's the pager. On my lab coat. That's the bomb. The pager's the bomb. I electronically activated it. The beeping's going to stop pretty soon. And that means you have four minutes thirty seconds left. That's it. Oh, you'll get a thirty-second warning at the end so you'll know.'

Grace stared at the pager. Her mouth went dry. The beeping stopped. There was only the sound of the vent machine. Red numerals whirred on the face of the pager: 4:27. 26. 25.

'You have less than five minutes before you and your precious daughter blow straight to hell. How do you like *that* Timer Game?'

Above them Grace heard a clattering roar and a scraping sound. A helicopter was landing on the roof and Opal lurched away from the window, one arm around Warren. They'd leave within minutes. Lift off into the sky.

With the hard money, the down payment from Belikond. Warren had that, but not the rest. Not the millions more he was counting on that came with the closing.

In the end, it was about money. And Warren had lost the only part that mattered to him.

But Grace was losing everything. A swelling rise of panic and pandemonium echoed dully through the sealed room and in front of her, numbers whirred in the last Timer Game she'd ever play. She was alone with her daughter. In a locked space with a bomb set to explode in less than five minutes. She'd die there with Katie.

There was no way out. They'd won.

48

Terrified pandemonium greeted Mac in the halls, throngs pressing toward the stairwells. The alarm shrilled, the sound merging with the deafening cries and shouts of people fleeing. Lights flickered in the hall and over the stairwell, creating an eerie convergence of shadows and form.

'*Attention, all patients. We are beginning a medical evacuation. Ambulatory patients, please move in an orderly fashion toward the exits. Medical personnel, please assist all patients off the ward before exiting.*' The voice through the speaker was calm, disembodied.

Patients in stretchers and wheelchairs jammed the hallways, as medical personnel worked at evacuating the most critically ill. Mac worked his way around a nurse bending over an old man on a gurney, holding an IV bag on his sunken chest.

Mac shifted Lee's heavy body and made his way slowly against the current, pressing toward Warren and Lee's lobby, screaming every time someone banged into his damaged arm.

The glass doors stood cracked and open. The steel door was sealed shut, the labs unreachable. The sirens had set off the phones; six lines at the receptionist's station blinked impotently. The retina scanner glowed like a red eye.

His arms were tired now and his legs were starting to give way. He shifted Lee's body so that he held it in front of him, and when he reached the red eye of the retina scanner, he gripped her with his good arm. Her head lolled back on his chest as if she were a lover. He was panting now, his face slick with sweat. He tilted her beautiful face and pushed open her eyelid, positioning her eye until it hit the red beam of the scanner.

For a moment he was afraid it wasn't working, and then the door slid open and he laid her on the ground and went through.

★ ★ ★

No way out. Four minutes left. Less. Grace ran into the scrub room. It had been built out of cement blocks and was bare except for double sinks and a supply cabinet. The cement wall separating it from the operating room didn't extend all the way up, but it would still afford them some protection. She wondered if she could squeeze Katie under the sinks, but what would happen if the sinks came loose in the blast?

Red emergency sockets had been placed in a wall to the left of the sink, so it had to be that wall that was structurally the most solid. Those were sockets powered by a generator during an earthquake. She'd remembered that from a sleepless night rocking Katie, when she'd channel-clicked to a public television station; red sockets meant emergency generators.

Okay, she'd put her on the floor next to that wall. Make a bed. Out of what? She pulled off her top and folded it. The cabinet. Had to be towels, something. She raced to it and yanked it open, praying it wasn't empty.

A small set of towels sat on a metal shelf and she swept them up and feverishly carried them to the rough bed and added them to what she had. No time. She ran back into the main operating room. There was a cabinet in there and she found fresh sheets and towels, stopping only long enough to glance at the pager: 2:49.

In less than three minutes, the room would explode, taking her and Katie with it.

★ ★ ★

The hall corridor on the other side of the steel door was deserted. From here, the cries were muted. The building rumbled with the volley of footsteps in stairwells. Mac limped down the hall, pain coring his arm like an ax. '*Attention, this is not a test. Evacuate immediately. Do not delay.*'

He pushed open a door and found himself in what had once been Warren's library. It still had paintings on the walls, and some books, but it had the feel now of a set, something manipulated for effect, not real. He moved as quickly as he could. The pressure of blood pumping through his damaged arm was stronger the faster he moved, but it was a necessary trade-off.

Katie wasn't there. He wasn't going to allow himself to think about Grace, what she'd done. What she'd thought. He only hoped it hadn't cost him his daughter.

He found a small bathroom and an adjoining conference room. Both empty. He went back into the hall and tried Lee's lab. Empty and vacant. No shelves of beakers, DNA thermocyclers. No prop created to look like a heart-in-a-box. Mac gripped his arm and padded down the narrow aisles, looking for Katie, and it seemed in that instant he'd always been looking for some part of her, something small and new that needed his protection and care. The lights in the building flickered as he lurched back into the hall.

Another lab, Warren's. Empty, empty. What was going on?

The alarm shrilled and Mac knew time was running out. Where was she? What had they done with his daughter? The power surged. Shadows flicked and he held on to the wall, chasing it to the end. A second hall came off the long one at the end and he rounded the corner, moving faster. There was a door at the end of the hallway and it stood ajar.

Mommy. Was that Katie?

Mac pushed the door open.

Mommy. Was that her voice?

The room was dark with eerie cubes of light, Plexiglas cases, cubes of lightweight polymers, a high-tech art museum. His throat closed. A high-tech horror show.

Lights pulsed and in the strobe of flicking power, he saw twisted coils of neon, lighting exhibits. He took an involuntary step back. Ahead of him spread a huge wall of glass.

He limped closer and looked down.

49

She could use the gurney as a shield, a metal lean-to protecting them, providing she could lift Katie safely to the ground. She wheeled the gurney close to the wall where the vent machine was plugged in, and slid her arms under her daughter's body. Katie seemed so much lighter than she'd remembered, and she wondered if they'd fed her anything while they were keeping her body alive. No, they had to be giving her fluids, her veins were good, and they wouldn't want to risk sending her heart into cardiac arrest because of potassium deficiencies.

She had to believe Katie was okay, the way she had to believe she could save them.

'Okay, sweetie, I'm going to lift you and put you on the ground. I'll try to be careful but it's going to feel hard, the ground, but I won't leave you there long.' She was talking out loud to comfort herself, a whistling past the darkest graveyard she could ever imagine.

She lifted Katie free and shoved the gurney out of the way, awkwardly settling her daughter on the floor next to the vent machine. Katie looked even more defenseless lying on the ground without the trappings of the gurney. At least a gurney gave the appearance that all was well, that something clinical and organized was about to happen; here, on the floor, with her small white face and her still small arms, Katie looked inert, like a fallen angel.

Grace stole a fast look at the pager. Less than two minutes left. She grabbed the gurney and pushed it toward the scrub room and banged it onto its side. It took precious seconds to figure out how to get the legs to fold up, and then she hoisted the gurney against the scrub room wall and raced back to Katie.

She wheeled the vent machine as far as the cord would allow. This was the tricky part. The scary part. She was going to have to yank the cord on purpose, detach Katie from the ventilator and seamlessly vent her manually as she pushed the vent machine and carried her daughter to safety.

And she couldn't let herself be terrified by the sound of the shrill alarm the vent machine would register as she pulled the plug. Alarm bells had shrilled in Guatemala, as everything fell apart.

'Okay, sweetie, here we go.' She was going to yank the plug and start venting by hand at the same time. Venting by hand involved squeezing a bulb and she could do this. It would only be thirty seconds or so until she could reattach the outlet to the red socket in the scrub room, and she could do this. The last time she'd vented someone by hand, after Sister Mary Clare physically could not continue, the patient had died.

Her mouth was dry. She crouched down and scooped up her daughter, carrying her to the vent machine and locating the bulb she'd use to manually inflate her lungs. About every five seconds, she needed to squeeze it. That would be twelve breaths a minute. With her other hand, she reached for the cord and yanked it hard.

A warning alarm cut the silence, coming out of the vent machine.

'It's just an alarm, nothing big,' she muttered. Five seconds. She counted them out and squeezed the bulb and heard the sound of air rushing into her daughter's chest, so she was doing okay. She was carrying her daughter, counting and squeezing the bulb, half pushing the vent machine forward with her knee. It was on rollers and that was good.

She half hobbled through the scrub door — *breathe, Katie, breathe* — and laid her daughter down onto the pallet of towels, and then she had the vent machine close enough to plug it in. She heard the reassuring sound of air rasping through the machine again.

She'd kept back a couple of towels and she used those now to stuff between Katie and the cement wall, a flimsy cushion against compression and death.

Her ears, she thought. They'd lose their hearing, it would blow their eardrums out.

They were going to die and she was worried about ears.

She found the gauze roll and lay down next to Katie and tilted the gurney over them. Her fingers wouldn't work and she fumbled with the gauze, nicking it with her teeth, ripping off a chunk, a second strip, two more. She balled one strip and stuffed it into Katie's ear, then tipped her daughter's head and inserted the second gauze strip, and then she was out of time, her fingers *icy God icy cold trembling.* Her fingers were shaking badly as she ripped a strip with her teeth and inserted it in an ear.

Grace knew, then, what happened when the first hunter lay bleeding and trampled by mastodons; what happened when fighter jets corkscrewed out of a crackling sky with pilots cranking useless controls; the dull surprise on the face of a kid dogging a ball into the street and looking up startled and facing two thousand pounds of steel; the secret thing shared by all, every last one: the AIDS patient gargling in a hospice, the construction worker thinking about lunch as the bus roared out of nowhere, the ninety-year-old great-great-grandmother dreaming of the boy in the white linen suit who said the sweetest things.

I want to live.

Grace pulled the metal gurney down and angled it over them.

'Katie!' It was a wail straight from the gut.

Mac's voice. It was coming from the other room.

He must have found the secret room and was looking down right now on the empty OR.

He was going to die if she didn't warn him.

She would die if she did.

In OR, the pager started beeping.

⋆ ⋆ ⋆

Mac pressed his hands against the glass. He'd seen too many OR's not to recognize it. Even

445

though there wasn't a tray of surgical tools or a Stryker saw, the lights were OR kliegs and a heart and lung machine stood at the ready. Toward the rear there appeared a separate cement room that had to be a scrub room. Was he too late? Where had they taken his daughter?

Something was beeping and it was coming from that room.

He ran the length of the window, searching for a way in, and found the steel door with the keypad code. There was no way in.

He ran back to the window and smashed it with his fist. The glass held, not even a spider crack.

'Katie!' He screamed her name.

Grace staggered from the scrub room, face smudged, stripped to her tank top. She looked as if she'd survived a nuclear blast. She raised her head, eyes unfocused, her gaze traveling in the direction of his voice, her face white, shocked.

'Mac?' Her voice rang with exhaustion and panic.

'Up here. How do I get in?'

'There's a bomb. Run.'

Her face was blank and then she saw him, and she went bright with a look he hadn't seen since they'd been together in Guatemala. It was the pure, transforming look of love. He understood, then, what this warning had cost.

'Save her!' he cried.

And Grace ran.

She ran in despair and terror back into the cement scrub room and squirmed in next to her

446

daughter, wrapping her arms around Katie and pulling the metal gurney over them. A tremor of heat streaked up the gurney and Grace closed her eyes. The room exploded in crackling light and a blast of thunder.

50

The volley of heat shot up the wall and the floor shook. Something metallic and huge cracked and smashed to the ground. The sink. Grace cried out. The temperature in the tiny, enclosed space spiked into a broil and subsided, and Grace feared the tubes keeping Katie hooked to the vent machine would melt. Grinding noise. Pain sliced her ears. She braced herself and held on. Rain fell. Hot rain. Scalding rain. The sprinklers. She'd been caught in earthquakes before; everybody in San Diego lived with the tremblers, the sudden rocking, pictures cracking off walls, dishes hurtling off shelves, but not this.

This shivered along some invisible fault line like an electric snake. A beam crashed against the gurney and slid, and Grace could feel the shock bang up her back. She pressed herself against the small still body of her daughter and held on as the floor heaved and bucked.

It stopped. Pitch black silence.

Rain fell, warm pelting rain mixed with choking dust and grit. She squeezed an arm up and pulled the gauze from her one ear and rubbed her unprotected ear, rotating her jaw, trying to get hearing back.

She carefully moved her hands along her daughter's body, searching in the braille of love for any damage and finding none. She tentatively tried pushing against the shield with her back to see if she could get more room for them. It wouldn't give and she realized they were enclosed in a small prison now, wedged against the wall by the same gurney that had shielded them from the blast.

In the dark close by, a warning beep sounded. It was coming from the direction of the vent machine just outside the gurney. There hadn't been room to protect the machine under the gurney and now she panicked, worried that it would shut down and that Katie would die after all.

She had to find the hand pump. She was certain she'd taken it in with her but now she wondered if maybe she'd left it on the cement floor next to the vent machine when she'd gotten it running again. She patted Katie's body and her own, a sense of urgency welling up that was hard to control. She couldn't find the pump.

She took a slow breath and this time moved a single hand over her feet and carefully up her body. She found it wedged under her left leg and she just had to figure out how to get it attached to Katie's vent line. She would get it ready now, so when she needed to make the actual shift she'd be able to do it smoothly. Her daughter needed air whooshing in every five seconds. Oxygenate that sweet brain.

The beeping stopped.

Katie's life support was gone and she had five seconds to save her.

Five.

Her hands were shaking badly as she touched Katie's face in the dark and found the trach tube. They were curled spoon fashion and she was going to have to reattach the pump from behind her.

Four.

She located the trach tube and pulled it out of the useless machine.

Three.

She shifted Katie slightly and moved her fingers over the pump, locating the hole where the tube would be inserted.

Two.

Her first try missed.

One.

She found the hole again and shoved the tube in hard.

Zero.

Squeezing it.

The merciful sound of air rasped through the tube and filled her daughter's slack lungs, air oxygenating her brain, air singing through her body.

Grace exhaled, her face damp, and realized she'd been crying.

When does a person give up all hope?

How long does it take?

She wouldn't allow herself to ponder that. She had to keep Katie alive and that meant squeezing the bulb every five seconds from now through eternity.

The thought of that filled her with fear followed by a sense of detached, floating calm. No, she couldn't be calm, couldn't allow herself. Being calm probably meant deep shock and if she was in shock, she'd forget to —

Squeeze.

She started counting again. She cradled Katie's head in the bulb-holding arm and wiped off her face with her other hand. Katie's skin was moist and clammy. She shifted the bulb to her free hand.

The sprinklers were easing off. Debris sifted like damp snow. Far away, an alarm sounded. No voices. The floor groaned and shifted imperceptibly, and Grace wondered how long it would hold or if there were aftershocks that would crumple the floor like a —

Squeeze.

Tin can. Cold air was coming from somewhere. A chunk of something — a beam? the floor? — banged nearby, the sound reverberating, crashing against canyon walls, ricocheting off heavy metal, the noise fading into, *squeeze*, silence.

She smelled something burning and, almost as frightening, the sudden raw smell of seaweed and salt water. Would the building collapse into some secret sea fissure? Or would they burn in a fire?

She wondered if Mac was dead. He had to be. There was no way he could have survived a direct hit.

She was going to have to shift things around because the arm under Katie's head was already going to sleep. It just meant putting Katie flat again and maybe, *squeeze*, rolling next to her so that her arm could still reach the bulb. She shifted Katie down and nestled next to her.

She couldn't afford to let her eyes close. If they closed, Katie would die. It was as simple as that.

Did anybody even know she was here? She thought about that.

Oh, God, *squeeze*, nobody even knew the room was there. But Mac had found it.

Something deep in the bowels of the building twisted and cracked and Grace stirred next to Katie, worried about what would come next.

How long would it take for somebody to get to her?

She tried to calculate that and couldn't. She was getting into a rhythm, *squeeze*, now with the bulb, squeezing and resting, squeezing and resting, her thoughts skittering. She checked her watch face, the small glowing numbers a comfort in the dark. An hour had slid by since the explosion.

Somewhere far away there was a sound she hadn't heard before and couldn't place.

She shifted her body. She was going to have to see if she could squeeze in against the wall and work on the other side of Katie. That way she could use her other hand.

She cautiously rolled a knee over the top of Katie, *squeeze*, and shifted her body until she was on the other side. The bulb came loose in her hand.

She let out a small cry and patted for the trach tube, finding it, hurriedly fitting the pieces together, despair and relief catching in her throat, *squeeze squeeze*. Air whooshed through the tube again.

'It's okay, honey, it's okay, I've got you right here.'

She was going to have to let go now. She was

getting tired. She bent down and carefully laid her head next to Katie. She found her small hand and kissed the palm.

She was tired, that was all. She'd just close her eyes.

'Grace. Grace. Can you hear me?' A bullhorn, from the sound of it, faint and coming from the wall where the sinks had been. That's what the sound had been that she couldn't place.

It was the sound of a human voice.

'I'm in here,' she half sobbed, half shouted and, *squeeze*, waited, hoping.

Silence met her and she shouted again, afraid now.

From somewhere close came the smell of acrid smoke.

She heard the faint sound of a buzz saw, grinding cement. 'Here!' she screamed again. 'Something's on fire.'

'We're breaking through.'

Flames roared up from some ruptured place, bellowing, ripping air out of the room, and suddenly the gurney moved and Grace pushed it off of them and saw a wall exploding in a haze of debris, outlining the shape of Paul Collins from the crime lab in a Tyvek suit, the power saw etched in red fiery dust.

Grace knelt and scooped up her daughter. Paul dropped the saw and held out his arms as heat rippled through the pallet of towels and sheets. She pushed Katie into his arms as behind her the wall burst into flames.

EPILOGUE

Mac had reacted with a split-second instinct that had saved his life. After Grace had warned him about the bomb, he'd hurled himself into the anteroom and the steel door had protected him from the worst of the explosion, but the ceiling had buckled above him and he was pinned under a beam in a pile of rubble.

The bomb, for all its ferocity, had been planted in a contained space: Warren's goal was to kill Katie, and Grace, if she intervened. Even though he was leaving the Center, the building itself was too important to Warren's ego to destroy. So while the Center sustained major electrical damage, structural damage was centered on the research side, leaving the hospital side without power or running water but reasonably intact.

Two people died, one in the transplant unit, the other a prominent bioresearcher.

★ ★ ★

Katie came back to life and remembered nothing from the moment she'd taken a long, faintly bitter drink of lemonade in the bathroom, until waking up in a hospital bed, her mother at her side.

Grace sat with her arms around Katie, struggling with how fragile it was, the small,

454

slippery moment that darted away, the sweet smell of Katie's breath, the rhythmic swell of her chest, those early sleepless nights jouncing a howling infant, certain Katie would never sleep and Grace would have to kill her; growing overnight into this child, long-limbed and pale, already leaving, dreaming her own quiet dream.

★ ★ ★

Across town at Scripps, Mac's arm needed pins and traction that would keep him in the hospital for another week. He looked pale on the bed and new gray threaded his temple. Grace shuttled between Scripps and Sharp, feeling the tug of both places.

With Mac, she did a cautious dance, filling in random bits from their lives, talking about tuna boats and concerts at Humphreys and the peculiar color of gray that hung over San Diego harbor when the water was churning and the wind blew.

Pete and Aaron stopped by, and it gave her a chance to thank them. Mac had text-messaged them at the Center and they'd helped locate where she and Katie must have been. Theo Sullivan, the homicide detective who'd taken her statement and kept her away from Senator Loud, stopped by the hospital room briefly, but he had a sick wife keeping him busy.

The third morning, Grace had just settled next to Mac as Paul Collins wandered in, chewing on a Subway sandwich.

'Marcie was easy to turn, I'm sorry to say.

Remember when she replaced you for that CSI that went south when those samples got slopped?'

'We never slopped samples,' Grace reminded him tiredly.

'Still got you both investigated.' Paul took a long draw from a Dr Pepper.

'I had to pick up Katie from the sitter. I'd been working straight for twenty-four hours and Jeanne had to go out of town. I didn't have anybody else.'

Paul nodded. 'Yeah, well, Marcie was pissed. Felt you pulled her into something that affected her family, cost her overtime. Her mom was sick and they were building that addition.'

Grace thought back over the good times with her friend and felt a wave of sadness. 'It was just the money, then.'

'A million bucks is a million bucks. That would have been her cut when the deal went through, so yeah. Nothing personal. Opal made the approach so Warren was once removed. It was supposed to be just a couple of easy things, at least it started that way. The first was to switch the sheets.'

'So it was Marcie who gave Dispatch the wrong sheet?'

Paul nodded. 'Yeah, and then her job was to simply turn off Larry's pager, so they went right to you. Then it got a little dicier, but by then, she was already involved and afraid it would come back on her if she backed out. Plus they'd already given her a hefty down payment.'

'Warren must have loved it when I called her from the road.'

'Oh, yeah. Asking Marcie to find out if I'd ID'd the palm print in the taco van, Warren loved that. It made it easy for him to implicate Mac.'

Grace shot Mac a look of chagrin and he nodded. They'd been over this before.

'Ever find out who the print belonged to?'

'You mean inside the cabinet? A vendor. It wasn't part of anything. And there weren't any little handprints from kids, either.'

'God, I was stupid.'

'You were afraid. Your kid had been snatched. This whole thing could have — well, I don't need to tell you how this whole thing could have gone.'

It woke her up nights, thinking about it.

Mac lifted painfully on his good elbow. 'What was Opal doing in the basement room at the halfway house?'

'The one with the lights and bed? Exactly what you thought. Using clients for porn she sold on the Internet. Apparently Warren wasn't in on that. It was just a side business she ran on her own. I hate to say it, but it's going to shoot your ratings through the roof when you air it, not that you need help in that department.'

Mac shrugged and grimaced from the pain, and Grace knew he was thinking about news, and the vagaries of his business. He'd had a full production crew on site to tape Hekka's surgery, a surgery that never took place. Instead, they'd had a ringside seat to a massive hospital evacuation, a bomb explosion, and the death of a prominent bioresearcher who'd been manipulating data and killing kids. They'd taped it all, including the rescue of Grace and Katie, and Grace's role in saving her daughter's life. The only thing Mac had kept back was his relationship to Katie, and Grace was grateful to him for that.

Neither of them wanted Katie to find out from the media who her daddy was.

But Mac was thinking about something else. 'He got away, didn't he? Warren.'

Paul chewed on his sandwich and swallowed it down with a Dixie cup of water from Mac's pitcher. 'For now.'

Grace could see Mac was getting tired. She gathered up the lunch wrappers and shooed Paul out. Then she sat back down and looked at Mac. He reached for her hand. 'You think we'll ever get past this?'

'You mean my trying to kill you?' She tried to make it sound like a joke and failed.

He studied her hand, the small nails. 'My *work* almost killed you. That AP story in Guatemala.'

'Warren set it up, remember? Even if you hadn't done the story, General Velasquez would have found me.'

'I've been thinking about what the general said. That I used you as a cover. That's not true. I did go there to meet a man who promised to take me into a ring of organ thieves. I also went there to interview you. I had heard about you. And when I met you — I didn't want you touched by anything I was doing. That was my

458

mistake. Lying to you. About anything. But the piece I ended up writing about you — well, that's what I do. I go into places and find stories and write about them. Grace, I know how you feel about the work I do. You've made that clear.'

'It's not fair, though.'

'Oh ho,' Mac said. 'You're talking fairness. Okay, can you intellectually override your emotions when it comes to supporting my work?'

Two nurses chatted in undertones as they walked by the room. Mac lowered his voice.

'Because, see, the problem is, even now, knowing how a piece so well-intentioned, so benign, hurt you so badly, even now, I still love my work. It's what I was called to do. I won't give it up, Grace. I can't. It's a good part of who I am. But there's a whole other part of who I am I haven't even explored. The part with Katie. I need time with her.'

Grace had been expecting it. She kept her voice steady. 'Tell me when.'

'Not while I'm here. I won't get out for another week. She doesn't need to see me here.'

This was hard. Impossible. She'd never had to ask this before of anyone. 'If it's all right with you,' she said. 'Katie's getting out tomorrow. I'd like to take her away.'

'Away.'

'Belikond's underwriting a small trip. Any-where I want to take her. It's their way of thanking me for uncovering the fraud. It's just a couple of weeks.'

Grace realized that from then on she'd be sharing her time on this earth with this man. It stunned her. 'If that's okay,' she said again.

He nodded and let go of her hand. 'The question I asked, about getting past this. It's an honest one. We have a kid together. A history. Maybe more. What are we going to do?' His tan had faded and in the hospital bed, he looked gaunt.

'It's complicated. The only work I've felt that passionate about, I guess I've decided I can never do again. And that makes me sad.' She looked at him steadily. 'I don't begrudge you your work. You're good at it. Maybe I'm just jealous of the joy you find in it and yeah, it's tied up with my feeling that I can never again do the work I loved. That it's gone from me. But that's my problem. And the other part . . . ' Her voice trailed.

His eyes were a rich green. He was looking at her with a deep, abiding tenderness. It scared her. It pressed something deep inside, some old wound, and she looked away, past the water pitcher and scattered books and the food tray, past the open door and into the quiet hall.

'Is anybody ever happy, ever?' Her voice was low. 'Are there ever any little families that work?' She felt close to tears and she got up and walked to the window.

Mac's room was on the third floor, facing a Hillcrest shopping center and busy street. She stood facing it as she spoke. 'Sobriety's the linchpin for me. I don't have words for how much your daughter needs you in her life. Your absence is the biggest hole in her heart, and I'm so sorry I did that to her. To you. To all of us.'

460

She took a moment to compose herself.

'I don't know, Mac, yet, about us. I need time. To get strong again, if I can. If I ever was. I won't come to you damaged.'

There was lonely pride in her voice. She turned and faced him. Mac was pulling himself up, reaching out his good hand to her, and she went to him and took it.

'Remember one thing,' he said. 'You came back for me. In the scrub room with the bomb. After everything. You came back.'

★ ★ ★

They were on a wide expanse of empty beach in the Bahamas on the island of Eleuthera. The island had a reputation for being a family-oriented vacation spot, but it was the name that had drawn her. It came from the Greek word *eleutheros*, meaning 'freedom.'

Sailboats dotted the calm sea and small hotels curved along a distant shoreline, but here it was quiet, peaceful. Grace had opted for a family-run bed-and-breakfast; no television, no newspaper, no alarms. Every morning, they climbed into their rented car and went exploring, and when they'd found this one, Ben Bay Beach, tucked away down a dirt road past a field of papayas, they took it as their own.

She'd called Jeanne then, and given her explicit directions on where to find it, for what had changed forever was taking any of it for granted. From then on, she would never think of her moments with Katie as anything less than a gift, and there would be times when just the simple sound of Katie shifting in her sleep would be enough to bring tears.

Grace had spread out a blanket and arranged the simple meal she'd brought along: bread and cheese and water. Katie ran toward the water, holding a small boat in her hands.

Grace watched her go. Katie ran tentatively toward the waves, slowing as the warm water swirled around her ankles. She looked taller, somehow, since the kidnapping. Leaner. She'd lost weight and her swimsuit bagged in the rump. She waded out until the water was even with her knees. She lifted the boat high. Silhouetted against the cloudless sky, Grace could see teetering in the boat, almost alive, the tiny figure of a deer dancer.

Don Jose had left the carving wordlessly on Grace's car hood one day at the hospital. Now Katie would send it out to sea, a tribute to the gods in honor of a child who was gone.

Grace felt his presence and she turned and saw him. Mac was pale and gaunt, arm in a sling. They looked at each other silently across the clear turquoise water. Grace instinctively moved to him. Mac crossed the beach and they were close now.

'Jeb's always up for flying. I realized something that couldn't wait. Something I needed to say in person.'

'How did you find me?'

'Jeanne told me where you were. She said to tell you, it's not too late.'

'For what?'

'She didn't say.'

In the water, Katie squealed and pushed the boat farther out.

'I don't know how to get it right.' Her voice was low.

'Nobody does, Grace. None of us escapes this world undamaged. That's what I wanted to say, the moment you left. And if that was the criteria for strength, we'd all be alone forever. Leaving is the easy part, Grace. It's the *staying* that's hard. So maybe the key is promising when we're not sure.'

Her eyes filled with unexpected tears. She looked at him.

'Maybe the only sure thing is staying, even if we're not sure, staying even then. We're going to hurt each other again, Grace. It's going to happen, no matter how hard we try.'

Grace stared over the water at Katie. With strong clean movements, Katie shoved the boat away. It rose on a swell of water, the light glinting against the wood.

'So maybe the key is trying,' Mac said. 'Sticking around.'

'For her sake.'

'And for ours.'

She looked at him and felt a fierce wonder. He reached awkwardly for her with his good arm, and she raised her arms, wrapped herself around him. The familiar texture of his skin, his smell. He bent down and cupped her face with his good hand. His lips found her face. Her neck. Her mouth.

'You,' she said. 'You.'

A wave caught the boat and it crested, tilted. The wave foamed. When they looked again, it was gone. Mac was staring at Katie with a look of longing and loss and transfixed joy, and Grace took his hand and led him out to sea where their daughter crouched in silty waves.

'Katie.'

She glanced up, looked at them. 'Yes, Mama?'

Mac's hand was heavy in hers and Grace saw his throat move.

'There's somebody here you need to meet.'

Katie waited warily, her hair gold against the vivid blue sky.

'Katie.' Mac's voice was thick, barely heard over the waves.

A gull screamed high overhead and dived.

'It's me, honey. It's your dad.'

He held out his good arm and Katie ran into it, and Grace lifted her up, her strong young legs scissoring, her glad cries mingling with the waves and gulls. Grace took a breath and held on.

Acknowledgements

First and always, my family. My husband, Fred, for his love and serene faith in me, for gate-keeping so I could get the work done, and at the end of the day, for being so much fun. My children, Aaron Arnout and Martha Smith, who each read versions along the way and made helpful and illuminating comments. Aaron, you are an extraordinary writer, funny, compassionate, complex. Martha, you are an extraordinary writer, generous, fearless, filled with light. Thanks for sharing your singular voices, and more than that, your lives. You three are the greatest gifts in my life.

My extended family. My mom, Florence, who encouraged creativity and whose own creativity is a constant inspiration, and my stepdad, Bruno Johnson, whose calm presence brings so much to our family; thanks, guys, for your love and support. My sisters, Nancy Wike, Neva Hutchinson, and Bonnie Hawley. Thanks for your laughter, counsel, stories. You're each a good friend and the very best sister. They're married to good, strong men: David Wike, Peter Hutchinson, Tom Hawley; and I thank them for making my sisters' lives so happy. Uncle Didrik Mydland, for your enthusiasm, and Aunt Katie Mydland, who taught me how to be an aunt; I hope I can live up to it. My mother-in-law, Dorothy Smith, for your love and kindnesses.

Jack and Dossy White, close friends as well as family, who've shared many adventures: thanks for folding us in. Jerry and Jill Smith, whose company we cherish and who live too far away; Carol and John Landis, for your friendship always and encouragement when I needed it most; Sandra and Rich Kersulis, who teach me by example what it means to live with grace and courage; and Barbara and Bill Graham, for more reasons than I can name, not the least of which is every meal Barbara's ever made, and a dazzling day spent flying with Bill in a Cirrus.

My remarkable agent, Nancy Yost. None of this would have been possible without you, and I am deeply grateful for your belief in me, your friendship, and for you shepherding this novel through to its life in the hands of readers, both here and in other countries. Your insights shaped the book in significant ways and your talent took it way past what I could have imagined. You are simply the best. Barbara Lowenstein, Tom Mone, Norman Kurz, Natanya Wheeler, and Zoe Fishman, thank you all.

Kelley Ragland at St. Martin's. I need an entire page just for you, but you've been reminding me of the value of reduction, so here it is: you are a superb editor, with a light touch and penetrating eye, and my novel is so much better because I've been graced by your gift. Thanks for the care and thought you put into making my novel shine and for your belief in what this book could do. Hector DesJean, thanks for hitting the ground running and for spreading the word; Lauren Manzella and Matt Martz, for your help and heart; my copyeditor Karen Richardson, for your meticulous attention to detail; and Andy Martin, the head of this fine imprint, who helped me find the path.

Thanks to the others on my team: Ed Stackler, for a careful reading of early drafts; Sarie Morrell, for your fresh ideas, game plan, and hard work; Marc and Elaine Zicree, supermentors of the first order — you've taught me so much; Gayla Nethercott, my terrific Hollywood agent — for your friendship, integrity, and passionate belief in my work; Cheri Bowers, friend and accountant; Kai Soremekun, amazing webisode director; and Amy and Justin Knupp, Stonecreek Media, for my Web page, www.susanarnoutsmith.com.

And thanks to the gang at ITW, especially Gayle Lynds and John Lescroart, gracious guides into a new world.

I've been blessed with a life of many friends. Thanks to the preschool group, Colleen and Kevin Morse, Gale and Jim Krause, and Joanne and Bruce Leidenberger, and the comfort of going through time.

I especially want to thank Terri Lynn Christianson, a true friend since our girls were galloping ponies in ballet, and Joanne Newman, an artist in her own right — members of the 'birthday club' and friends I trust with my stories; Anne Sparks, friend of the heart whose insight and compassion I cherish; Mary Nagel, who tells the truth and always makes me laugh; Paul Neff, who encourages my art and reminds me that it takes many forms; Susanne Friestedt, who pushes me to enjoy more and fear less; Herb Shaindlin, a friend through several lifetimes; Shelly Mecum, a force of great good in this world and whose voice always makes me think harder, go deeper; and Dawn Troup, who believed in a fourteen-year-old girl, and has never stopped believing.

A novel is always about creating a world out of random bits, and many experts have given me freely of their time and expertise: first, with great thanks, Randy Gibson, San Diego Police crime lab, who read many drafts, answered questions, and opened numerous doors for me — all with graciousness, humor, and tact; Steve Cowman, San Diego Fire and Rescue, for talking about bad things that can happen and what to do; Dr. Don Tecca, emergency room physician, for describing the basics; Dr. Asa Morton, for his stories about the beauty of Guatemala; Dr. Genaro Fernandez, cardiologist, for his careful read and excellent suggestions; Andrew Holtz, longtime friend and former television colleague, for his thoughtful read and sidebar notes on what it was like working for network TV news; Janine Miller, San Diego Police crime lab, who helped me shape Grace's world by sharing her own and was generous with her feedback; Larry Dale, San Diego Police crime lab, for his time and tours; Nick Vent, San Diego Department of Environmental Health, for his careful read, helpful comments, and terrific stories that added so much; Wood Erwin, for helping navigate the bewildering world of biotech and making it look easy; Jerry Keeney, for generously sharing 'bits' that make a novel come alive; Robert Griswold, for taking time during a busy part of his life to answer questions; Denys Williams, San Diego Sheriff's crime lab, for early on welcoming me into her world; Sue Bishop, for filling in La Cholla Airpark colors, and Bill Graham, for the window into flight; Captain Fred Schroeder, Public Information Officer, Folsom Prison, who patiently answered in detail all my questions, even the stupid ones; architect Tim Martin, for answering building design questions; BillyJean Vollman, for describing Mather Field; and the incomparable Dr. Ken Heying, for reminding me how resilient children can be, even in the face of evil.

The mistakes, of course, are mine.

I also want to thank the men and women at St. Martin's whose job it is to take this book and see that it actually gets into stores. Headed by Jeff Capshew, they are the often unsung heroes of any writer's tale and I'm honored to remember them here.

FACT

Almost three hundred children in America at any given time are waiting for a heart transplant. A third of them die waiting, or from transplant rejection.

FACT

Scientists have grown skin, teeth, ears, noses, bladders, chest cartilage, thumb bones, and heart valves in labs and successfully implanted them. Over fifty universities, among them Harvard, MIT, and the University of Colorado, now have tissue-engineering programs.

FACT

In 1998, researchers met in Toronto to set up a ten-year plan for creating a lab-grown human heart. The National Institutes of Health launched a multimillion-dollar effort to create that heart. And now, as the deadline approaches, work continues at a feverish pace around the globe. The revenue value for creating a lab-grown heart has been placed at well over a billion dollars.

We do hope that you have enjoyed reading this large print book.

Did you know that all of our titles are available for purchase?

We publish a wide range of high quality large print books including:
Romances, Mysteries, Classics
General Fiction
Non Fiction and Westerns

Special interest titles available in large print are:
The Little Oxford Dictionary
Music Book
Song Book
Hymn Book
Service Book

Also available from us courtesy of Oxford University Press:
Young Readers' Dictionary
(large print edition)
Young Readers' Thesaurus
(large print edition)

For further information or a free brochure, please contact us at:
Ulverscroft Large Print Books Ltd.,
The Green, Bradgate Road, Anstey,
Leicester, LE7 7FU, England.
Tel: (00 44) 0116 236 4325
Fax: (00 44) 0116 234 0205

Other titles published by
The House of Ulverscroft:

WHEN SHE WAS BAD

Jonathan Nasaw

Lily DeVries suffers from DID, a psychiatric condition known as dissociative identity disorder. Her mind has fragmented into different personalities known as 'alters'. There's the child-like Lily, the sexually aggressive Lilah, and Lilith — the violent psychopath. Now she's found herself in the Reed-Chase mental institution where another patient is undergoing treatment. Fellow DID sufferer Ulysses Maxwell faces life imprisonment for the rape and murder of dozens of women. When Lilith and Max (Maxwell's psychopathic alter) meet, the reaction is dynamite. Then the ingenious lovers engineer an escape — it's only ex-FBI Agent E.L. Pender, and psychiatrist Irene Cogan, who have any chance of stopping the potential carnage. Together they must take on a pair of killers who win hearts as easily as they slit throats . . .

RUN

Jeff Abbott

Everything changes the day two government agents appear unexpectedly at his door. Ben's business card was found in the pocket of one of America's most dangerous assassins, who has just been shot dead. Whoever killed him now has their sights set on Ben. With no idea why he has been targeted, Ben has to act quickly. And in a world where suddenly nothing is as it seems, and no one can be trusted, Ben's only option is to run for his life . . .

THE PAYBACK

Mike Lawson

Sent to investigate what he thinks is a case of fraud at a US naval base, Washington trouble-shooter Joe DeMarco soon realises that he's stumbled on something even more lethal. Accompanied by Emma, an ex-Defence Intelligence Agent, DeMarco comes up against a ruthless and vengeful woman, whose hatred of his colleague stems back to when they were submerged in the cold war. Their encounter destroyed the woman's career and turned her into a ruthless operative intent on revenge. DeMarco has never been a spy in his life, and now he is faced with one of the deadliest in the business — and what's more, he's not convinced this is someone he can fight. But this time, it's not just his own life at stake.

THE ASSASSIN

Stephen Coonts

While on the trail of an Al Qaeda lieutenant, ex-burglar turned CIA operative Tommy Carmellini photographs an American mobster on the island of Capri. Tommy's boss sends him to investigate an alleged link between the mafia and Al Qaeda. Soon they are caught in a deadly tangle of terrorists and the mob, and the clock is ticking . . .

CUT HER DEAD

Iain McDowall

Brady, Annabel, Maria, Adrian. Four bright, sexy, nice-looking twenty-somethings leading the high life at other people's expense. Fighting their perpetual apathy with an interesting hobby: abducting and terrifying young women, burying them alive — and calling it 'art'. Except now they seem to have moved their creative base of operations into Crowby. And unless DCI Frank Jacobson and DS Ian Kerr can crack the case in time — Brady and company may soon be graduating to murder.

THE KILLING GROUND

Jack Higgins

When intelligence operative Sean Dillon stops Caspar Rashid at Heathrow airport, it's only a routine passport check — but it's the start of a bloody chain of events. Rashid is born and bred in England, but has family ties to a fiercely traditional Bedouin tribe. Rashid's thirteen-year-old daughter, Sara, has been kidnapped by his own father and taken to Iraq to be married to one of the Middle East's most feared terrorists, known as the Hammer of God. Then, when the distraught man begs Dillon for help, Dillon has his own reasons to comply. However, unwittingly he is about to unleash a terrible series of consequences and gain implacable enemies. Before his journey is done, many men will die — and Dillon may be one of them . . .